Enjoy

CHRIS BERRY
TOUGH
SEASON
in the sun

GREAT NORTHERN

TOUGH SEASON by Chris Berry

First published in Great Britain in 2020 by Great Northern Books

A CIP catalogue record for this title is available from the British
Library

ISBN: 978-1-912101-98-6

Cover design by Caroline Berry

Great Northern Books
PO Box 1380, Bradford,
West Yorkshire, BD5 5FB

www.greatnorthernbooks.co.uk

Chris Berry is from the north of England and lives near Leeds. He has written for the Yorkshire Post for over 20 years. He is the author of crime thriller novels and several autobiographies. He's a keen sportsman and runs several distances from parkruns to half marathons. Born in Kingston upon Hull, he is a staunch Yorkshireman. His hometown rugby league club is Hull Kingston Rovers. *Tough Season in the Sun* is his second novel.

Also by Chris Berry

FICTION

TOUGH SEASON
TOUGH SEASON IN THE SUN

NON FICTION

THE MAKING OF FARMER CHRIS
  – The Official Autobiography

TONY CHRISTIE The Song Interpreter

JOE LONGTHORNE The Official Autobiography

SUGAR IN THE MORNING Joe Longthorne

LES BATTERSBY & ME Bruce Jones

BOXSTER'S STORY The Truth Behind the Bull

THE J.D. IRELAND STORY

www.chrisberry.tv

PRAISE FOR 'TOUGH SEASON'

Chris Berry has broken the rugby league literary mould. Berry's novel is the first to use the game as a vehicle for the genre of crime. Berry uses short, in-your-face chapters – 69 in all – and staccato sentences to speed up the narrative, somewhat in the style of James Patterson. The down-to-earth and no-nonsense language quickly draws the reader in to what is a definite page-turner. *Tough Season* is a convincing thriller in its own right.
Ros Caplan – Forty20 Rugby League Magazine

I am an emotional wreck with all the twists and turns. It was a tough season all right ... and not one for the faint-hearted, either. You'll soon find yourself dodging bullets from all directions. Fast-moving, breathless action. A steamy summer read and one which keeps you on the edge of your seat right up to the final whistle.
Darryl Wills – Yorkshire Evening Post

A novel that rolls rugby league, sex, politics and scandal into one.
Matthew Shaw – Rugby League World

Well, I've finished Tough Season that I'd saved to take on holiday. Read it in two days, couldn't put it down. What a read! Keeps you guessing. Can't wait for book 2.
Sharon Butterfield

What a brilliant holiday book! Great plot and very well written. Looking forward to the next one!
Roddy Hamilton

A plot that slithers its way around a great game, full of ups and downs, keeps you wondering where the plot will go up until the last few pages, lots of players in this storyline to keep you going back for more!! I'm now waiting for the follow-ups!! A great read!!
Stax Green

Wow, Chris Berry. Your book is a fantastic, can't-put-it-down read. Well done Chris. Yet another on its way soon?
Pat Harrison

Just struck chapter 36 Chris, enjoying it immensely, love a book with short punchy chapters.
Dave Morley

Just back from me jollies and wanna say thoroughly enjoyed ya book. T'was a truly good read pal. Here's to *Tough Season 2*!
Gary Walker

Just to let you know I have read *Tough Season* and loved it. Grilled me right to the end and I didn't guess who the villain was!!! Can't wait for the second book in the series. Hope it continues to be the phenomenal success that it is proving to be.
Margaret Grant

Excellent read! A real page-turner.
Amanda Clarke

Well Done Chris. It will be a Movie before you know it.
Kevin Gairn

I felt as though I was actually stood on the touchline, feeling every failure and cheering every triumph. The plot is full of twists and turns and it certainly kept me on my toes because it never went in the direction I was expecting. Congratulations Chris on publishing your first novel and introducing me to the wonderful and charismatic Greg and the world of Rugby. I sincerely hope this is not the last we have heard of him!
Tina Jackson (Amazon review 5 stars)

Excellent read, fast-moving and great plot, shades of Dick Francis keeps you guessing until well into the story and even then has a few unexpected twists and turns. Looking forward to the next in the trilogy and I'm anticipating another action-packed adventure into the world of rugby.
Ken Knott (Amazon review 5 stars)

Excellent! A really good thriller based around Rugby League – the sport that I know and love. Perhaps a little far-fetched in places but well worth reading all the same. Well done Chris!
Steve (Amazon review 4 stars)

Great book, can't wait for *Tough Season 2*, would make a great movie.
Mel (Leeds Rhinos fan)

Tough Season is a great read from start to finish, enjoyed the storyline, cannot wait for the next one.
Patricia Murray (Amazon review 5 stars)

I enjoyed reading this book a great deal. It was fast-paced, with well-developed characters and much of the action was very plausible. Being a rugby league fan helped understand some of the on-field action no doubt, though equally this would not prove to be an obstacle to anyone else's enjoyment.
Dave Pointon (Amazon review 4 stars)

Just finished it. Sitting in 42 degrees in Majorca. A really good read. Can't wait for the next.
John McCarter

AUTHOR'S NOTE

Tough Season in the Sun is the sequel to *Tough Season*, for which I was delighted to be nominated in the CWA's Dagger Awards 2020. It follows the trials and tribulations of Greg Duggan, a rugby league hero in the mould of Bruce Willis's *Die Hard* and Sylvester Stallone's Rocky Balboa, with a dash of football's *Roy of the Rovers*. Like Willis's character John McClane, Greg has a habit of finding himself in the midst of troubles not of his own making and attempting to bring his foes to book.

In *Tough Season* the action centred around a struggling north of England club at the foot of the sport's professional ladder. In Tough Season in the Sun I have moved the scenery from that archetypal 'grim up north' scenario to the sunshine and warmth of the Canary Islands, more specifically Lanzarote.

By moving the location to 'sun, sea, sand and …' this allowed me to open up a whole new can of worms. I have stayed in Playa Blanca several times and it is a fabulous resort that is very much 'on the up'. The Papagayos Beach Hotel where Greg stays is based on where I have spent vacations, but this is not its real name. There is a tract of land between the Rubicon Marina and the most easterly of the hotels in Playa Blanca where I imagined the audacity of a new stadium.

The Ghost Hotel is a real place to the far side of Playa Blanca and really is a decrepit building that was never finished. It provided a great setting for some of my more dramatic action.

Lanzarote is a beautiful, iconic, unique island with one of the most fantastic post-volcanic landscapes in the world. It really is, as I make great play of in this novel, the only island in the world to have its whole surface – towns, villages, beaches, everywhere – designated UNESCO World Biosphere Status. There have been dangers it may lose this due to corruption in the island's high offices in the past. Mayors and politicians really did receive their comeuppance. This played into my hands when coming up with Greg's heroics here.

I have also wilfully played fast and loose with what many generally see as corruption in any sport's governing bodies, regardless often of fact, but which still make for powerful and manipulative characters. There is no suggestion intended that any character portrayed here is based upon anyone occupying high office in any sport or for that matter in Lanzarote, but who knows whether some may see similarities.

I'm extremely grateful once again to Ross and David from Great Northern Books who have taken considerable care in looking after this second book in the Greg Duggan trilogy – and also my beautiful wife Pauline for all her support, including the pouring of much single malt whisky, and my beautiful daughter Caroline for her superlative work once again on cover design.

Happy reading! See you again in the third book of the series!

Chris

TOUGH SEASON
in the sun

CHAPTER 1

She'd stayed away. It hurt. Deeply. Didn't matter how hard she tried to dress it up as one of those things. That it had never meant much. Never been long term. She had never believed in going back. Move on, put him behind her, at least that's what she'd thought before now.

New chapter, she'd done it all before. This time it had been different, hard, she hadn't realised quite just how much she would feel.

Stupid. Smiled as she thought of him. She was naked on her bed, blonde hair caressing the soft pillows. Another night on the road. Pictures flashed into her head as she closed her eyes, she could hear his voice, feel his breath. He'd taken photographs of her, selfies of them together on his phone, she'd never taken any herself and had never asked him to send any, preferring not to have anything about her that others could see. She saw him clearly now as she drifted off to sleep, she smiled again.

She pictured those days when they had enjoyed each other sensually, sexually and, even more importantly to her now, as two people very much in love and happy to be together, laughing and talking about anything and everything. She'd called him Mr Cool. She laughed inside at herself when she remembered. He'd loved it. She knew.

He'd held her hand and had told her she was beautiful. She had enjoyed his words, his playfulness, but she had been careful not to get hurt. She was a good deal older than him. He'd said it wasn't a problem, but she had worried that it would be, in time. She enjoyed being with a younger man, she knew that much about herself, but what about when he grew tired of her? She had known in her head that day would come. Some day. She'd shielded herself, as she always did.

She wished now that she'd been able to show as much love back to him as he'd shown her, but she hadn't thought it possible given the circumstances. He hadn't been truly available. And when he'd tried to show that he could and would be there, she'd rejected him, not out of the way she felt, but the way life had been.

She'd moved on, they had lost contact, she had another man, younger than him, come into her life. She'd thought that was enough. She kept coming back to him in her head, the times they'd had, those memories, the way she truly felt.

Tomorrow would be another day, another fresh start. But for now, as sleep took hold, think nice thoughts about him. Nothing wrong with that.

Maybe she should call him after all. She was hurting, more than she'd ever felt before. Sleep, think nice thoughts.

Same time. Another place. Another person. Different country.

'*Juan? I need your help. Can you meet me? I'm on Avenue de Papagayo,*' she was out of breath, close to tears, of heartache, of distress, so near they'd already been quelled once, but they were hurrying back to her already moist eyes as she walked, checking behind her as she made her way in the semi-darkness. She flinched, thinking she'd seen something, an outline of someone briefly. She wasn't normally one to panic, but right now she couldn't chance anything.

'*Just come, quickly please.*' She began to pick up her pace from simply walking as best she could despite her figure-hugging red leather strapless dress and immodest heels.

Another place. Another person. Another phone. Same country.

'*So, what's stopping you, mate? ... Listen, just get on a plane and get over here. Put it all behind you for a few weeks. It's great out here. Sun, sea, sand and ...*' He left the rest hanging with a laugh very nearly under-his-breath. If only he'd known how close his next word was to being so accurate. He lost connection.

Back at the first place. First country.

The phone had been flung after she'd hit the button. Other

buttons were now certainly being pressed and with appropriate results. The breathing said it all.

'Oh … Oh… Oh, ba-by yes, mmm …'

She hadn't anticipated this, given all that had happened, all that had passed. She was astride him now, in control, her hands on his expansive and perfectly toned, chiseled chest, her eyes closed. *'That's so … oh … nice and slow darling … oh … yes … just … there … oh … oh, yeah … don't stop … mmm … yeah … that's it …'*

Next day. Back in the other country.

Clear blue skies, blazing sun and a beautiful sandy beach greeted the young couple as they made their way down from the lone bar where they had enjoyed a carafe or three of sangria. They had been taking in the area known as El Papagayos just a mile and a half from their beach resort in Playa Blanca to the south of the island.

The beach in this sheltered cove was deserted. The bar now out of sight. They stripped naked. It wasn't unusual here. He with blond hair, a swimmer's physique, a carpet of dark brown chest hair and endowed in the most established of ways with six-pack and inches more than the norm swinging between his legs. She, also blonde, slender, perky boobs and 'smooth to the south'. They held hands as they made for the ocean. Warmed by the tropical climate, Lanzarote's waters were welcoming. They embraced, kissed passionately, tongues dancing in each other's mouths. Luca lifted Lucia who wrapped her legs around his body.

They collapsed into the sea and kissed again. Then they no longer kissed.

CHAPTER 2

'How soon can you get here?' She waited for the reply. 'Something's happened. Can't talk now. Not on here.'

Her tone was purposeful, calm. Calmer than the previous evening. The conversation from the other end was similarly brief. She replied.

'Great. WhatsApp or Snapchat me. Snapchat better. See you tomorrow.' She smiled. Looked out of her penthouse towards the sea.

Greg Duggan took one step out of the Jet2 plane that had landed at Cesar Manrique Airport three miles south of Arrecife, Lanzarote's principal town, to be greeted by the warmth of the Canary Islands. This was especially welcome given the Pennine climate he'd been used to. It felt good. This was what he needed. Time away. Get his head straight.

'Mr Duggan?' Greg couldn't believe his luck as he made his way out of Arrivals where the package tour holidaymakers were looking for their Jet2 or TUI representatives.

Clutching a laminated sheet with his name on it was a gorgeous, raven-haired, fabulously attractive woman of around 28-32. Greg was no good at guessing ages. She was wearing denim shorts that Greg had already imagined showed a hint of bum cheeks if he cared to look behind, and check shirt tied at her midriff that displayed a generous cleavage. The combo, accentuated by curvaceous hips, made her look as though she could have been doubling as Daisy Duke from *Dukes of Hazzard*. He had to stop this, lusting after every gorgeous woman he came into contact with, and she was gorgeous. He had to stop it. He smiled to himself. He knew he wouldn't, probably couldn't.

This girl's lush, deep green eyes, hair, cherry lips and gorgeous smile caught more than just his imagination. He smiled the broadest smile he'd managed in months and proffered to shake hands, very British. He was on his best behaviour, while it lasted.

The girl, whose radiant personality shone through her 5ft 2in, elevated by what seemed like six inches of cork heels, shook her head mockingly at this, rolled her eyes and embraced him warmly, kissing him on both cheeks. He was beginning to enjoy himself already. He'd made the right decision.

'I'm Ciara. Welcome to Lanzarote.' She smiled her huge smile. *'Kenny asked whether I would meet you. I've to take you to the ground, but perhaps you would like to see your accommodation first?'*

There were several thoughts going through Greg's mind and, given the question and who had asked it, not one of them was pointing towards being in a hurry to see Kenny. Her voice, her smile. And was there a slight trace of temptation? Or was it just him?

Why did he do this all the time? His cock and balls once again ruling his head. Then he smiled. Shook his head at himself.

'Let's go and see Kenny.' They made for the ground.

Greg was travelling light. Everything he currently had in the world was inside his carry-on bag he'd had at his feet on the plane. He'd had a bad run since playing what had turned out to be his final game for Hopton Town, and for the club itself, at the end of the previous season. He'd been their rampaging, ball-handling hero, team captain and player coach. But now Hopton Town no longer existed.

So much had happened. His world had been turned upside down and inside out. He'd lost his wife, his son, his job and very nearly his life. A few more inches and the bullet he'd taken would have pierced his heart.

Kenny's call had come at just the right time. Greg had thought about not coming, but here he was, in the warmth of a tropical climate, being driven in a massive Dodge pick-up by this beautiful, vivacious young woman. Greg found the combination very much to his taste. Maybe he could just lose himself here for a while, and hopefully find himself again. Rebuild his life. Sod the rebuilding, maybe just losing himself for a while was good enough.

CHAPTER 3

'Bloody great mate! Aww great hands boys! Jordan, massive play; Manny, aww now that's an offload Bassey, that's pretty footy boys!'

Kenny Lomax was watching from the sidelines as his Lanzarote Eruption rugby league squad went through a full-on practice game at the newly-built 7000-seater Estadio de Lanzarote.

The club, in another plank of expansionist policy from the game's hierarchy, had been handed what had amounted to a golden ticket straight into the second tier, just as Greg's previous club Hopton Town had been disappearing forever.

Lanzarote Eruption had been parachuted straight into the championship, just one step away from locking horns with the big boys in Super League.

Clubs in New York, Spain and Eastern Europe were also being considered. They had massive populations to work from, but rugby league in Lanzarote? An island with a resident population of less than 150,000?

Social media had been full of negativity particularly from those who had followed their small-town clubs in Yorkshire, Lancashire and Cumbria for generations.

Lanzarote Eruption's volcanic rise without ever playing a single game and with no infrastructure, youth policy or development plans had for many been a step too far.

'Another example of the utter twats ruining our great game.'

'It's a fucking joke!'

'Lanza-bloody-rotty??!!!'

'Money talks once again!'

'I've followed rugby league all my life, but never again, the lunatics have taken over the asylum!'

It was certainly a departure from previous start-ups away from the sport's traditional hotspot of the north of England but social media had also brought the opposite end of the spectrum.

'Holiday in Lanzarote? Watch your team playing without getting your tits frozen? What's not to like?'

'Great call! I'm an Eruption fan already! Sunshine rugby, bring it on!'

There was concern that the original criteria set down for where new clubs to be based was being flouted. Lanzarote has just 8,000 resident Britons; and 75 per cent of the islanders are Spanish with either no knowledge or at best limited experience of the game.

Money had played its part. There was no way this was going to fail so far as the rugby league powers were concerned and Lanzarote socialites Juan and Maria Cavaleros.

The Estadio de Lanzarote had been widely reported as having been wholly funded by the club's illustrious owners and was light years away from what Greg had been used to as a home venue. Everything here was fresh.

The ground had been slotted in between the also recently built, 6-star La Cala – a hotel for the rich and the ever-so rich that featured individual small plunge pools and the elegant, luxurious Rubiconia Hotel.

Estadio de Lanzarote's main stand featured seating for 4000 facing seawards, or indeed Atlantic Oceanwards, across to the island of Fuerteventura. The sea side of the ground had shallow terracing, rising to no more than a few feet high.

The Cavaleros had understood this could work against them with those out of the ground being able to watch the games without ever coming in, but they wanted the Estadio and Eruption to attract everyone. Their hope was that what they might lose in revenue from those who simply stood on the promenade they would gain back in long-term interest in the club and its facilities, which included a gym and an Olympic size outdoor pool.

Eruption's first season was going well.

Australian Grand Final winner and international Kenny Lomax had been lured as player-coach having originally landed in the UK the previous season.

He'd spent the last six weeks of the previous season playing alongside Greg in what had turned out to be a failed mission to save basement rugby league club Hopton Town from extinction.

Kenny had assembled a squad that included players from Australia, New Zealand, France and Papua New Guinea plus established English players, including a handful from his brief spell at Hopton Town where Greg had been his coach.

Eruption were challenging hard for promotion to Super League, sitting second in the table with just two games to go before the play-offs and the winners guaranteed to be promoted.

'Greg!' Kenny's famed gap-toothed grin spread right across his face. 'Great to see you, mate'. The pair embraced briefly on the touchline after Greg had been deposited by Ciara.

'Just five more minutes and we'll go and get a tinny.'

Kenny and Greg had been within seconds of saving Hopton Town from finishing at the foot of rugby league's professional ranks. It hadn't worked out, but not for the want of trying and with a hugely dramatic finale.

Hopton Town's fate had been sealed in the most startling and horrendous of fashions when bullets had struck Greg, the club's owner Bob Irvine and Greg's teammate Tony Estorino. Kenny had been alongside Greg as he had approached the culprit, former coach George Ramsbottom, who had later been apprehended. The scoreline had read 28-20 in Hopton's favour at that point.

They had needed to beat their opponents Ensideleigh by nine to stay up and send their opposition down. The game had been abandoned with three minutes on the clock. The result had stood at the scoreline the game had reached. There was no way it could have carried on. The crowd had run for their lives. It had been mayhem. Greg's life had been in tatters since.

Hopton had scored a try to go to 28-20 and were supposed to have had the opportunity of a conversion kick that if successful would have brought about another two points and safety from extinction, but there had been no opportunity to kick the conversion. Hopton's fate had been sealed.

Fortunately, Greg's injury had been merely a flesh wound to his right arm, bad enough to keep him in hospital for observation and requiring a skin graft to repair but not life threatening. He'd taken time to recover but had done so from the end of the season to the start of the next. He'd not signed for a new club. His head hadn't been right.

Tragically, Bob Irvine and Tony Estorino hadn't been so lucky. Tony had lost a leg and was now an amputee with a prosthetic on the way.

Bob Irvine had died instantly on the field, hit straight through the heart. Previous Hopton coach George Ramsbottom was awaiting trial.

Greg had been hounded and harangued by those who had been determined that Hopton would finish bottom and in so doing go out of business in the lead up to the calamitous final day of the season. He could never forgive Ramsbottom for ruining Tony's life, taking Bob Irvine's and his own wound, but he'd also known it had been the money men behind the scenes, robbing Hopton of their only professional sports club, that had pulled the strings and had brought about George's state of mind.

George had been the one brandishing the gun. The others, those with the power and the money, who had pocketed millions from cash generated over the sales of the club's ground when Town had finished bottom had all come out squeaky clean.

Greg, his family, friends and teammates had suffered at their hands during the season.

George would no doubt end up locked away for years, regardless of any diminished responsibility tales a solicitor would offer in mitigation – and those bastards were in the clear.

Greg took his mobile from his pocket to check messages, calls and social media while waiting for Kenny to finish up. That was at least one thing Greg had improved at in the past months, social media and technology. He shoved it back in his pocket. He exhaled. The kind of exhalation that was borne out of bewilderment. But he was out here in the sun. Away from it all. Time to, if not forget, then at least enjoy. Relax.

Normally – before the end of last season – he'd have been under a car at the Victoria Street garage where he had worked since leaving school at 16. He was now 28. Normally he would have been training with and playing for his home town club. Normally he would have been with his wife Diane and their now three-year-old son Kyle.

And from time-to-time he would have been with Susie, an older woman than him by several years. Okay, this may not have been exactly normal in most people's lives, but nothing was now normal for Greg.

Diane had lost their second child she was carrying due to a near hit-and-run, which Greg knew was linked to threats he had received, there had been explosions at Hopton's ground. He'd been beaten, bound, abducted. Nothing normal at all.

His life had turned upside down. Diane, sick and tired of his dalliance on more than one occasion had found another man. John. Greg had lost his job at the garage. Hopton Town had folded. The Parrot Lane ground had been bulldozed last week. End of an era.

'*Senor Duggan!*' Greg turned.

Wow! What was it about this island? His first contact on Lanzarote had been curvaceous Ciara, his next new introduction was to be a second stunningly attractive woman, blonde and with another magical smile. Stop it! he managed to say to himself. I've only been on the island for five minutes and already I'm like this. He smiled inwardly, laughing at himself. Concentrate on the job in hand – and that's being here, playing rugby league … and enjoying myself!

'*It is so good that you are here,*' said the woman dressed in tight-fit bleached jeans, white heels complete with sparkling rhinestones and skin-tight white T-shirt/body that accentuated her boobs.

Greg couldn't help but return her smile. Her soft Spanish accent was as alluring as the way she looked. Her cool-blue eyes were entrancing.

'*I am Maria. Maria Cavaleros.*' More kisses on both cheeks. Sod the shaking hands bit now, Greg was getting into this already.

He may well have been on a downer for much of the past months but suddenly here, within his first hour or so on the island, things were perking up.

Greg realised, even though she hadn't spoken to him in Spanish, that he perhaps should use a few words like senor and senorita when being introduced. The rest of his Spanish vocabulary consisted of paella, sangria and mucho. Was mucho a real word? Inside he shook his head at himself again.

He smiled at Maria and offered a very simple, '*Great to meet you,*' but hadn't even managed 'senorita'. Maria spoke in a kind of broken English.

'*Senor Lomax. Kenny. He has told me so much about you ...*' again that smile.

Kenny would surely have talked up his playing exploits, but maybe he'd also given out other information?

The Cavaleros weren't just involved in Lanzarote Eruption and the Estadio. Maria and her husband Juan had earned their wealth through construction and ownership of land and property, or at least that is what the headline notes said on Wikipedia that Greg had checked out before flying.

The events of the previous season had brought about a new Greg Duggan, one that was more alert to situations off-field in the way he was at times imperious on-field. There was more to him now. He wanted to know about what he might be getting involved with.

Other stories on Google painted quite different pictures of nefarious, but unsubstantiated, activities that had led to how the Cavaleros' wealth had been acquired.

Greg hadn't been unduly bothered about any of it. Whatever might be going on behind the scenes, as there always was, Greg's main driver had been to come out to the island, enjoy the sun, play rugby league and hopefully get his life back on track.

'Your husband … is he here too?' ventured Greg, by way of conversation as the practice game was still in action. He was enjoying this beautiful woman alongside him. Maria's expression became straight-faced giving a different aura that Greg hadn't intended.

'He is always busy. Here, there and everywhere. I never know when he will be here…' She left the words hanging. She smiled her beautiful, pink lips ever so slightly at Greg as Kenny arrived, the training session over.

'Greg!' A young player bounded up to the trio and others were just behind. *'Couldn't believe it when Kenny said you were coming. Brilliant timing. We're on a right run.'*

Eighteen-year-old Stu Wainwright was brimming with confidence. He'd had a fantastic season after having only made his debut for Hopton in the last few weeks of their fateful season.

Kenny had taken a gamble on the teenager being able to perform a tier above where Hopton had played, but he had proved a sensational signing. Stu was on the verge of the division's young player of the season award and had just received a call up to the England Knights U21s.

'Hey really cool news man!' was the next voice as the Hopton reunion took shape. *'This ain't nuffin' like Parrot Lane is it!'*

This was already more words than Greg had heard from his winger Vincent Venus in the three months he'd worked with him back home. Vincent and Stu were two British bright young things that Kenny had spotted at Hopton.

Experienced centre Ron Rigson, who Greg had signed in the lead up to their near phoenix-like rise that had been close to saving Hopton, was next to shake Greg's hand, along with Welsh centre Alan Thomas the club's leading try scorer.

New Zealander, Warwick Player, who had added more experience in the final games was on board too. It was great to see them all. Others from the Eruption squad welcomed him. Aussie stars Greg had seen over the past decade, Mannion Roberts, Shirley 'Bassey' Fastleigh, Elton Richards and Ellard Vellidale.

'*Kinda makes you feel at home, doesn't it?*' said Kenny, as he and Greg now sat overlooking the splendid new ground from the bar and restaurant area above the seating in the grandstand, Maria having said her goodbyes.

Kenny was enthusiasm and positivity personified: '*Two games to the play-offs. We've already qualified, but we want top spot in the league, win the championship. That will give us home advantage in the play-off semi-final.*'

Kenny sensed his mate perhaps wasn't where he wanted him to be. He knew Greg, understood what he'd been through. In the immediate aftermath of 'that match' last season it was Kenny who'd been there for his friend.

He'd seen Greg's world unravel. He'd understood because he'd had events occur in his life that he could relate to Greg's. But nobody could have had it quite so bad and dramatic as Greg had suffered in the lead up to that game and the ending.

Tony (Estorino) had obviously suffered more physically and poor Bob Irvine of course, but Greg's problems went way beyond being shot – even though that should have been traumatic enough. Kenny was measured with his approach. Calming his voice.

'*How are you doing mate?*' Kenny let his words rest. What he'd learned about Greg was this man didn't want hundreds of questions. It was best to give him space.

Kenny also knew he had to quickly assess where his friend was at. He'd told Greg to come, partly as a way of helping but also because he knew Greg could do a job for him. He waited.

'*I'm doing okay.*' It was all Greg could come up with. He knew it wasn't enough. He knew if he was in Kenny's shoes he'd want something more. This wouldn't get him on the park. Greg tried to get the words.

'*I'm on this long hard road at the moment … trying to get my life back together …*' He paused, took a drink – they'd both settled on water – and smiled just a little, while giving a slight nod. '*But I'm up for this. It's what I need …*'

It was the answer Kenny wanted to hear, but even though it

was he who had inspired Greg's appearance he had his own doubts about just how much he might be ready for action.

But he also had his own concerns too. While Eruption had been playing well injuries had been piling up. He'd thought about approaching Greg earlier in the season when he hadn't been as stretched, but had felt it may have been too soon for him.

'How fit? I know you've not been playing.'

Greg was nowhere near match fit, but he had been working out. His arm was fully recovered, but his fitness was probably around 80 per cent right – and he'd not played for nearly eight months, since that last game.

Greg wasn't going to pass up a chance to play even if he had more or less just hopped off the plane. He nodded. 'I'm good. Not 100 per cent, but not far off.'

'Good enough for two spells of twenty tomorrow night?'

Jesus! Greg hadn't expected something so immediate, even though he knew there was a game, but it set his heart racing in a good way, adrenaline pumping.

'I've eight players out Greg, and while I've just about got the numbers, there's not a lot there after the first choice seventeen. I could do with another good head and with a good go-forward. I'll spell you with Manny (Mannion Roberts) or EV (Ellard Vellidale).'

He looked Greg hard in the eye.

Greg knew his body might not be in the best shape, but what the hell, this was a game. He wanted it.

The smart talk, when Greg had been in his teens, was that he would play in Super League one day, but he'd remained faithful to his home town club. Now he had an opportunity to make good.

'Yeah. I'm good. Just put me on the park.'

Kenny smiled. He wouldn't have expected any less. He knew Greg certainly wouldn't be match fit but he also knew two twenty-minute spells from a man who could turn a game around in just a split second was worth it, especially if Eruption's winning run was to be maintained. They'd won seven on the bounce.

The Papagayos Beach Hotel is the last hotel in Playa Blanca, Lanzarote's fastest expanding resort. It sits just before the sparse, arid and historic El Papagayos promontory that leads to some of the island's and indeed the world's most beautiful golden sandy beaches.

Costa Teguise, Puerto del Carmen and San Bartomole all have larger populations and the island's biggest town, Arrecife is home to nearly half of the islanders, but Playa Blanca's continued growth has made it a developer's paradise and the all-new Estadio de Lanzarote stadium was another status symbol marking its continued development. It had been built specifically for Lanzarote Eruption.

Greg was now in his Royal Elite apartment, less than a quarter of a mile from the ground at the Papagayos Beach Hotel having arrived after his earlier meeting with Kenny who had introduced him to the backroom staff and had shown him the dressing room, treatment room, gym and pool. The whole thing was light years ahead of what Greg had been used to back in England.

This was something else. Lanzarote Eruption had ensured his stay was certainly going to be comfortable. He checked out the mini-bar. He took the water, sat on the side of the bed. Opened the bottle, drank a third. Went out on to the balcony.

Beyond the blue swimming pools below was the Atlantic Ocean and completely blue sky, with the island of Fuerteventura framed clearly in the far distance. After what Greg had experienced in recent months back home this was much improved, idyllic and warm.

'*Senor Duggan.*'

Greg had heard the voice before. He knew it before he turned around.

CHAPTER 4

'Tackling him is like tackling a sack full of knees and elbows.'

Ralph McBalingfour was Cloud TV's rugby league pundit for the evening. He'd played in Super League a decade ago and had retired to the Canary Islands to run a beach bar.

Since Lanzarote Eruption had been formed, Ralph had been an easy choice for the TV channel when they covered Eruption's home games. Cloud TV had committed to covering every Eruption home game for the next two seasons. They were also working in partnership with Canaria TV.

Ralph was currently eulogising over the form of Jordan Garrett who was 'pulling up trees' for Eruption's opponents Leverfield Lynx.

'He's unstoppable at the moment and with Eruption just looking as though they may wilt under a logjam of injuries, the last thing they need is for Garrett to add to their roster with a few massive hits …'

The TV screen showed Eruption's starting line up: Longchamps, Estapol, Rigson, Thomas, Venus, Peters, Wainwright, Vellidale, Lomax, Borsoni, Ortega, Fastleigh and Roberts. And then the bench: Richards, Ramos, Rodriguez-Perez and Duggan.

'But look at that name on the bench,' McBalingfour was ready for this. He'd been primed by Kenny. 'Greg Duggan – I'm sure all of us in the game wish him well. He's such a good player to have been languishing in the lower divisions for years and tonight, well it's probably too early to expect too much of him, but if he's fit, he could be a powerful and important player for the Eruption.'

'I couldn't agree more Ralph.' The Saturday Night Big Match host was Joanne Collingwood. 'Our best wishes go out to his former teammate Tony Estorino and of course the family of Hopton Town's owner Bob Irvine.'

Joanne left an appropriate pause before announcing they'd be back with the kick-off after the ad break.

'All right boys. Like we talked about, let's get in their faces and knock young Garrett out of his stride before he gets into it.'

They broke from the huddle out on the park, all seventeen including Greg. Kenny had delivered his words, his gumshield now in place.

The crowd was a decent size. Leverfield were in one of the play-off spots at present and had a good away following – when in the north of England.

Many of their fans had seized the opportunity of the cheap break offered through Lanzarote's Tourism & Business Affiliate of 3 days for the price of 2 including subsidised air travel from Odd Shaped Ball Holidays set up by the Rugby League Authority.

'It's wonderful to see the Estadio de Lanzarote getting towards three-quarter-full or maybe even more tonight.' Joanne Collingwood was on a talking up mission for the game as a whole. 'I'd say Leverfield Lynx have brought around 2,500 with them and the atmosphere around Playa Blanca has been fantastic today.'

'Yes, it has,' McBalingfour interjected. 'When the Eruption played their first game I don't think the locals really knew what was going on, but this island is developing a real passion and love of the sport ...'

'And tonight's crowd is probably being swelled even more by the locals as three of their own are in the seventeen. We've seen Jose Maria Estapol a couple of times this season when he's come off the bench, but this is quite a night. The first ever full start for an islander – and also two other islanders making their debuts on the bench.

'Right, we're under way. Eighty minutes of all-action rugby league. Let's go to our match commentators – Karen King and Robbie Robertson.'

Kenny Lomax didn't need a commentator or pundit to tell him how his red and blue hooped shirted players in blue shorts and red socks, Lanzarote's island flag colours, had performed by the end of the first half. But he did tell his team!

'Under the pump boys! This is the worst we've played all season,' he included himself in what had so far been a drubbing. He wanted to make certain that this was seen as a collective performance and that he was as much to blame. *'We are letting young Garrett run this show.*

'17 missed tackles. Completion rate 65 per cent. No busts. It tells the story boys.' Kenny's assistant coach and former Aussie teammate Malky Shannon had supplied the stats that had seen Eruption finish the half 0-18. The wily Shannon, who had plotted many comebacks took over from Kenny.

'… but here's how we win this game …'

When Eruption took to the park for the second half, Borsoni and Ortega had been replaced by the two Eruption debutants, the island-born players Raul Rodriguez-Perez and Angel Ramos at prop and second row; Elton Richards had come on at full back to replace Philippe Longchamps; and Greg had replaced 'Manny' Roberts.

Four changes as an interchange at the start of the second-half rarely happened, but they'd made none in the first half. That much had been part of Kenny and Malky's game plan.

Go the first 40 minutes as one unit and hit Lynx with four sets of fresh legs at the start of the second – a very different plan to other games they'd played, but they'd monitored Lynx all season and they'd seen they usually faded in the second. That's when young Garrett faded.

They hadn't anticipated being as far behind as they were right now. It was always tough to come back from an 18-point deficit, and this would have to be a first for Eruption.

'Well here we go.' Karen King was ready. *'The first score in this second half could prove crucial.'*

'Absolutely Karen.' Robbie Robertson was a former player who had played for Lynx among his many clubs. *'This is definitely Lynx's game to lose. I don't think I've seen The Eruption play so poorly.'*

Karen King took over once again. *'Let's go pitch side to find out what was said to both teams at half-time with our reporter Max Sunderland.'*

While Max gave his account of the information given by the coaching staff of both Lynx and Eruption the game exploded into life.

Locals who had turned out to see their island heroes had whooped with delight as Ramos and Rodriguez-Perez had taken to the field.

The island's Aussie population had been growing during the season as Eruption had six guys who had all played first-grade in the NRL.

They had been more than delighted to see young pin-up star Elton Richards hit the turf for his first start of the season; and then there was Greg. His was the only emergence that had received no big reception.

'*Ooof, what a hit!*' Robbie Robertson might have been a former Lynx player, but that's where it ended. He was by no means partisan. His reaction was part grimace and part humour, in awe of the tackle. '*Now that's how to stop young Garrett.*' He chuckled ever so slightly at the teenager's expense. '*Well, hello Angel Ramos and welcome to this game.*'

'*That's something we've not seen all year,*' was Karen King's response. '*Oh, and now Garrett has knocked-on at the play-the-ball … the boy is human after all.*'

It was Eruption's head and feed at the scrum on Lynx's 40-metre line. Stu Wainwright fed the ball. He collected it out of the base of the scrum and flew around the side, ducking under one despairing tackle and running into the gap, flicking the ball out to stand-off Jordan Peters who was hauled down at the Lynx 20-metre line.

Garrett, still stunned, had to his credit returned to the defensive line. Kenny received Peters' play-the-ball and set off straight for Garrett who may well have had youth on his side, but Kenny Lomax had experience, guile, turn of pace, side step and much more in his locker, including the ability to crunch. He also knew the last thing Garrett needed at the moment was another hit.

Kenny bore down like a guided missile into Garrett's ribs,

then turned quickly as he made impact … Another collective 'Oooof' from the commentary team and the crowd alike and he spread the play on an inside run to bring thunder raining down on the Lynx defence in the shape of Raul Rodriguez-Perez as the islander made his first impact!

'*I don't know what Eruption have had at half-time, but I want some of it.*' Robbie Robertson was loving this.

'*Three Lynx players are down in back play after that charge by Perez.*' Karen King was into the moment.

'*And the ball has gone through a series of hands. Now it's Rigson, Estapol – he's cut back inside – he's jinked, he's got it to Fastleigh – big charge. Lynx are struggling here. They've not got him. He's a colossus. Now Vellidale. Eruption are battering the Lynx line. Now Wainwright. He's dummied, he's shimmied, he's … ohh, right on the line now.*'

Greg was at first receiver. Kenny nodded to him at acting half back behind Stu Wainwright. The ball flew straight into Greg's grasp. Greg's life momentarily flashed before him. His last game for Hopton. It was the last thing he'd needed.

In a split second to everyone else in the ground, but a slow-mo of epic proportions for Greg, he spilt the ball. Lynx recovered it. A suddenly resurgent Jordan Garrett took the pass from his teammate and performed a Lazarus-like comeback that saw him fend off four would-be tacklers on the way to a 90-yard run that extended Lynx's lead to 22 points and with an easy conversion they made it 24.

'*Stand up Jordan Garrett. Almost dead in the water one second, length of the field try the next. I applaud you, young man!*' Robbie Robertson wasn't wrong. It had been a brilliant, sparkling return. Greg's first touch of a ball since that last game had been anything but.

Kenny had taken immediate control behind the sticks as Lynx's conversion goal was being taken. His words were positive.

'*Great play boys. Forget this try. We had them. We'll have them again. Now this time let's get that ball over the whitewash, or on it.*'

Kenny gave Greg a wink, a smile – and as they were heading

back for the restart a quick, '*You all right mate?*'

Greg hated being a second-class citizen, but at that moment that's exactly how he felt, out of condition, out of place and out of his head.

'*Just give me that ball.*' It was as firm a statement as he had made for months. Kenny slapped him on the back as they set for the restart.

Lynx now knew one more score should nail it completely. The older Lynx heads on the park set about taking play back sufficiently into Eruption's half with their aim simply to tag on a drop goal that would mean even if Eruption scored four tries and converted all four kicks, they would still come up short.

Estapol restarted the game for Eruption with a towering kick-off.

EV, Fastleigh, Ramos, Richards and Rodriguez-Perez had been on a mission. Winning the ball had been their start point with collision a secondary benefit. As the ball came back down to earth the Lynx player destined to receive it, Ben Hogan, momentarily caught the onrushing Eruption attack in his eyeline.

He jumped but Ramos had reached him and went airborne at the same moment. Ramos swiveled spectacularly in the air and managed to palm the ball back to his compatriot Rodriguez-Perez, who in turn flicked the ball out of the back of his hand to Jordan Peters, who scampered through flailing Lynx arms, broke clear and dived under the sticks. Within seconds Estapol had converted the try. Eruption 6 Lynx 24.

Lynx restarted with a kick deep into Eruption's half. Ramos and Rodriguez-Perez both made headway, seemingly brushing off would-be tacklers at will. Their two runs brought Eruption back inside the Lynx half from where Peters, Wainwright, Rigson, Thomas and 'Bassey' weaved their respective magic.

The Eruption support was getting louder by the second, their confidence resurrected by their team's renewed spirit and determination.

'Bassey' (Shirley) Fastleigh was tackled fifteen yards from the line. The green and yellow shirted Lynx defence was under pressure, but one more tackle completion and they were back in possession. Keep their discipline. Get the ball back.

'Oophhh!' Karen King gave a grimaced howl. 'My goodness. That's an awful hit!'

Greg had caught up with play, he'd been struggling to keep pace but had managed to get behind 'Shirley' to feed the ball out to Kenny, which he'd managed but was now laid spark out.

He'd been hit head-high the split second the ball had left his hands which, in the millisecond previously he'd been moderately chuffed with as it had been his first meaningful contribution.

As he laid there it looked to everyone else as though it would probably also be his last touch.

The big screen was in operation at all Cloud TV matches and re-runs were being played as the game had been stopped by the referee. The crowd had made a collective gasp as the impact was shown again.

This hadn't been in Greg's plan. He stayed down. The physio was on, the Lynx physio too. A brace appeared around his neck. Greg blinked, stars circling his head.

A stretcher appeared. Greg was lifted on to it, but in the same instant he made his own decision. He wasn't about to be strapped on to the bowl-like stretcher. He had work to do. It was time to get back in the game.

Greg sat up, taking off the brace before it had been applied properly, shook his head as though to clear everything. The physio looked him squarely in the eye, checking for any form of concussion. Greg rose to his feet.

The crowd applauded. The warrior in Greg wasn't about to let things lie. He shook his head once more, as if shaking the hit away, then rolled his head from side to side. Nodded that he was okay.

Greg was now in the mood. And he was in the mood for retribution. His assailant had been put 'on report', the referee not even sin-binning or showing him a red card.

Karen King was ready for the next drama.

'Greg Duggan is back up. And looks as though he is ready to right a wrong. Robbie, this could get tasty!'

Eruption had been awarded a penalty. They were fifteen metres out from the Lynx line. There was plenty of time left in the game even though they were 18 points behind.

Greg took the restart and charged headlong at the Lynx defence making a beeline straight at his previous assailant sending him reeling back and managing to launch his knee at incredible force into the groin of the man who would later wish that he'd been given a yellow or red card after all. The trio that also had been hanging on couldn't haul him down either. Greg twisted, turned in their would-be tackles and burst free of them all. Five yards to go.

Just one Lynx player was left to beat – Jordan Garrett. Kenny was in support on Greg's right side. Vincent Venus was making good time to his left.

Greg's razor sharp rugby league brain was about to hand out a lesson to the upcoming young superstar. He feinted to slip a pass to Kenny, stepped off his right foot and slipped past a despairing Garrett, touching down for a try bang under the sticks and leaving Estapol with the easiest of conversions.

'Unbelievable!' Karen King was in raptures. *'Greg Duggan, the man who was shot, literally took a bullet for his club just last season and was about to be carted off the field just two minutes ago after a blatant head high smash … and now … Wow! Wow! Wow! … explain that Robbie …'*

'We've just seen something that is beyond words.' Robbie then went on with further words, he was a commentator after all.

'That was world class! And I mean world class. This may be the league below Super League but I promise you, you will never witness a more complete, instantaneous comeback to a game than that … and he managed to take out his own revenge on the player who caught him with the head-high tackle AND make Scott Garrett look like a schoolboy player at the same time … plus score the try … Amazing … Game on!'

Kenny and Greg simply nodded at each other before Kenny had to say something. *'Just what you needed, that hit mate!'*

Eruption were still twelve points adrift, but Greg's impact had a profound effect. Stu Wainwright was next. He went on a razzle dazzle move that saw Eruption back into Lynx territory.

Many of the islanders may have turned out primarily to watch their compatriots Estapol, Rodriguez-Perez and Ramos, who were all performing well, but they now had Du-GAN! That was their combined shout from the terracing as Greg received the ball once again, this time 20 metres out from the Lynx line, as a result of running on to a ball propelled by Ramos.

'Oh, I just cannot believe that.' Karen King was in ecstasy.

'Greg Duggan is running a master class, right here, right now. Robbie, explain to me what is happening here, because I have never seen a transformation like this.'

Robbie Robertson was chuckling along in similar astonishment. Greg had handed off two more tacklers and had then rounded the now hapless Jordan Garrett for the second time in under three minutes. No feint to right or left needed this time.

Greg had simply looked him in the eye on his approach, sped straight at him and at the moment when Garrett had intended making his tackle Greg had stepped off first his right and then his left leaving the young wannabe clutching at thin air. Greg deposited the ball under the posts once again.

'I've only one question in all of this. Why has Greg Duggan not been playing at a higher level all his career? This guy has got everything. He is demolishing Lynx. I bet they thought they had this game in their pockets. Look at it now.'

Estapol once more slotted over the kick.

The game still had over twenty minutes left. Eruption were just six points short of Lynx. 'Du-GAN! Du-GAN' rang out the Eruption supporters. Greg hadn't felt this good in years. He'd gone from zero to hero in the space of twenty minutes – dropping a ball with his first touch, clothes-lined by an opposing player and now two tries within three minutes.

Leverfield Lynx were still six points up. But Greg and his new teammates were now in the ascendancy. Lynx lasted a further ten minutes before Greg once again opened them up.

This time it was EV (Ellard Vellidale) wrestling free of two tacklers and offloading to Jordan Peters, who fed Elton Richards and found Greg on his inside.

Greg smashed through one tackle, avoided the despairing lunge of another, before once again setting his sights on Jordan Garrett, Lynx's last line of defence.

By now the crowd was baying for Greg to beat him once again. Greg was up for it, but at the moment before impact slipped the ball immaculately out of the back of his hand to Jose Maria Estapol. The winger did the rest from the remaining ten metres out and placed the ball in its now customary position right under the posts.

Estapol was ecstatic! A try on his full debut. Seconds later, his fourth conversion. The comeback was complete. The match now all square. 24-24.

Ten minutes still to go on the clock. Either side could yet win the game but Greg, his Eruption teammates and his new, adoring fans were seriously not going to let this slip.

Malky Shannon made three more interchanges. Bassey, EV and Ron Rigson made way for the return of Roberto Ortega, 'Manny' Mannion Roberts and Philippe Longchamps.

The next six minutes became about both sides creating the right position to attempt a drop goal. Greg had kicked plenty for Hopton and knew his range for popping one over comfortably but he didn't have the ball yet.

Instead it was Lynx who were finally making long overdue headway. It was the first time for an age they'd had anything near reasonable possession inside Eruption's half and the first time they had been able to even think about earning the extra point they had felt, half an hour ago, would categorically win them the game. How times had changed.

Four minutes to go. Alarm bells rang in Greg's mind. His last game had only reached seconds beyond this point. He remembered poor Tony Estorino, now crippled. Bob Irvine going down instantly, unmoving. He mentally shook his head again.

Lightning, or at least gunshot, wasn't about to strike twice. He didn't believe in that. And he didn't have time for it as he launched himself at the Lynx forward who flipped the ball out just a millisecond before they collided.

Alan Thomas became the eager recipient. He'd watched the move develop and was a master at interceptions. As the Lynx player released under heavy fire from Greg, Thomas darted on to the ball before it could reach the now hapless Jordan Garrett the intended receiver.

Right now, Thomas was scorching away from the despairing lunges of the opposition. Vinny was the only other player who could live with him at this speed and duly appeared. Lynx wingers were both in hot pursuit. Thomas dragged their defenders towards the corner and popped the ball deftly into the hands of Vinny Venus, who had come inside Thomas' run after having tracked on his outside. It was a clever move that saw Venus go in right under the sticks and with another easy conversion for Estapol it was pretty much game over. Eruption had come from 6-24 down after just a couple of minutes of the second half to lead 30-24 with just a minute and a half now left on the clock.

There was to be no way back for Lynx, but Greg hadn't finished with them yet.

Lynx put up a high ball from the kick off. The ball made the required ten yards' distance. Players from both sides went up and 'Manny' Roberts tipped the ball back to Ortega who threw a cut-out pass to Estapol, who in turn darted back into the Lynx half before being hauled down. Kenny took the ball at acting half back and pushed a delightful pass straight into the hands of free-running Rodriguez-Perez, who charged a further ten metres before he too was tackled.

Kenny and Greg were now back to their old routine of just nine months or so ago. A quick look, a little motion from Kenny as he flicked a hand behind his back as he received the ball at acting half again. Greg was 5 metres to his right and 40 metres out from the goalposts. 10 seconds left on the clock. The last kick of the game. They didn't need it to win. The game was already up.

'*And Lomax swivels to his left, dummies a pass before turning to his right,*' Karen King was enjoying every move. '*And Greg Duggan receives. He's set back especially for this. It's something like 43 yards out. And he's launched it! It's a towering kick. It's got the direction, has it got the legs? … Yessss! … What a kick … and what a show from the man who has turned this game on its head!*'

Jordan Garrett was the first of the Lynx team to congratulate Greg at the whistle. Beaten but wholly in awe.

'*Fantastic bud! You were outstanding,*' and he wasn't stopping there. '*I saw you play in a Challenge Cup game when I was 12 years old and knew I just wanted to be like you. That was really something out there. See you next time!*'

As the young pretender clasped hands with Greg, Kenny dragged him away where the Eruption players were heading towards their fans.

'*See this mate! You've done this! That's why I knew you had to come. You and the three Lanzarote boys. You're bloody Gods to these people already!*' Kenny put his arm around his former player-coach's shoulders. '*We couldn't save Hopton, but here … we can really have some fun!*'

Pitch side reporter Max Sunderland was ready for Kenny and Greg in front of the Perspex Cloud TV and Canaria TV promo screen adorned with the sponsors' names. He'd just completed the post-match interview with shell-shocked Lynx captain Dave Greensward.

'*And now Lanzarote Eruption's head coach Kenny Lomax; and new signing, fresh off the plane yesterday, match winner Greg Duggan. Greg, it's easy this game isn't it? Just hop on a plane, get off four and a half hours later, add a bit of sleep, get knocked out on the field of play, then score two tries, make another and kick a drop goal from forty yards.*'

Greg smiled at Max's words. He'd never had a post-match

TV interview before, loads of radio, but this was different.

'*You missed the ball I dropped. The one that brought about their fourth try,*' he said with a smile and enough well-intended humour. He wiped away the sweat from his brow. '*But hey, the boys all played really well. It was great to be back on the park again.*'

'*Kenny, you've gone top of the league with tonight's win. That's now eight on the bounce. Just one game left in the regular season. Home advantage is what you're looking for in the play-offs?*' Max Sunderland left the statement hanging in the air as Kenny responded.

'*Aww mate, we're not looking at the table. We know what we have to do – and that's win matches. We've done well so far, but there's a long way to go. Hudderford next, that's all we'll concentrate on now.*'

'*And what about this feller?*' Max motioned at Greg.

'*This man!*' said Kenny. '*This man is the real deal. That's why I wanted him to come here. You've only seen him for 40 minutes. Listen to that crowd!*' The Eruption fans were chanting 'Du-GAN' once again.

'*Kenny, can we ask you, on behalf of Cloud TV viewers, to present this man of the match award to Greg.*' Kenny duly passed it to Greg and with a quick word for his new signing then mouthed to the camera 'Du-GAN! Du-GAN'.

CHAPTER 5

Post-match celebrations were the order of the day at the Estadio Rooftop Club, that looked out over the ground and beyond to the sea. The sun was finally going down on what had been a momentous evening. The Lynx players and officials were there too, warmly received by the Eruption players, coaches and staff.

Eight wins on the bounce was to be celebrated but coming back from the dead in the second half had lit the blue touch paper so far as the local support was concerned. Greg's outstanding contribution and the island boys had ignited something far more powerful, a sense of belonging from the top to the bottom in the club.

As Kenny had said, Greg and the three Lanzarote-born players were the headline news of the night.

'Senor Du-Gan. Let me make my introduction. I am Juan Cavaleros.' Greg hadn't known what Senor Cavaleros would look like but he'd had a mental image of someone in their 50s or 60s or even late-60s, black haired, heavy set, swarthy businessman wearing a well-tailored suit and sporting a heavy black moustache.

Juan didn't fit that mental image at all. He was slim, around 5ft 10 and dressed in jeans, a black short sleeved and buttoned shirt and was bleach-blond. Hardly the high-powered executive look Greg had in mind.

'What a player you are. Magnifico!' Juan Cavaleros seemed very natural, easy and delighted. Maria was currently laughing along with a group of her fellow Lanzarote socialites. Juan followed Greg's eyes, which had momentarily followed the laughter.

'Maria is the reason we are here Greg. She sees opportunities and potential where others do not. She may give an impression otherwise, but she is also a powerful, determined woman. Don't underestimate her.'

Greg's tendency in the past had been to pretty much ignore getting involved in small talk, but had he just been warned off Maria by her husband Juan? Or had Juan simply offered up his own acknowledgement of her talents by way of making conversation? It had seemed an odd comment to make as an introduction, but Greg had read it as a targeted message.

'I hope you enjoy becoming a part of our legacy to the island Greg. I myself only arrived for the second half of the game. You have set yourself a high standard judging by what I saw.'

And with that, plus other congenial nods and half-smiles from Greg and a murmuring of something Greg hoped sounded like 'okay, Mr Cavaleros', why hadn't he said Senor? Juan moved back towards Maria's group, his champagne flute in hand, and began talking with more of the social gathering.

'That was some game feller.' Ellard Vellidale (EV) clinked glasses with Greg. *'Kenny bigged you up with us when he knew you were coming, but man, what you just did out there …'*

EV left the words hanging as his and Greg's attention suddenly went towards a beautiful blonde who had lit up the room dressed elegantly and exquisitely in a Roland Mouret white satin gown and Stuart Weitzman shoes, eat your heart out Jimmy Choo, with at least 5 inch heels.

The dressmaker's or shoe manufacturer's names would make no difference to Greg, but for the Lanzarote socialites this was even more stunning than Senor Du-gan's display. This would be talked about for weeks, an entrance that poured glamour ten times over anything or anyone else in the celebrations.

There was a hush around the room, even at the club bar, as the head-turning beautiful woman in killer ensemble walked with purpose straight to Greg, put both her hands to his face and kissed him. Greg responded. The kiss becoming increasingly passionate.

CHAPTER 6

'That was so much fun,' they were laughing now, back in Greg's room at the Papagayos Beach Hotel. 'As soon as I got your message I just thought, what the hell, I'm on my way.'

'I wondered what you were planning when you asked where I'd be after the game – and when would be best to turn up.' Susie smiled and raised her eyebrows in the same alluring way that had Greg enchanted by her when they had first met.

'I don't know what you mean Senor Duggan. I was just passing by … and you just happened to be there … now come back here Mr Cool … I saw you play, I was watching on the television back here. Senor Du-gan is a big hit already! And your big muscles and your big … oh my!'

Seductive and sexy was most definitely the way, tinged with her lightness of humour Greg never needed a second invitation.

This had been just what he needed. He'd not just played the game of his life, he was also in the sunshine of the Canary Islands playing the sport he loved and now, with the woman he simply adored.

It couldn't be better. Who knew where they were heading, all Greg felt was happiness being with Susie. She made him feel good and they laughed. That was enough. They were enjoying each other, drinking the champagne the hotel manager had supplied on their return from Susie's spectacular entrance at the ground.

Pablo-Marizio Gonzales hadn't realised the significance of who he had staying at the Papagayos until he'd been enjoying drinks in the Estadio Rooftop Club after the game.

The Papagayos Beach Hotel was one of the club's sponsors. He knew little of the game except that Lanzarote Eruption's matches were bringing in regular additional trade. He'd introduced himself to Greg and Susie just after their embrace had finally come to an end and had ensured they had champagne, compliments of the hotel, when they had returned.

'*Pablo likes you, you know …*' Susie said it with such a straight, deadpan expression as she propped her head up with her hand after what had been a satisfying conclusion to her appearance. Greg was open mouthed. Susie saw it immediately. She laughed. '*You don't know what to say, do you …*'

'*You mean? … Noooo …*' Then he saw her look, that tell-tale shift of her head slightly to one side, that smile. God, he was hooked every time. '*Really? … how? … I mean, how can you tell …?*'

'*Come on Greg … why do you think we got the champagne? … it wasn't for my looks … yours, sweetheart … don't you feel the same?*' Susie teased.

Greg couldn't be arsed with the conversation any longer. He wasn't one for beautiful, sensitive words. He let his actions speak louder. He may well have played his heart out for 40 minutes, and they may well have already enjoyed each other, but stamina was his strong point.

After not seeing Susie since a few weeks before the end of the previous season and having had no contact at all for the past nine months Susie had sent him a message. Hardly a message at all, just an 'x'. At first, he hadn't responded. He'd sent an 'x' back a couple of days later.

Greg's head had been a shed. He'd only recently found out his wife Diane was with this new feller John and apparently perfectly happy. He'd lost his now 3-year-old son Kyle, although that was slightly over dramatic as Diane had called and had told him she would let him see his son. Greg had agreed with her terms. He still held a love and fondness for his wife, and she for him. He loved Kyle to the moon and back, realised he hadn't a leg to stand on over his rights, given his actions – but now at least he had Susie back in his life.

It hadn't been he and Susie that had caused the end of his marriage. There had been a press story about a one-night fling he'd had with his brother Colin's girlfriend. Colin and Patsy had split up later. Colin hadn't been in touch since. Diane had simply had enough of Greg's meanderings.

The one thing that had worked in Greg's favour had been

that his affair with Susie, almost twice his age, but with a body, as he always told her, of a twenty-year-old, had never seen the light of day in print.

Greg had found it strange, bearing in mind the determination of those who had been trying to ruin Hopton and him, that his relationship with Susie hadn't been uncovered, but he wasn't complaining.

He had seen Kyle, and Diane, before flying out to Lanzarote. They'd talked reasonably and he'd explained that

Kenny's offer had come with a reasonable contract to the end of the season, bringing back income since losing his role at Victoria Street Garage.

Greg's mind returned to matters in hand.

'I loved that call you made … you know … that's what made me come … here,' Susie smiled, she knew he'd love the innuendo. They were entwined, relaxed, satisfied, once again for the night.

It had been out of character for Greg, such a spur of the moment decision, to call Susie after the initial single kiss text. He was used to having to make quick decisions on a rugby league field.

Susie had made the most minimalistic of contacts. It was something she had said she didn't do, go back.

When Greg had first rung her he'd had no idea what he was going to say, but Susie had told him what she was wearing, or more accurately what she was not, and that had sparked Greg into a verbal seducement that he'd never known he had in his locker. That's when she'd ridden him, from over 2500 miles away. He smiled back at her now.

'I knew you'd love it.' Greg shook his head at himself in good humour. *'Don't know what made me do it, but I could tell you were … you know …'*

She looked into his eyes. He loved the way they sparkled, he'd always seen that. Her eyes smiled. They just did the trick every time. It wasn't as though either Greg or Susie had to try. *'And when you came over to me in the bar tonight. Well, wow! What an entrance! … and that kiss … you looked sensational.'*

This was the best he'd felt in months.

CHAPTER 7

'Are you sure? … no, he doesn't need to know … it's between us … and I don't want him getting to know. It's better he doesn't … for now.'

'I don't know. I honestly don't … but I can guarantee you this … if he does, then God help us all … talk tomorrow.'

Back in England

'Where are we at then? Are we any closer to nailing these bastards?' The voice was authoritative, holding court in an office where he ruled supreme. But despite everything he still hadn't been able to break it down. He felt nowhere nearer now than when they'd started months previously.

He thumped his desk in frustration. *'I want these scum! I want to hang 'em out to dry. Ruin them. Give me something. Anything.'*

He switched from heavy handed, to calm and assured in a heartbeat.

'I cannot believe that we have nothing to pin on these guys. There has to be a way of exposing them.'

Unbeknown to Greg at the time, it was this meeting that was to put him into the firing line once again.

Back on Lanzarote

Juan, we need to talk. As the text was sent the sender looked out to sea in desperation. This couldn't go on. Questions were bound to be asked. The sender thought again and sent another. The sender put down their mobile and looked back out to sea. Within seconds looking at the screen again. Nothing. It had been the same all day. Calls had been ignored. Messages too.

CHAPTER 8

El Papagayo is a historic tract of land that today features just one building near to the end of Lanzarote's most southernmost punta. It is situated at the foothills of a now dormant volcanic mountain range Los Ajaches, with the Hache Grande towering ominously in the background, and is just beyond the easternmost end of Playa Blanca.

Its barren, arid appearance is something you might expect from the set of *Planet of the Apes* or even a fictitious moon landing. Two and a half miles of varying rolling landscape, a plateau across its middle and an underfoot ground of gravel, stone, shale, rock, lava and sand, giving way to the sandiest beaches on any Canary island, have lured generations. Everyone who ever finds it invariably keeps coming back for more, due to its coves' shelter from wind and its turquoise waters. It is an unspoilt paradise that, along with the rest of the island, led to Lanzarote being awarded UNESCO World Biosphere Reserve status in 1987.

The beaches here are still regarded by many as the island's hidden gem.

The Papagayos Coves, hidden from the rest of the island and isolated from the larger beaches along this shoreline, made this a favourite site of pirates looking to sequester goods between Europe, Africa and the Americas over many centuries.

El Papagayo saw the island's first settlement of Europeans in 1402. French adventurer Jean de Bethencourt's arrival signaled the commencement of the bishopric and cathedral of San Marcial del Rubicon. It was reputed to have been the most important of all cathedrals on the Canary Islands.

While little of that time remains, the original medieval wells are still there – five of them – situated only a hundred or so yards from the largest beach on this shoreline, Playa de las Mujieres. For safety reasons the wells were covered by cast iron grilles.

Chiquitita's Chiringuito is the only permanent enterprise of any kind on this otherwise desolate landscape. It sits above the smaller beach of Playa de la Cera and also looks down on the only beach that actually carries the name Papagayos with two coves to explore within yards of the bar/restaurant.

While Chiquitita's is the name on the whitewashed building it is known by the locals simply as *Al's*, having long ago been taken over by Scotsman Alisdair Mackie who had made his money back in the UK through tarmacadam contracts in the north of England in the 1980s. Everyone knew Al's no matter where you were on the island, and not simply for its seafood and a carafe of sangria.

Al had been an intrepid walker in the Munros of Scotland, he'd ascended any hill worth walking in England and Wales and legend had it he had completed the ascension of both Montana Roja, that looks down on Playa Blanca to its north, and Hache Grande when he came across Chiquitita's. He had fallen in love, not only with the area, the beaches, the bar, but also with its owner, or rather the owner's wife. Legend also had it the owner then mysteriously disappeared. There had been many rumours.

Al took the owner's place in all ways. He and the previous owner's wife Juliana made a far more harmonious couple and nobody asked questions.

Legend also had it that although the previous owner was never seen again Al received warnings relating to him having to leave the bar or he would find himself separated limb from limb, his butchered body delivered to each individual cove or beach on El Papagayos. Al eventually also disappeared and was never seen again.

Greg and Susie were currently on their second carafe of sangria having enjoyed a generous helping of calamari at Al's. Greg had run there. Susie had hired a Suzuki Vitara.

They were laughing once again, this time with Greg relaying his moment of the morning when he'd dropped down to Playa de las Mujieres and had witnessed more than he had bargained for as he had run across the beach. Swinging appendages of various male and female equipment were fully on display.

'*I hope you didn't ogle too much …*' Susie teased. '*Pablo would have loved the sight of you in your birthday suit, showing off your glistening abdomen …*'

Greg shook his head slowly at Susie's cheeky smile and turn of her head lightly to one side, her chin raised in that way she had of doing it that he'd always loved. He rolled his eyes and feigned disgust. They clinked glasses.

Al's was busy. Every table taken. Colombian, Carlos Cuadrado had taken over the bar/restaurant three years ago. Carlos was sturdily built, not tall but heavy set. He made no secret of his love of food and wine and had added to the largely fish-based dishes with some of his own South American-styled platters.

His affable manner would soon turn what was going to be a half-hour break from the beach to a couple of hours of drinking and eating, and he would often lead everyone in song with oldies like *Y Viva Espana* and *To All The Girls I've Loved Before* at which point he would visit each table serenading the assembled diners.

He was also one of those had been at the game the previous night and flew into full-on fan mode when he emerged from the kitchen.

'*Senor Du-Gan!*' Carlos's arms were outstretched as though he was about to welcome home a long-lost brother. '*Senor Du-Gan!*' Greg looked across at Susie wide-eyed. He wasn't sure what to do. Carlos had it all under control. '*Adriana! Bring more wine. You'll have more wine? What can I prepare for you? Anything you want, for you and your beautiful lady.*'

Carlos was all for the big show, his booming voice as always attracting the attention of everyone at the tables, but it was as though he'd realized it was time to adopt a filter as he softened his voice to a conversational tone.

'*I am Carlos. I am new to this sport you play and I enjoy. But last night … Pow!*' Carlos acted as though his brain had just exploded. *I never see anything like it before in my life. You are amazing player. You eat and drink here on me!'*

He held out his large chubby hand and clasped hands with Greg as he was summoned back to the kitchen, while also acknowledging Susie. *'Senorita.'* He beamed. *'You are a beautiful lady. You have beautiful smile. You are both welcome here any time!'*

'Well you're certainly making an impression on the men of this island sweetheart,' Susie was continuing her tease. Greg shook his head at her once again. This woman was everything to him right now.

His next game was in three days.

Sure, he had training with Kenny and the Eruption boys, but right at this moment he was happy to be in his and Susie's bubble. The two of them. Susie being playful. Greg being his usual man-of-few-words self but smiling more in her company than any time he ever remembered.

Right now, he couldn't imagine trading Lanzarote back for England, but he knew this particular idyll with Susie probably wouldn't last. She hadn't said anything about when she was going back. She worked in cosmetics. He knew nothing of the trade and little of her role except she travelled around quite a bit as an area manager.

'Carlos is dangerous man. Be careful,' the words were whispered into Greg's ear as he and Susie left Al's.

They were from the woman Carlos had called Adriana. She was possibly in her mid-to-late thirties wearing an Al's shirt, black with the name of the restaurant/bar on the jacquard. It sounded somewhat melodramatic to Greg but, bearing in mind his previous experiences and threats with Hopton Town and what they had led to, he was taking nothing for granted. The woman went back to customers as quickly as possible.

It was 33 degrees, the sun blazing from a brilliant blue sky at around 2 in the afternoon. To any normal, sane person especially after around a carafe's worth of sangria, a run up and down some rocky hills and over stamina-sapping sand would have been readily swapped for a bumpy ride back along the track in the hired Vitara with his beautiful girlfriend, that would take all of five minutes rather than the twenty-two Greg had managed with the initial run out from the Papagayos Beach Hotel.

Greg was now on a mission of full match fitness. If he had impressed in his first forty minutes as an 'Eruptor' – it sounded like being called a 'Terminator' to Greg – with only limited training time Greg knew he would have far more to offer once he was back up to speed.

The previous evening's game had given him increased motivation. This move, although nothing was permanent beyond the end of the season, could prove to be fantastic. He could be playing in the Super League next season if this ended in promotion for Eruption. He couldn't help himself.

Greg set off at a steady pace across the beaches, the rises and falls from cove to cove and take in the pleasure boats anchored just a short distance offshore. He was taken with the landscape, the sea, the mountains, the sand. He imagined spending the rest of his life there, something he'd never thought of anywhere previously. Him, Susie together, playing the sport he loved, sunshine, and hopefully, eventually having Kyle with him for a week or two, bliss.

'Senor Greg!' Pablo was waiting for him on his return. He was uncomfortable, looked afraid. Pablo had been prowling the reception area of the hotel and alternating between walking outside into the coach drop-off area and reception for the past half hour. *'You need to come with me now. I must take you.'*

Greg stared at him dumbfounded. He had no intention of going anywhere but in the shower, and preferably Susie joining him too. He had evening training coming up in a few hours and relaxation was very much on Greg's agenda, preferably relaxation involving extra curricula exercise with Susie. But Pablo was adamant. This was quite different to the Pablo he had talked with the previous evening, who had been all over him like a rash. This was much more urgent, frantic.

'Senor Greg,' Pablo now adopted a deathly serious stance to get his message across. *'All I know is that I must take you to Arrecife. And that I must take you as soon as I have seen you return.*

I have been waiting for you coming back for the last two hours.'

'Okay. Okay.' Greg was keen to get more information about where he was to be taken. He was certainly not getting into some random car with some random guy on some spurious assignation. He recalled only too well what he'd gone through with abductions and beatings at the hands of dubious characters only a year ago.

'Look at me! I need a shower and to get changed before I go anywhere. And I need to make a call.' Greg started to make his way across the marbled reception area.

'Just get in the car!' Pablo's patience was over. 'Get in the car, now, or none of us – you, me and your lovely lady will be safe.' Greg was shocked by Pablo's manner – and his final words. Pablo then turned apologetic. 'I just know I must take you straight away.'

Greg stopped and made his way back to Pablo. He looked his hotel manager in the eye. 'Look mate. I am not going to simply get into a car with you. I don't know you or what you will do to me, or what others might do to me, but all of this sounds very dodgy – and you sound very stressed about it, which from my experience of these things means this isn't going to be a good thing.'

Greg let his words settle. 'Now, I'm going to take a shower and I'm going to find out what's going on. I'm going nowhere.' With that – and with a modicum of pride at the way he'd handled himself he turned and walked directly through the doors that led to his apartment.

Greg wasn't to reach it.

CHAPTER 9

'Yes. He was here. I made a show. He'll come back again, like you wanted. What? The girl? The woman? … yes.'

At around the same moment as the mobile phone conversation, flight LAN52383 was arriving at Cesar Manrique Airport. On its outbound journey back to the UK it was set to be almost completely full of still shell-shocked Leverfield Lynx fans who had spent the early part of the day on the beaches and bars around Playa Blanca before heading home, but the inbound flight was to be more of Greg's concern, albeit that he wouldn't be aware of it for a while.

Greg was in Pablo's Seat Arona. He was still in his running gear. Pablo had hit him, not physically but with the words that would always turn him around no matter what else happened in his life. *'Your wife Diane and your son Kyle. Do you really want them hurt?'* The fact that someone like Pablo could know that information about him told Greg he had no choice.

It also brought back bad memories, what had happened last year, the heartache Diane had gone through losing their unborn child as a result of something that couldn't be proven, the victim of an attempted hit-and-run while out with Kyle, who could so easily have been killed.

He may well now be estranged from Diane but he'd never want anything to cause harm to her and of course Kyle.

In Greg's world, Kyle and Susie were his two most precious people. Susie was always in his heart. Diane was still there too. They may no longer have been a couple, but he still cared how she was, how she felt and would never forgive himself if something happened to her that had something to do with him.

'Do you know this woman?'

Greg was now opposite a man whose face resembled the flat end of a battering ram. It wasn't that his tone was overtly aggressive. He was just keeping po-faced.

'*Have you ever met this woman?*'

The interviewer tried asking it differently. Irish accent. Greg wasn't sure where this was leading. So far as he was aware Pablo hadn't brought him to a police station.

'*These are simple questions.*'

The questioner was becoming annoyed. Greg was generally a man of few words, more about action, but maybe he could appease this guy if he at least answered. Yes, he knew the woman in the photograph that had been shoved in front of him. Yes, he'd met her. What did she have to do with Diane and Kyle?

Greg had learned from his previous run-ins with those who threatened him that he had just as much resolve as they. Maybe it was time to turn the tables a little.

'*Why am I here?*'

He left the question hanging. If this had been a police matter then the local cops would surely have come to the hotel?

'*And what the fuck are you doing with my wife and my kid?*'

His tone now was starting to make him the aggressor.

'*And why the fuck am I here?*'

Greg was on a roll now. He wasn't finished.

'*And while we're at it, who the fuck are you?*'

All of a sudden it was now questions from both sides with no-one answering.

'*Come on! These are simple questions.*'

Greg bounced back the phrase battering ram face had uttered.

'*I will ask you again. Have you met this woman? Do you know this woman?*'

Battering ram face was sticking to his guns. He wasn't about to be intimidated by Greg even though he'd looked as though he was about to blow. He was about to land another bombshell.

'*Do you know this man?*' He shoved another photograph Greg's way. '*And this man?*' Another photograph appeared. No, he didn't know either, but what was it all leading to?

'*Why should I answer you? You haven't told me who you are. I want to know why you want to know?*'

Greg didn't want to get too cocky. The threat to Diane and

Kyle was still uppermost.

They were at an impasse. Neither side giving information in this room that looked no more than an office, certainly not some kind of police interview room given Greg's limited knowledge of such places, garnered mainly from TV shows.

Greg had been brought to what appeared to be an office block.

He'd not been manhandled. Pablo had dropped him off at the doors of the building. He hadn't stuck around.

Greg hadn't yet thought about how he was going to get back to the hotel. He'd ring Susie to collect him in the Vitara or he'd order a taxi or contact Kenny. That bit was easy enough. He'd not had his mobile phone taken from him. He'd made a call to Susie to let her know that he'd had to go somewhere as he and Pablo had left the hotel.

'*Hey, come on now, just answer the questions about these photographs. What's the big deal?*'

Greg was sticking pontoon-style with the hand he held. In his head it was a case of show me your cards, why you're asking, and then maybe I will show you mine. He fired back at BRF – he'd already given this guy a label, BRF, battering ram face.

'*What's the big deal with you? Why did you give Pablo the names of my wife and my son?*'

Greg looked around the room at nothing in particular. He had no intention of looking out for anything, until he focused on the camera up in the corner, trained bang on him. He then looked past battering ram and found another. Little cameras attached to the wall. There were probably more. What the fuck?

'*Or maybe I should be talking to you!*'

Greg asked directly into the camera before turning his attention back to BRF.

'*Is that why you can't answer me? Because you don't know?*' Greg looked back at the camera.

'*Because if you don't give me reasons why I should answer then I'm on my way …*' Greg made to move.

CHAPTER 10

LAN52383 had been cleaned, spruced, refueled, re-laden with passengers and was taxiing down the runway ready for takeoff as those it had deposited made their way in various directions to locations throughout the island, some by coach transfer, some by private taxi. One car, a brilliant white Maserati Levante, was headed on the L2, cruising at around 70mph on the island's main road southwards destined for Playa Blanca with someone who was well known to many.

At around the same time the Lineas Maritimas Orlando ferry from Corralejo on Fuerteventura was reversing into Playa Blanca harbour.

Training night was fast approaching at the Estadio. Kenny was assessing injury situations and watching videos of Eruption's next opponents in his office with Malky.

Eruption were already assured of being in the play-offs but winning this final game would assure them of the championship trophy. After that, just one more game, winning the semi-final play-off, would assure them of being in the Grand Final. Three games from Super League next season.

Their last regular season game, in three days' time, was against Hudderford Gladiators. Eruption had only just scraped a win at Hudderford's ground three months ago. It was all set up to be a 'battle royal' as Sir Roger Ingham, doyen of Pennine fell racing and rugby league, would regularly use in his commentaries at famous old grounds like Farbridge, Hudderford's home.

Eruption's players were either making their way to the ground or were already there in the fantastic gym facilities that the Cavaleros had provided, or they were in the outdoor pool or hot tub exercising or relaxing after exercising.

Hudderford fans would start arriving tomorrow. Their club was just as excited as Eruption. Years ago they had ridden high, in the early days of Super League, winning in the Grand Final twice and once crowned World Club Champions. Their downward spiral had seen them on their knees, nearly going bust twice. They were now back on their way up. This was their year – and for many of the diehards in the sport there was more feelgood in the game about them than there was about Eruption.

Kenny had given everyone pretty much 24 hours following the 'Du-Gan Dramatico', as the fightback against Lynx had been reported in the island press, before reassembling at the ground. Now he wanted them back and focused as they concentrated their efforts on achieving what had been the number one objective at the start of the season – immediate promotion.

After a great start where they had won five on the bounce they had stuttered a little mid-season, had then regained their confidence but had now become stretched with injuries. That was why Kenny had been so keen to get Greg in.

The Maserati Levante rolled up to the gates at La Casa Grande de La Flamenco on the outskirts of Yaiza near to Playa Blanca. Smiles were all around as greetings were made between the host and the passenger in the white car who had arrived at Cesar Manrique. They had business to attend to, but for now it was time for wine and relaxation.

'Tomorrow we start … but now we dine … and enjoy all the good things …'

As the Lineas Maritimas Orlando ferry docked the young woman looked over towards Papagayos. She took a deep breath, closed her eyes briefly then opened them again with a steely determination, mouth closed, breathing slowly through her nose. She'd arrived.

CHAPTER 11

'Go. We will get you back to your hotel …'

BRF had had enough. He stood, but made no attempt to block Greg's way.

'Your driver is waiting for you.'

Pablo must have returned.

Greg couldn't work this out. Why bring him here, travelling what had seemed like around forty minutes from Playa Blanca, and what had seemed further than he had travelled when arriving on the island, ask him questions that could have been asked at the hotel, then not get anything from him when they must have known he at least knew the girl in the first photograph, then let him go? It didn't figure.

Greg made his way to the door, made his way down the corridor that led to the exterior doors and was putting his hand towards them.

'You'll regret you gave me no answer …'

BRF had been walking around five yards behind Greg, who now turned. BRF stood, solid, waiting for Greg's response.

The young woman from the ferry embraced the somewhat older man as she disembarked. They were both now heading towards the harbour car park. The guitar case she had been carrying was now safely stowed in the rear of the vintage Sapego Z-102, the classic car that had been built to challenge the Ferrari and Jaguar but had stalled at a production quantity of just 68 cars. This was a brilliant red sports car built in the 1950s and car number 1 out of the 68. Only seven had survived in the sixty-plus years.

Its current driver was Ricardo Rubio, son of legendary engineer Javier Rubio who had designed the car and who had worked alongside Enzo Ferrari at Alfa Romeo before WWII. Ricardo was a proud man. Proud of his car, his home island and his business. He smiled at the young woman alongside him now.

'I am so pleased you are here darling. It has been too long.'

The Sapego was a real head-turner as was the young woman with long, flowing flame-red hair and a face that could easily have graced any film set. She smiled back, but then turned her head to look in the other direction. She wasn't here for him. He probably knew that.

If BRF had wanted a reaction, he got it. No more playing games, so far as Greg was concerned.

Greg strode up to him, nostrils flaring, tension rising. He stood slap bang up to BRF and

gradually raised his voice as he responded to the threat.

'Do anything to my family and I will find you. And kill you. And you won't regret that you didn't answer me …' Greg let it lie a second. *'… because you won't be here.'* BRF stood, impervious. His face didn't move a muscle.

'She was murdered this morning … the girl …' His face still held the tightness. *'You were with her. Your first evening on the island … the girl … is my daughter.'*

CHAPTER 12

Finally, battering ram face's face cracked, but he had no intention of breaking down. He wanted justice. These were his offices. The cameras were for training courses. There was nobody watching elsewhere. His daughter was Ciara Cortelli-O'Grady. He was Paddy O'Grady. He told Greg all of this after explaining Ciara was his daughter.

Ciara. It had been she who had said 'Senor Duggan' as he'd returned to his room from the Eruption ground on that first night, amazingly still less than 48 hours ago.

Ciara had been in his room waiting for him when he'd returned from meeting Kenny and the boys. She had made herself comfortable and had been wearing nothing more than her smile. It had all been so easy, effortless and at the same time highly energetic.

Greg had had no idea Susie was to turn up the following day, make such an entrance at the ground and that his hours to follow were to have been so special.

Now Ciara was dead and Greg was facing her father. No wonder he had used the threats. Greg reassessed the man. They had moved to Paddy's office.

'I own the Papagayos, the hotel,' Paddy explained as another piece of the jigsaw fitted into place, the reason why Pablo had been the one who had to do his dirty work for him and also perhaps how Ciara had found her way into his room.

'I am not stupid Mr Duggan. I know how my daughter ...' Paddy reined himself in. 'I am well aware of how she enjoyed herself, in lots of ways.' Paddy raised his eyebrows, giving away some of his thoughts about his daughter's lifestyle. 'It was Pablo who told me he had seen Ciara, and that he'd seen her heading toward your room.

'No, Mr Duggan,' Paddy raised his hands as Greg looked as though he were about to offer some form of condolence. 'I am not seeking pleasantries, nice words. I am seeking retribution.

Whoever killed my daughter will pay. And as you say: 'I will kill him, them, whoever they are.

'There is some bad shit going on in Lanzarote at the moment. It may not affect the tourists, those on holiday, or those coming to watch your team – but it is there, it is like a cancer going on around the island.

'This is a small island that is becoming richer every year as more people come, that's certainly true of Playa Blanca. There are many who see Playa Blanca and the Yaiza region as the jewels in the island's crown, and that includes the Cavaleros!

'I thought I recognised one of the men in the two photographs you showed me,' Greg offered.

It was the least he could do in the circumstances.

Yes, he had enjoyed a highly charged session of unbridled raw passion with Paddy's daughter. It had been so athletic Greg had felt later it had been as useful as a training run, except infinitely more enjoyable, memorable and desirable.

'I just can't place where I've seen him, but it can only have been in the three days I've been here.'

'The Comisaria de Policia are not cut out for any of this – and the police commissioner is in bed with the Mayor of Yaiza. It's all corrupt, so there's no way I can trust them to find out what has really gone on.'

Back in Pablo's pale blue Seat Arona gaps were filled in Greg's island education.

'Senor O'Grady has many businesses on the island. Like the Papagayos Beach Hotel, his vineyard interests in La Geria, the Lanzarote Aquapark, his business management training centre, where he has invested in new technologies. He is also the man behind the online concert tickets group Gigagogo.

'I am sorry Senor Greg, that I could not tell you why I had to take you ...' he paused. 'Ciara was a beautiful young woman,' he was driving, concentrating on the road.

'You are an extremely active man Senor. Such vigour, for your sport ... and your ladies ...' They both smiled.

Ciara's death had nothing to do with Greg. His conscience

was clear on that score. Sure, he'd been with her the night before she'd been killed, but she hadn't been killed because of an involvement with Greg. Or had she? Either way the fault wasn't with him, of that he was pretty certain. For fuck's sake he'd only been on the island five minutes!

So far, all he knew was that Ciara had been murdered, not the circumstances. He hadn't thought about asking Paddy and hadn't wanted to get involved in a discussion over the whys and wherefores. He'd just wanted to be out of the building, because he was probably going to be running late for tonight's session at the Estadio.

But Ciara and he had had mad, passionate sex. He couldn't just act as though it was nothing. They'd had a fantastic night, but that was it, that's what it had been. Animal attraction, both willing partners. There had been no hint of taking things further the following morning. No discussion over a bedroom breakfast about what they might do together the next day. Ciara had gone by the time Greg had woken.

Of course, if he'd known Susie had been arriving the next day, he might have thought differently about what he and Ciara had enjoyed the night previously, but Susie hadn't given any indication she was on her way at the time and coming back into his life.

And she had. Sod's law. Like waiting for buses and they all come at once. It didn't seem right thinking that way with Ciara now gone, but that's what had happened.

'It's off!' Stu Wainwright looked about as cheesed-off as it was possible to be that training had been cancelled as Greg approached the gates having been dropped directly at the ground by Pablo, for fear of arriving too late. He'd tried ringing Susie on his way back from Paddy O'Grady, but again to no avail.

Greg still had his same running gear on from the morning. It would do for the time being.

He shrugged his shoulders and gave a quizzical look at Stu asking why training was off.

'*Dunno.*' The teenage half back was glum. '*Just got here …*' Greg again asked the question why with his shoulders. No words.

'*It's Ciara mate …*' EV butted in as he was stowing his kit bag into his car. '*Kenny's girlfriend …*'

Greg's world stopped. For fuck's sake! His head started spinning and wouldn't stop. No way, no fucking way! Jesus H Christ! This had just become a whole lot worse!

Ciara had said when she'd picked Greg up from the airport that it was Kenny who had asked her to pick him up. He hadn't twigged that they were together, an item. Shit. Fuck's sake. He'd had sex with his best mate's girlfriend!

That's how it would play out, how Kenny would see it and anyone with a brain, unlike me thought Greg. And now she was dead. Jeez! No! No!

EV didn't see Greg's face. He was more intent on getting off wherever he was headed. Greg was thankful for small mercies. His face would surely have given way to suspicion at the very least.

'*The Cavaleros have closed the ground, the bar, gym, everything … you should have a text, email, Facebook message. I've just had them all …*' EV slammed the boot of his car shut. '*See you tomorrow mates.*'

The atmosphere couldn't have been more different from the previous evening's euphoria over the amazing turnaround at the Estadio.

Dear God. Not so long ago he'd had a great one-off with his brother's fiancée Patsy, now he'd bedded his best friend's girl. And now she was dead and presumably murdered.

How could the space of less than 24 hours turn his life around so much? For a second, he felt like driving straight to the Cesar Manrique and boarding the next flight out, but then he looked at the now beautiful red and golden sky glistening off the sea and decided on a swift but steady run back to the hotel and into the arms of the woman he loved.

CHAPTER 13

If Greg had thought his day might return to its sheer pleasure of the previous evening with Susie, and then this morning and as far as lunchtime at Al's, any hope was short-lived. His half-mile run back to the Papagayos Beach Hotel had been no problem. Vincey Venus, Alan Thomas and Stu were all staying at other apartments on his route back to the Papagayos and Greg gradually shed them as they reached their destinations. Some were going to take advantage of a night without training by having a more relaxed glass of wine or a long cool beer. Vincey and Stu were meeting up to play some computer game. Maybe, thought Greg idly, he'd have been better advised doing the same, certainly on the night he'd had with Ciara.

'Senor! Senor Greg.'

Greg had come through the hotel gate, taken the stairs rather than the lift to the fifth floor to reach the swimming pools. Dusk was setting in. He had reached the pool bar that during the daytime was the epicentre of the hotel holidaymakers' lives – lounge in the sun, repair to the bar, and then back to lay in the sun once again. Repeating the exercise several times during the day.

By evening it was a relaxed bar with live music usually involving either a saxophonist, solo singer or keyboard player.

Currently the bar was in transition mode from daytime to night-time activity. Pablo was overseeing the staff and, in particular it seemed, a new under-manager. He acknowledged Greg as he made his way to his apartment. 'Are you okay?' Greg nodded and gave out the briefest of sounds that could have almost been taken as yes or no but was a muffled yeah.

Oddly, for a man so eager to grab Greg's attention, this was all Pablo had to say.

When Greg reached his apartment all he wanted was to get out of this kit he'd been in now almost the whole day, get a shower, something to eat and see his girl.

CHAPTER 14

'You know why I'm here,' the flame-red-haired girl was now laid languidly on the bed, propping her head up with her left hand, her left elbow resting on the mattress. She was talking into her mobile phone. She laughed at the comment that came back. 'You must be joking … OMG … No way. I'm here for one thing and one thing only. Well, maybe two or three.'

She giggled as the other side of the conversation also saw the funny side. *'Right, he's coming. Talk soon … bye.'* She was whispering the final words as Ricardo walked into the room armed with glasses and champagne.

Ricardo was around his mid 50s, grey distinguished hair, well-tended. An amorous man of about 5ft 11, he had been married several times. He'd made it his business to collect the remaining Sapego Z-102 cars and now had five of the remaining seven.

Collecting his father's cars was an obsession, as it seemed was collecting wives.

Ricardo had qualified in construction, built a successful business he'd started in his early 20s and had been hugely instrumental in the growth of the Yaiza region and in particular Playa Blanca. Popular talk was that he had been responsible for over 50 per cent of the new hotel complexes built there in the past thirty years.

Ricardo opened the champagne as the flame-haired girl of little more than 22 years of age made little attempt to cover her pert, perky breasts. She didn't need coverage. It was a family thing. Here. Champagne was their go-to family sustenance. In the same way that others had a cup of tea, the Rubios imbibed unmercilessly in the bubbly.

One of Ricardo's other obsessions was nudity. Within the walls and beyond the security gates he was nearly always naked. She'd grown up with his dangly bits wafting along as he walked and she had to confess, now she was older, that his rather substantial tackle swinging like the balls of a prize-winning bull at an agricultural show, combined with a relatively large trunk was an impressive playset – for anyone who was keen on that sort of thing.

She wasn't, but the nakedness was all simply a part of the way he lived, he meant nothing with it, just transferring his love of it from displaying on a beach to feeling free at home. She'd been encouraged to do the same. Her mother too, now long since back in the UK, the fifth Senora Rubio. Ricardo had moved on to numbers six and seven before realising that payments for an eighth divorce may just be one too many alimonies. He now lived alone.

They clinked glasses. She was now standing alongside him before turning toward the view she had of the sea from their elevated position, the homestead being set in to a hillside looking back down to Playa Blanca about half a mile away. It hadn't been too long a run for the vintage Sapego, which had been just as well as the car that once boasted the fastest production car speed in the world had laboured.

'I am so happy you have come, darling.'

Ricardo, now joining her, looking out, was always cautious.

Her temperament often matched what many believe comes with the territory of having flame red hair, so he had learned to take things carefully. He would always want her to stay. She never did. Life had been good when she was younger.

'You know I'm not staying.'

She delivered the line casually, not a threat and no malice intended, or at least if it had been that was a while ago. Ricardo smiled, gave the faintest of nods.

'You know I can't.'

She said it without an ounce of regret. He let it slide. He knew she would tell him why she was here in her own time.

'And you know I will always be here for you. Whatever you are going through.' He was trying hard to play everything cool.

'Tell me about this new sports team,' she could see the Estadio in the distance from where they both stood and changed tack, looking for levity. 'Fit young men with muscles to match and the talk of Playa Blanca, or so I've heard.'

CHAPTER 15

'You bastard! You pommie fucking bastard!'

Greg had just come out of the shower and had a towel around his midriff. He'd taken those minutes in the shower to simply let the water cleanse, and also wash away any kind of thought. Now he was being pushed hard in his well sculpted chest by his best mate, or at least best mate until a short while ago.

Kenny had launched himself into Greg's apartment having run from his half a mile away. There were no tears, just rage.

'Why couldn't you keep that dick of yours in your pants for once! My girl for fuck's sake! You'd only been here a couple of hours! Even in your world that's some going.'

Greg had been preparing himself for going over and talking with Kenny, not that he could offer much. He had hoped Kenny wouldn't have known about he and Ciara but clearly he already knew only too well.

Kenny wanted to hit him. He'd only heard about Ciara's death around an hour before training was due to start. His world had been rocked.

Ciara had met Kenny from the plane as he'd come to the island, in much the same way that Greg had been picked up by her too. Kenny and Ciara had become a couple very quickly and Kenny had thought they were going great.

It had been his first meaningful relationship since splitting from his wife Sheila, true, a real-life Aussie Sheila until three years ago. He didn't hit Greg. Instead he kept on pushing him around the apartment. Pushing him with force.

'Why Greg? Why? What is it about you that just seems to want to have it with any woman you come into contact with?'

He stopped pushing. He knew this was futile. He stood, eyeballing Greg.

'Why, Greg? Why screw your best mate's girl? Do you not have a filter?'

Kenny held out his hands in dismay.

'Screwing your brother's fiancée, now my girl. Don't you have something, anything that kicks in to your brain, telling you that what you're doing is going to cause problems?'

Greg's day was getting better all the time – not. Kenny was right of course, despite being no angel from what Greg had heard. But Greg's instincts of self-preservation were now kicking in too.

How would Kenny have known about that night? Ciara surely wouldn't have told Kenny? Or would she? Maybe she was all about conquests. Greg didn't know her. He knew he hadn't made the running. Ciara had been not just his willing partner. It had been her who had been there for him.

Greg had no idea about her and Kenny, even though now he thought about it there were signals that maybe he should have noticed? But no. There weren't any. He wasn't being stupid. This wasn't his fault.

It wasn't as though he could make a balanced opinion about her. They'd only just met. Shared a car journey from the Cesar Manrique. She'd then been in his room later. They'd done what had obviously come naturally to them both. And it had been great.

But other than Ciara, who would have told Kenny about her night with Greg? How would Kenny have known? Kenny certainly didn't know yesterday. He hadn't confronted him before or after the game, he hadn't mentioned anything.

'How?'

That's all Greg started with. He'd sat on the edge of his bed, toweling his hair. Following swiftly with:

'How did you know about me … and Ciara? Who told you?'

Greg was careful in his questioning.

Kenny, after his enraged entry, was now calming. More so than that, he was close to sobbing. He sat alongside Greg, on the edge of the bed, head in his hands. His fingers were splayed coursing through his tousled hair.

'She's dead.'

Kenny had no idea how or why.

'All I know is that you were banging her the night before she died.'

Greg didn't say anything for a while.

Yes, he had been 'banging her' as Kenny had put it, but she'd been doing the same with him. It wasn't all one way. But nothing he could say right now would help his friend.

They passed the next few minutes in silence.

He felt the need to say something, even if it was minimal. He said it low-key, matter-of-fact and deliberated over his delivery.

'I didn't know … about you and her … she was here … I didn't plan it.'

Kenny almost laughed despite himself. He'd been in quite a few scrapes during his career and had his share of similar attention. He didn't want to admit it at the moment, but if he'd been in Greg's position would he have acted any differently?

They were quiet again for a while. Kenny looked down at the floor, then towards Greg. He shook his head at him, but not with the kind of venom earlier.

'And then last night you're with Susie. Man, she is hot, but mate …'

Kenny couldn't hide his frustration with his friend. He then changed the conversation.

'I don't know how I can let you run out on the paddock with me in the next game …'

He shrugged.

Greg was already ahead of him.

'I'll go.'

It was unequivocal. Greg didn't mess around. No long diatribe, just two words. No sense being around if it wasn't going to work. He'd had a great 40 minutes on the park, one of those things. He'd go back to England. Find a job. Maybe his TV performance the other night would help.

Greg's mobile phone suddenly sprang into life. The pings, chirrups, ringtones and whatever other sounds signaled messages coming through. It then hit what seemed an accelerator button.

Greg had put his phone back on charge after returning from the cancelled training session.

'Do you know how stupid I would look if you're not on the paddock after last night?'

It was Kenny's turn for the matter-of-fact approach.

'You're a twat, Greg, but you're going on that park no matter what I think. You're a bloody hero to the guys on this island after what you did last night. I'd get castrated if you weren't there.'

Something didn't feel right that he'd moved to talking about the next game instead of talking about Ciara.

'Listen mate. Ciara … I know it's not down to you … why she's not here … why she's dead … there are other things … going on …'

Greg had been listening, as well as reading. Taking in his emails and social media messages. He'd added a great deal more social media nous to his repertoire in the past year.

Greg held up his hand to Kenny by way of letting him know to stop talking or at very least to tell him he wasn't currently listening as intently as he should. He read from the text that had been sent, that had also been doubled up on a Messenger text.

'Susie's gone.' Greg, man of few words had put them, once again, into that briefest of sentences.

CHAPTER 16

You think you got away with it, but you didn't. I know you hired the man who killed Jeff Markham and were responsible for George Ramsbottom's state of mind in murdering Robert Irvine. I intend to destroy you.

The letter containing these words arrived in the old traditional manner, via the postal service, marked 'strictly private and confidential'. There was no name, no signature.

Jeff Markham had been the journalist on the newspaper owned by Bob Irvine, Hopton Town's enigmatic owner who had done all he could to keep the club's professional rugby league status. All three were now dead – Markham, Irvine and the club.

GPK had been the editor of Irvine's big city newspaper. His initials were those of Grahame Pythagoras Kraft so named, it was said, because he worked every angle to get his stories.

Markham had never been GPK's best mate, in fact that they had hardly ever seen eye to eye, but they had been colleagues. Irvine had been his boss. His mission now was akin to when one of the police force is murdered. Everyone in the journalistic world was keen to help when it had involved a death of one of their own.

GPK had relinquished his editorship and had been given special dispensation from his newspaper group, to set up a special ops team that had worked night and day for the past nine months on bringing those who had orchestrated events that had led to the two murders.

GPK knew the three perpetrators he needed to hang out to dry. His journos had dug around. He'd had them watched. He knew their movements, but he had nothing substantive enough to make anything stick.

They were currently, it seemed, still beyond reproach. Julian Jardine, the major player in the rugby league hierarchy; Geoffrey Quinigan QC and Brent Dugarry.

Geoffrey Quinigan QC had planned Greg's abduction to his family's estate in Scotland. The head of rugby league Julian Jardine had been uncovered through the work of Greg's brother Colin and fiancée, at the time, Patsy. Threats, intimidation, pay-offs had all been used in a bid to ensure Hopton were finished and their pockets could be lined.

Shortly after the season had ended scumbag brewery owner Bryan Caill of Caill's Ales had sold Hopton's ground for millions, just days following the fateful game where Hopton had secured a win, but not by sufficient points to stop them finishing bottom, and ex-coach George Ramsbottom had lost his marbles with a shotgun.

Greg's quick thinking and resultant actions had managed to restrict the mayhem to a bullet wound for himself, for teammate Tony Estorino and a fatal shot for Bob Irvine, plus a minor wound for Josie Penzance, ironically the gun-toting George Ramsbottom's friend. He

would have loved to see Quinigan, Jardine and Caill get their comeuppance, but had enough problems of his own at the time.

A failed marriage, a bullet wound, recuperation, losing his job at the garage, his beloved rugby league club no longer in existence. Coming to Lanzarote had been a blessing, or at least it had seemed that way for the first two days.

He now read a copy of the letter that had arrived anonymously on an email on his laptop in the Papagayos Beach Hotel. 'For fuck's sake,' he spoke to himself. Now what?

CHAPTER 17

Geoffrey Quinigan QC was currently wet shaving. It was he who had landed at the Cesar Manrique and had been picked up in the Maserati Levante. He'd spent a wonderful evening in the company of his business colleague and occasional partner Hugo Silva at his palatial La Casa Grande de la Flamenco. He was now looking forward to the days ahead and securing even greater wealth.

'Seguramente no me vas a dejar hoy querido.'

Hugo's voice was provocative, alluring and the words 'surely you are not leaving me today, darling' very nearly convinced Quinigan he should stay a while longer, but he was in business mode. Things needed to be done.

Wheels needed to turn – and he was about to turn them. There were some things you could do via email and mobile phone, but others still required the old methods of conversation, negotiation and if all else failed extreme aggravation and blackmail.

He smiled back at Hugo as he toweled down, sprayed sweetness and dressed to impress. He had no qualms about making others' lives a misery if it meant his was comfortable.

Eton schooling, law studies at Trinity College, Cambridge and a stellar career as a barrister with one of the renowned magic circle of law firms had secured him the 'silk' at just 30 years of age, a Queen's Counsel. As such he'd effectively blown himself out by forty-five but had by all accounts amassed a personal fortune, in addition to his family seat in the Speyside region of Scotland.

He'd also learned enough about the law and the nefarious activities of his clients, to realise life would never be fair. The rich would always become richer, poor would invariably become poorer and justice was very rarely meted out where lucre ruled.

But life for Geoffrey Quinigan QC had been anything but

easy recently. His personal life was a mess. He needed to be here. He needed the next big deal.

'It will all be worthwhile babe. When this is done, we won't just be able to go to that little island you love so much, we might even buy it.'

Quinigan stood at the mirror, admiring himself. He was only wearing a white shirt, jeans and shoes, but they were a Turnbull & Asser £250 white shirt acquired from London's finest shirtmakers in Jermyn Street, Emporio Armani £200 slim-fit jeans and a pair of £400 Crockett & Jones Connaught brown calf shoes. He was in casual QC mode, on holiday yet ready for business.

'My God I look good,' he said as he saw his reflection and blew a kiss at himself. The response from the bed was just as impressive.

'Ven aqui, no vas a ninguna parte, te quiero ahora' meaning, *'Come here, you're going nowhere. I want you now.'*

CHAPTER 18

Ferry girl was on the move. She'd left Ricardo to his swaying appendages and was heading for Playa Blanca with her guitar. Weirdo Ricardo her father? That's how he saw himself to her. What a load of mush.

Ricardo had been her stepfather for what had amounted to just a couple of years in her early teens and she'd not seen him at all for five years, but his place was an amazingly fortuitous bolt hole right now for what she had to do.

She'd been playing guitar and singing in bars all around Spain and the Canaries the previous summer playing some of her own songs as well as plenty of covers by the likes of Jess Glynne, Katy Perry and Ellie Goulding; as well as newer names such as Halsey and Alessia Cara; alongside the classics like 'Son of a Preacher Man' by Dusty Springfield.

She'd arrived from a stint in Australia earlier in the year where she'd had a residency in a new bottle shop bar called Luna in the surfers' town Byron Bay on the east coast run by an English guy Russell Stewart. She'd then secured a spot on the 'first-timers' stage at the legendary, internationally-renowned Byron Bay Bluesfest where Kool & The Gang, The Doobie Brothers and Van Morrison had headlined.

It had been while she'd been out in Byron that her eyes had been attracted to one of the TV screens in a bar where she'd been having a drink, hanging out with friends, Russ, the bottle shop bar owner and his fiancée Alex.

She'd seen Kenny Lomax's face appear on screen. She knew the face from the previous year back home when her natural father had been alive. It had come up at what must have been half-time in a game from the NRL.

The sound was difficult to hear, but the caption below had told her about the new Lanzarote Eruption entering the British competition and everything had clicked into place about what her real father had spoken about months beforehand.

That's when she had made the decision to make her way to the island. She might find out nothing, but at least she would try. She had been close to her father.

Greg had slept well. He very rarely didn't, but now that he was awake his mind was back with Ciara and Susie. How had Ciara been murdered? Why?

Susie. God he would miss her. They'd only been back together for such a brief spell. She had sent a text he'd read while Kenny was with him, telling him she'd waited as long as she could.

Susie had explained that an urgent family issue back home meant she'd had to get straight to the airport. By sheer good fortune there had been a flight available with seats untaken.

Susie's family? She had never talked about family. He let it pass. *'Great to see you darling. I'll be back just as soon as I can. xxx.'* Susie had ended her text.

'Training session tonight 5pm. Be there,' was this morning's text, from Kenny, or rather a text from last night. It wasn't friendly, nor unfriendly either. It had probably been sent to everyone.

While Greg would have wanted to wake up alongside Susie, and to have gone to bed alongside her, he also saw the positive side of her suddenly not being there.

Concentration on the task in hand would be improved, his mind solely set on winning games.

He hadn't wanted her to go back, certainly not as quickly as she had done so, and he most definitely wouldn't have asked her to go, but now she'd gone it cleared his mind. He'd loved seeing her again. Too short a time, they'd been together less than 24 hours, but it had still been worth it. He wondered what the 'family' problem would be, but let it pass, quickly reconciling himself to preparation for the next game.

He'd called Diane. John was fine, thanks for asking, which he hadn't. Diane's talent for sarcasm was undiminished.

He'd found out what he needed to. Kyle was great, but

currently at nursery so Greg couldn't talk with him.

Train, run, fitness, work with the rest of the boys.

It was morning 9.30am. Light breakfast then a run. There was only one way he was going to be heading. A light lunch at Al's Bar was beckoning, after a decent workout that this morning would take in every inch of the Papagayos beaches and coves. It was time he put in a shift.

It was all back to being about Eruption today.

'He's on his way.' There was no drama. The voice was monosyllabic. The listener at the other end of the call was even more brief. *'Gracias.'*

The players met just outside the entrance to the Papagayos Beach Hotel.

'Just like old times!' was Stu's welcome as he arrived. *'At least we're not going to get soaked, like just about every time we ran back home.'*

It was good natured stuff including a fair degree of playground humour.

Training night was for later. Kenny had sent another text to everyone late the previous night after his earlier message about 5pm training.

'Morning run. Meet at Greg's. 9.55am latest.' Greg had mentioned about his proposed run once Kenny had calmed, and Kenny had latched on to it for additional training.

All the ex-Hopton Town boys were there, along with the Antipodean contingent. A few of the bigger lads were missing along with those carrying injuries but they formed a sizeable battalion going out on to the dusty landscape.

Alan Thomas, Vinny Venus and Jose Maria Estapol trailblazed with New Zealander Warren Entish and Papuan scrum half Popoli Baru just in their wake. Stu Wainwright, Ron Rigson, Jordan Peters, Angel Ramos, Elton Richards, Roberto Ortega and Philippe Longchamps made up the next group.

Greg, Kenny, EV and relative newcomer Tonito made up the rest with Raul Rodriguez-Perez at the back of their group. Sixteen out of a squad that numbered 28 might not normally have been considered a success but having only given short notice, plus the injury list, there were only five missing. Everyone was expected at training in the evening, including the injured players.

Typically, Vinny, who never went anywhere without a ball had turned up with one and he, Alan Thomas and Jose Maria Estapol were not just moving at pace but also running inside and outside of each other passing the ball and occasionally kicking ahead with a race on for who was to get there first.

By the time they'd reached Playa Muerto, one of the beaches used more by the locals, they were close to Al's. The sands of Playa de las Mujeres had found out a few of those who chose to run on the softer, wetter sand.

Playa Muerto was pretty well deserted. They had a ball. It was as good a time as any for a few drills and moves Kenny was keen to work on. It hadn't been intended that way, but Kenny was quick to seize on the opportunity.

This was also Greg's first real opportunity to get to know some of the rest of the squad. He'd arrived, played the next night, then they'd had a day's break and training had understandably been cancelled the previous night. It was Greg's first time to work with his new teammates.

'Look fellas, tomorrow night's game is not going to be any kind of walk in the park. We're certainly not invincible and we're running out of fit players. We could easily have even less if we're not careful running around out here, so watch how you go in to each other and how you twist in the sand.

'The Glads (the shortened nickname for Hudderford Gladiators) want it probably just as much as you and me, but I want this bloody title. We've worked hard for it and I want us to play at home in that first game in the play-offs.'

Vinny put up his hand as though he were still in a school classroom. Kenny dealt with him as though he still was.

'Yes, tall lad at the back. Question?'

'Please sir, can we have our ball back now?' The gathering descended into hilarity as EV intercepted the projectile from

Kenny only to be mobbed by nearly everyone else. So much for Kenny's words.

They played a sevens game on the beach with Kenny watching on, and each player taking a breather every few minutes. Greg was breathing hard but no more, he noticed, than the rest after around twenty minutes.

Young Tonito had been showing impressive handling skills and EV had been seeking to search and destroy everyone in his wake in retribution for his earlier receipt of the combined mass tackle. Fortunately for the rest his giant frame didn't move quite so well in the sand.

One pair of eyes looked down on their gathering. She was watching for now, preparing herself. She didn't want to be noticed by the Eruption guys. Not that they would have known who she was.

For the meantime she would observe, get to know. She wasn't about to charge in anywhere without good reason. Ferry girl would become known to people when she was ready. She had plans. She was ready to set the ball rolling, but wanted to know who she was dealing with first. This was a reconnaissance mission.

Ferry girl made her way up the slope from the beach to Al's.

'*Senor Du-Gan! Senor Lomax! Come! This is great day.*'

Carlos was having his photograph taken with the pair and the rest of the players with his Al's sign. He'd been waiting for them as they came up the slope. Kenny had called from his mobile earlier to let him know they would need several tables.

'*Everyone! This is our wonderful island team the Eruption!*'

Carlos had announced proudly. If he'd expected a rapturous reception the response was somewhat muted. The Germans and French around the other tables didn't understand what was going on and had little interest if they did. Some of the locals and a few English gave a smattering of polite applause. Carlos wasn't bothered.

'*Whatever you want boys. It is all on me.*'

'*Been coming here since I arrived,*' Kenny told Greg as they were together at one table with EV and Jordan Peters. Understandably given the circumstances of the previous day, they weren't exactly thick as thieves, but they weren't cold to each other either and it had been Kenny who'd spoken first at Al's.

'*Great place,*' Greg had already fallen in love with the whole of El Papagayos. He found Carlos a bit much, too over the top, but he enjoyed being at Al's. His mind was now wandering back again to yesterday. He and Susie had been here around the same time and it had looked like it was going to be the best of times. It had all ended too soon.

Since yesterday it had all gone pretty much pear-shaped. Ciara and Susie both gone, different reasons but gone nonetheless. Paddy on his case, and then Kenny. He chose not to mention to Kenny about being at Al's with Susie the day previously. He didn't want to make matters worse.

Kenny either read his head or simply wanted to get things back level with Greg.

'*Look mate, I'm sorry I flipped at you …*'

Kenny let whatever he might have been going to say just hang in the air for a second.

'*… I just couldn't believe it, you know … still can't …*'

'*Do you know how? …*'

It was Greg's turn to pause.

'*Or where?*'

He wanted to ask more, but these would do for starters. He'd been wondering why neither Paddy nor Kenny had said, not that they had to, but it was odd that they hadn't.

EV and Jordan Peters had been having their own conversation, mainly about Aussie RL, but couldn't help themselves listening to Greg and Kenny. EV had known Kenny for many years, they'd locked horns several times on the footie field and had both represented their country in the green and gold, rooming together while on tour. EV also looked after his mate and was there for him now, protective. Kenny was suddenly struggling, he'd started biting on his bottom lip to maintain some form of decorum. He didn't want to break down. He shook his head as if to shake away any tears that may have been coming.

'You okay Ken?' said EV. The gentle giant off-field was straight there for his good friend.

Kenny nodded. He steeled himself once more. He motioned with his head for Greg to follow him as he left his seat. He and Greg moved away from the rest of the players and out beyond the restaurant by around twenty or thirty yards, looking out to the sea.

Their walk was wordless and so too their first few seconds near to the cliff edge. Greg waited. Kenny was facing the sea when he started.

'You know, I was in the best place I'd been for the last few years, since Sheila.' He shook his head, looked out to the ocean again but this time his face further out of Greg's range. 'I really felt she was the best thing to have happened to me for a long while. This place, the club, Ciara, it all felt good.'

'Then I come along,' said Greg, also looking out to sea and down to the cove below.

Kenny couldn't resist responding, but not in words. He turned to Greg, eyebrows raised.

'I can still go,' Greg reaffirmed.

'Don't be such an arse.'

Kenny turned away from him again. They fell silent as they looked out back to the sea, but there was a grin from both. Whatever had gone before, their friendship was still intact.

The shriek that rang out below where they were standing wiped the smiles from their faces. Instinctively both Greg and Kenny made their way down to the beach, the smallest of the coves.

CHAPTER 19

Ana Cristina Magdalena's family were 'old money'. They'd built their wealth when Lanzarote had begun attracting holidaymakers in the 1970s as the 'package holiday' had become popular. Her father and his brother Francisco and Antonio had arrived from Madrid in the 1940s after WWII, settled inland in San Bartolome where they bought significant tracts of land very cheaply and had returned to their first love on the Spanish mainland of construction.

The brothers had been responsible for a sizeable quantity of hotel construction in Costa Teguise and Puerto del Carmen during the 70s and 80s, aided by some of the El Cabido, the island's local government, who had benefitted personally from helping secure lucrative contracts for them.

Ana Cristina, now 56, was the sole heir to the Magdalena fortune the brothers had accumulated, being the only child to Francisco and Carmen, and Antonio having never married. She had been fiercely protective of the wealth she had inherited when her father was the last of the three to pass away in the early part of the new millennium and although she had had partners there was always the proviso that there would never be marriage, any prenuptial agreement, even if she relented, if someone swept her off her feet, would see everything remaining with her.

Film star quality good looks, trim figure, kept so by a daily routine of running, swimming and yoga, raven black hair and not a 'botox' in sight.

Property was now owned in Costa Teguise, Puerto del Carmen, Punta Mujeres and Playa Blanca, but Ana Cristina's time was mostly taken up on La Graciosa, recently heralded as the Canary Islands' official eighth island, a rocky outcrop of an island covering 11 square miles, half an hour's ferry trip north of Lanzarote's north east tip with a resident population of around 700.

This is where she planned, plotted, kept herself fit and, largely, herself to herself, north of the island's harbour and main village of Caleta del Sebo. La Graciosa was home of the white sands and aquamarine waters that enticed 25,000 visitors each year.

The AgustaWestland helicopter that now sat on her lawn, alongside her own, decanted a man on a mission. She'd been expecting him for a while.

'Could you believe that?'

Kenny was incredulous, couldn't keep his face straight. *'No way!'* Greg was similarly in hysterics.

'That guy has some serious issues'.

EV and the rest of the squad had also sprung to life on hearing the wail of pain that had reverberated around the cove and above, where Kenny and Greg had been standing.

'Who does that kind of thing? And in broad daylight!'

Kenny was still processing what they had just seen.

'So, it would be alright in the dark, is that what you're saying bro?'

Vinny Venus had made it to the scene quicker than the rest.

Ferry Girl had been careful not to make herself more visible by running to the cliff edge as the Eruption players and some of the restaurant crew and customers had, but had also not simply sat in the restaurant when others moved to take a look.

Important to go with whatever flow, be a part of the crowd, not to stand out.

It had been a bizarre incident that, from what she gathered from the hubbub, had involved a man, his appendages and a voracious albino cave crab, endemic to the island and the animal symbol of Lanzarote. It had proved more than a symbol to the nude bather!

Even Ferry Girl couldn't help but smile at the victim's misfortune. It appeared she wasn't the only one either with winces turning to sniggers as the story was retold of the poor incumbent's similarly nude and highly well-endowed lady partner's several hard hitting attempts at extricating the crab, that appeared to have taken a liking to his now engorged penis and swollen testicles.

Exactly what the now relieved-but-battered, bruised and

broken man and his heavily-boobed good lady had been in the process of beforehand was hardly in question, however the woman's aim, having finally got her eye in after three previously failed attempts with her impressively large hair brush, had finally dislodged the varmint.

Her earlier forays had all made contact, not with the perpetrator but in and around the man's nether regions, leading to the squeal heard above. The final whack, that had done the trick, had been landed with even greater ferocity, had sent the crab on its way and had left the unfortunate man doubled over, not quite knowing which had been the most painful – the crab or the brush, bejeweled as it was on the whacking side.

The crowd had returned in good humour to the restaurant. Ferry Girl easily slinking back into her chair and burying her head back into the book she had little intention of reading.

She saw who she reckoned to be the restaurant manager, the man who had made a big show of Senors Du-gan and Lomax. There was something about him that she saw as maybe more sinister, as though he had some other agenda. It was only a fleeting thought.

It was his reaction once he returned from the furore, that reaffirmed the thought, but she didn't know him, had only been on the island five minutes, and was already jumping to conclusions. She parked it to one side.

'Haven't you lot had enough of me?'

The man delivering the words was world-worn, weary.

George Ramsbottom was being charged with the murder of Bob Irvine, the owner of Greg's hometown club Hopton Town when they played their last fateful match at the end of the previous season. His trial was scheduled in two weeks.

There was little doubt he'd shot and killed Bob Irvine, maimed Greg's teammate Tony Estorino and had injured Greg. He'd also somehow winged his friend Josie Penzance. There had been at least one thousand witnesses if not more at the game.

Ramsbottom's solicitor was going for a verdict of manslaughter on the grounds of what he took to be George's diminished responsibility through his state of mind at the time. He'd suffered at the hands of the conspiracy to ensure Hopton Town finished bottom of the league and lose their professional status.

That one element alone had returned Bryan Caill, owner of Caill's Ales, one of the town's major employers, back into the land of millionaire. It had also increased the wealth of a triumvirate of others: Brent Dugarry, property magnate; Julian Jardine, head of the rugby league governing body; and Geoffrey Quinigan QC, the man who was presently in Lanzarote.

George had been granted bail on the grounds that he wasn't a menace to society and would not travel further than 10 miles from his caravan home at the Coniston Glades site in the Lake District.

He'd agreed a meeting with a man he'd never met before, one of GPK's team, who had promised that, although he was with a newspaper this was not about writing a story and dragging George's name back through the media.

After the pleasantries on arrival, they walked to a viewing point through the glades looking down on Coniston Water. George looked out across the lake rather than directly at the man who had come to ask questions. He exhaled long and deep, as though he was deflating, keeping calm.

'I can't believe I may never see this again.'

He continued to look out over the lake.

'Makes you wonder, when you're here, why we do the things we do.'

The other man left him to it, let him expand.

'I loved the bloody game, played it since I was a kid, followed my dad and my grandad. My brothers played. It was all I ever wanted. But now ...' George shook his head in disbelief. He turned to the journalist.

'I'm not expecting miracles. I killed Irvine. Ruined Tony's life. I'm expecting to get sent down. But if you can find a way of making sure these others suffer, that they are exposed, that's some consolation, I suppose.'

He turned back towards the lake. *'Ask me whatever you want, tell me what you need. I'm going nowhere.'*

CHAPTER 20

Carlos Cuadrado was not a happy man. He was currently not the gregarious, friendly restaurateur he liked to portray. He was on his mobile phone, noticeably agitated.

'*They are leaving now … no, it was not possible … they all came, and then there was something going on down in the cove, nothing to do with Du-gan or Lomax, but they went there … and now they are on their way …*'

Ana Cristina Magdalena was returning from her daily run as her visitor landed. Five miles long by two-and-a-half miles wide with largely sandy tracks – there were no roads as such and only limited motorised transport, generally clapped out Jeep taxis – meant she could take in most of the island on every run. She had seen the helicopter heading over and had been aware of the time he was due to arrive, but her morning run was a ritual, a circuit this morning of ten miles taking in rocks, a testing run up one of the two volcanic hills, beach and tracks.

By the time her visitor had been frisked and checked over by her security patrol – everything was tight, nothing left to chance – she'd be back. She looked at her running watch, good steady pace today, she was in good shape.

'*Ana!*'

The formalities on arrival had been completed. The two highly attractive female security guards, dressed as formally as shorts and T-shirts with firearms could allow, had been an interesting take on the archetypal meatheads who usually took this kind of role.

Geoffrey Quinigan QC had stored the idea for future, although he wasn't quite sure the Baywatch-style approach would be appropriate up on the Speyside estate. His arms were now outstretched to the radiant, lycra-clad female athlete before him who had been handed a towel from one of her staff on return from the run. They kissed, both cheeks, in customary style.

'You look absolutely stunning, darling, even given for the perspiration.'

He kept himself in shape too and had run for St John's College in Oxford, the wealthiest college of them all. It was while he was there that Quinigan began realising the combined power of the legal trade, land and property rights. And it was also where he had first met the overseas student in law, Senorita Ana Cristina Magdalena.

'Senor, you are so kind. Perhaps you would like to join me in turning my perspiration into something more?'

She raised her eyebrows, turned to walk, slinging a provocative smile across her shoulder as she took a glass of Dom Perignon from another of her team.

Quinigan followed suit. Life with Ana was always carefree and wild. He couldn't help himself but play along when they were together. She brought the best and worst out of him. She always had from their first dealings as under graduates.

Ana could read him. He put it down to her similar upbringing, from 'old money', as well as her Machiavellian tendency.

'Come on, grumpy! We can get your immaculate clothes steam cleaned and pressed while we take a shower … and then we can talk about our latest investment … while we enjoy our day … Come on!'

She led the way and Geoffrey Quinigan QC was transformed into a different man once more. He felt himself changing colour like a chameleon. Only hours earlier he had been laid in the arms of the current man in his life – Hugo. Now his hi-end designer clothing was disappearing on the lawn as he fell under Ana's intoxicating spell. Batting for both sides was an accurate description.

Greg's mobile phone held a multitude of messages when he returned to the Papagayos Beach Hotel from the morning's and now early afternoon's activities. It would not be long before he was due back for Kenny's later session.

Susie had called, Diane too. There was a message from Pablo. The rest were a mix of Facebook messages, Twitter feeds and

Strava updates on the distance he'd run that morning. Another update from Kenny, even though he'd only just left him. He listened to and read each one, which included hearing Susie's voice, which he always loved. It really didn't matter too much what she said, he couldn't explain it, he simply felt good when he heard her.

Typically, Susie hadn't gone into what the family detail had been for her swift return to the UK and also typically hadn't given any indication of whether she would be back any time soon. That was nothing fresh. Greg accepted it. They accepted each other.

Diane had rung for Kyle to talk with his daddy. Said she'd call back later.

Kenny had recognized that to have two sessions in one day, for those who had been out earlier, may be too much, but still wanted everyone at the ground at 5pm. This too was not a request, more an edict.

'Hola! … Buenas tardes, Senor Greg!'

Maria Cavaleros had looked stunning the first time Greg had seen her, but here, now in his room, she outshone even her initial appearance.

Whenever Greg came back to his room it was already occupied. Surely that wasn't right?

He recalled a similar, but less glamourous regular attendance in what had been his office at Parrot Lane, Hopton's ground, the previous season – only then it had generally been a succession of male visitors. He preferred this kind of intrusion, at least on the grounds of female company.

'Pablo allowed me a key, I hope that is okay?'

Greg shrugged his shoulders in a non-committal way. He was concerned but had nothing to hide. There was no real problem, he guessed. But why was she here?

She looked amazing, wearing a white lace off the shoulder crop top with white Prada skirt, not that Greg would have known whether it was Prado or ASOS. She had a red rose in her hair that matched her Jimmy Choos. On anyone else they would have been too much, but Maria carried everything off.

'*I need to talk with you, Greg. This is not, I am afraid, a social call.*'

Maria motioned for Greg to take a seat in the sitting room of his apartment. She was already perched on the arm of the other. Where the hell was all this leading?

How come Greg couldn't just play for a team anymore without all of this? Whatever this was.

At least Maria wasn't offering herself. Mental note. Don't be an idiot, this woman is talking seriously. He should reciprocate. He sat.

One day soon he'd finish some exercise and be able to jump into a shower like normal people. On his own.

'*It is about Ciara.*'

Greg felt this was the first time he had seen her look anything like vulnerable. She looked upset. Why was she talking this way?

He looked back at her, into her eyes. He gave the slightest of nods. She didn't know whether this was some form of acknowledgement, she went on.

'*Juan and I …*'

This was clearly proving hard for her, searching to find the right words. She nipped her bottom lip with her front teeth as she sought to keep her emotion in check. She exhaled.

'*Our relationship has not been good for some time.*'

Greg had no idea where this one-sided conversation was heading but he let it go. Let Maria get whatever she wanted off her chest. Maria shifted on the arm of the chair.

'*I am here because of you and Ciara …*'

Christ! How did she know about him and Ciara? He'd only been on the island four days. Who was broadcasting on Greg's behalf? This was enough. It was time for Greg to give something back.

'*Mrs Cavaleros …*'

Greg stopped himself from elaborating too far.

'*… I didn't really know Ciara.*'

It was time for Maria to show her own mild amusement at Greg's response, despite her earnest, serious and near tearful approach she couldn't help herself. She countered his answer quickly, in a manner that proved both humorous and yet polite.

'*You knew her well enough …*'

Maria left the line hanging for a second as she deliberated over her next words.

'*… from what I understand, well enough in your bed …*'

She stopped again, for effect, before slinging her hair back as she moved from her position.

'*… but that is not why I am here, Greg …*'

Greg shrugged slightly. This was going nowhere. Sensing his nonplussed nature Maria finally began offering more.

'*There are many bad things happening on the island at the moment … your team, our team, is one of the good things, but there are people who do not want to see us – Juan and I – become bigger than them.*'

Again, Maria awaited some form of reaction from Greg. Again, she saw none.

'*I cannot say for certain but Ciara … her murder … it may be involved with the problems we have been facing lately*'.

'*Why?*'

Greg was trying to process the information Maria was giving, but it appeared there were some vital pieces missing in his education.

'*I mean why Ciara? Why would she be a part of whatever you and your husband are going through? I don't get it.*'

'*You have only arrived a short time ago. How could you?*' Maria moved to a position where she was once again in front of Greg to gauge his next reaction. '*Ciara was my daughter.*'

CHAPTER 21

Bombshell! Greg thought what had happened months prior at Hopton had mentally prepared him for anything. But whaat? His head was suddenly scrambled. There had been no mention of Ciara being Maria's daughter. Why should there be? For one thing, Maria didn't look old enough to have a daughter of Ciara's age. For crying out loud! He'd not only had a fantastic night with Kenny's girl, which again he had no right to have known, he'd also made out with the boss's daughter!

This was all still percolating through as Greg realised his jaw must have hit the floor.

'*Before I married, my name was Cortelli.*'

'*And you had an affair with Paddy O'Grady.*'

For once Greg's interpretation was fast. The one piece of information he had been given had been that Ciara's father was Paddy O'Grady. Now it turned out she was Maria Cavaleros's daughter. His daughter. Her daughter.

'*No, not an affair.*' She flicked her hair once again as a smile returned to her face. '*I married him. We married when I was 19. I married again, becoming Cortelli, before marrying Juan.*'

'*Do you want me to leave?*'

Greg didn't know where his words had suddenly sprung from. It was his gut reaction, not just on behalf of Kenny and now Maria, but also for himself, his own safety.

'*I can go now, back to England.*'

It was half-serious, half-lame as though he was offering it but had no real intention of following it through. Greg had been enjoying Lanzarote. He'd loved his first game and was looking forward to the second. Maria was shocked by his response.

'*No, no, Greg. This is not what I mean by coming here …*'

Maria was animated. Her well-manicured hands outstretched in a kind of stop sign.

'*I need your help.*'

CHAPTER 22

Kenny's best-laid plans of an easy training night at Estadio de Lanzarote in Playa Blanca were in tatters.

Tomorrow evening's regular season finale versus Hudderford Gladiators was gathering momentum as the 'Glads' supporters had begun arriving at Cesar Manrique Airport earlier in the day.

Playa Blanca was already heaving with summer tourists and it had been estimated that around 3500 fans from the Pennine-based club that was 'on the up' would be at the game, which was being billed as 'El Partido Mas Importance' by the Lanzarote media.

It couldn't have worked out any better by the fixture planners. The best supported club in the division, with one hundred years of rugby league history behind them, and the newest, brightest, most affluent team in the game at present, head-to-head in the final league game of the season.

Eruption vs Gladiators. They were level on points, both sides having only suffered two defeats all season, and with drawn games having to be settled by the first score after normal time there was no way they could finish level, something had to give.

Disaster had struck before the evening training session had started. Jordan Peters had pulled his hamstring on the way to the ground. There was no way he could play tomorrow.

Victor Borsoni and Ron Rigson had collided during light training in what had initially seemed harmless, but their innocuous clash had broken Victor's thumb and had given Ron concussion as they had fallen awkwardly.

Three of Kenny's starting lineup out – and an injury list that was already stretching his now meagre resources. From a squad of 28 players he was now down to less than 20 fit to play, with some of those carrying knocks and minor strains.

One of Eruption's two defeats had been at the hands of the 'Glads' at their Farbridge ground. The 'Glads' had been worthy winners, but Kenny had seen enough that day to recognise his team's weaknesses and he had been confident, up until half an hour ago, prior to going into the final training session before the game that they could avenge that result.

They'd gone down 28-10 that day but he knew at that time his charges hadn't played enough together and their match fitness hadn't been at the same level as they had reached particularly in their now eight match winning run.

He and Malky Shannon had to front it up, give their players as much belief as possible. It was going to be a tougher ask right now. Nonetheless, Kenny had seen it all in the game during an illustrious career that had seen him win everything in Australia and play for his country many times.

Kenny finished the session with a team talk.

'One game. That's all I'm asking from you boys. One game. Eighty minutes. Get a result tomorrow and we have just one more game before the final. That's it. Lose it and we're done, simple as.

'Warren, Elton, Raul – you're all making your first starts of the season tomorrow – you all deserve it. Tonito, Popoli – you're on the bench for the first time. I've seen the way you've worked. Get a good night's rest and let's do this out on the paddock tomorrow night.'

This wasn't the way Kenny would have wanted to have gone into the game. Putting together a new half-back pairing was always a step into the unknown.

Young Stu Wainwright had played out of his skin all season and had built a great understanding with Jordan Peters. Now he had precocious poster boy teenager Aussie Elton Richards making his first stand-off appearance alongside him.

Raul was different gravy again. Raul Rodriguez-Perez, along with his fellow Lanzarote-born teammates Jose Maria Estapol and Angel Ramos were now becoming a major part of the remarkable story of Eruption's campaign.

If some in the sport had been concerned that this small island could not produce rugby league talent, then they were already having to think again.

Kenny had seen enough from Raul's debut from the bench

in the previous game to know that he was more than worth his full debut this time around.

Far more concerning was the bench. Rugby League had become a 17-player game, not purely the 13 out on the paddock.

Kenny had Greg, who he had so very nearly put in at stand-off instead of Elton Richards, and Angel Ramos. They were both absolutely sound.

It was the other two players who would sit alongside Greg and Angel that were more of a forced hand.

Under normal circumstances he may even have put a couple of the guys carrying little knocks and twinges back in, rather than two untried and untested players but Kenny knew it was more important that all of those who were either coming back from injury or nursing new ones should take more time before being put back on the front line, especially with even bigger games to come.

He'd already lost so many of what had been his regular starting line-up in recent games. This was time for Popoli Baru and Tonito.

Popoli Baru from Papua New Guinea was one of the two who would be ready to make his first appearance. Baru had arrived with his compatriot and much better known international centre Manuwai Manuai.

Even in his native southwestern Pacific island Baru was an unknown. He'd been a member of the Port Moresby Vipers youth team but so far as Kenny and Malky had been able to ascertain that had been where his career had ended up, until arriving with Manuwai. His natural position was scrum half. Kenny had gone with him on the bench as the other three were all used to playing in the pack. It gave him an option, along with Greg, if Richards didn't click with Wainwright.

Tonito was the biggest gamble. The lad was Spanish-Australian. Nobody knew much about him. He'd arrived in Playa Blanca with a backpack and the clothes he stood up in.

Kenny and Malky had been impressed with his attitude to training, he'd fitted in well with the rest of the boys and on signing they had been pleasantly surprised to find that he'd played for Pacific islanders Vanuatu in the Emerging Nations World Championship in Sydney. His position was hooker.

Putting him on the bench was more about having four fit players there, but if they could give him a spell it might at least help one of the others get a breather.

Kenny's only other non-injured options were to blood two more young Lanzarote lads, who were in the squad to bring on new island talent and form the basis of a youth squad for the following season.

The senior players were gathered in the Estadio bar after training, looking out over a glorious sunset, when the entrance of someone new to the proceedings took Greg's eye. And not in a good way.

It was Juan Cavaleros. Jeez. Juan had entered the room unflustered, business-like yet also relaxed. He appeared amiable, but Greg was immediately on his guard.

Not that anything of any kind of sexual nature had occurred with Maria Cavaleros, but Greg could see that if it had been reported by someone, it may have caused unnecessary problems.

'*I have no wish to interrupt your meeting gentlemen,*' Juan began.

'*I just wanted to wish you well for the game tomorrow evening. For me, this is big too. We have all achieved so much already and I just wanted you to know how much it means. Tomorrow is the first major step towards where we all want to be next season and in future years. To Manana!*' He smiled and made to leave.

A moment later he turned back towards them briefly to deliver one last line. Shit, this was it thought Greg. This is where it becomes about me, about the meeting with Maria, the death of his stepdaughter.

Juan came back towards them a step.

'*Oh yes, I knew there was something else ...*'

He smiled, cleared his throat, took a deep breath and announced.

'*In honour of this game being so important, 'El Partido Mas*

Importance' as our island is calling it, and because today I have just agreed a partnership with another major sponsor, you may find something even more to your advantage in your bank accounts should you be successful in winning tomorrow. Buenas Noches Senors!'

It was 'Bassey' who was first to speak once Cavaleros had gone on his way.

'They're all the same, owners. Smarmy bastards ...'

And then with next breath. *'I'll take his money though, anytime.'* The rest of the players laughed with the big Aussie.

Shirley Fastleigh had little to no respect for those who felt any sport was some kind of cash machine even though his own career had been a mercenary affair. He'd played for half of the NRL teams in Australia and four Super League clubs in England. As soon as the money wasn't right he'd slide off to the next club, but maybe not this time. He was getting near to the end of his career.

Greg stuck around as the other players gradually left. He wanted a word with Kenny again. They walked out of the stadium together. Greg, for once, took the lead. Straight to it.

'Ciara.'

It was a marker. He cared about Kenny's feelings. He looked at him. They had been walking. They now stopped. Kenny waited for the next line, or often in Greg's case purely the next word. He came up with three.

'Maria Cavaleros's daughter?'

Kenny waited again. Greg continued.

'Maria visited me earlier. Yesterday I had Paddy O'Grady, her ex-husband, on my case. Did you know Ciara was his daughter?'

He let the first question settle, watching for reaction.

'And then her husband comes swanning in tonight and I'm certain he's about to have a word with me about Ciara, or Maria in connection with Ciara following her visit and that he's come to take me to task in some way, and then all he talks about is the club. What's that all about?'

'Woah, big feller, that's a lot of words for you all at once ...'

Greg saw the humour in Kenny's mickey-take. Kenny carried

on.

'Maybe he's just able to deal with things, you know, compartmentalise them. He came because of tomorrow's game.'

'Maybe Ciara means fuck all to him.'

'Greg. We're all different. Anyway, what does it all mean to you?'

Then a thought suddenly sprang to his mind.

'Oh, no way! You've not screwed her as well? I don't believe it! ...'

Kenny was playing it through now, as though he'd hit the nail on the head. Greg shook his head, quick to dismiss it.

'It's not that.

'I just feel there's something more to it. I don't know what it is, but no police brought in; an Irishman who interviews me like he's the police; a strange meeting with one of the club's owners; and her husband doesn't mention my meeting with Maria when he comes in just now. Something isn't right.' Greg shook his head in a show of dismay.

'Maybe it's just me. Reading too much into stuff after what happened before. Take no notice.'

The pair clasped hands before casting out their separate ways.

Ferry Girl had been there all along, watching the players come and go. She was still watching, calculating, now in totally new gear, all acquired via a quick call to Ricardo to meet up for coffee, followed by a swift flash of his debit card at the Rubicon Centro.

He might be weird, but he had his uses. Today had been a reconnaissance job, tomorrow would be too. She wasn't sure what she would learn, but she knew that by being around she would learn more.

CHAPTER 23

Geoffrey Quinigan QC hadn't intended to stay, but Ana Cristina had been highly persuasive. She had plied him with a heady cocktail of champagne and caviar and hired in The Thai Knight Masseur to provide the sensations he enjoyed.

Ana Cristina had also invited Hugo Silva over for dinner.

'So, where are we?'

This was Ana Cristina's opening gambit at the El Marinero.

'I do not wish to spoil the party. We are going to have some fun tonight, but humour me for the present.'

It was to be the start of a highly satisfactory evening as they looked out towards Lanzarote over the Strait of El Rio.

As the trio began their entrees Cesar Manrique Airport was welcoming its largest influx of Jet2, EasyJet and Ryanair flights touching down on its runways as Hudderford Gladiators supporters – and their team – flew in from England.

If the Lanzarote Business & Tourism Affiliate had not been aware previously of the impact of rugby league and its supporters, they were now. Many had not been able to book into Playa Blanca, such had been the demand.

'The Glads' had arrived on a late-night flight in order that their players were rested up during the day and ready to go in the evening. They'd secured a Playa Blanca booking and, thanks to their wealthy owner, had booked out part of the 6-star La Cala.

But there was one visitor who had only booked their ticket an hour before their scheduled flight was due to leave the UK, having taken a late cancellation.

Accommodation had been found above a seafood restaurant in the old town near the harbour. It wasn't where the visitor would have chosen, but that wasn't a concern right now. A taxi drive from the airport, followed by a short walk as the accommodation could not be reached by the taxi, brought the visitor to a location that would perhaps at least offer greater privacy than a hotel.

CHAPTER 24

The Glads were in town! It was Game Day! They were taking over the bars and restaurants of Playa Blanca. Claret and primrose shirts were everywhere.

By midday yet more visitors were reaching the town, with the arrival of those that hadn't been fortunate enough to book into the resort making their way from Costa Teguise and Puerto del Carmen.

The new resident above the seafood restaurant had not arrived for the game, but the flood of supporters and activity acted as an ideal additional assistance to invisibility – and for the moment that would do just fine.

'*Are you going to the game tonight?*'

Ferry Girl had returned to her stepfather's luxurious home on the hill and had taken up an easy start to her day, emerging for coffee and croissants.

Ricardo was one of many businessmen and women who had taken an interest in Eruption. She knew he wouldn't miss it, for the socialising opportunity and business contacts.

Mercifully, he was dressed. No jacket but smart, white shirt and solid royal blue tie matched up with equally smart black trousers and stunning brown shoes that gave the whole ensemble a quality look. When Ricardo made an effort he could really stun. He'd already acknowledged her question with a little nod, as he too had been eating when asked.

'*I wondered …*'

Ferry Girl expanded, in a kind of daughterly fashion when a 7-year old wants something from a parent. This wasn't the way she normally spoke, but she knew he'd appreciate the effort.

'*I wondered … whether it would be okay if I tagged along?*'

Ricardo was already nodding as she added.

'*I won't get in the way … it would be nice to go.*'

'*Darling, of course you may join me. You know how much I love having you around. I have a business meeting I must attend that will probably run into the late afternoon. I can meet you back here around 5pm and we can go to the game together, have a meal.'*

She was indeed going out again. She hadn't made much headway as yet in her quest, the reason she had come from Australia, but she wasn't dispirited. She hoped for more, but today was also about getting back to her first love of playing guitar and singing. She'd picked up an afternoon gig in one of the bars in the old part of the seafront.

Greg had woken, breakfasted, swum, run, FaceTime'd Kyle and spoken with Diane by 10am. He'd had to leave a message for Susie as she wasn't available. She didn't do social media that much, never had. It was a drag that she didn't.

With his early tasks out of the way Greg had just two that would occupy his brain for the coming hours – Maria Cavaleros and tonight's game.

The game was the easier to get his head around. Focus on the match. Give everything to help achieve the result.

Maybe he was finally growing up. He shrugged and laughed at himself over the thought. Not bad for a man of 28 years of age. His phone sprang into life on his bed as he came out of the shower.

He looked at its screen. It wasn't a stored number. In which case maybe he shouldn't answer – wait for whether a message was left. Too late, he slid his finger across the screen, waited for a voice. The caller seemed to be waiting too. They were at an impasse. Greg decided to hit the red button. Whoever it was would have to leave something if they wanted a response. He threw the phone back on the bed and continued drying off.

It rang again.

This time a name appeared on the screen.

'Hi sweetheart! Is this a good time?' Susie. Greg flopped on to the bed, immediately relaxed. She was the only person in Greg's world that could do this for him. Just hearing her voice was enough. *'I'm sorry I had to leave so soon, but like we always say …'*

Their conversation was light, fun and took Greg's mind away from Ciara, Paddy, Maria, Juan and everything that had happened since Susie had left.

He was here to play for Eruption and get away from everything else. Of course, if he'd said no to Ciara on his first night on the island none of these other things – Paddy grilling him, Kenny almost braying him, Maria pleading with him and Juan, well nothing there as yet but he was anticipating – would have happened.

At least with Susie it was cheekier conversation. Both laughed and Greg could feel Susie's smile as he enjoyed the moment.

Not once did Greg ask about what had caused Susie to go back almost instantly, and not once did she offer. It wasn't as important as hearing her voice. Although both were concerned for each other, there was an unwritten code they had accepted without ever talking about it. The times they had together were precious, special, just about them, nobody else.

There was no plan mentioned for when Susie might come back over. He could never understand why, but her voice, her ways, her easiness were all he really ever needed. Susie's call set him up for the day.

Or at least for the next two minutes!

'Duggan? Greg Duggan? I've been trying you, but the reception here isn't great. Have you got a minute?'

Greg had seen the caller's text after having finished up on his call with Susie. Greg hadn't even decided whether he would call back as the text had not said who was sending it. It was purely a note to tell him there was nothing at all to be worried about and that it was in connection with what had happened last year and 'nailing these bastards'.

'My name is Grahame Kraft. I'm the editor of the newspaper that Jeff Markham worked for, the man who was shot in Hopton Town's car park, and the newspaper that Bob Irvine owned. I'm trying to uncover the people who were really responsible for what happened to you, him, Jeff and Tony Estorino. I'm in Lanzarote, in fact I'm in Playa Blanca. I'd like to talk with you, about what you remember, what you know.'

It was nearing 11am. Greg had been planning on sticking

around the hotel for the best part of the day, avoiding any hubbub of Hudderford supporters in and around the town. Go for another swim, maybe another run on El Papagayos, a light meal around 3.30pm then make for the ground for 4pm. Kick off was 7pm.

Kraft tried to make any possible meeting easier.

'I could come to you? But if you don't want me to see where you are staying you could come to me?'

Greg had gone straight to Google on his MacBook Pro. He saw Kraft's journalistic achievements.

He could never forgive George's actions. For God's sake, the man had killed, maimed, caused utter carnage. But he'd also known this hadn't been the real George, not the George Ramsbottom he'd played under.

Even an old schoolmate-turned-sports-reporter Darryl Wills had reported: 'Who would have guessed George Ramsbottom would turn into a gun-toting madman?'

Greg had wanted retribution against Quinigan and his fellow conspirators and now, Kraft

was offering him his opportunity to bring about that justice.

Kraft would want it for Markham and Irvine; Greg wanted it for Irvine, Tony, himself, for the love of his hometown club and for the loss of his unborn child, that he was certain had been caused by a runaway car.

This was a chance. This man – GPK. He could do things. Greg had faith in him already.

They decided on Al's. GPK hired a jeep. He picked up Greg from the hotel's drop off point. Heavy set, but by no means overweight, GPK was a good-looking man in his early-mid 60s. He'd kept in trim, he'd tell friends he'd done so by having taken a wonderfully lithe, young wife Wendy, whose golf was also far superior to his own. He decanted stories, such as this, as part of his natural bonhomie that would have worked wonders if he'd ever been a pub landlord.

'He is here … Du-Gan … I have no idea … I never received a call …' The words were said as Greg and GPK took their seats at a table looking out to the sea. It was a quiet start at Al's.

'*My problem Greg is getting the story so that everything sticks. I want to see them all go down. George Ramsbottom was used and yes, he ultimately did the deed. But he didn't kill Jeff Markham. Different killer. George was pushed, over the edge. We believe we know the men who were involved, but we have no proof.*'

GPK let his words settle. Greg was, true to form, letting the other half of any conversation carry it forward.

'*So, why am I here? … Geoffrey Quinigan QC, who I believe you had problems with yourself last year, has connections on Lanzarote …*'

Greg was listening even more intently now.

'*Eat your calamari* (which had just arrived) *… Greg, I want everything you've got on Geoffrey Quinigan, Julian Jardine, Brent Dugarry and Bryan Caill.*'

Greg proceeded to fill him in with all that had gone before. Diane, their still-born baby; the abductions, the beatings he'd suffered. He told him of the undercover work that Patsy and Col had tried, that had gone catastrophically wrong for Jeff Markham.

None of this possible retribution would bring Greg's hometown club back to life, repair any long-term damage done to Diane, but it could bring these bastards down and Greg was well up for that.

'*What did you think to Bob Irvine?*'

GPK's question took Greg by surprise. It sounded as though Kraft had softened him up and was now watching for his reaction.

'*I didn't like the guy … at first. He just seemed all show. I don't get people who are like that.*'

GPK was about to interject.

'*But he came through for us. Gave me and Bill* (Bill Garside had been the club's chairman and had passed away of natural causes during Hopton's brief revival under Greg's equally brief career as coach) *players to work with, brought a belief back.*'

Clarity, through vocalising what he thought, also gave impetus and increased conviction to Greg's next words.

'*We were going to win that game. All we needed was to kick the conversion. We'd already scored the try. That kick would have kept us* in the league, it would have ruined everything for them. Caill would have gone bust. We would still be playing. The ground would still be ours. We even had time to score again, if we'd have missed the kick.'

Greg was surprising himself at just how much he was letting go of his feelings, but this was because for once he had the impression that there was an opportunity to set everything straight. Someone who could do something about it all.

'Senor Du-Gan!'

Carlos Cuadrado had busied himself with other customers after initially seeing Greg and GPK making their way from the Jeep. He'd now recalibrated, having initially flapped into making a call on his mobile.

'Senor.'

He nodded to GPK by way of acknowledgement of his presence. He turned back towards Greg.

'Tonight's game. El Partidos!' he announced with a flourish. 'I think the whole island is looking forward to it. Everyone talks about it.'

Greg smiled back at him. Carlos stopped.

'I'm sorry, you are busy. I will leave you gentlemen to your business ... can I get you anything?'

'Let's go shall we?'

GPK was up out of his chair in the time it took for Carlos to disappear back into the kitchen. He left cash, enough so that there was a generous tip, and also no need for the bill. It was a quick move.

'Something about him, call it a reporter's nose if you like, but that guy did not just come over to pass the time of day.'

Greg hadn't even thought anything of Carlos, apart from him being a bit over-the-top. Now that GPK had pointed it out he remembered the woman telling him that Carlos was dangerous.

GPK thought he sensed a reluctance in Greg.

For Greg any sense of reluctance he conveyed was more down to not knowing what the hell was going on. GPK wasn't about to put Greg off from helping him.

'No bother. It's these twats I'm bothered about, but if you need me to do any digging for you ...'

CHAPTER 25

Ferry Girl was coming to the end of her set at the bar overlooking Playa Limones in the older part of town between the harbour and ferry terminal of Puerto de Playa Blanca and Puerto Deportivo Marina Rubicon. Her mix of singalong standards and more recent hits from some of the world's best-known acts had hit the mark with the Hudderford following and the 'Glads' were more than impressed when she had belted out their club song 'Take Me Home Country Roads'.

'*One More Song! One More Song!*' was the all too familiar refrain as she finished, with the also customary '*Two more songs! Two more songs!*' from those who were prepping vocally for the evening's game that was now only three hours away.

Ferry Girl played one more – a rousing rendition of Oasis's '*Don't Look Back in Anger*' – as she'd intended anyway. She was used to British bar audiences raised on a diet of singalongs. It was easy money. She enjoyed it.

'*If you're still here tomorrow afternoon come along, and we'll do it all over again – have a great night! See ya!*'

The punters had been great and quite a few couples had obviously come over for the game, including the more regular groups of blokes. Ferry Girl was putting her guitar back in its case.

'*You sing and play really well.*'

She looked up to see who was supplying the compliment.

'*I just wanted to say thank you. It has been a lovely afternoon.*'

There were no names exchanged, just an attractive woman talking with her.

'*Maybe see you again.*'

Ferry Girl offered pleasantries in response but was more concerned with getting back to Ricardo's villa, showering and readying to take in her first experience of The Eruption.

She felt that going to the game might help her put things more in order. So far, she'd followed Kenny and Greg. She had read everything she could on her phone or iPad, every media story.

The Greg Duggan link, Greg having arrived at the same time she had been making her way over to Lanzarote, had been a bonus. She'd initially started her travels from Australia on the basis purely having seen Kenny Lomax on TV in Oz.

Her research had brought up that her father had been responsible for taking Kenny to Hopton Town after having flown to the UK for surgery. He had signed on a short-term contract, which would allow him to regain match fitness. Her father had also been responsible for Greg Duggan's appointment as coach.

She and her father had always been close, even when they were far away. Bob Irvine and his daughter Gina – pronounced 'geena' not 'ginner' as some unkind, supposed girl friends would call her when at school, on account of her flame red hair – had an unbreakable bond.

Ferry Girl was Gina Irvine, or Jen Juniper, her stage name.

'Do you mind if I ask …'

The same attractive woman had lingered.

'Do you do private parties?'

Gina was closing her guitar case. Like every other singer-guitarist or band she was always on the lookout for any type of gig, and party gigs usually paid a little better than pub and bar gigs. She'd done plenty of them, but it was the emphasis on the word 'private' that sent bells ringing in Gina/Jen's head.

It might be just the way she speaks, thought Gina, but it sounded more like 'will you come over to our room and play – and don't bring your guitar'. Gina gave the woman the benefit of any doubt. It was a possible gig after all. She rose up, her guitar case now in hand.

'I do all kind of gigs. What kind of party?'

Buoyed by a smiley response the woman was emboldened to go further. She was joined by her partner.

'How are you fixed for tonight?'

He leaped in to the conversation. Now this was weird. Gina wasn't used to being hustled for a gig. And certainly not to play for just a couple. And the same night.

The young man was handsome, equally smiley. He was good looking, but this was still weird. Gina already had her answer.

'Sorry. I can't. I'm going to the game, Eruption, with my dad.'

She had thrown her stepfather in at this point. There were times when Ricardo could come in useful.

'Come later.'

An immediate response and, as though anticipating a second rejection the attractive man followed up.

'600 quid if you do … or the appropriate in Euros. No pressure.'

He grinned back at Gina, smiled at his partner.

Nobody offered that kind of money. Nobody threw out an offer of money straight away – and certainly not 600 quid.

Gina looked at them, smiled. She was usually up for anything. She wasn't averse to something extra curricula to her guitar playing and singing. Christ, she'd been around enough with pot being smoked, drugs being sniffed, love-ins, swingers and 20-something parties not to get fazed by a couple of good-looking people with obviously too much money to burn.

'Here's my card. Check me out. I'm David, as you can see,' he passed Gina his card – David Pickup.

She laughed instantly on reading his name.

'Seriously? Pickup?'

She spread her arms, shrugging her shoulders.

'And this is what you're doing? Living up to your name?'

Gina shook her head and continued smiling.

'It is pronounced 'pic-wah' by all of my friends,' David 'Pic-Wah' laughed, adding additional stress to 'friends'.

'And I'm Pen – short for Penny, which is short for Penelope. My dad loved watching Thunderbirds as a kid, but I never got the pink Rolls Royce that Lady Penelope had.'

'Ahh, but you got your own version of Parker, didn't you m'lady?'

David was sharp. Either that or this was some regular performance the couple gave wherever they went. Gina was enjoying it, come what may.

'Well, Mr Pic-Wah … and Miss Pitstop.'

Gina had added her own children's TV programme reference of another Penelope, this time from a TV cartoon called Wacky Races.

'I would need to know what you would anticipate I would have to offer in return for the rather generous sum you have ... negotiated. And I would appreciate the fee being paid by BACS prior to my appearance ... I'm Jen.'

She held out her hand to Pen. This would smoke them out.

Pic-Wah wasn't to be assuaged.

'Text me your bank details. I'll have the money in your account straight away. Just what you've been playing will be great.'

Now this was getting even more weird. This guy was so sure of himself, but at the same time disconcerting. Gina decided to back off. She had to go.

'I'm sorry guys.'

She smiled at them both.

'It sounds great, but also kinda weird and I don't have the time to work out whether I'm putting myself in some kind of danger here, so I'm going to have to say no. Thank you, but no.'

David. Mr Pic-Wah was deflated. He'd clearly thought the money would do it. Pen continued smiling, shrugging her shoulders.

'No worries. See you back here tomorrow?'

'Yeah.'

Gina saddled her now stowed away guitar to her back, picked up her cash from the bar manager, put the tips she'd earned into her pocket and away she went.

500 quid, she thought, as she counted the 40 Euros from this afternoon. I've just turned down 500 quid. Then she laughed at herself. Right decision. Weird proposal.

But a short while later she managed to convince herself David and Pen were genuine. She had no reasoning other than they had appeared fun. The more she considered it, the more she felt she should do it. 500 quid after all!

Greg reached Estadio de Lanzarote three hours prior to kick off.

'Hiya boss!' Stu Wainwright enjoyed calling Greg by his

previous title, from when he'd come from nowhere to play for Hopton.

Stu's past ten months had seen a constant upswing in his career and he was loving every minute. Vinny (Venus) was next. No words. He had his white designer headphones on, lost in the vibes.

The 'Glads' weren't due to arrive for another hour, the distance they had to travel was never likely to be a problem being next door at La Cala.

The Eruption boys had made their way in to the ground and within twenty minutes were all involved in light training with Malky.

Teenage half-backs Wainwright and Elton Richards were on fire. They'd been full of it since the previous evening when they'd heard they would be playing together. They'd been over on the ground earlier working on moves and what they could do on the paddock.

For all their youth and exuberance neither player was taking anything for granted and nor was Malky's coaching team. Injured Jordan Peters was working with them. Jordan's seasons in the NRL were something special for both Wainwright and Richards. If they were to reach Super League or NRL status they would need to learn far more about the game from guys who had played in those leagues.

Nobody was expecting them to come up with a bang-on partnership immediately, but they had confidence and it was up to the coaching staff and more experienced players to ensure they maintained their buoyant approach to the game when things did not go their way.

It was a vibrant atmosphere all around the Estadio as the bar staff, club officials and stewards of all types from working on the gates to programme sellers and cleaners all prepared for The Eruption's biggest game yet.

There was even talk of the match being a sell-out, such had been the influx of 'Glads' fans in the past 24 hours.

Playa Blanca was alive with a fervour it had never

experienced. It had been an old fishing port that had developed and was still fast developing into becoming Lanzarote's major resort, putting the likes of Costa Teguise and Puerto del Carmen in the shade.

GPK had always followed the story, wherever it led, and there was something about his meeting with Greg that told him he had to follow what was happening here, in Playa Blanca.

Greg hadn't wanted to confide in him about Ciara and hadn't, but Kraft had felt there was something. It would probably have nothing to do with what he was currently trying to uncover but somehow instinct told him to follow.

Since their meeting earlier that day GPK had spent the past few hours in a restaurant/bar near the harbour taking a closer look at Greg on his laptop. He'd gone through everything from Greg's playing career, a bit sketchy with being lower league; his personal life, which at first hand had made him appear the regular family man, with a wife he'd known from school days and a young son, but now estranged and several hints at possible affairs through social media gossip; work life, other than rugby league, in a garage as a mechanic. Hardly the most earthshattering resume he'd ever heard.

But it had been the digging around he and his team had done since meeting him that had added the colour to Greg Duggan's life.

Within the space of a few hours after their meeting Kraft had switched all the resources of his small team back in England on to focusing their efforts on everything Greg had ever done.

'I want everything. I want to know what he's done, where he's done it, who he's done it with. Every game, every meeting, every girl, every affair, every enemy he's ever had, every friend. I want to see his bank account, where he gets his money, what he does with it.'

Kraft was motoring now. He was always like this when he hit what he felt was some kind of pay dirt. He'd gone out on to the beach to deliver these words to his team. They'd been going nowhere fast and now GPK had found them a way back into their endeavours.

'I'm not saying Duggan is our man, God knows he suffered at the hands of Ramsbottom. A couple of inches to one side of where he was wounded would have meant he wouldn't still be here, but there is something about this man that seems to attract trouble – and I'm certain it is happening again over here.

'I've come to get the inside track on Quinigan, but ...' He stopped himself momentarily as people passed him by on the beach.

'... I don't know, but there's also something over here ... no, hasn't told me a thing, but you know ... I just have this feeling ... and he's our only real link to what happened to the guys we're after ...

'What I want from you, by this time tomorrow or even tonight, is a complete record of Greg Duggan's life ... and don't just get it from the Internet, I've already exhausted that. You're going to need to get on the phone or go and talk with anyone and everyone who has come into contact with him. Start with his wife, Diane, and the garage where he worked.

'Also, take a look into the affairs of a guy who runs a bar/restaurant on the El Papagayos, east of Playa Blanca. It's called Al's. Find out all you can about the man who runs it. Nothing to do with our affairs, but definitely something to do with Duggan over here.'

Perhaps Greg would have a different feeling about Kraft right now.

Currently he was enjoying the build-up to the game – the biggest of his career. It seemed unreal that he was on the precipice of picking up his first trophy in the sport.

The atmosphere around the ground was of optimism, from everyone. Hudderford Gladiators' fans were streaming in. Cloud TV and Canaria TV were in position, cables all in place, the sound and cameramen going through their pre-game dispatches with the producers who were in the articulated truck studio in the car park.

The Cavaleros had arrived looking immaculate, every inch the proud owners, basking in their personal achievement in having come so far in such a short space of time.

They were talking with Hudderford's chairman Glen Witheford who'd made his fortune out of golf tees. Having initially started out from his bedroom selling to local clubs he'd become 'The Golf Tee King of Europe' and had built his now thriving business through developing a whole range of branded golf products.

'*Ricardo!*'

Maria almost ran to her good friend of many years. He was the equivalent of a lifebelt to cling to rather than face even more conversation about little pegs that were forced into the ground. Profitable though it may have been, she had lost the will to live after having listened to the whys and wherefores of various lengths.

'*You're a life saver.*' Maria now said in more of a whisper, explaining her getaway, '*I am sure what the gentleman is saying must be very interesting ... to some ... but I'd rather find out more about this beautiful young lady ... who if I'm not mistaken would be ...*'

She paused more for dramatic effect, but also to reassure herself that she'd got it right. '*... Gina!*'

Gina had been enjoying her anonymity. The less people who knew her the better at present, but she had known it wouldn't be long before any advantage she held over people not knowing who she was would disappear. She was impressed by Maria's deduction nonetheless. As, it seemed, was Ricardo.

'*I knew your mother.*'

Maria was quick to explain.

'*I liked her very much. She was a very good friend ...*'

Gina was delighted. This was a real bonus. She was here to assess Kenny and Greg at closer quarters and hopefully make herself known to them, but to hear nice things about her late mother and make acquaintance with a friend of hers from way back was a bonus.

Ricardo had pointed out Maria and her husband when he and his stepdaughter had entered the Estadio Rooftop Club. Gina, looking very different to her jeans and T-shirt from her afternoon gig had favoured a simple, but alluring and flimsy, floaty red dress. Another of her acquisitions earlier thanks to her stepfather.

While Geoffrey Quinigan had stayed on La Graciosa, Hugo had returned to Lanzarote and was also present at Estadio Rooftop Club.

GPK was there too. He didn't quite know what opportunity might present itself just yet and was flying by the seat of his pants, a common state as he undertook his research, but he knew he had to keep following wherever Greg led him at present.

The guy in the bar on El Papagayos. GPK had instantly known he was dodgy.

Since he'd put in the call on the beach his team had been moving with greater speed than they had managed at any stage in the past months. Greg's life, digging for anything, was meat and drink to the reporters who were part of Kraft's 'spotlight' team. They were compiling a dossier on Greg's every traceable movement, telephone records, friends, relatives, fellow players, lovers, workmates. And they had already decided their boss was on a worthwhile cause.

Texts and emails had begun flying around. Background was being built on the man they didn't necessarily suspect, but who might provide them with the evidence they needed for what had happened to their colleague Markham and owner Irvine. But maybe Duggan had been involved in some way? They weren't ruling anything out.

'Money or sex, that's what will lead us to the answer, or both,' Kraft had said to his team as a parting shot before he reached Estadio.

'We all know it's one of those two – and often both of them. Like I said, we've two stories here. And I'm bloody certain that sorting one out will lead to sorting the other.

'I don't believe in coincidences, and this boy Duggan. He's our link. I'm certain of it. Follow him and where he leads us and we'll find our answers.'

CHAPTER 26

Kraft knew there was only one other person in the ground who was aware of him at that moment, and Greg was now in the dressing room with the rest of the team. This was ideal. He could be as invisible and inconsequential until such time as he wanted to crawl out of any woodwork and get in the faces of the ones he would choose.

'Senor!'

Fuck! Correction, only two were aware of him. It was the loud guy from Al's.

'Senor Du-Gan is amazing player. Tonight is a great win I hope.'

'I hope so too, if you'll excuse me Senor ...'

Kraft made his way from the man. He really didn't want any kind of show.

'Si, Si ... Senor, you come back to Al's tomorrow and we celebrate, yes?'

Kraft really didn't want this right now. He waved and smiled as he moved across the Rooftop Club in the direction of the press area, which looked out on the ground and was already well populated.

'He is a bit loud isn't he?'

Gina was looking out over the ground, the Estadio Rooftop Bar canopy being where the best seats in the house were situated for the game, with magnificent views of the ocean and a fabulous sunset in prospect around halftime. She was cradling her drink and had moved on from Maria Cavaleros who was doing the rounds, chatting with other less golf tee obsessed Hudderford officials, and the Lanzarote glitterati who had turned out in their finery, particularly as the island looked as though it was in the process of achieving something.

Kraft smiled at the young woman. He raised his eyebrows and slanted his eyes as though he concurred.

He really hadn't wanted any type of conversation just at

present, but she was a northern girl, clearly. He responded.

'*Do you know who he is?*'

Gina looked directly at him. Kraft was getting ready to follow up the question by way of giving a reason why he was asking but thought better of it. Years of training told him to stick with what he'd just asked. Another question now might sound too much.

'*Why?*'

The way she elongated the word made him think the girl was playing him already, he could sense it. She smiled. Then turned back to her drink and looking out over the ground again.

She's gathering her own thoughts, thought Kraft. He waited the split second necessary. She spoke again.

'*I've no idea.*'

She was either good, smashed or didn't give a damn. Maybe she just enjoyed messing. Whichever it was, Kraft wasn't one for being played or being the cause of someone's fun. He dropped it, moved on.

Maria was back.

'*Gina, darling, I've someone I want you to meet …*'

And the red-haired girl was gone, to meet with more of the Lanzarote hoi polloi.

'*Senor Jardine! It is wonderful that you are here!*'

Juan Cavaleros was beside himself with pride as the top man of Rugby League's governing body entered. He'd invited him over to watch the game and had arranged hospitality for his visit.

'*You already know my wife Maria …*' He went on to introduce other of the Lanzarote glitterati.

Julian Jardine. Here? Oh yes!

This was a bonus for GPK. Sure, he'd perhaps anticipated some nugget turning up by being around this lot, but one of his targets? Great news.

Kraft recalled George Ramsbottom's words that had appeared in his and every other newspaper's front and back pages, that 'they' were destroying the game he'd loved.

Ramsbottom had meant those in the sport's hierarchy. Here

was one of them. Julian Jardine, served up on a plate for him, but GPK wasn't about to wade in.

Approaching those in authority in the wrong manner could easily blow up in his face. He needed to have something more substantial before he started on Mr Jardine. He needed information. But here, where he wasn't known, there was no problem with sticking around, gathering in what he could while not drawing attention to himself.

Gina wasn't by any means smashed. She'd clocked GPK a few seconds earlier, before Carlos had spoken. She'd been scanning, watching the room, letting Ricardo do his bit in talking with some of the island's leading businessmen.

She'd enjoyed Maria's recognition of her and talk of her mum. She was back enjoying talking to some of the other women from the island now, along with Maria.

But the intervention of GPK, the older man who she didn't know, coming over, who she'd already spotted beforehand not exactly looking nervous but clearly, it seemed to her, on his own and trying to work out what to do with himself, was a new element.

Now she watched him again, from the comfort zone of having others around her.

He left the room.

CHAPTER 27

'El Partido Mas Importance' was being beamed across the world and the ground via the big screen as Cloud TV and Canaria TV began setting the mood. The 'Glads' supporters were adding a vocal soundtrack for the evening that those who had followed the Eruption found entertaining, even if they couldn't match it as yet.

Glads' supporters were giving out their rendition of 'Country Roads'.

It had only been three days since the match against Leverfield Lynx. In that time the islanders had thoroughly awakened to the game and their island heroes, the players born and bred on Lanzarote – and the man everyone now simply referred to as Du-Gan!

The Eruption following may not have been in full voice as yet with any particular favourite club song, but they knew how to voice a name and 'Du-Gan' was heard ringing around the ground.

'Listen up fellers!' Kenny was stood perfectly still. *'Do you hear that?'* There were now trumpets blasting on the terraces.

Kenny had spent the last few days assembling what he hoped would be a great addition to the crowd.

Musicians from Arrecife and others from Tenerife and Gran Canaria were playing a Spanish and Brazilian-influenced version of 'Can't Take My Eyes Off You', the classic song made famous by Andy Williams and Muse.

'You're just too good to be true!'

Kenny was using the lyrics as part of his team talk.

'And you have been for nearly all of this season, but this is now the business end. This is where it matters.'

Kenny looked around the dressing room, checking for reaction. He couldn't always tell what everyone was thinking. Players had their own way of preparing, motivating, but he was watching for anything he recognised as negative, too contemplative.

He wasn't certain that his message was getting through. He knew he'd find out soon enough when they hit the turf, but he wanted reaction now.

'Remember, these boys gave us a lesson earlier in the season. I want everyone – and I mean everyone, including you ...'

He turned to Tonito and Popoli Baru specifically.

'... to be ready from that first kick of the game. Even if you're not on the paddock you need to be all set as though you were about to receive the ball or make that tackle ... you could be on within seconds, minutes.

'Now, let's go and make Lanzarote proud!'

GPK had been annoyed with himself. He'd not been as ready as he might have been when the girl had probed him. He hadn't needed to ask what the loud guy's name was, the bar owner. He'd find out soon enough. His question had hopefully been sufficiently throw-away.

In the meantime, facts were now starting to stack up back in England and some of them were being sent across already with the premise that there would be one extensive dossier later. His team were working hard generating as much as they could find.

'It has been billed as 'El Partido Mas Importance' over here in Lanzarote ever since the amazing fightback last weekend ...'

Cloud TV's Joanne Collingwood was back in high energy mode.

'... and the talk has all been about that ... but tonight that counts for nothing as the Gladiators meet the Eruptors at the Estadio de Lanzarote ... Ralph, what are we expecting from both sides tonight?'

As Ralph McBalingfour began his roll call of players from both sides and the Estadio de Lanzarote edged ever nearer to capacity two Policia de Lanzarote cars entered the ground.

There were already police present, but this was different.

'This is another landmark night for rugby league on the island.'

Joanne Collingwood resumed her presentation just prior to the last ad break before kick off.

'… it is the first time two islanders will have started a game with Jose Maria Estapol again starting on the wing and Raul Rodgriguez-Perez starting a game for the first time, taking over at prop forward from the injured Victor Borsoni.

'Raul had a fantastic second half at the weekend. But all eyes, inevitably, will be on Greg Duggan's appearance. It was his introduction in the second half against Leverfield Lynx that transformed the game and brought about the remarkable victory that has set this game up tonight.'

As Cloud TV's presenter talked up the game right up to the final ad break the Policia de Lanzarote entered the Rooftop Club, where all but a dozen or so guests had yet to make their way to the hospitality boxes, that looked on great vantage points of the ground.

The Policia that had arrived were a uniformed team of four with a plain-clothed officer at their head.

'Senor Kraft?'

This was an angle Pythagoras hadn't planned on.

GPK had only just finished chastising himself over his brief discussion with the flame-haired girl and had returned to the bar for another drink before the kick-off.

He hadn't been too bothered about the game, but there was something about this that had drawn him in. He sensed another story. He'd already sensed it while with Greg earlier in the day and was eager to drink in the atmosphere, be around Greg's world, watch what was going on.

The on-field activity might provide him with some kind of insight, he didn't know what, but recognised it was better to be in and around it all.

His first thought as he'd seen the uniformed police striding toward him, as he'd turned, glass of wine in hand, had been that there must have been some mistake or they were looking through him to somebody else.

'Senor Kraft.'

His identity was now effectively rubber stamped.

'I am Detective Sergeant Alba Marta Arteta with the Policia de

Canary Islands.'

This was formal. Kraft had been around enough police in his journalistic career to know that a visit did not necessarily mean they thought the person they were approaching was guilty of anything, but the mob handed nature of this made him bristle.

Just why they would be on top of him, having only arrived the previous evening, he had little idea. His brain quickly ran through where he had been in his short time on the island, who he had seen. It all kept coming back to bloody Duggan!

Detective Sergeant Arteta was quite possibly the most attractive copper GPK had ever seen, with Hollywood-style film looks not far away from Julia Roberts, but he wasn't one to leer.

He'd always prided himself on his journalism, upheld his own standards and, despite being regarded as 'old-school' due to age and experience, had maintained a professional approach throughout his career and had never once been accused of being sexist or demeaning women in the workplace. He certainly wasn't about to start now.

Detective Sergeant Alba Marta Arteta took the lead:

'I am aware that you have only recently arrived in Lanzarote, but we have received information …'

A roar went up in the Estadio as the players must have been making their way out on to the pitch. Loud entry music for the teams was being played. Detective Sergeant Arteta recomposed herself, as the roar had stopped her from delivering her next line.

'Perhaps we can go somewhere, here, where it is quieter?'

Neither she nor Kraft knew the stadium, but they were directed to one of the meeting rooms by the bar staff.

CHAPTER 28

'Well, here we go!' Joanne Collingwood announced, as Cloud TV's coverage returned from its ad break.

'Eighty minutes of hi-energy rugby league football to determine who will win the championship league title – and the right to a home tie in the play-offs, with that Super League prize the ultimate pot of gold.

'It's the league's new boys Lanzarote Eruption up against the long established and rejuvenated Hudderford Gladiators. Let's go over to our commentary team Karen King and Robbie Robertson.'

'Thank you, Jo. Strap yourselves in everybody.'

Karen King was revved up and ready to go. Robbie was quick to add his words.

'Yeah. Whoever wins tonight takes the title. The only form guide we have between these two is that game three months ago at Hudderford where the Glads took the spoils.'

Wayne Dorringe, Hudderford Gladiators' full-back, launched the ball into Eruption territory as he kicked the game under way. The atmosphere was like nothing the Lanzarote crowd had witnessed previously.

The Hudderford faithful hadn't come all this way for a holiday. They wanted their team to bring back the glory days of yesteryear – and their coach, former player Gary Hopewell, had assembled a team that was, on paper, stronger than the Eruption's.

'And it's a massive, towering, spiraling kick from Dorringe.'

Karen King was already in full flow.

The ball eventually came down, having been watched intently by Jose Maria Estapol who gathered it safely into his hands and chest, just prior to the onrushing 'Glads', centre Aussie Chris Rice and second row Martin Huff who succeeded, despite the sterling efforts of Pierre Longchamps and Warren Entish, in bundling him straight into touch.

'That's a fantastic effort from Rice and Huff, one of their trademark plays of the season.'

Robbie Robertson was full of praise for what had just occurred.

'We've seen that Dorringe kick and Rice/Huff rush operation work so many times, but that was perfection. Scrum-down on the Eruption 10-metre line and Gladiators' put-in, Eruption already under pressure. This will be a test for them this early on in the game.'

'That's right Robbie. The Lynx put Eruption to the sword in the first half last weekend. They really don't want to get into that sort of position again, but it's a brilliant start by the Gladiators … oh, hold on, something's started …'

The crowd had erupted near to the touchline where Estapol had been bundled out of play. There had been a melee of arms and legs as several players had ended up on the ground together, Estapol, Longchamps and Entish from Eruption and Rice, Huff and stand-off Schoular from the Glads.

The touch judge had seen it all. Referee Paul Caden had had a more restricted view. The crowd was baying. Mr Caden was taking advice.

'Well, to say this game is charged up is an understatement.'

Karen King was still trying to make out who was in trouble with Mr Caden. The operators of the big screen were attempting to give the best possible angle so everyone in the ground and watching at home could see exactly what had gone on. Karen King and Robbie Robertson also had the added advantage of their own TV monitors.

'We're only in the first minute, the hang time on the ball was counted as 4.5 seconds, Estapol was bundled into touch in 2 seconds. That's 6.5 seconds worth of play and we could have our first sending off of the game.'

Referee Caden was about to impose his authority when the crowd saw it, the evidence!

'Oh, hold on a second. And this could be very bad news for Jose Maria Estapol. It looks to me as though he's lashed out at Martin Huff.'

'Karen, I think both of them could be in big trouble here. Mr Caden isn't known for his patience. I don't see anything but cards being shown here … Here we go!'

Referee Caden had directed traffic away from him, from both teams as each protested the innocence of their players. Kenny feared the worst. This wasn't going to end well – and yet the match had hardly started. Caden drew the players over to him.

'It's Estapol and Huff he's asking for – and he doesn't usually take long over this kind of thing. No words … There we go! He's brandished red cards to both of them. But that's not all. Oh, this looks very bad for Eruption. He's now signaled for Longchamps.'

'Yes, Karen. If you see on the screen, he took a shot at Rice. It wasn't visible in the first angle, but now it's clear and that's what the touch judge must have seen.'

'And he's off too! Amazing! The game is less than a minute old and three players are off for the whole game. 79 minutes and 45 seconds on the clock and the Gladiators are down to 12 and The Eruption are reduced to 11. It's going to be a long night for Eruption's defence.'

Kenny turned instantly he saw the second red card. Moved to Malky, who had come to the touchline.

'Tell Greg to get ready. We'll see how it goes for 10 minutes.'

And he was away. Back into the fray. Kenny needed all the experience he could muster on the field right now. Referee Caden had given the Gladiators a penalty on the Eruption 10-metre line. Kenny was back in the line marshalling his shell-shocked troops.

Rodriguez-Perez and Richards were on their first starts of the season and Ortega, Venus and Wainwright were all young and maybe too inexperienced to know instantly how to handle this kind of situation. He needed guys that wouldn't be looking for retribution and wouldn't incur further wrath from the ref.

This was going to be an uphill task. The Glads' halfback combination of Aussie Elliott Schoular and former England international Paul Revere was one of the reasons Hudderford were now dreaming of days gone by. They were playing behind a solid, professional pack with the likes of Kiwi Hillman Ward and former Super League players in hooker Ray Erikkson and second row Paul Pratt.

'*And, not surprisingly, the Gladiators are running the ball rather than taking the kick for two points. They want to hurt Eruption, run them all over the park making use of their one-man advantage. Here they come, with prop Steve Hardy hammering at the Eruption line.*'

Karen King was in commentary high gear.

'*He releases the ball to Wells who finds Revere. He spins off one despairing tackle, lunges for the line. Oh!! What a stop. They've held him just inches short. It's the play-the-ball. Revere to Schoular, who turns, twists on his heel and feeds it to the onrushing Ward who steams back at the Eruption line. Eruption are stretched out wide. He releases and there's Easterly to score the opening try!*'

Kenny motioned immediately for Greg to come on. It was blatantly obvious he needed more tackling ability. Poor Warren Entish had played just shy of two minutes but was sacrificed in favour of Greg. Fortunately for Eruption, the Gladiators had scored out wide, which made the kick more difficult and Dorringe had missed the conversion attempt. 4-0 to the Glads.

The fans went crazy when they saw him!

Du-Gan! Du-Gan! Du-Gan! The place took on an even higher charge. Along with their island homegrown heroes this was the man who had put the increased numbers on the Lanzarote supporters' attendance.

The island's radio stations, press and Canaria TV had been full of 'Du-Gan' since the last game. They adored him, and the other Canary Islands were joining forces too. A boat load of Fuerteventurans had added to the gate.

The next 20 minutes saw the battle become a war of attrition. Kenny knew that the big time in the game was yet to come, in the final stanza, the last 20 minutes when tired legs would take their toll of 12 fit men versus 11.

Kenny had felt they would be more secure with Greg on the park – and they had been. It hadn't become the mountain he'd felt they might have to climb if they'd shipped more points.

Greg hadn't played a full competitive match, or indeed any match until the one he'd played three days ago. When he'd landed on the island he had not even known how fit he was, and the answer he'd found since, he thought now, was that he was nowhere near 100 per cent.

He'd played 40 minutes in that first game.

Now this. A whole game! For a championship title! He had no idea whether his body was up to it.

Kenny, relieved his side had come through the first quarter of the game reasonably unscathed, decided to get back to his plan. He wanted his forwards as fresh as possible and at the same time didn't want to lose the vital quality of experience on the field. He interchanged Rodriguez-Perez with Angel Ramos.

'You know, darling, we may have to reconsider what we are trying to achieve here.'

Juan Cavaleros had spoken gently into the ear of his wife Maria. It had come totally out of the blue. They were both watching the game, but it was Maria who seemed more intent on the on-field action.

Maria knew he must have been planning this as soon as he uttered them. He'd been waiting his moment. She was shocked, but so far as she was concerned, this was another crack to add to the several in their relationship. She chose to ignore him. She didn't want to give him the satisfaction of acknowledgement. He was a bastard and she knew it. In truth, she'd known it since before their marriage but their passion when together had been sufficient initially.

So, he wanted out of their involvement with Eruption? Or the Estadio? Or the sports centre? Or the buildings themselves? Really? Why?

There was only ever one reason in Juan Cavaleros's world. Financial gain. Money. She'd seen it before in him. Behind that friendly, affable outer persona lurked a heart of stone. There wasn't much he wouldn't do to suck up to anyone where he felt a better deal was to be had. She continued watching the game. Let him stew on his words. Maria was a tougher cookie than he, and she knew it. But for now, she was engrossed in the game – and it was about to kick into another gear.

'The game has now settled into a pattern where both sides are constantly using up their six tackles, there's no quarter being given either way.

'It's Erikkson, running up the ball to the Eruption defence. Oh, there's a mistake. No, Wainwright has stolen the ball, quite legally and he's away! He's evaded two, three now four tacklers,' King couldn't help but chuckle.

'He's a handful this young, scrum-half – and they can't get a hold of him. He's twisting, turning off one heel, then the other, now he's in the clear! This is sensational stuff by Wainwright, he's running it out for the corner, oh, he slips the ball inside … oh, that's brilliant … and young Vincent Venus scores right underneath the sticks! Amazing, Robbie!'

'Absolutely tremendous work from the lad, Karen. He did everything there – and that flick-out pass from the back of his right hand as he knew he wasn't going to make it into the corner. Just brilliant! You know, these lads played together very little at Hopton Town last season as Wainwright only came into the side near the end of the season. He was stacking supermarket shelves just under a year ago. Now look at him, on the verge of international honours, and you can see why.'

Greg stepped up for kicking duties. The two players who'd been given their marching orders so early on in the game – Longchamps and Estapol – had been the club's recognised kickers until now, but Greg had always kicked the goals for Hopton. He popped over the conversion as easy as you like. 6-4 in favour of Eruption.

Gary Hopewell, the Gladiators' coach, was incandescent. Erikkson was immediately interchanged with Kiwi Mike Bleasdale, centre Dave Solly and second row forward Paul Pratt, who had both missed tackling Wainwright were replaced by George Millson and Phil Hoggers.

'It's a bit early to say the wheels have fallen off, but I don't think I've ever seen Gary Hopewell as angry as that, look at him, and he's coming down from his normal position in the stands. He's thrown his earpiece out. He's had enough of this, he's coming to the sidelines. He's angry!'

Karen King loved talking up the drama as it unfolded, and there was nothing more she loved than when it was a normally placid individual losing it.

'You know, there's a lot of expectation on his shoulders at the moment. You can see how much it means to him. He was a great player in a side that continually under-achieved. I think that's in his head. He doesn't want second place in anything.'

Robbie Robertson's assessment wasn't just speculation. He'd been on one of those winning teams that had caused Hopewell's past frustration. Kenny Lomax had experienced it too. He'd played against him in an Ashes game where Hopewell had gone off the deep end against a Great Britain teammate when the Kangaroos had waltzed in for an easy try.

Kenny caught sight of Hopewell coming to pitchside, hollering at his players.

'Eruption have the ball again!'

Karen King sounded almost ready to charge at the Gladiators herself.

'It's speedy centre Alan Thomas, ohhh he's skipped past one tackler as though he was hardly there, and he's found his centre buddy Greg Duggan to his inside. Eruption are putting on the style. They've just gone past halfway and look at Gary Hopewell! He's down by the touchline giving his players some right stick!'

Greg had taken the tackle. They still had work to do but the hard working centres had laid a foundation.

'And Gary Hopewell is having what can best be described as a moment here. I don't think he will want to analyse this in playback. He's kicked the drinks bottles in his frustration.'

Karen King was warming to this moment in the game.

'Duggan plays the ball. Lomax is at acting half back. He's received the ball and he's … no, he's still in possession, he's dummied, the Gladiators have taken the dummy … and Lomax is in the clear, he's only Dorringe left to beat … ohhhhhh, that's glorious

… Lomax has rolled back the years here to when he showed us all what he could do in the NRL Grand Final … and that try is as good as anything he has scored … What a wonderful try!'

Within seconds another two points had been added as Greg tagged on the extras. Eruption were down a player but up by eight points. 12-4.

'Well, who would've believed this after the first minute?'

Karen King never ceased to be amazed by the way rugby league games turned out.

'We're not even at thirty minutes and it feels like a lifetime, but listen to this, it's bedlam here! I don't think they've ever had sport like this on the island and they're enjoying this ride!'

'You know we could do very well out of this Maria.'

Juan was trying again.

'What does this game, this sport mean to us? We come out of this, we sell, make some money, no-one gets hurt, what is there not to like?'

Maria set her face towards the game. She had no compunction to turn towards her husband. What was he about? There was something more here. And why make his move now? While the game was on? She was livid.

Someone else was not just watching the game, but also what was going on amongst the Cavaleros.

Gina had no idea where anything was heading. She'd come to Lanzarote under the auspices of finding out more about Kenny Lomax and Greg Duggan – how they may be implicated in the death of her father and what that information would lead her to. But this other thing being played out with Juan and Maria Cavaleros?

With three minutes left on the clock for the first half Kenny signaled to the bench for the introduction of Tonito and Popoli Baru, in place of Wainwright and Richards, who both appeared distraught at being withdrawn. Warren Entish came back on too, with Alan Thomas taking a breather.

'That's quite an interchange,' was King's response. *'We know nothing of Tonito or Popoli Baru.'*

It was EV – Ellard Vellidale in possession on Eruption's 20-metre line. He shipped it to Warren Entish who avoided one tackler and was hauled down at the 30-metre line. Popoli Baru was instantly behind him at the play-the-ball. Dummying a pass to his right, he stepped off his left foot and found a hole in the Gladiators' defence. The collective groan from their fans spoke volumes for their confidence, but they cheered as Baru was immersed into the arms of Schoular and Ward.

Tonito appeared from nowhere alongside him at acting half-back and proved just as astute on his feet, bouncing and jinking, looking for another opening – and his strength took his tacklers back further yards. Three tackles down and Eruption had made it to just across their 40-metre line.

Kenny had signaled in backplay for Greg to get himself in position. Eruption were going to make the Gladiators sweat coming up to the halfway stage. Hopewell hadn't calmed. His arms were everywhere trying to direct his players. The Eruption fans roared their appreciation for the Herculean effort their team was putting in.

Baru had followed Tonito and was now ready at the play-the-ball as Tonito played it back. Baru fed Lomax and Kenny didn't mess around. He propelled the ball straight to Greg, who kicked for touch from just inside the Eruption 40-metre line.

'Ohh, look at this! Eruption have pulled another rabbit out of the hat ... and that ball is going towards the left side touchline ... is it going to make it inside the Gladiators' 20-metre line? I think it is you know ... and the crowd tells you that's exactly what has happened! ... Robbie, Eruption should be out on their feet by now the way they've had to defend this half, and yet it's the Gladiators who look more fatigued ... and look at the man who has suddenly burst into this game, well we don't need to tell you here, just listen!'

Du-Gan! Du-Gan! Du-Gan! rang out from all sides of the ground.

'Just a minute and half left on the clock before half-time and the Lanzarote fans are loving it.

'The ball will be fed into the scrum by Popoli Baru, the Papua

New Guinean scrum half, who only came out here by way of piggy-backing on their signing of his fellow Kumul, Manuwai Manuai, who is injured ... he's run around the scrum ... and, would you believe it, Tonito has exploded on to the ball ... these two seem to know exactly where the other is going to be and what they are going to do ... Ohhh! ... now that is another fantastic slice of rugby league artistry ... and Tonito has a smile as wide as anything I've seen for years, he's scored bang underneath the posts! Wonderful try!'

Tonito had taken a delightfully flipped inside pass from Baru. He had feinted with his left boot, turned off his right and somehow, he'd contorted his body, avoiding despairing lunges to stop him, and had beaten three players. It was a mesmerising run.

Kenny had seen the way they had interacted on the beach, one of those immediate understandings that form superb partnerships.

And that was it for the first half. Eruption had weathered the storm. They'd suffered two sendings-off, had played the whole half with one player less than the opposition, they'd brought on two players who had never played first grade and they were coming off at half-time with an 18-4 lead, Greg having tagged on the extras by converting Tonito's try. Amazing didn't seem to do justice to their efforts!

CHAPTER 29

'How much more of this can you take?'

The atmosphere was sexually charged and the question purposely loaded with imaginative innuendo on La Graciosa, where Ana Cristina Magdalena and Geoffrey Quinigan QC were enjoying each other's company in role reversal.

Ana Cristina was presently positioned intimately behind him and was providing an intensity of sexuality, and proving a worthy substitute for what Quinigan was missing with Hugo having returned to Lanzarote 'on business' at the Estadio de Lanzarote. Additional non-natural appendages aside, as indeed was now the case, this had been a rather different workout to Ana's daily run.

They collapsed in a heap of laughter as both saw the humour in each other and their current state of heightened passion.

'Darling Ana, you do know my most sensitive areas …'

Quinigan spoke as he relaxed and the black-leather-catsuit-clad Ana Cristina unstrapped her rather girthy addendum. She looked back seductively over her shoulder.

'And it's certainly not your heart is it my sweet, responsive yet singularly determined handsome man-girl …'

She returned to the side of the bed, offering her hand to his-her hair and a glass of Moet to the normally suave, exceedingly well-presented barrister who was currently sporting bright red lipstick, eyelashes, eye shadow, make-up and tousled ash blonde wig to complement his outfit of white leather and lace and over-the-knee white stiletto boots.

'You know me too well …'

He smiled back.

'Like a sister …' she responded.

'So, in answer to your earlier rather heavily breathed question, when and what exactly do you have in mind?'

Quinigan smiled back as he brought the conversation back

to his favourite subject, making money.

The Rooftop Bar in the Estadio was a hubbub of noise as the great and good, and not-so-good, of the island plus their guests, took a break from the proceedings on the ground. It wasn't all talk of the game, by far, but there was an enthusiasm fired by what had just been witnessed.

'A *que demonios crees que estas jugando?!*' Maria whispered it in Juan's ear – what the hell was he playing at? She then swiftly sought short-term solace elsewhere. Their marriage had been tempestuous, particularly in the more recent past. This, though, was not about husband and wife, but their relationship as business partners – or was it?

Maria was, as her husband had pointed out to Greg on his first meeting with him, a woman who had great inner strength, awareness and acumen. Juan had chosen his moment to strike.

It had hurt. But she was ready. Maria knew she had to find out what had brought about her husband's comment, and she also knew that his words would have been lingering for some time. And because even then he hadn't chosen the right time, she knew instinctively he was working to a deadline. That time had to be approaching otherwise Juan wouldn't have chosen this time, a poor time. She wasn't impressed. As usual she would have to sort out whatever was going on.

'Gina!'

Maria's game face was back on, bitterness turned to sweetness in one turn. She had been passed her 'go to' Johnnie Walker Blue Label on the rocks as she made her way to Gina across the bar area.

'How is your diary?'

Maria smiled an ever-sweeter smile. It was warm and welcoming. Gina had seen this kind of smile before, one that looked genuine but you felt was fuelled by something else. But she was happy to smile back. You never knew where a smile would lead – and she was looking for leads. This could work very nicely, inside the Lanzarote Eruption camp she would get to know more.

'What is it you have in mind?'

She answered in as coy a state as she could without sounding something like an over eager teenager.

'Perhaps you would like to come to the house. I'd very much like to hear more about you and your lovely mother? We could share stories?'

Maria was careful not to come over too heavy. She had no agenda. Her offer had been a spur of the moment invitation.

Gina could see and hear that Maria had delivered her words with an affection. It warmed her soul.

'Let me just check my dairy.'

Gina replied instantly. She had no diary.

'I'm free whenever, name your time.'

They exchanged numbers on their mobile phones.

Juan was talking with the Gladiators' owner Glen Witheford who was doing a great job of being big about his team's current half-time plight. Ricardo was with them too; while Hugo Silva had taken up conversation with Julian Jardine.

There was little of these people that held any relevence for GPK, who had finished helping Detective Sergeant Arteta around the same time as Kenny had put Baru and Tonito on the field. As such he'd not seen any of the game so far, not that he was there to watch the rugby league. He was people watching. That, and watching his mobile for any news from the team.

'Did you find out who he was?'

She'd caught him out again, the flame-haired girl. He didn't like coincidences.

'Your man. The one you were asking about.'

She added at his initial quizzical look, before he had chance to process. God, he must be getting old. Surely, he'd never have been as inept in quickfire situations years ago. She held a definite edge.

Fight fire with fire, usually a handy way of working out of a corner, was his response.

'And who might you be then?'

He'd delivered his question in as nonchalant manner as he could manage. She turned as she'd done previously, away from him and then:

'*Jen Juniper.*'

She held out her hand, he shook it.

'*As in the Donovan song?*'

'*Go to the top of the class, Mr …?*'

Gina had saluted him with her glass. He clinked his with hers. He didn't answer immediately. He was thinking. Gauging. She could tell it would be a lie before his lips even moved.

'*Gilmour … Gary.*' It was the first name that came to mind. A story he'd covered years back about a lovable rogue who had set himself up on the Isle of Man selling advertising for a colleague's magazine publishing company. It was as good a name as any for the time being. He was certain Ms Juniper hadn't been around when the Canary Islands Policia had asked for him by his real name.

'*A pleasure to meet you Gary.*' She gave no indication that she'd sussed his nom de plume.

'*Are you on holiday?*' GPK/Gary was now politely fishing. He'd ping a message back to the UK shortly, get them looking at who Jen Juniper was, if that was her real name. He had as much confidence in her reply as she'd had in his.

As far as GPK was concerned she wasn't merely passing the time of day with him, or rather, passing part of the half-time break with him, coincidences meant agendas in his book.

Gina was not passing the time of day. She was her father's daughter, and she had issues here. She'd find out who this guy was. He was from the north of England, that much was certain, from his accent.

'*You ask a lot of questions Gary.*' She too was fishing. GPK wasn't about to get hooked. He was enjoying the game playing.

'*Do I?*'

She laughed. He smiled. It wasn't a bonding, more a mutual respect for their respective dancing around handbags in getting this far with a somewhat staccato conversation.

'*You do … I'm travelling and performing. I play the bars, pubs, basically anywhere that pays …*'

There was a shift of foot traffic as the announcement came that the second half would be under way in two minutes. They went their separate ways.

Kenny Lomax had seen Stu Wainwright's face as Malky had swapped him for Popoli Baru, and the combined reaction from Elton Richards. He knew, from his own teenage years, the performance of Baru and Tonito in that brief spurt at the end of the half may have the potential to dim their spirit.

Wainwright had hardly been interchanged all season, he'd already made one try in this game, been as involved as he could have been. His face had said he wasn't happy, even if he'd refrained admirably from saying so. Kenny had taken him to one side in the tunnel as they had come off the park after the first half.

'Stu? You okay mate?'

Wainwright was sulking, he knew the feeling. He'd often had the same feeling when he was younger. It was time for hard words, straight to both his heart and his head.

'Listen mate, you don't own that shirt. Nobody does. You've played great all season, don't fuck it up now. Team game. Understand?'

Wainwright nodded. It wasn't sufficient. Lomax wasn't impressed. He wasn't about to let it pass.

'When was it you became a Diva? ... If you're done, had enough, let me know, now get in there and get your head back on! This is a team game!'

The half-time briefing had been a much happier affair. Malky Shannon had been giving individual one-to-ones with Alan Thomas and Vincent Venus, something about Gladiators' right side defence that he'd spotted. There had been initial back slapping and high-fiving among the rest of the crew with Tonito and Baru. It was largely a happy ship. As well it might be at 18-4 with one man down.

'Welcome back to El Estadio de Lanzarote!'

Joanne Collingwood had brought a brightness and freshness to Cloud TV's coverage since she'd taken the helm as anchor for their rugby league coverage.

'This is El Partido Mas Importances. And if you missed the first half, I have to tell you, you've missed incredible drama, which all started inside the first ten seconds ...'

As Jo continued her eulogy to the first half the teams re-emerged.

The band seemed as though it had somehow now grown in number and 'You're just too good to be true ...' was ringing out throughout the ground as the Hudderford Gladiators' fans launched into 'Country roads, take me home, to the place, I belong!' but without the band accompaniment.

It was as though they'd had a meeting at half time and had decided more noise was required. Everyone in the ground knew it was the next forty minutes that counted.

'18-4, Robbie, it's by no means all over.'

'No, Karen. And as we know from last weekend, it probably won't be right up until that final hooter. Remember, whatever show the Eruption put on they are still down by one player and believe me that makes all the difference, especially in the final quarter of the game. This has many twists and turns left in it.'

Glads' coach Gary Hopewell had calmed somewhat as he returned to his position in the stands for the restart.

'Yeah. Jen Juniper. Anything you have on her let me know. And that restaurant owner called Carlos at Al's. I've just run in to him again. And he's caused me problems.

'And I want anything you can get on the owners of the club and their allies. There's definitely something going on here. Oh yeah, and Jardine. He's here. He might have come here for a jolly, but that's not his style. Him too. And find out who's in charge of the Canary Islands Policia. I've just been interviewed by a Detective Sergeant Arteta, yeah like the footballer.'

'And Kenny Lomax is keeping faith in his new halfback pairing of Baru and Tonito for the opening of this second half. Entish retains his place too. It's Eruption to kick off – and we all know what happened at kick off in the first forty minutes.'

Both sets of supporters roared the approval as the ball soared high into the now floodlit arena as it now approached dusk.

Wayne Dorringe took the ball under no pressure and fed to his Glads' teammate Richie Wilkins, who had been somewhat anonymous in the first stanza, most unlike him. He was eager to redeem himself and revved as high as he could to blast a hole through the Eruption defence, but he was met with as solid a double tackle from Manny Roberts and Roberto Ortega.

The game became an arm wrestle of possession by both sides for the first fifteen minutes, each gaining territory before handing over to the other side or kicking the ball without success over the whitewash.

'*Twenty-five minutes to go and this resolute Eruption defence has remained firm since that try in the opening minutes when they were regrouping after their double red card. But here come the Gladiators.*'

Karen King was ramping it up for the viewers.

'*A try for Gladiators in the next ten minutes and this game will be a nail-biter right to the end.*

'*Phil Hoggers has possession for the visitors on his side's 30-metre line. They're looking lively here. Mike Bleasdale takes the pass, ducks under what looked like a swinging arm from Fastleigh, he's still got the ball. He's a stepper, trying to find that opening, again the Eruption are swift to cover. He feeds it out to Revere! Who darts away!*'

Paul Revere knew instinctively that when he darted, he usually had Eliott Schoular or Richie Wilkins close by, or on their way. This was one of those moments. He flipped the ball out of the back of his hand just as Greg and EV were into him.

'*Oh, hold on right there! What a pass! And Wilkins is in acres of space as he opens out his stride, pins back his ears and goes for the line! Forty, thirty, twenty, young Venus is in his wake, but he won't catch him. And there it is! A try to the Gladiators and they've doubled their tally!*'

Seconds later, the conversion was successful too and the game was very much back in the balance.

'*18-10, Robbie. It's game on!*'

There were no recriminations from the Eruption, no cataclysmic fallouts of a Gary Hopewell nature. Kenny Lomax had predicted this in his head. He knew, especially the way the teams were unbalanced numerically that something had to give. It was that calmness that he'd tried to transmit to the rest of his charges. This was a to-the-wire battle again.

No words had been spoken between the Cavaleros since the break.

Maria was calculating Juan's words while watching the game. Did he have a point? Or was this just another of his business dealings in which the Estadio and Eruption were just a couple of chips in a game?

Kenny had persisted with Tonito and Baru for a reason, not merely because of their impact in the last minutes of the first half but because he knew he had Stu Wainwright and Elton Richards as keen as young greyhounds, ready to come back fresh; and he wanted whatever a huge swathe of island pride would do to the crowd when Angel Ramos came back on field and joined compatriot Raul Rodriguez-Perez for the last stanza.

Eruption just had to last out another three or four minutes, until the final twenty, they would come on.

'Oh, that's a horrible high shot! And he's in trouble here!'

Karen King sounded dismayed.

'Hillman Ward was very nearly decapitated with that clothes-line stiff arm by Vellidale – and he knows! EV is apologizing immediately. Hillman Ward took that ball perfectly and Vellidale was a bit slow, puts out his arm, and when he puts his arm out it is Goodnight Vienna. I wouldn't be at all surprised if it isn't the same for Vellidale. Referee Caden is reaching for his pocket.'

'And we know there's only one colour he can show him after that.'

Robbie Robertson's words were followed by a collective 'ooooffff!' around the stadium as the incident was shown on the big screen for all to see.

'Maybe he'll be lenient, maybe a yellow card ... I've not seen three players from one side given red cards in any game ... but I have now!'

Referee Caden had no doubt. It was a red card all day long, he had to go.

'10 players! Richie! 10 players versus 12. Eruption lead by 18 points to 10, but ...'

Karen King looked at the clock for confirmation.

'Just over 20 minutes to go. This would be unbelievable if the Eruption could hold out.'

'And fairly embarrassing if the Gladiators weren't able to win from here,' was Robbie's quick retort.

EV was a giant of a man, 6ft 6 inches of meat, bone and muscle, he was one of Kenny Lomax's best mates, probably his best over so many years. He stood with his hands on his hips. He wasn't questioning referee Caden's parentage over the decision. He knew only too well he was late with the arm. He knew in that split second of doing it that he was in trouble and he also knew Hillman Ward wasn't someone who looked to get other players sent off. EV was downcast, he shook hands with Ward in a show of sportsmanlike behaviour that each understood. He left the field with his head hung low as he trudged from the arena.

'Gladiators now have possession inside the Eruption 20-metre line – and there are now just too many holes here for Eruption to have to fill surely?'

'Yes, Karen, they're ready to make some changes. I can see movement on the bench from both sides. Gary Hopewell is freshening up his attack again as he seeks to make the most of this two-man advantage. Malky Shannon, Lomax's off-field general, is preparing to bring back Ramos, Richards and Wainwright.'

GPK was on his way back to the Rooftop bar area. He'd seen enough. It was just a game to him, regardless of its nuances and on-field drama. His phone had been reverberating. News was coming through and news was his stock in trade, not the flight of a rugby ball.

'Eruption are stretched. Gladiators have the two-man advantage, they are also a very good team, and this is most definitely their time, right now.'

In Karen King's world this was now the Gladiators' game to lose, even though they were still eight points adrift.

'Fantastic cut-out pass from Bleasdale, who has played exceptionally well since he came on, to Millson, who has also

impressed. He looked like he was going to be wrapped up by Duggan and Venus but he's traded their tackles with a cheeky little flick pass out to big Aussie centre Chris Rice who only has the try line in front of him and places it down, cool as you like, over the whitewash.'

'This could be the beginning of the end for Eruption.'

Robbie was echoing Karen King's earlier thoughts.

'Eighteen minutes left on the clock. The Eruption boys are going to have to dig even deeper now.'

Kenny signaled for Malky to hold on with the changes, as the Gladiators tagged on their conversion goal for two more points, bringing the score to 18-16, still marginally in favour of Eruption.

'Country Roads! Take me Home!' rang out from all around the ground as the Gladiators' fans now sensed victory.

But the home crowd lifted themselves too, as the band started up again. They wanted to believe their team could hold on, but it was getting harder to do so given the circumstances.

Pitchside commentator Max Sunderland gave his assessment of what it was like around the respective team benches as the game entered its close.

'Both teams are set to make changes, Karen, as Malky Shannon and Gary Hopewell bring back what they hope will now be players recharged for the finish and the championship title. To those who think it is only Super League glory that these teams are after you really should be down here now. Changes on their way!'

The crowd's noise level rose again as Tonito was smashed in a tackle inside the Eruption half.

'Ohh! That was a terrific hit-up by Bleasdale, who has played out of his skin since coming on. Tonito has been hit hard there. And the referee has stopped the clock. That looks bad.'

'I'm not sure if he will know what day of the week it is when he gets up, Karen.'

Robbie was quick to point out Tonito was not as bad as first thought.

'That was a truly big hit by Mike Bleasdale who is showing exactly why he was called up by the Kiwis a few years ago.'

Eruption and the Gladiators both made their changes. Alan

Thomas was nursing a strain, so couldn't come back, but Stu Wainwright, Elton Richards and Raul Rodriguez-Perez all made their return to action in place of Popoli Baru, Tonito and Warren Entish.

Eruption were in possession when referee Caden restarted the clock and the game. Eleven minutes left. Two points the difference.

'Possession boys. Get them down their end of the paddock,' Kenny was marshalling.

Stu Wainwright took the play-the-ball from where Tonito had gone down, thankfully still clutching the ball. Behind him was Elton Richards who dummied from acting half back, sending the Gladiators' defence on the wrong foot. He turned back inside – and was immediately hammered down by Steve Hardy, Gladiators' prop.

Richards rose groggily but managed to play the ball back to Wainwright who fed Angel Ramos with a short pass that he charged on to like a raging bull. Ramos had no care for who was in front of him, he just wanted to run over them. He blasted into Mike Jefferson who had just come on for Gladiators and Hillman Ward, sending them both sprawling backwards as they clung to him before going down together with them.

Eruption were now within the Gladiators' 40-metre line with three tackles of the six left to go.

'That was some run by Angel Ramos!'

Karen King was ratcheting up her commentary.

'And he's played the ball back to Roberts who has gone straight from acting half back. He's fed it to Lomax, who's off on a mazy run. He's running crossfield, trying to find an opening. Duggan has come on his inside. His knees are pumping.'

'He's taken the ball at pace and … ohhh … he's shot through the Gladiators' defence. He's in the clear, thirty, twenty metres from the line. Ohh …'

The crowd was finding its voice with Eruption on the attack at last. The chants of 'DU-GAN!' were just about to be back in full flow when …

'That's a fantastic tackle by Richie Wilkins. He's had to come across field to make it and he's taken Duggan into touch! Tremendous action. But really, Karen, the Gladiators shouldn't be getting caught out anywhere on the park.'

It was a scrum on the Gladiators' 20-metre line, time was ticking down, they still trailed by two points. Juan and Maria Cavaleros were sat together but on Juan's left was Hudderford Gladiators' owner Glen Witheford and to Maria's right was Julian Jardine.

With just ten players left on the park the last thing Kenny had wanted was a scrum, which committed over half of his remaining players into a huddle. They'd have to disengage pretty quickly when the ball came out from the scrumdown if they were to cover all bases.

Revere put the ball into the scrum so adroitly that it was out and into the hands of Chris Rice within a second. There were only three Eruption players not involved in the scrum in some way as the six in the pack and Wainwright were all in close proximity. It left Greg, Richards and Venus as the only players to string a line across the pitch where normally there would be six, three generally each side of where the scrum was formed. Venus was to one side, Greg and Richards to the other.

Chris Rice was a pacey centre with a lot of class and great feet. One little shuffle and he was away. He went to Venus' side. Vinny had developed into a cracking winger on attack, but his defensive game still needed work. He knew it, the coaches knew it and were working on it. One second Venus thought he had him as Rice rushed headlong in his direction, the next second he'd gone and Vinny was grasping at thin air.

'Oh my word! That was electric feet from Chris Rice! He left Venus for dead there in back play. It's been a stubborn resistance. But it looks as though, for all the efforts of this Eruption side, it is going to be for nothing. That's 20-18 as Hudderford Gladiators take the lead once again, and an easy kick for the two points in front of goal. There it goes. Four points in front now and six minutes left on the clock.'

Karen King was seemingly administering the last rites.

Finally, the game looked up for Eruption's championship hopes.

Some of the Eruption fans started making their way to the exits. It had been an uphill struggle with fewer players for what amounted to seventy-five minutes of the game.

It was even better news for the Hudderford support a minute later when straight from the restart Dorringe collected the ball from the kick and remained unchallenged for twenty metres as Eruption attempted to calculate who to cover. Dorringe was hauled down by Mannion Roberts and Elton Richards inside Eruption's half.

Rice took the ball up and again made a surging run. He was now inside the Eruption 20-metre line when he was tackled by an increasingly stretched but game Lanzarote defence. Milton Easterly now had the ball and went for the line.

It was try time all the way, but from nowhere and with legs deceiving him Greg appeared, covering as though his life depended on it. Easterly, determined not to go into touch, flicked the ball back to no-one in particular.

It was a move that horrified Hopewell. Why the f**k weren't they running down the clock? 'Keep hold of the ball,' he muttered under his breath. 'Keep hold of the f***ing ball'.

Stu Wainwright had been one of the other Eruption chasers, fleet of foot to get over to Easterly – and he scampered on to the loose ball, picking it up deftly in one hand and setting off, diverting quickly from would-be tacklers.

The Eruption support, seemingly on their way home just a minute or so ago, roared their appreciation. They were out of their seats. Wainwright jinked, bobbed, weaved, searching for an opening as more Gladiators appeared in front of him.

Elton Richards was on his shoulder just as the tackles were becoming effective. Two were around him now, but somehow Wainwright managed to sneak out the offload. Richards claimed the ball.

Maria Cavaleros was out of her seat, finding a passion that would surprise herself later when she saw the playback of herself punching into the air, hollering at the top of her voice.

'*Richards takes an audacious ball from Wainwright who looked all wrapped up there. There is still time for this game to go either way, especially while Eruption have the ball in their hands. And Richards has avoided one tackle from Darren Wells, and now another from Steve Hardy. It's now Gladiators who are looking leggy ...*'

Elton Richards was a good-looking lad. He'd played the sport from being seven years old, always free from blemish, always a star of a junior club or glitzy, flash player in his early teens. He'd prided himself on looking in the mirror and staring back at him was this pristine face.

'*Ohhh!*'

Karen King was wincing as she saw it, as Richards' nose splattered on impact. It was like a giant strawberry exploding with claret everywhere. But as much as he'd held pride in not having suffered previously, Richards held even greater resolve in the ultimate reward Eruption were chasing.

'*And Elton Richards has really taken one for the team, but nothing is stopping him. He has blood across his shirt, streaming from his nose and sparks must be flying around his head right now, but he's still holding the ball. His legs are going like pistons. Mr Caden hasn't stopped play. He's not seen anything wrong, or if he has, he's playing an advantage.*'

The young Aussie stand-off was finally felled just inside the Gladiators' half with both sets of fans raising the volume to a new level for the Estadio de Lanzarote. The place was a cauldron of excitement and hopeful anticipation from the Eruption fans willing their players to the line; and of excitement and hopeful anticipation from the Glads' fans that they could hold out.

'*This is unbelievable play by the ten from Eruption.*'

Karen King couldn't help herself. She was trying to keep neutral in her commentary but it was proving more difficult.

Kenny was back directing traffic. He was ready at first receiver as Ramos took the ball from behind Richards. The clock ticked down to three minutes on the screen as he glanced up. There was a chance they might get another opportunity in possession if they didn't make it this time, but that's all it was, just a chance. This had to be the time. One move, just one move.

Angel Ramos duly delivered the ball to Lomax, but Gladiators looked to have regrouped. They were back in the line, coming up as one. Mannion Roberts was to Lomax's right with Ortega next in line. To Lomax's left were Wainwright and Greg. He went with the Roberts option.

'Roberts is out on his feet here. He's been on field throughout the game as have most of the Eruption pack. He's taken it back into the tacklers. He's taking time to get to his feet. These are precious seconds.'

Kenny had followed Roberts. Caden hadn't brought out his blood-bin card for Richards, he was so caught up in the momentum of the game reaching its tumult. Kenny brought Richards back into the game. He looked like a man who'd just gone ten rounds in a heavyweight boxing championship fight. If Kenny had wanted to see the boy's temperament in the big moments, he was seeing it now.

'It's Richards! His face might be a mess but that's some run at the Glads' defence. Ohhh! My word!! Not again!'

There was a temptation to bring out the humour in Elton Richards's nose being blasted for a second time inside a minute or so, and Karen King's voice betrayed the thought ever so slightly, she hoped.

'And this time referee Caden has taken action. If the first one went unnoticed this one certainly hasn't. Oh! And now what's happening here? Richards has lost it!'

Sure enough, Elton Richards had cracked. He'd taken out Gladiators scrum-half Paul Revere with a shuddering jab to his jaw. Caden, with the deftness of a magician, propelled red cards in front of both players and Eruption were down to just nine men! Gladiators down to eleven. Caden hadn't stopped the clock immediately, which had continued ticking down to less than two minutes.

'I have never seen a game like this before in my life!'

The Cloud TV commentator was now in complete bewilderment at having now witnessed six red cards in a game.

'This is stupendous! It's a good job it has little time left. If it was to carry on much longer we wouldn't have enough players on the park to finish. They're both making their way. Revere and Richards – and they're still at each other with the verbals as they go. Robbie, over to you!'

'Karen, if this is what they're like playing for the championship just think what these two sides would be like contesting the play-off final, as we anticipate they will.'

'It will also depend on whether they have enough players either fit or unbanned after this. But back to the action. Referee Caden has restarted the clock. Duggan has kicked for touch from the penalty awarded by Caden. He's found the edge of the Gladiators' 20-metre line.

'Eruption have six tackles to get the ball over the whitewash – Gladiators have six to stop it. That's all there is left. Hold on tight everybody, this rocky ride is coming to its end, but who knows which way it will go?'

Maria Cavaleros hadn't moved since Elton Richards was in possession. She had stood transfixed by the action. She was in her own bubble, didn't care what was going on in her world with Juan. This was a game, a moment, filled with far more passion than she'd experienced in either boardroom or bedroom lately.

Gina too, hadn't thought she would get caught up in the atmosphere, but the action was intoxicating. She could now see why her father had been drawn into it and she now wondered why she had never been interested before.

She'd watched Greg and Kenny specifically, but she'd also found herself watching the whole game, the tactical, strategic side. She was hooked. As well as being hooked up to other matters, on her smartphone.

Juan Cavaleros and Glen Witheford were by now no longer mute bystanders with other things on their minds. Their respective clubs were fighting lock, stock and barrel for supremacy and that was something both saw similarities with their business dealings.

Witheford believed in sport and was a true British sportsman. He held out his hand to shake with Juan.

'Whether we win or you, Juan, we have two fantastic teams. I

*look forward to us hopefully meeting again in the play-off final – and
I thank you, for you and your wife's generous hospitality.'*

'*Senor Glen* (Juan couldn't quite manage the pronunciation
of Witheford) *it has been a privilege. Perhaps this is a taste of what
is to come?'*

Both men raised their eyebrows and turned their attention
back to the final throes.

Gary Hopewell had gone back to manic. His team led by a
slender four-point margin. A try would bring Eruption level.
And if they converted it? That thought didn't bear thinking
about for Hopewell, to be beaten by a side now playing with just
nine men. He was urging his players to be vigilant, to keep some
form of composure. This was not the time for infringements.

Kenny Lomax had his gumshield out, giving instructions, as
Greg kicked for touch.

'*On three!'*

It was all he'd mouthed to his limited charges left on the
field. They knew what it was about.

'*Lomax takes the ball and here comes Lanzarote's Angel Ramos
running at speed taking the pass and aiming to make a hole in this
Gladiators' line … That's a great surge by Ramos, and an equally
fabulous stop by Schoular and Bleasdale … They've put him to the floor
… He's up and plays the ball back to Wainwright this time, who darts
away to his right side and gets an off-load away to Rodriguez-Perez,
who charges back at this resolute Gladiator defence. He turns in the
tackle, his hands and upper body are free, he's looking for support, still
the Gladiators' defence stays firm. They wrap him up now.'*

The band struck up again. The crowd joined in. Islanders
who had never known the game existed until a few weeks
previously were now in the same land as supporters who had
followed the game for forty years.

'*That's two tackles gone, not much ground made up, I'd say
they're about four metres from the line, if that …'*

King looked at the screen.

'*And fifty-five seconds left. Something has to give here. Lomax is
back behind Rodriguez-Perez as the island warrior lifts his tired body*

from the ground. Lomax has taken the ball ... he's on a run! ... he's straightening up ... and the Gladiators are struggling to hold on to him here! ... he has one, two, three on him now, though ... and he's wrapped up ... and he's down!'

Forty-five seconds left. The Gladiators' fans launched into 'Country Roads ...' the stadium was burning with anticipation of a try from Eruption or a shut-out from Hudderford.

'And what's this?'

King was going from one sense of amazement to another.

'Eruption have brought back Popoli Baru and Tonito! With forty-five seconds on the clock? And it is Ortega and Fastleigh who have made way quickly from the battle ... and they're straight into the action! ... Lomax plays the ball back to Baru, who dances as though he's a boxer readying for offloading a punch, he jinks, turns, finds Tonito, who darts at the Gladiators defence ... ohh!! ... he's gone under one tackle, he's through! ... but Jefferson has caught him, he's going to ground five metres from the try line. Four tackles gone, five metres to go, two tackles left in this game ...'

King looked at the clock again.

'Thirty seconds, less than that now ...'

Kenny Lomax had his gumshield out again. He nodded at Greg. Called for Baru.

'Tonito plays it back to Baru. Baru to Wainwright, they're still five or six metres away. Wainwright feints to his left, comes off his right, steps inside a tackle, but the Gladiators are holding firm here. It's a heap of players with tired limbs.'

And this is what the championship game had come down to – one last play, fifteen seconds on the clock. This wasn't even about getting into Super League, but it was for a trophy.

Greg had held back from the play throughout the six tackles until now. Similarly, Vinny Venus. Kenny took charge once again, this time behind Wainwright.

'Well ...'

King took a deep breath.

'It all comes down to this. One play. One moment. Lomax receives the ball – fourteen seconds – he swivels to his right so he can

now see his runners … and it's Greg Duggan! … Duggan has his legs pumping high and crashes into Hillman Ward! … but he releases the ball, basketball style over the top to Venus, who cannot make ground – ten seconds – as he has nowhere to work it – he makes an amazing pass as he's going to ground, throwing it as he launches himself to avoid contact with the pitch before offloading … seven seconds … Tonito receives it … wow, he must have gathered that with his fingertips no more than an inch or two from the floor … but he's back to his feet … and … oh here we go … he's gone for a little grubber kick … the hooter goes …!'

But the ball was still alive and the crowd was almost suspended in disbelief. Tonito's kick through had gone behind all except one of the Gladiators' defence. Only Wayne Dorringe remained as the one defender who could see it initially. But even he couldn't see it fully because …

'It's hit the bottom of the post!'

King was way beyond caring about her voice now, which was developing into something resembling a hoarse throat and squeak.

'It's still in play! Dorringe's view is obscured by the post protector, he can't get to it, but Duggan can, bloody hell how did he get there after that earlier tackle? He's managed to gather it in one hand and he's … ohhhh! … he's been horrendously taken out by a massive hit by Steve Hardy – and it's not at all legal – you saw Duggan's head rock back as he was going down for the try … but amazingly he's got the ball away, he was going in, of that there's no doubt, but he's managed to flip it as he was being sledgehammered – and Kenny Lomax now has it … now it's his turn to burrow away at the line … he's pushed back … he flips it out to Tonito! … Gladiators are back holding firm again … we're well over the time since the hooter sounded, but it's still alive …'

Greg shook himself back to consciousness. His legs were like jelly from the high shot, but he had to keep going. This was his time – Duggan Time – the time he had lost ten months ago when the last Hopton game had finished early and had decided his club's fate – and his life. Never again. Every second counted, even when the hooter had gone. Dig deep! And when you've dug, dig deeper again!

'*Tonito rounds a static Darren Wells. These players are out truly on their feet. He's ducked back inside. Popoli Baru takes it from him. They're still three metres short! Baru cuts back inside, finds Wainwright who finds Lomax. Surely, they cannot sustain this. Ohhhh! Lomax throws out the most audacious pass of the game! He's propelled the ball crossfield over twenty metres ... there would normally be some kind of interception tried by Chris Rice, who has made that one of his trademarks, but he's out on his feet too ... the ball is in the hands of Venus once again, he's ten yards out now ... but he skips inside from the left wing, takes two Gladiators with him ... and ... TRY!!!! ...*

'*I just do not believe what I am seeing here! ... Greg Duggan was felled like a big oak tree only seconds ago, he's got back to his feet, not only that, he's trailed the play, he's followed Venus ... just how has he done that? ... the man is a colossus! ... he's taken the ball from what I have to say is another fabulous offload from Venus whose game improves every time I watch him ... and Greg Duggan, who only arrived on the island less than a week ago may just have won this game for Lanzarote Eruption and earned the islanders their first trophy in any sport, outside of a Canary Islands competition. Although I may have to verify that ...*'

Karen King was more than in a lather. It had been a commentary like she had never given before.

Greg was mobbed. In all honesty he could have done without it, but the adrenaline he'd produced withstood the impact of everything coming his way. Tonito and Popoli Baru were being congratulated too. In the space of a day they had introduced themselves into the first team and were seemingly set to become very much the club's future. But for one man the air was full of his name.

'DU-GAN, DU-GAN, DU-GAN!!!' The crowd was not just on its feet, there was hugging, kissing, high-fiving, dancing. But the score was only now levelled at 22-22. Legs still like jelly – or even blancmange, thought Greg – he had to kick the penalty to win the game, otherwise the match went into extra time to decide, when the first team to score would win. There was no way either side wanted that, but right now that was Gladiators' only choice. Greg had the kick, from way out near the touchline, as he'd scored near the corner. This was it. Big moment. A trophy at last in his career. Maybe.

He heard his name ringing around the Estadio. It was a fabulous feeling, something again he wished he'd had in the same numbers when he'd been playing for Hopton, but this was far different. A fabulous sunny land, his thought flashed to how life could have been for he and Diane and their son Kyle had he done this kind of thing earlier in his career.

He had to let that thought go. His thoughts flashed to Susie, how good it had been with her again for that one day, but maybe that wasn't meant to be? She'd disappeared quickly, too quickly he now thought.

Greg teed up the ball. He was crouched behind it, looking at the posts, putting the right panel of the ball – he always hit to the side with the manufacturer's name, didn't know why, but he'd always done it that way – so that he could see it. His legs didn't feel clever at all, and his head was still a bit blurry. He got to his feet.

'Duggan doesn't look quite right here, and I'm not surprised.'

King had calmed now.

'He took one hell of a knock from Hardy. I don't know of many – or any – that have got up, and back in play in the same play, taken the ball again – and scored the try. It will probably go down as the most inspirational passage of rugby league I've ever seen, but this kick?'

Kenny Lomax had watched it too. He'd seen Greg's legs buckling. He knew his pal would attempt it, but he also knew it was too much to ask. He headed across the field to change kicker as Greg stared at the ball. From nowhere, it must have been somewhere, Greg girded up his loins, gave strength and stability to his legs and made towards the ball. The crowd was hushed for both sets of supporters.

'You cannot be serious!'

King watched as Greg gave it everything he could as he sent

the ball high into the night sky. The crowd caught its collective breath. Maria held hers. Gina too. The band had stopped playing. The ball spiraled towards the posts.

'It's a good kick, but it's … it's just sailed wide … the game goes on!'

The groans of the crowd were followed by uproar as both sets of supporters realised the game was, even now, still alive.

'… that was a fantastic effort from a remarkable player … but maybe just a step too far for the man now known simply as DUGAN around El Estadio de Lanzarote … ohh … hold on! … don't go anywhere! … there's another kick at goal!'

'Mr Caden has certainly played his part in this match from the very beginning and it looks like he's having the last word here. He's waited until Duggan's kick at goal. Now he's signaling for a penalty goal!'

This was all new territory for King and would have been for most rugby league commentators.

Known as the 8-point try, but unknown by most, the ruling was that if, in the process of a try being scored, there had been a severe infringement by the defensive team the attacking team would be awarded the try even if it had not actually been touched down, which it had in this case, plus the attacking team would be given an extra kick at goal, following the conversion attempt, that Greg had just missed.

Even worse news for the Gladiators was that the penalty kick was bang in front of the posts!

'And that's not all either! Steve Hardy has received a red card for his smash on Greg Duggan, that's seven players red-carded in all. And this has reignited the crowd – the kick and the latest sending off. And after what is now well over the eighty minutes we just might be down to the final kick of the game.'

Kenny had stopped in his tracks, in trying to get over to Greg, when he'd seen him set off. He was now with Greg as he made his way towards the sticks in readiness.

'Hey mate! I don't know how you do it!'

Kenny had his arm around Greg's shoulder.

'The try, that attempt … but let me slot this one over … I saw

your legs just before it …'

Greg looked at Kenny as though he was stupid. There was no way he was not going to take this kick. This was the championship. One kick. In front of the posts. He could do it with his eyes shut! And in the next second they were, as Greg slumped to the ground!

'And Greg Duggan is down!'

King, whose concentration had been on the monitor, watching the infringement again, to give a more detailed analysis, saw him on the floor and looked desperately at Robbie Robertson, who shrugged, also having not seen.

Kenny called to the bench, but the medics and physios were already on their way. They'd all been stood watching the action and had been readying themselves for celebrating Greg's kick. Now they were deeply concerned.

'I'm okay.'

Greg protested, like many other players before him who had suffered post-hard knock syndrome. By the time the infantry had arrived he was sitting up, dazed.

'Greg, you can't take the kick mate. I'll do it.'

Kenny was adamant. He marched towards the sticks as Greg avoided the gang who were approaching him. He shook his head as though shaking it would make it clear.

'And it looks as though Kenny Lomax, the coach and captain, will be taking the kick that should win this most eventful game. I think we could all do with a nice lie down after this, maybe with a glass of something close by … but … no, I don't believe this!'

Greg hadn't just returned to the perpendicular, he'd also broken into a run that took him past Kenny, and with Kenny howling at him in his wake Greg received the ball from the referee and undertook another unique moment in rugby league history.

'No, no, no, no, no …. That is f …'

King very nearly let her professionalism go out of the window but managed to correct herself in time.

'I would love to have carried on with a certain word because it seems so opportune right now, but I have to think of our viewers who

may be offended … that was audacious and amazing, but in the context of this game it fits right in as the most bizarre ending!'

Estadio de Lanzarote was in mayhem. As roller coaster rides go the islanders were starting to get used to this with two consecutive fantastic finishes, and they were also getting used to Senor DU-GAN who seemed to be making a habit, not just of winning games at the death, but also pulling out plays that were causing near heart-attacks due to his ingenuity for the breathless.

Greg had taken the ball from the referee, checked the mark from where it was to be kicked, kept the ball in his hands, stepped back five paces and two to his left, he'd then set off and had calmly released the ball to drop-kick it between the posts.

It was almost unheard of in rugby league, but it was legal, and he'd used it once before in a match for Hopton Town years ago when he'd been so inflamed with the way the match had gone that he just couldn't be arsed to place it down properly.

This time he'd taken it so quickly because he knew if he took any longer Kenny would be at him – and he also felt if he crouched again he might not get up to launch the kick.

'You bloody mad man!'

Kenny's famous gap-toothed grin was set as wide as it could be.

'That was …'

He shrugged his shoulders, kept them shrugged and lifted his outstretched palms of his hands.

'I don't know what it was, Jeez Greg …'

Kenny slapped his team mate on the back, then held his arm up with Greg's to the adoring crowd.

Greg, still teetering and with medics waiting to see him, concerned about his sparking out less than a minute prior, was enveloped by a sea of Eruption players and the crowd, fans who all wanted to show the love for their heroes invaded the pitch.

'Du-Gan! Du-Gan! Du-Gan! rang around the ground as the band launched back into action with yet another round of 'You're Just Too Good To Be True'.

CHAPTER 30

'We Are the Champions!' blasted out over Eruption's public address system and along with fireworks that didn't quite match those that had just taken place on the park.

Julian Jardine and his team had brought the trophy over, knowing that, whichever way the game went, it was going to go to one of these two teams. Jardine made his way down to pitchside where a small stage had been hastily put into place with sponsors names adorning it.

Cloud TV's presenter Joanne Collingwood was to make the on-field announcements and on this occasion would interview coaches Kenny Lomax and Gary Hopewell, prior to the raising of the trophy and the champagne soaking that inevitably ensued. Superlatives abounding, Joanne started:

'Ladies and Gentlemen, I'm sure you will all join with me in your appreciation for one of the most astounding, astonishing games rugby league has ever seen!'

The applause from the crowd was deafeningly loud.

'We've all been through something incredibly special here tonight, and I still cannot for the life of me believe what I've seen from two tremendous teams.'

Again the applause.

'Now I know it's not often any of us will see seven red cards in one game …'

Collingwood paused for effect as the pantomime style boos started up.

'But I think when we all watch it back, we won't look on this as a dirty game. Our referee Mr Paul Caden and his team have dealt with every decision the way they have seen it and have worked as hard as anybody.'

There was derision as one might expect. Paul Caden, his bristly chin and smiley face, had been invited by Joanne to give his comments, not often done, but he wanted to say it like it was.

'Ladies and Gentlemen. Senors et Senoritas ...'

The likeable referee received a cheer for his acknowledgement of the locals.

'Like Joanne says, this was not a dirty game, but when I see something that's not right I take action. It just so happened that involved seven red cards tonight, but it was a fabulous game played, largely, in a fabulous spirit. Commiserations to the Gladiators' lads, congratulations to the Eruption boys! Thank you!'

And he handed back to Joanne.

'Thank you, Mr Caden! Excellent job. Next up, here's the Gladiators' coach, Gary Hopewell. Gary ...'

Gary Hopewell held firm to the typical rugby league club losing coach discipline of admitting the better side had won and his boys would take a good look at where they had gone wrong. He thanked the club's supporters for their faith throughout the season and gave an assurance his charges would be ready for their play-off match. And he was gone.

Next up was Kenny. The cheers when his name was announced and when Lanzarote Eruption were officially announced as champions made Greg's hairs stand on end as he watched, clutching a water ball by the sidelines with his teammates.

'Kenny, how do you explain what just happened out there?'

Joanne Collingwood held the microphone towards the player-coach, who ran his fingers through his tousled hair shaking his head.

'Jo, I have no idea!'

He shook his head again.

'When I came here six months ago this island didn't even know the sport, now look!'

He raised his arms to the fans. They cheered again.

'Para Ti! ... For you!'

He cried out with gusto, and the crowd roared its appreciation, then he returned to his summing up. Taking time to take occasional slugs of water.

'Aww look, this game does your head in at times, but we love it.

Tonight? ... Phew! ... First, I gotta say, hard lines to Gary and his team ... we all know sometimes it can put more pressure on you, when you know you've a man or two advantage ... great game ...'

Polite applause reigned for this part of the proceedings.

'But our boys! ... Hey, you guys saw what you saw ... and that is the most amazing last minute I've ever played in my life, it lasted a month out there ... but WE DID IT!!'

Kenny punched the air, saluted the crowd and left the podium.

'There's just one more thing before the medals and the trophy presentation, which we're pleased to say will be made by the Rugby League Authority's Mr Julian Jardine ... and that's tonight's Man of the Match award ...'

Immediately the crowd took up the chant of 'Du-Gan! Du-Gan!' ... there was no way it could go to anyone else, but Joanne Collingwood toyed with them ever so slightly.

'We've had some fantastic performances tonight ... for the Gladiators two fabulous tries by Chris Rice, Mike Bleasdale came on and made a massive impact, Hillman Ward played the whole 80 minutes giving everything ... and for Eruption ...'

The roar was building. One name was being increased in volume every time it was shouted.

'For Eruption ...' Joanne continued. *'Outstanding contributions from Vincent Venus, Stu Wainwright, Elton Richards, Mannion Roberts and Kenny Lomax ... amazing debuts by Popoli Baru and Tonito ... the local boys ... Angel Ramos and Raul Rodriguez-Perez ...'*

Joanne left a pause while the crowd carried on its deafening chant. She smiled. She waited her moment.

'... but, who will ever forget that last minute? ... He did much more besides, but that last minute, Wow! ... and I mean Wow! ... the El Partidos Mas Importance Man of the Match can only be one player ... it's ... Greg Duggan!'

Greg received his award from the Cloud TV presenter.

'DU-GAN! DU-GAN! DU-GAN!' was hollered out once again, and again, and again. So much so that Julian Jardine – who had been waiting in the wings to make the championship

trophy presentation – and his officials, perhaps fearing the applause and that the DU-GAN celebration would never end, stepped forward for Kenny Lomax to receive the silverware. Once again 'We Are the Champions' blared out from the speakers all around the ground.

GPK had found himself drawn back into the game, having earlier retired to the Rooftop Bar to receive emails and texts from his team. He'd returned for what had been the last two to three minutes when the noise levels had begun rising with Elton Richards' tremendous efforts. He had been in awe of Greg's match-equalising try and of the man's inner strength in coping with the conversion attempt and then the penalty goal.

Whatever impression he'd formed of Greg Duggan previously this showed a man who could sustain incredible performance under extreme pressure, a man who had remarkable fortitude, courage and a quick brain. Strength of mind coupled with physical prowess.

Greg had told him at Al's about his escape having been abducted to Quinigan's Scottish highland estate to the beating he'd endured from those who were working with Quinigan & Co. He now knew what the man was capable of either on a field of play or anywhere else, no matter how strange and far-fetched.

He also had work to do. Somehow, he needed to set a ball rolling with Jardine, start giving the guy a bit of grief.

Jardine would get him to Quinigan. Whether that was a good thing to do right now bearing in mind what Quinigan was capable of was another thing entirely. It would need careful handling.

GPK wasn't about to rock any boats unless he knew he was likely of success, scratch that, he thought, he was always about rocking boats, it was just a case of how you rocked them. Nonetheless Jardine was a target.

Jen Juniper, on the other hand, was another matter. It hadn't taken long for his team to find her Facebook page, Instagram and Twitter feeds. And it had taken them even less time to track through her friends and followers to find the connection that led her to being Gina Irvine, daughter of Bob Irvine.

CHAPTER 31

Well, well! What was Gina Irvine doing here? GPK didn't like coincidences and this was too big a coincidence. Why would she be here on this small island of 150,000 people, watching a rugby league game that involved people her father had been involved with? She was here for a reason.

He hypothesized that Greg and Jen/Gina may have been together at some stage. Possible, certainly given Duggan's track record, or maybe Lomax and her? His team had told him of Duggan's recent and Lomax's far less recent marital splits. The team were working on both players' ex-partners presently.

Anyone else with whom Gina could have a connection? Well, yes actually. Gina had a stepfather, Ricardo Rubio on Lanzarote. Shit, that might be the whole coincidence. Nothing to do with Duggan or Lomax at all.

But no, surely the coincidence had to be her father, Bob Irvine. Two men who played for her father's team in England were now here, and now she was here too.

Shit, that might even mean a relationship with the other players in the team that were ex-Hopton Town. The coincidence surely had to be Bob Irvine and Greg Duggan or Kenny Lomax. Given his time spent with Duggan everything seemed to revolve around him, everywhere he went it was drama and trouble.

'Gary! Hey, Gary!'

At first, he didn't respond at all. Hadn't heard, in the way that you don't when it's not your name, but then realised it was his name!

It was her again, Jen, now also Gina. He was losing his touch here.

Gina was high on the emotion from the game. *'Did you see THAT?'*

Despite swallowing a modicum of professional pride at the

realisation he might be losing what sports players often refer to as that half-yard, but in his case that half-second of brain power, GPK couldn't help but be captivated by her smile, her enthusiasm.

She cocked her head slightly. By now they were alongside each other. Her voice lowered and she held her hand cupped to one side of her mouth as she spoke into his ear like a granddaughter confiding with her grandfather.

'*You know, you might do better if you loosened up a little …* Grahame?'

She left his name floating in the air as she smiled back.

'*And then maybe we could quit this dancing around?*'

Her voice was now no more than a whisper.

'*I'm sure your team back at Castlegate Press would find it much easier if they just called me?*'

No matter what kind of expression GPK might have attempted to pull he couldn't get away from how this girl, Gina Irvine, had given him the runaround. He admitted to himself to being pretty impressed by his former boss's daughter. She seemed to know what he was going to ask next.

'*I'm here because I aim to find out who was really responsible for my dad being killed, not the hopeless man who pulled the trigger. You're here because of what happened to Jeff Markham, as well as my dad.*'

She let her words settle.

'*You don't need to be a journalist to find out how I found out about you, Greg Duggan, Kenny Lomax or anybody else. It's all out there, on here –* Gina held her smartphone as evidence.

'*It's a brave new world, Grahame.*'

It was a cheekily delivered line and although GPK wasn't quite yet prepared to be cast as a dinosaur of the media world he felt she was dragging him steadily closer to the precipice. He smiled with her.

'*We need to talk, Gina …*'

Kraft then changed tack. Gina might be having fun, but he was working.

'But I want to try something that may help us both, right now, shake a tree or two, over there …'

He shifted his head slightly in the direction of where she saw Maria. This was Pythagoras coming up with one of his 'angles'.

He'd succeeded in throwing Gina for a half second. She looked inquisitive. He reassured her.

'Just back me up …'

GPK had wanted an angle, something to get him in front of Julian Jardine. Scare the shit out of the twat. Shake his tree. Gauge his reaction. He hadn't had a good enough reason for doing this previously, but now that Gina had presented herself his plan had come together. He had his angle.

Jardine was in conversation with Juan and Maria Cavaleros, Gladiators' owner Glen Witheford and Hugo Silva. Champagne was flowing from the umpteenth bottle of Dom Perignon.

The Cavaleros had prepared for victory with several crates of 'bubbles'. Regardless of any of their behind-the-scenes problems they both had enough business and professional nous, plus an island mentality, to recognise that a party would always provide a great atmosphere and they had every reason to celebrate.

The air was filled with laughter and high spirits all around the Rooftop Bar. GPK and Gina made their way toward the group.

'Mr Jardine …'

GPK spoke his name genially, upbeat, he didn't want anything coming across negative and sinister for his opening gambit.

Julian Jardine turned his position slightly to greet the man who had come up to his right side and was holding out his hand. Jardine responded. The kind of thing he did all the time at functions. Kraft grasped it tightly. Firm handshake, business class.

'Grahame Kraft,'

GPK announced as he then held out his open palm of his left hand and stepped slightly to his right to make room for Gina.

' … and Gina Irvine … Bob Irvine's daughter …'

He wanted to see how acute it struck a chord with Jardine, who chose, interestingly felt Pythagoras, not to be deliberately obtuse. He'd half expected a certain coldness.

'I ... err ...'

Jardine floundered.

'I am so sorry ... Miss Irvine ... your father had great passion for the game ... I hope you are okay?'

This was, although a little messy in the way Jardine was coming across, a little more warmth than GPK had anticipated. He'd thought he would be more a cold fish.

Maria's attention had been immediately alerted, on seeing Gina and now hearing of her father.

The Cavaleros' world in Lanzarote was not one that had included much about the north of England up until this season when they had visited on half a dozen occasions as Eruption had played away games, but she knew Bob Irvine.

Jardine knew it was always best to appear concerned. The introduction from this man Kraft was loaded, he knew that much and he was searching for some easy way out of this conversation, to get back to the fairly nondescript chatter of a few seconds ago. Another easy night, another nice stopover all paid for through the Rugby League Authority. Easy number. He'd spend time checking this man out afterwards.

But for now, he had to deal with the situation currently and sensed, in the eyes and body manner of this couple, that they were looking for something from him, and so he offered a little more.

'It is always difficult to know exactly what to say ... I was there myself ...'

Jardine wasn't unduly perturbed, he was just a little uncomfortable. Maria provided his lifebelt, deflecting the attention to herself and Gina. She moved closer to her friend's daughter.

'Gina, darling. This is terrible. I did not know ...?'

GPK felt the focus shifting from Jardine, however well intended Maria's words were to Gina.

He sought to redirect the conversation straight back at

Jardine. He wanted reaction, to see what he was dealing with, how Jardine would play things.

'*Dead, yes.*'

Gina nodded briefly, lightly biting the bottom of her lip to accentuate the emotion she was holding back. It played its part with Maria and gave GPK an opportunity.

'*He was shot … on the pitch.*'

GPK emphasised for Maria's and now the rest of the assembled group's information.

'*At a rugby league game. Last year.*' Kraft let the words settle, then turned directly towards Jardine.

'*Miss Irvine would like to know, Mr Jardine …*'

He had no time for buggering about here, he now wanted to see the whites of Jardine's eyes.

'*… just who the fuck benefited from my father's death …*'

This wasn't the line GPK had decided upon, but it also wasn't him speaking it.

Gina had not just played her part, she'd now taken charge. She had this recurring ability of knocking Kraft off his angles, and had provided an angle of her own as sharp as any.

The evening was turning decidedly sour for Jardine. But if either GPK or Gina had expected some form of capitulation, it wasn't about to come. Jardine had been around enough serious stories, bad news and hard negotiations. He also knew he did not need this.

Maria stood open-mouthed for a second at Gina's words.

'*I have no idea what you are trying to accomplish here, Miss Irvine, nor you Mr Kraft?*'

Jardine was the epitomy of calm whatever else was raging inside him.

'*And you have my sympathy over what happened to your father, but I'm afraid …*'

'*Maybe Jeff Markham then …*'

GPK succeeded in getting Jardine to turn his head back in his direction. He wanted to see how this affected the outwardly impervious skin of the man. He drew a blank from Jardine who simply shrugged.

'*I'm sorry, you've lost me there …*'

And swiftly, Jardine decided on retreat. He turned back to his hosts.

'*… now, it has been a lovely evening … Maria … Juan … you have been the perfect hosts … and what a finish! …*'

Jardine was quickly back on his own territory. He'd cut Kraft and Gina from the conversation.

'*Glen, good to see you too … maybe see all of you again in the play-off final for Super League …*'

He shook hands with Glen Witheford, two-cheek kisses of goodbye with Juan and Maria, then turned back to GPK and Gina ensuring he was not cast as someone without breeding.

'*A pleasure to meet you both.*'

And he was gone.

Kraft knew he'd hit the mark. Jardine had been on his team's radar all along, but he hadn't had such an ideal opportunity to see him in action, his body movements, always a giveaway. If this guy truly had nothing to hide, why was he looking to get away so soon? He turned to Gina, and cupping his hand this time, replicated her conspiratorial fervour.

'*Good job, Gina. We work well … bear with me a second …*'

He left her with Maria. He had other fish to fry. Next up, the guy from Al's. He'd been watching for him.

'*Carlos!*'

It was time for the gregarious GPK once again. He was developing his own agenda, which at present consisted of finding out who everyone was, making himself noticed. See what kind of ructions he could instigate.

Carlos Cuadrado was with a couple who frequented Al's. Before Carlos had time to put a face on, GPK was in his. The couple faded away as Kraft approached.

Carlos was not instantly on his mettle, but he wasn't about to give anything up to this man who he'd only seen earlier in the day, this man who he also now knew was a journalist. Seconds after initial impact, he beamed back at GPK.

'*Senor.*'

He bowed his head ever so slightly in Kraft's direction. Then went into another higher gear, as if he'd only just realised with whom he was about to talk.

'*Senor Greg, wow!*'

He raised his arms out wide, beaming even more. '*He is amazing player!*'

'*Yes, he is …*'

Kraft was keen to set the ground rules. It was time to see what this man was made of. Kraft's genial outer persona was designed to disarm.

'*Tell me, Senor Cuadrado. How long have you had Al's?*'

Carlos's face straightened.

'*Why do you ask this question, senor?*'

He forced a smile, and then offered a concerned expression.

'*Just asking, Carlos. Just making conversation.*'

He let it lie a second. It hadn't been a difficult question to answer and he already knew a reasonable amount about Carlos.

'*What is going on, Carlos?*'

This was direct.

'*Or maybe, Que esta pasando, Carlos?*'

Carlos could feel himself tensing and didn't like it. He knew Kraft was looking for a reaction and he knew his face was giving himself away.

'*I am sorry Senor …*'

It was weak, he knew.

'*I am not … how do you say it? … I do not understand?*'

Meat and drink to GPK. Meat and drink. He took Carlos by the elbow, then spoke gently but firmly.

'*The police, Mr Cuadrado. You think I don't know who arranged for them to question me? Why, Carlos? Why?*'

It was delivered complete with what he considered an appropriate dollop of venom. He released his elbow.

'*I … I …*'

Cuadrado had been knocked off centre. GPK knew he was dealing with the monkey not the organ grinder. Carlos quickly brought himself back round.

'*Senor, I know nothing of what you say … policia?*'

'*Carlossss! …*'

GPK offered a voice that sounded as though he was trying to soothe a tormented animal.

'*Nobody else knew I was here … I saw you earlier today, you're here when I arrive, I see you on your phone, I see the way you talk, the way you move, how you look at me… and Detective Sergeant Arteta arrives 20 minutes later with her little army … you, Mr Cuadrado, are …*'

'*A fucking fake!*'

Gina was back alongside GPK. She'd been watching, had caught Kraft's words about halfway through, and was ready to double team again. GPK hardly flinched on her intrusion. He'd half expected she might. Carlos thought he recognised the girl but couldn't be sure.

'*You, Mister Big Man at your little restaurant, you are …*'

'*Not who you say you are … isn't that right?*' There was an amused glance of raised eyebrows from GPK/Gary Gilmour and Gina/Jen Juniper at this moment over their earlier nom-de-plumes, as GPK delivered his next salvo.

'*Perhaps your passport may need some attention, Mr Cuadrado?*'

Carlos knew enough about putting on a brave face. The charge of illegal immigrant now being levelled at him from Kraft had hurt.

'*I have no idea what you are saying. I think perhaps in the circumstances it is best for me to say goodnight …*'

Carlos made his departure. The new pairing watched him go.

'*People seem to want to get away from you.*'

Gina spoke with a similar sarcastic style as Kraft, and with a glint in her eye.

'*I have that effect on people who have something to hide.*'

GPK preened himself over having set a couple of balls well and truly rolling. Trouble, he interjected to his own thoughts, may not be Greg Duggan's monopoly now that he was in town.

CHAPTER 32

Way below the Rooftop Club, which was still in full swing with high spirits fuelled by the night's excitement on the field of play, the Eruption team party had begun some time earlier.

Greg, although knackered by his exploits and collisions, in common with the rest, was on Cloud Nine! After all his time in the game and now at 28 years of age he had his first winners medal, his first championship, he'd won a trophy!

Okay, he'd only played in the last two games of Eruption's league season, he'd only arrived less than a week ago, but he'd come out Man of the Match in both, he'd saved tries, scored tries, kicked goals. Chuffed was as good a word as any to describe how he felt right now.

After having been drenched with champagne along with the others, so much that his eyes had stung, he was now showered and in the dressing room smiling, just a towel around his shoulders.

Kenny dumped himself down alongside, just as shattered, but also just as high on the win and his first trophy as a coach.

'We did it mate.'

It was all underplayed. They held no tinnies, no glasses of bubbly, no bottles.

The rest of the guys were either in a similar state, or in the case of Stu, Vinny and Tonito a whole lot more hyper. They'd partied with the fans when the game had finished and when the trophy had been presented and they were due upstairs in the Rooftop Club sometime soon, but right now it was time for exhaustion to take a hold. They'd achieved what they had set out to achieve.

'It's Ciara's funeral tomorrow.'

Kenny hadn't intended to bring the enjoyment of the evening down. He just wanted Greg to know. Greg was quick to respond.

'I'll come if … you know, if you need some support …'

Kenny continued looking forward, now grabbed one of the

bottles of bubbly that appeared to have enough left and gave an easy, non-offensive, friendly reply.

'*Yeah, why not mate.*'

They both rested back against the dressing room wall. Kenny handed Greg the bottle. He took a little, handed it back. He also looked forward, not at Kenny.

'*How did she … die? O'Grady never said, you've not said … I never asked either, do you know?*'

Kenny exhaled slowly. Took another glug.

'*I have no idea … none at all …*'

This was strange territory.

'*There are things on this island that stay on the island, Greg …*'
He paused again.

'*The people here. They deal with things in their own way. The murder rate is published as zero for the tourists and those Rough Guide books and Trip Advisor, but there's a whole bad and weird scene going on. The crimes are usually among the islanders themselves. I'm guessing Ciara was caught up in part of it in some way, maybe because of her father … all I know is she's gone …*

'*I only really got to know her in the past few months … we started fooling around at first, then it turned into something I'd have wanted to have made even more …*'

Kenny took another breath. He was calm, matter-of-fact.

'*I think she might have gone for it, for us, but she had issues … I don't know what they all were, but I knew she did a bit of weed to get by, a few other things … being a drug dealer's daughter and all …*'

Greg couldn't help but give away his immediate shock. Kenny had seen it instantly.

'*You think Paddy O'Grady ended up here as some kind of Brit abroad? I don't know how she died, except it was murder. All I know is what you know, but, come with me tomorrow. We can get a beer or two after it. Better make the most of tonight and tomorrow.*'

They clinked two of the remaining bottles.

'*Anyway, your public awaits! … How you ever scored that goal, after the try. Genius! Come on, let's give them the man who brought you here and the man himself … Senor DU-GAN!!*'

CHAPTER 33

Despite 'the GPK effect' of zealous interviewing there were still many guests around when both sets of players made it to the Rooftop Bar.

The party had taken on a fresh lease of life with the remnants of the all-new Lanzarote Eruption band, that had made their debut earlier, having struck up with a few improvised performances of classic hit songs including 'Delilah' and reggae classic 'Hot Hot Hot' with everyone singing the 'Ole, Ole, Ole, Ole' part leading into the song title.

That number would definitely be added for the next game and the band had promised to add even more players and songs to its repertoire.

When Greg, Kenny and the Eruption team arrived the air was once again filled with 'You're Just Too Good To Be True, Can't Take My Eyes Off You'. The Hudderford Gladiators were in good form too, considering their defeat not quite an hour or so ago, and loved it when the band struck up an impromptu version of 'Country Roads' for their fans and officials.

'Senors, Senoras, Senoritas ... Ladies and Gentlemen!'

Juan Cavaleros was finally able to hold court. He'd invited Canaria TV and Cloud TV to film the gathering. Cloud TV had politely declined, although match commentator Karen King and pundit Robbie Robertson had joined the proceedings, along with presenter Joanne Collingwood and pitchside reporter Max Sunderland. Summariser/pundit Ralph McBalingfour was a regular after-match guest.

Canaria TV had taken up the offer. They shared the camerawork for the games which were relayed in Spanish by a presenter and commentator – Gabriel Garcia and Alejandro Hernandez. Garcia had interviewed Juan immediately after the game.

'Gracias amigos! For coming here tonight on this wonderful evening and being with my beautiful Senora Maria and I ...'

He paused for the anticipated, desired and duly confirmed reaction. *'We started on this journey nearly two years ago. We built this fabulous stadium to give something back to our island. And we took a very big chance on a sport hardly anyone on the island knew …!'*

'He loves this, doesn't he!'

GPK was taking in the club owner's spiel.

'Loves himself, more like.'

Gina and Kraft were now installed as almost a father-and-daughter or father-and-granddaughter double act.

While Juan Cavaleros continued Greg made his way over to Kraft. Greg nodded to Gina, not knowing who she was other than she was with Kraft.

'Great performance.'

GPK had intended his words as a compliment. Greg knew what he meant but was on form.

'Personally, I think he's spouting a load of old crap.'

They both smiled.

'Gina.'

Kraft cocked his head to where she was stood, by way of introduction.

'Gina Irvine.'

He watched Greg's eyebrows extend to reach his hairline. But there was little time for anything else to be said as Juan Cavaleros hit an even more rousing part of his address.

'… but tonight, there is one man whose name we all want to shout out loud … a man who scored that most amazing try … and kicked that goal that made us, Lanzarote Eruption, champions, and maybe in two more games a Super League team … Greg DU-GAN! … Come up Greg! …'

'For fuck's sake …'

Greg muttered under his breath, while putting on that plastered smile that sportsmen and women have adorned from time immemorial when they've done what they are paid to do on the park, but in many cases have no drive to talk about it interminably until perhaps long after their career is over.

'I'll be back.'

'*You sound like Arnie,*' Gina offered, and seeing Greg's rather blank reaction, followed with, '*The Terminator! Doh!*'

He liked her immediately, spunky, earthy, funny.

Kenny took the lead as Greg approached. The players joined together as one to applaud their skipper and coach. The Hudderford guys applauded heartily too. Kenny acted as orchestra leader.

'*Calm down guys, just a sec … and before Greg launches into his speech, which will probably consist of a whole sentence if we're lucky …*'

The ex-Hopton Town lads knew what Kenny meant. Greg was not known for using a hundred words when he could usually convey what he felt with a minimum of the Queen's English.

'*I just want to say this is only Part One of the job being done, as these guys know.*'

He nodded to the Gladiators squad.

'*We could well be playing this lot again in the play-off final for one of us to get into Super League – and if that game is anything like tonight's well … phew! …*

'*But back to tonight … first I'd just like you all to join with me in toasting every single player from both sides!*'

Warm applause and cheers rang all around the room.

'*I could go through everyone, but some really special mentions. I promise not to do everybody. First, the Glads' lads. Hey mates, great show tonight. Especially a couple of my old mates Chris Rice and Hillman Ward, but also Mike Bleasdale, great game mate! Gary, you've worked hard with this team all year and it shows, first-class.*'

Gary Hopewell and his boss Glen Witheford, although choked to lose, were royally saluted by all.

'*Our guys. Jeez. I didn't know how many we had left at the end, or even after the first minute!*'

There was good-natured laughter. Referee Caden joining in.

'*But first, what a debut by Popoli Baru and Tonito tonight. It's like you guys have been playing together for years.*'

The applause was starting again.

'*Vinny and Stu, amazing as usual, Elton, fantastic courage … all*

*the boys in the pack, the big fellers, we couldn't do this without you …
and of course the island boys Angel, Raul and Jose Maria … but …'*

The applause that had been rising with each mention was
suddenly quietened by Kenny's conducting. His Aussie drawl
was about to go into overdrive.

*'This man is a magician on the rugby league stage … last season,
for those who don't know, he was shot, wounded, saving other
players' lives, saving my life … for years he's played in grades way
below his talent … I played with him last season … I knew I wanted
him here … and in these past two games he's proved everything I ever
thought about him … I'll let him tell you just how he managed to
score that miracle try …'*

He waggled his finger at Greg, who was scratching the back
of his neck and shaking his head.

'Senors and senoritas, ladies and gentlemen, Greg DU-GAN!!!'

The rallying cry went up around the room as Greg came
forward, careful not to raise his hand aloft too high. The room
rocked.

It continued rocking as Greg smiled, he couldn't help but
smile. He let it gradually die down. When the room finally
hushed, largely down to Kenny's orchestration again, Greg
rocked his head a little to each side, scratched some itch that
had suddenly demanded scratching on the back of his left
shoulder, cleared his throat, ran his fingers through his hair.

*'This is all a bit mad … a year ago I lost my club, my wife, my
unborn kid and nearly my life, others lost theirs …'*

Greg shook his head, shaking himself to move on. He could
see Gina Irvine, who he'd only just met. You could hear a pin
drop now.

'… then this!'

He still wasn't euphoric, still contemplative.

He looked down, came up beaming.

*'This is amazing! These guys are the best! It's a team game.
Thank you!'*

The spontaneity of applause as Greg waved a fist into the air
by way of his own celebration demonstrated the warmth felt

throughout the room and Greg shouted aloud while the adulation was in full flow.

'And I've no idea how the try happened, it just did, thank God!'

'Bloody hell, Greg, mate. You had us all in bits.'

Kenny was mightily impressed. Juan was next to offer his personal congratulations.

'You are an extremely talented and brave man, Greg, we will need you to remain so.'

Maria Cavaleros went not just one better, she made to kiss Greg on the cheek but used the opportunity to whisper into his ear.

'You are a good man, Greg. We will talk again soon.'

Greg looked Maria straight in the eye for a second. Then let it go. They'd both felt it. A bond, an energy. When Greg usually felt that, it invariably meant something else, but this time? Maybe, maybe not. He returned her smile before being swept off with his teammates.

'Oh, bugger!'

Gina didn't quite stamp her foot, it was more a movement towards stamping and with her fists clenched.

'I'm so sorry, Grahame, I've got to run … appointment I need to keep … catch you tomorrow, right?'

Gina wasn't Kraft's concern, although seconds after she'd left he found himself worrying.

He'd just given grief to Julian Jardine and Carlos Cuadrado, and he knew that those with something to hide did not always let things lie.

Which is why he was now, suddenly, considering Gina. She could end up being collateral damage in something he had set rolling.

Greg had seen Gina looked about to leave, or at very least her body manner had alerted him that she was probably going to be on her way soon, but he couldn't easily disengage from the attentions of Karen King and Robbie Robertson of Cloud TV who were keen to chat, giving themselves more commentary ammunition on him for next time. He saw Gina making her way to a man who he didn't know, pecking him on the cheek too, as she had with GPK.

'*Senor Du-gan … I am Gabriel Garcia, this is Alejandro Hernandez … we are with Canaria TV. We would like very much to interview you for tomorrow morning's breakfast show?*'

By the time Gabriel had finished his introductions and Greg had agreed, Gina was gone.

Gabriel made his introduction to the camera, in both Spanish and English but, thankfully, opened up to Greg in the language he understood.

'*Greg, wow, what a fantastic ending to a game!*'

Following a couple of questions about the game and Greg's last-minute magic act Gabriel expanded the interview, taking in more of Greg's background and what had happened at the end of last season. There was serious interest in the man who had become an island hero. It was easy going stuff, until …

'*… and you also have another reputation …*'

Greg did not know exactly where this was going, but didn't like it. He dealt with it calmly …

'*Sorry, that's all I have time for …*'

Greg waved into the camera and gave a big, beaming smile.

'*Keep coming to watch us, we need every one of you … thanks Gabriel.*'

He unclipped his microphone and walked off.

Kraft followed him out into the corridor/lobby area seconds later and was quick to ask.

'*What happened there? One minute you looked as though you were enjoying yourself …*'

Greg didn't answer him directly, instead with a question of his own.

'*Where's the girl? Irvine's daughter?*'

'*Some appointment or other.*'

Kraft came up with a solution for them both.

'*Let's get out of here, somewhere we can talk, without other ears. You may have had a productive night on the field, I've had an interesting one off it. This island is hot in more ways than the weather …*'

Greg looked at him quizzically.

'*Island police. Tell you more when we're out of here.*'

Gabriel was heading in Greg's direction, big smile right across his face.

'*Hey Greg, thank you for the interview, Alejandro's sending it now, talk again, adios!*'

Greg chose not to question Gabriel about the comment that had brought the interview to its end, he just smiled back at him. Gabriel had clearly been trying something out, seeing whether Greg might bite. He was a TV journalist after all.

The party was now on the wane. A few stragglers, regulars from the crowd who held Eruption in their hearts, diehards from their inaugural season, many of them ex-pats from the north of England, but also some native islanders too.

Greg signed a few autographs, chatted with them, constantly surprised at how their eyes lit up as they spoke with him, finding his new stardom a little bewildering. Ten or eleven months ago Greg would be under a car repairing something or other in Victoria Street Garage the next morning.

Some of the lads were still there and looked as though they might be set in for a while yet. They were signing autographs. Those fans who were still around were enjoying having selfies taken with Greg, Kenny, EV, Manny, Jordan Peters, Bassey and Stu.

Little Stu was already wasted, along with Jordan Peters. Their morning was liable to be in the afternoon or evening tomorrow, but there was no game to be concerned about, no training, day off, back the following day for light training and analysis of how four red cards had been flashed and must never happen again, that much Kenny and Malky had already said.

There was no sign of Maria Cavaleros. Greg smiled inwardly as he thought of the words she'd said and the looks she had given. Was she coming on to him?

Susie. He'd loved hearing her voice again earlier. He longed for her to be back soon.

CHAPTER 34

'Well, this beats my place above a fish restaurant. Must be quite a change for you. From Hopton to this … I don't know how you cope?'

GPK delivered the line with his trademark sarcasm, as they entered Greg's suite in the hotel.

'I'm getting used to it.'

Greg's reply came as the pair looked out from Greg's apartment at the Papagayos Beach Hotel.

'It's a bit different from Parrot Lane and my old day job, I know that much.'

'But trouble follows you doesn't it, Greg?'

Kraft hadn't meant to put Greg on his guard, but he couldn't help himself. He wanted to poke him, find out whether there was anything Greg hadn't been telling, or probably more likely find out information Greg hadn't thought he knew, that was relevant.

GPK elaborated. Greg could cope with this. They had already formed a bond. Greg was relaxed back in his suite.

'Your girlfriend, beautiful looker, mature lady, great figure, comes over. She stops just one night, goes back the next day?'

GPK paused for Greg's reaction. He saw it. It was a nothingness. Greg was waiting for the rest.

'The girl you bedded the night before she came, first night you're here?'

GPK raised his eyebrows, Greg looked back out towards the ocean.

'Ends up dead next day.'

GPK went on, adding a little more pace.

'You meet a known felon, her father; you're playing for a team owned by people of dubious means; I turn up; Bob Irvine's daughter turns up, do I need to go on?'

None of GPK's words were delivered with anything in mind other than piercing something in Greg, to see what was there.

Kraft was on the hunt.

'And tonight, before the game, I get some island police come to interview me while I'm here.'

Greg wasn't quite certain where all this was heading. GPK carried on. Now trying to bring his own reflections, he spoke calmly and as a friend.

'I know nothing, or at least very little about rugby league, Greg, but I can see you are a talented bloke, extremely fit and you're going places in your career.

'I can also see that you sometimes have a problem in the trousers department. That is keeping them on when attractive women come your way. Good luck to you I say, but whether you can see it or not, trouble is written on your forehead … as well as in your cock and bollocks.'

Kraft let his words rest. Took a sip from his brew. They were drinking tea, very British.

'While you've been playing tonight, so have I. My guys back home have been busy. And I've just given Julian Jardine and our friend at Al's a bit of a wake-up call. Want to know something else?'

Greg was rubbing the thumb and forefinger both sides of his temple now, eyes closed. How could such a euphoric win one-minute, always turn to something like this?

'Have a guess who else is on the island? Well, strictly speaking not quite on this one at the moment?'

Greg had no idea what this man, who he'd thought was becoming an ally, and still thought so currently despite the trousers lecture, was on to at this point.

GPK came out with it.

'Geoffrey Quinigan Q bloody C!'

Bryan Caill's name had created an impact from Greg earlier in the day. But this piece of news and Greg's breathing and body shape told GPK what he needed to know.

Greg's next words were delivered gravely, with all of the intensity with which he played the sport he loved.

'Where is he?'

CHAPTER 35

'*This man with Senor Du-Gan, he is asking questions. Si ... Si ...*'

Carlos had so much at stake here in Lanzarote where he had built a new life. Now it was in danger. He felt the need to do something and was hoping the other end of the mobile phone conversation would assist, as it had done so in the past.

Two minutes later he was relaxed, knowing what he had to do.

'*Darling, come back to bed ... I am certain there is nothing so urgent that it requires you to stay away from me for a minute longer ... tell Hugo to go away ...*'

Ana Cristina Magdalena was a passionate woman, in all ways. She was also nobody's fool. Sure, her family line had plotted her destiny, but she had added to her predecessors' reputation in the fields of law, wealth creation and island esteem.

Intellectually she was at least Geoffrey Quinigan's equal, something he knew only too well from their time together at college and their ongoing, albeit sporadic relationship over the years.

She knew what she was dealing with when it came to Geoffrey. Machiavellian wasn't the only word she would use outside of polite company. She called him El Bastardo to her friends. They also shared a commonality in sexual preferences, deviances and downright kinkiness.

Currently, however, they were back as nature intended.

Ana Cristina also knew Hugo well and had introduced the two then much younger men thirty-plus years ago when Geoffrey had first visited the island, at her father Francisco's behest, between semesters.

Francisco Magdalena had considered a match of the legal brains between his daughter and a dashing young man would serve everyone well, especially with his own varied business interests.

'*Hugo, I've got to go. Talk in the morning ... it looks as though we shall have to nip this in the bud ... love you, darling, goodnight ...*'

Geoffrey Quinigan QC paused just a second. He was looking

out from Ana Cristina's bedroom balcony on La Graciosa, not perhaps so much taking in the view as setting his mind clearly.

'*With you in a second, darling!*' he called through to Ana Cristina, before pushing buttons on his mobile.

'*I have a little job for you …*'

Julian Jardine was not a happy man. He'd returned to his sumptuous hotel room at La Cala, next to El Estadio, but his journey to Lanzarote was fast turning sour.

This little hop over to watch the game hadn't been on his original itinerary, but as it was a 'championship decider' he'd contacted the Cavaleros directly to say he would be coming. He'd been responsible for Eruption's acceptance into rugby league and their catapulting straight into the second tier.

Jardine saw himself as an innovator, someone who could propel the sport into the world game that others had hoped to achieve. He also saw where he could earn additional funds of his own through greater facilitation for those who bended a little to his ways.

Having a team on Lanzarote or anywhere on the Canary Islands had not been on his agenda initially, but it provided a glamourous, sun-kissed venue that looked good on camera and might also provide the sport with another strand in the coming years of perhaps even an Islands Sunshine League, including combined island teams from the South Pacific, Caribbean, Canaries and Mediterranean. Another new venture with the possibility of making more money for himself along the way.

Jardine had been delighted with the progress made by the Lanzarote club in its first season and he enjoyed being associated with success. But now, Kraft and Irvine's daughter were on his case.

He'd now made calls. He wanted to know precisely who the fuck Kraft was – and more about Irvine's daughter. And who the hell was this guy Markham they had mentioned?

He hadn't had contact with Quinigan for months. His involvement had only been a means to an end.

'*We have a problem,*' were his opening words. No texting. He used a pay-as-you-go phone. He kept several, for special purposes, in his briefcase at all times. '*Yes, that's good … yes, on here …*'

CHAPTER 36

By the time GPK had given Greg the sketchy detail he had on Quinigan being in Lanzarote, his team having been able to place him with Hugo Silva and Ana Cristina Magdalena, it was way past midnight. Greg became concerned for GPK, given what he'd told him.

Greg called Pablo to his room. He explained that Senor Kraft was not returning to his room elsewhere in Playa Blanca. Could Pablo look after him? Another suite perhaps?

Pablo had duly made the necessary arrangements. GPK was to stay two doors down from Greg. They would have breakfast tomorrow before he made his way back to the fish restaurant.

It was only when Kraft was ensconced in his suite that Greg took a look at his phone and laptop. He'd not looked at either since he'd left the hotel earlier in the afternoon. His missed calls included Susie, Diane and Kyle, Maria Cavaleros and Kenny. Missed texts or voice mails from each of them. Quinigan was playing on his mind.

Voicemails from Susie were a rarity. Maybe Kraft's words were impacting on his thoughts, making him think the worst of her. Kraft had only intimated it was odd that she'd stayed just the one night.

Greg had never questioned anything Susie had said. He'd just accepted that what she'd said was how things were. GPK had sent his mind spinning.

'*Sweetheart. Thought I'd ring, but you're not there ... nothing special ...*'

Her voice was as alluring as her body and her smile. Just hearing her speak gave him a good feeling.

'*... I'll try you again later ...*'

Greg immediately reasoned that she didn't sound like someone who had left because of some ulterior motive. Just Susie's natural voice. Or was he blinded because it was her voice?

Diane and Kyle's combined message brought a smile to his face, he could hear Diane in the background whispering into Kyle's ear.

'*Hi daddy!*'

Kyle sounded excited but struggled as Diane tried to prompt him. In the end Diane had taken over. She'd laughed off Kyle's efforts and hers. And congratulated Greg on the game, that she'd seen back home.

'*We will have to use FaceTime or WhatsApp next time so he can see you.*'

Diane then finished up with:

'*And what a try, superstar!*'

She used to call him 'superstar' affectionately when they were dating in their teens and when he was being touted as a great player in the making. It was nice of her, especially as she now had another man in her life – and rightly so. It still didn't stop Greg thinking of what could have been if they'd been out here together with Kyle. Ifs, buts and maybes.

Maria and Kenny had sent texts, both relating to Ciara's funeral.

His mind kept flitting back to Susie.

Could Susie have been with him because of something to do with Quinigan, Caill & Co all along? Was there a connection? It wouldn't leave him, the thought that Kraft had put in his head. The doubt.

He'd loved the call from Diane. Loved hearing Kyle. He turned his concentration back again to Maria's text.

'*Fantastic finish to the game, you were 'soberbio' (superb). See you at the funeral tomorrow. Kenny tells me you're coming. Hopefully we can talk afterwards. x.*'

Kenny's text was much simpler and to the point.

'*Pick you up at 10.*'

Greg went back to thinking about Susie again.

Susie had always kept her side of conversations fairly limited. Sure, they'd chatted and had fun, not taking life too seriously, and he'd never pushed. He'd been happy to nudge life along in her company without any thought of anything else. He knew of her family and she'd mentioned friends, but most of the time they'd been wrapped up in each other. Or had Greg simply been wrapped up in Susie?

But the visit? Out of the blue. The quick return back home? And Susie hadn't elaborated on why she'd had to go back almost immediately, she had apologized for doing so but that was all. But what sense would any of that make?

Greg tried to think back to when there were problems last season. When had Susie been in contact? When hadn't she? It kept festering in his brain. None of it made any sense. His mind drifted, heading towards sleep. He was knackered from the game. The euphoria at the end had been great, but now he needed time to recover.

When Greg's apartment door opened without force and as silently as possible some time later he hadn't moved when his uninvited visitors made themselves known with something sharp against his skin. His eyes opened briefly to a blur, after that he knew nothing.

CHAPTER 37

Gina's night had already been quite something. Not only had she witnessed a fantastic finish to a sport she hadn't given credence to previously, she had also made an ally in her quest, in the shape of the ageing, but caustic journo; she had wound up the egotistical restaurateur; and had been partially responsible for the flagrant questioning and unease of a man who may just have been among those ultimately responsible for her father's death.

She had found Greg Duggan an intriguing prospect.

It had been an active day throughout. The gig at the bar having gone well and then also meeting up with Maria Cavaleros, an old friend of her mother's, at the game.

Gina's last call of the day was to a holiday villa way beyond 5-star hotel status overlooking the beach of Playa Dorada, between Puerto Deportivo Marina Rubicon and the ferry terminal where she had entered Lanzarote at Puerto de Playa Blanca.

This was another wow!

It seemed Mr Pic-Wah (Pickup) and Pen were loaded, and hence the reason why money seemed no object when David had offered the sum he'd suggested.

Although Gina had been suspicious over taking the gig, she had been pleasantly surprised when she had arrived around 10.30. Far from being some kind of personal, private show for the couple, Gina found herself the star of the evening's proceedings with some of those who she had entertained in the bar earlier present plus quite a few more who it turned out were friends, relatives and associates of the Pic-Wah's.

This had ended up being one of those incredibly nice evenings and it had proved a delight to play for such appreciative people. The Pic-Wahs had their own sound system. Everything had been set up in advance, including lighting, mics and guitars.

'You do know who David and Pen are don't you?'

This had been Gina's first indication that the Pic-Wahs were something far more than a normal couple.

She'd finished performing for the night to the appreciative throng and was enjoying a well-deserved drink. She looked blank at the beautiful woman who had asked the question.

Gina looked over to where the couple were laughing along with their guests, clearly having a great time. Pen reacted with a little wave, mouthed 'well done' and smiled as Gina cast her eye over to her before turning her attention back to the woman, probably in her late thirties/early forties, with a curvaceous figure and gorgeous face.

'I'm sorry. I have no idea. Should I?…'

The woman, in a bright yellow catsuit who had admired Gina all evening, was keen to remedy Gina's lack of knowledge. By the time she had finished explaining the couple's success in social media advertising and their secondary career in music having scored a couple of hit songs in the Spanish charts Gina was even more impressed with her hosts.

'Don't believe everything Elena tells you.'

David was by Gina's side now, grinning like a Cheshire cat at the lady in primrose.

'She never knowingly undersells us.'

He put his arm lightly around Elena's waist. Elena appeared happy with David's attention and it looked as though they had been used to each other's company. She smiled sweetly into his eyes. David was full of praise.

'Jen, you were great, even better than this afternoon. We're so pleased you were able to make it. You do know we will all be in the bar with you again tomorrow don't you!'

These people seemed a completely different set to those at the El Estadio, a different breed.

'You will stay, overnight? Our guest? It's gone two (o'clock) now.'

David was on to any thoughts she may have had about different agendas like a shot.

'Hey, nothing to worry about there. We have lots of rooms and plenty of the others are staying. Anyway, the offer's there …'

Gina thanked David profusely, vowed she'd think about it, but had already made her decision. Staying with the Pic-Wahs in their villa was a real pull, and she could benefit from the Pic-Wahs' place being closer to Santiago's, the bar where she was playing again in less than 12 hours, but she was determined not to be naïve and felt there might still be extra curricula activity in some way if she had changed her mind.

She also had an assignation with Maria Cavaleros to look forward to as well as meeting up again with Kraft.

David, ever the gentleman it seemed, had organised a driver to take Gina back to Ricardo's, once he knew she wasn't about to take him up on his offer.

As Gina was preparing to leave, having spent another hour or so since finishing for the night in refreshingly pleasant company talking fashion, films and music, there was what started out as a low growl and had developed into a distressing wail from the woman in the yellow catsuit.

She crumpled, legs dying on her. Gone for Elena was her joie-de-vivre of earlier, her eyes now a sea of tears, face a fast-flowing river. She couldn't speak, it was as though her breath had been pumped out of her.

'*Luca, ohhh!*'

She raised her tearful head up from it having been in her hands.

'*Mi hijo, mi hijo, no esto no puede ser, noooooo!*'

David, Pen and others still around sought to comfort Elena and find out what was happening.

'*Esta muerto! Muerto! Muerto! Esta Muerto!!!*'

Each time Elena said the word 'dead' it was at a higher pitch. Her son. Luca. Dead.

'*Muerto!*'

'*Murdered?*' Gina whispered to Pen, who shook her head.

'*Muerto means dead,*' said David.

'*Asesinado is murdered, but who knows, maybe?*'

'*Asesinado!! Asesinado?? Si, Si! Eso lo explicaria!*'

Elena had overheard and concurred. Her beautiful boy, her son Luca murdered.

CHAPTER 38

Greg rubbed his neck. It was coming back to him slowly. Intruders. Two, maybe three. He'd hadn't been able to make anything out, it was all over very quickly. He'd had no chance of any kind of reaction.

He couldn't recall being manhandled in any kind of aggressive way and didn't feel as though anything was bruised or was causing him any kind of problem right now, just an itch to his neck.

What time is it? Where the hell was he? He knew he'd been taken somewhere. He had no idea where he was. No idea what had happened, except that he was no longer in the luxurious super king size bed at the Papagayos Beach Hotel.

But at least he was back in a bed. And it was comfortable. Whatever had happened, wherever he was, it could all wait. He was really too knackered after the game earlier. Right now, he could just do with some shut-eye. He closed his eyes again. Began drifting and dreaming.

Something sharp, in his neck earlier?

He remembered the old school joke explaining when a needle was to be stuck in you 'you'll feel a little prick'. He felt himself smile and drifted off again.

Greg had no concept of time when his eyes next began to see the light of day. He had no mobile phone with him. All he was wearing was a pair of grey jogger shorts, as he had been when he'd finally flaked out in the hotel, exhausted from the day's exertions, and after having organised the room for GPK.

He'd put his phone on charge in the room. He'd not made any effort to check on the time when he'd awoken earlier, and he made little attempt now. Judging by the light filtering through into his current accommodation and the feel of the day he made a guess at somewhere around 6am, but it could have been anywhere between 5am and midday for all he knew.

He couldn't recall whether anyone had been watching over him when he'd woken previously and it did not appear as though there was anyone with him now. Strange. Greg had become used to threats and violence where abductions were concerned, waking up with sweaty, heaving frames of those who never wished him well. He rubbed his neck again.

In some kind of bizarre and comedic thought process he decided he preferred this approach. He'd been taken from one comfortable bed and had woken in another.

He smelled what could be breakfast cooking. For him? And if so, why? If someone wanted a meeting why not just invite him over?

This method seemed a bit extreme, yet on the other hand it also had to be the most civilised abduction he'd had so far. He was now a serial abductee! Maybe the next one would be even better? Crazy thoughts again, that he was now in some way creating his own greatest hits of abductions! Idiot! Was he delirious?

Greg decided it was time to raise himself from the bed. There was no-one there to restrain him or tell him what to do. He touched first base by sitting up, to listen more intently for any other movement elsewhere. He sat on the edge of the bed, rubbing his neck. He closed his eyes again. He splayed his right hand, rubbing the fingers over his forehead and cheeks before bringing the hand down to his chin and on to his torso. He looked around the room and out toward the balcony.

No-one around and seemingly no movement close by, he walked across the room to look out over a completely contrasting landscape to that which he'd become used to at the Papagayos Beach Hotel. Wherever he was, it was an elevated position but with a vista that looked like some kind of moonscape, brought on by the volcanic activity he'd read about and why The Eruption had gained their name. It looked a little like El Papagayos but without the sea.

Greg felt his timing accuracy must have been about right. In the short amount of time he had been on the island he knew that the sun rose between around 7am-7.30am. It was coming up.

Run now? Away? In one sense it would have been easy. His

room had a balcony. The drop down below was not exactly the most difficult, just one storey up from the ground.

There seemed no-one to stop his escape, no-one guarding the premises from what he could see, but escape from what?

He wanted to be back in his hotel, that's for sure, readying himself for the day, to talk further with GPK, attend Ciara's funeral with Kenny, meet up properly this time with Irvine's daughter. But this? This was totally out of left-field.

'It is amazing, yes?'

Greg turned on his heel. He'd not heard anything, no footsteps.

'It is how the volcanoes changed the island over two hundred years ago, over there is where Timanfaya sent lava all around this area. It is a miracle that anything or anyone here survived.'

She talked as though he was a paying guest, someone with whom she was acting as a tour guide right now.

In common with most of the women Greg had seen on this island in his first week she was also uncannily beautiful, with jet black hair and olive skin.

Typically for Greg, he was suddenly more than comfortable with this. Whatever it was that he was involved in, it was always made better by female company.

The young woman in front of him now was somewhere in her late teens or early 20s and wearing jeans and a tangerine T-shirt. She was barefoot, hence the lack of sound as she had approached. She saw him assessing.

'Who are you?'

Greg found himself asking politely.

'My name is Naira.'

She smiled at him, there was nothing more in her eyes and smile than exactly that, her name. He'd asked, she'd given it.

'Where am I, Naira?'

'Yaiza'.

Greg had heard of the place. It was the name of the district that included Playa Blanca, as well as being a small town in its own right. He'd seen signs for it after returning with Pablo from the meeting with Paddy. He had no real clue as to the mileage but with Lanzarote being such a small island anyway, and Yaiza being in the same district, he couldn't be far from Playa Blanca.

'*You want something to eat?*'

Greg did. He'd not had anything substantial since the previous afternoon. The game and then the party in the Estadio Rooftop Bar had seen to that.

'*Am I being held here?*'

Naira, for the first time, appeared unsure about a question. Maybe the word 'held' had thrown her? Greg tried a different approach.

'*Can I go? Would you try to stop me if I did?*'

This was an odd situation. Greg had been in some weird places last year when all the shenanigans were going on with his captors in Scotland, but this was far different. Much more subdued.

'*No, Senor Du-Gan … Greg … you are not being held.*'

Greg's answer came from another voice, now in the doorway. It was altogether more authoritative than Naira's, but still warm and welcoming. More English than Naira's, yet still Lanzarote-Hispanic. This woman was possibly in her late-40s/early 50s, luscious lips, possibly Botox advanced, accentuated cheekbones, bounteous golden hair to her shoulders, smarter in appearance than Naira – skinny-leg white jeans, off-the-shoulder sleeveless black top. More money. She took the lead.

'*I am Yurena Aguilar, which will mean nothing to you at the moment, but I will explain.*'

She motioned for Greg to sit out on the balcony, and for Naira to bring coffee.

'*I am sorry we had to disturb you and bring you here, and how we chose to do it … it was not my choice, but we needed to move quickly and the drug we used has no side effects and was the smallest of dosages, enough to knock you out so that we could bring you here. Time was not on our side to explain.*'

She had been watching Greg touch his neck. She opened her palms wide in front of her and cocked her head slightly to one side, making a face that was meant to convey once again that there had been no option. Her words did not go unnoticed. All a bit dramatic. What was going on?

'*There are many good things happening here on the island Greg, and many bad things.*'

Greg had heard that phrase a couple of times now. It could be true of anywhere.

Surely drugging someone, he considered, whether minimal or not, without the person's prior acceptance, made her more a part of the bad things.

He felt saying as much wouldn't help his cause. Hear her out. It seemed Yurena was getting down to business. He kept quiet, allowed her to go on.

'*My family has been here for many generations, even before the volcanoes last erupted. Aguilar means haunt of the eagles, from the time when birds of prey inhabited this island more than humans. The Golden Eagle is still here, and we are fiercely defensive of our status as a UNESCO World Biosphere Reserve, working on conservation throughout the island.*'

Yurena was watching Greg now, clearly concerned that he was taking notice. Greg found he was keen to understand.

Anything that helped him find out more about the people on the island would help at present, especially in the situation he had now found himself. He'd read about the island's status, but hadn't found out what it meant to the islanders.

He also hadn't bought Yurena Aguilar's idea about why he'd had to be drugged, nor why there had been such urgency. Why hadn't she simply asked him to come over? She continued to further his education.

'*This whole island is a Biosphere Reserve. The towns too. We received this important status because of the island's relationship with nature, the land, the animals, the birds, the ways in which we have used the ash from the volcanic activity to create our unique vineyards, how we trap rainfall and water for agricultural use.*'

Greg had never been to university but she sounded like some batty professor at this point.

'*Cesar Manrique, the artist, the man whose name is given to our* airport, it was he who contributed much to our receipt of the status …

'But now …' Yurena raised her hands, palms wide, fingers splayed. 'Our status is constantly being threatened due to indiscriminate tourist developments, many that have never received authority to be built … and there is corruption all around, that is affecting everything … we are close to our Biosphere status being lost forever …'

Greg was tempted to say 'that's progress' but remained tight-lipped. He still wasn't sure where the woman was going with all this.

'The Mayor of Yaiza and Mayor of Teguise were both convicted of corruption ten years ago. Representatives of all the island's political parties were implicated and it hasn't changed today. It was estimated, when the mayors were convicted, that half of the island's hotels had been built illegally, by people in authority looking the other way.'

Backhanders, thought Greg, but none of this clarified why he'd been brought here.

'And there are many others involved, people of influence, people with money, some families who have a long heritage with the island. It is worse now than ever … and it is those families who are causing most of the trouble …'

Yurena's tone amplified her disgust at her fellow islanders of long standing having succumbed. Naira arrived with the coffee, cheese and croissants, set it all before them and left. What had Greg smelled earlier? There was nothing cooked here. Ah maybe the croissants, as they were warm.

'The Cavaleros and the Magdalenas …'

She exhaled deeply, shaking her head.

'They have been fighting with each other for years. You know of the Cavaleros of course.'

Greg nodded briefly, Juan and Maria.

'The Magdalenas go much further back than the Cavaleros, who are still seen as 'new money'. And then there are the Dominguez and the Torres families – and the Hidalgos.'

Greg recognised only the Cavaleros. He took a croissant as well as his coffee.

'Yesterday Luca Hidalgo's body was found. On El Papagayos. A week ago, Ciara Cortelli-O'Grady was murdered. Lucia Dominguez is missing. El Policia do nothing. They try, but this island is run by those with money and those in power ... but mostly, those with money ...'

Yurena stopped. She took her coffee. Sipped. Looked directly into Greg's eyes. Breathed in deeply. Put down her coffee. Stood. Moved to the balcony railing.

'My father worked tirelessly with those who gave the island this status. I worked alongside him. I am working again now to preserve it ... and preserve it I will, but ...'

She turned back to face Greg.

'... something else is now happening that is much more urgent ... people are dying ... being murdered ...'

Yurena paused again.

'... and it is something that affects what is taking place on the island, but is a very 'personal' feud ... It is something I cannot be seen to be involved with and that El Policia has no chance of uncovering, because they will not be allowed to by those who would have to help them ...'

Yurena again looked directly into Greg's eyes before continuing.

'You were with Ciara Cortelli-O'Grady the night before she died, you were at Al's on El Papagayos, near to where Luca Hidalgo was found just hours beforehand, Lucia was with Luca in the Papagaya coves, and they had been drinking at Al's beforehand when they were last seen together ...'

How did she know all this?

Before Greg had time to defend himself Yurena held up her hands to halt him.

'I know, I know. You were not involved in what happened to them. Although Luca's body was found last evening he was murdered a week ago, the day before you arrived on the island.'

Yurena composed herself once more.

'But we believe you are someone who can help.'

It was Greg's turn to look perplexed.

'Why me? Where do I suddenly come in?'

Help? How? Why him?

'You've had direct contact with Patrick O'Grady ... Maria

already trusts you otherwise you wouldn't be here now ...'

Yurena paused. She was fully aware that she hadn't mentioned Maria in this way until now. It was time she did.

'Maria is my sister, an Aguilar by birth, then O'Grady, next Cortelli, now a Cavaleros although for how much longer ...?'

Yurena let her sentence sing as he held out her palms once again. She continued.

'Through your team you are close to Juan.'

She was taking things step by step.

'You have been going regularly to Al's bar on El Papagayos ...'

Yurena was trying to be as methodical as she could in imparting the information.

' ... and you are, the way it goes, under the radar ... you are someone who has had connections or has connections, admittedly all very small ones over a short period, with all of these people. It means that nobody sees you as any more than you are ...'

Greg still wasn't quite 'on the same page' as Yurena, but he was getting there. He didn't know why, but he

already held a strange admiration for this woman who was now pouring herself another coffee.

'Like I said, there are many bad things going on here, on the island. Family ...'

She paused once more.

'... differences, mostly concerning money, but some have more of a Shakespearean quality ...'

She lost Greg at this point. Bloody Shakespeare!?

Throwing old Shaky his way in any setting would have been difficult for him to comprehend. She saw his look, decided to explain further.

'Romeo and Juliet? Two people in love? Two families determined to keep them apart?'

Finally, the penny dropped. Greg held up his hands. He'd got it.

'Luca and Lucia. Luca of the Hidalgo family. Lucia, the Dominguez. The Hidalgo and Dominguez families, like the Cavaleros and Magdalenas, they do not mix. They hate each other. It goes back years.'

'... and the Aguilars?'

Greg wanted to know why Yurena held such an interest in others. It was enough to make her once again take a deep breath, close her eyes. Steady herself once again.

'*I was married … to Sebastian Dominguez … Lucia is my daughter.*'

It all suddenly took sharp focus in Greg's brain. This beautiful, radiant woman was steadying herself at every word or line, not just for effect – he'd thought she had been acting like some kind of Bond villainess up until now – but because she feared for her daughter's life. It made sense, although just what she was expecting Greg to be able to offer seemed ridiculous.

'*Sebastian and I divorced some years ago. I returned to my family name. It was in the end a bad relationship, but we had some good times. When we divorced Lucia lived with me until she went to college where she met Luca.*

'*They had known of each other previously, but her father, my ex-husband and Luca's father Luis Hidalgo, kept their families apart … it goes back generations …*'

'*My ex-husband married again. He married Elena, Luca's mother, who had previously been married to Luis Hidalgo. Some say they had been having an affair for a while, in the time Sebastian and I were together …*'

Yurena threw her right hand out dismissively, as if this was of little consequence now.

'*… there are those who say Sebastian only had his affair with Elena and married her, to spite Luis. It is the way his twisted mind works.*'

This wasn't the best picture Yurena could have painted for recruiting Greg's assistance. Danger everywhere.

His mind skimmed back to Hopton for a few seconds. Not last season's ending, but more the days when he was a garage mechanic who played rugby league, had a wife and a child, and, okay, Susie too, but everything was a lot more low-key than this. This sounded like some kind of mafia thing.

'*Lucia is studying for her master's degree in Earth Sciences at Cambridge in your country. She has followed my interest in our island*

and has been extremely vocal in her admonishing of those who are threatening our Biosphere status. She and Luca met while at college in Madrid where he was studying law.

'*They were the perfect match, especially for our cause too, as he could apply his legal brain to the complicated processes we need to go through, but they were certainly not the perfect match for either Luis or Sebastian, who had once been friends, despite old family disagreements, when they were in their teens but now hate each other like a fire rages inside them both. Neither Luis nor Sebastian were happy with Luca and Lucia being together.*

'*And then there was Ciara.*'

Greg saw the way Yurena's eyes lit up at saying her name. They showed a warmth that perhaps she hadn't conveyed even when mentioning her daughter.

'*Ciara. Beautiful, cheerful, funny …*'

It was now that Yurena's voice cracked a little. She took a moment. Put her finger up to touch away a tear.

Greg thought of her too, at this moment. The Ciara she had described was the young woman he had seen when she had picked him up from the airport, now a week ago. A week for goodness' sake!

Yurena had composed herself again. She blew a little, exhaling to keep herself right.

'*Ciara was so different to Luca and Lucia. The party girl. Not so much the wild child, but certainly wild and free. She and Lucia had been friends, as well as cousins, since they were little girls.*

'*And the three of them, with Luca, were a great trio. They shared my love of the island and were fighting with me over the Biosphere status being maintained. This was not going well with several people, including Luis, Sebastian and Juan.*

'*The reason why I had Naira, her father and brother bring you here … and again I am so sorry the way in which we did it, but … it is to help me find Lucia … quickly … I am … I cannot … since Luca has been found … I had to do something …*'

Once again Yurena's voice cracked.

'*My daughter, she means everything to me. She has been missing for seven days. Luca's body has been found, but not Lucia's …'*

She paused again.

'I am not hopeful … Lucia would never go this long without making contact. I have tried all the ways … but I need to do what I can … and I am desperate …'

She looked once again into Greg's eyes.

'You are someone, like I said, who is under the radar … I need to find my daughter – and anything you could do to help …'

This, as well as Quinigan on his mind and on the island. He sure as hell didn't need to make life any more difficult or dangerous. On field it was all going well. Why put all that in jeopardy by causing problems for himself?

He felt for Yurena. He also felt that he owed something in some way for Ciara, Maria's daughter. Crazy. Yet he also wanted to walk away, relax and train before the next massive game. What happened last year hadn't made him want for any more danger.

He shook his head, slowly.

'I don't know what I can do …'

He was thinking of leaving it that way. He placed his hands over his face, breathed deeply, let his hands run down his face finishing with his thumbs and fingers acting as a crutch for his chin.

This woman had had him drugged for God's sake! He still couldn't work out why she'd felt the need, but she'd said she was desperate, that she had to do something and quickly. That's why he couldn't say yes.

Yurena nodded. She rose from where she had sat.

'Think about it, please … Come. I will drive you to your hotel.'

CHAPTER 39

*'Julian, dear chap, you are worrying about nothing ... remember the
case is closed ... there is nothing to prove ... yes, I'm certain ... have
a good flight ...'*

Quinigan had waited until morning to respond to Jardine's
message on account of another night of incredible activity with
Ana Cristina. He'd now left La Graciosa and was making his
way back to the mainland of Lanzarote, and Hugo.

'Hugo darling, I'm on my way. Are we ready?'

There might well be nothing to prove, or at least that's how
he'd quelled Jardine's worrying for now, but it didn't do any
harm to take out a little insurance. Hugo confirmed that the
steps they'd discussed had been taken.

'Hi sweetheart! I've missed you again. I'll try later.'

Another missed call from Susie. To ring, now a few times,
for whatever reason, when they were not due to meet, was out
of character for her, or was it? They had just spent a lovely but
short time together. If she had been called away urgently family-
wise, what the heck. After all, they had just rekindled their
relationship and were now thousands of miles away. Perfectly
natural. Why should he be suspicious of the woman he always
wanted to ring him now ringing him?

He'd told her so many times how much he always liked
hearing her voice? He'd rather hear it than not.

Screw what had been put in his mind by Kraft. Journo just
trying to fish!

Greg had picked up Susie's latest message on returning to
the hotel, freshening up, getting dressed and being ready for
Kenny turning up at 10 o'clock to go to the funeral as planned.
Greg had only returned less than an hour ago after being
deposited by Yurena.

Greg thought about trying to ring Susie, but she'd said she
would ring back, both times. There had been no expectation of

him ringing and somewhere inside him he felt that by calling he would only be doing so because of what Kraft had said. Nope, leave it. Susie would come back. He had a funeral to attend.

GPK had left the hotel. There was a message at reception and on Greg's phone thanking him for arranging the room for the night and letting him know that he was going back to his room above the fish restaurant and would call Greg later.

'It is done … Si … Si …'

The caller felt able to return to his day-job now. He was looking out from above the Papagayos Coves, taking in the view out to sea towards Fuerteventura.

Carlos Cuadrado cherished the life he had built on the island. He loved Al's. He would do whatever it took to keep him there. And he had been busy. He hadn't festered for long on Kraft's words from the previous evening at El Estadio. He'd found out the information he'd needed.

As he looked out on the beautiful golden sandy beaches he breathed deeply and calmed once again, prepared for another day as the gregarious restaurateur.

Ciara's funeral was to take place in La Geria, in the middle of the island, at Ermita de Nuestra Senora de la Caridad, The Chapel of Our Lady of Mercy.

'Juan! I am so pleased you have managed to come. We have much to discuss. Come.'

The lithe-bodied Ana Cristina had no sooner off-loaded Geoffrey Quinigan QC 'El Bastardo', whose company she enjoyed but whom she had never trusted an inch, than Juan Cavaleros had arrived on La Graciosa. She was drying her hair after her shower, following her morning run.

The funeral was a purposely small-scale affair, typifying everything about Paddy O'Grady's desire to keep contact to a minimum. Hence the reason for somewhere out of Arrecife and the main towns.

La Geria fitted the bill, being in an area where he owned a vineyard and where the small church was built on a hill. O'Grady wasn't one for any media spotlight and with good reason. The last thing he wanted was to draw attention to himself.

There were few present. O'Grady, Maria Cavaleros, Yurena, Kenny, Greg and one or two others that Greg didn't know at all, but who looked as though they could have been a similar age and were possibly school friends or those Ciara had grown up with.

Juan Cavaleros would never be present in the same place as O'Grady, even if she was Maria's daughter, but he also had other things on his mind.

O'Grady acknowledged everyone's presence in a gentlemanly manner. Maria shed tears and her sister Yurena comforted her.

'Fuckers!'

He didn't shout the word, keeping it more or less under his breath when he looked at his room. He immediately rang his team back in the UK.

'… yeah, we're on to something alright, if you could see what I'm looking at right now you'd know how much I've got under someone's skin … keep digging on this Carlos guy … and Jardine … they're the two I targeted last night …'

GPK's room had been ransacked. It had been a fairly spartan affair above the restaurant, but anything that could have been turned over, ripped apart or slashed had been, and anything he'd brought with him had been taken. He'd travelled relatively light, but for a man who was slightly larger than the average and weighed in at around 16 stones he'd always found the need for an adequate amount of clothing. Even that had gone.

' … Not a thing … everything I had here, apart from the clothes I have on, my smartphone and my wallet, which fortunately I had with me last night … no, I'll get clothes easily enough but my laptop is gone … they'll do well to get anything out of that with all of the protection we have … no, I'm fine … just get me more information on these guys and the others I gave you … we're rattling cages …'

Kraft had speculated on whether there would be any kind of response to what he had set rolling the previous evening. He'd been impressed by the speed with which things had happened, but he wasn't about to bring in Det Sgt Arteta. She had not exactly given him confidence that she would see things his way.

His more instinctive thought had been whether the carnage inflicted on his room had come as a result of taunting Carlos or trying to shame Jardine, or both somehow. He'd smelled something bad on the island.

His suspicions were with the former, purely on the basis that for this to have happened in just a small matter of time after the party at the rooftop bar presumably the islanders like Carlos would have a quicker source of finding out where he was staying.

But had they thought they would find him there? And if so, what would have been their actions? He made a snap decision. Reinforcements.

'I'm going to check myself in to Duggan's hotel. In fact, get me checked in now. If you can get me the same suite as I had last night or next door to Duggan's so much the better … and I need support on the ground here … tell Ken, James and Jan to get themselves on the next available flight … and get me another laptop … I'm going shopping …'

Gina Irvine, who was still Jen to the people she'd been playing for the previous night, was also on the move.

Although the Pic-Wahs had been most generous in their offer of accommodation, which she had been on the verge of accepting until Elena had found out about her son Luca, she had returned to Ricardo's. David Pickup had been true to his word and had found her a driver to taxi her back the short distance.

Having breakfasted naked, with her stepfather of the swaying appendages plus his similarly unattired girlfriend, a mature lady, well-endowed in the breast department and hirsute to the south, Gina was now back fully-clothed and determined to find out more about her father's demise.

She'd arranged to meet with GPK around 11am at the bar where she was about to play again from around 1.30pm.

She'd taken a car, not one of Ricardo's prized family possessions but a little runaround white Seat Ibiza Cabriolet.

Ricardo never declined her anything except the use of one of the Sapegos.

Gina was only bothered about wheels, not the model or its history. Normally she would stick with walking rather than drive and if longer distances were involved she used rail, ferry or plane, but today was different. After meeting GPK and playing for a couple of hours in the bar she had arranged to meet Maria. She was also keen on fixing up a meeting with Greg Duggan.

The previous evening had been enlightening. She'd enjoyed seeing Jardine squirm, and even though that didn't mean he was guilty of being involved with what had led to the killing of her father he had looked uncomfortable. She was certain there was something there to follow.

As the gates opened from Ricardo's mansion and Gina appeared in plain sight, her hair tied into a pony tail, another car pulled out around 100 metres away. The driver was careful. Playa Blanca was not an area of high activity on its roads. It would be easy for someone to work out they were being tailed after a short while.

'… Si … Si … *solo sigue … adios!*'

Just follow, had been the instruction. Gina was Ricardo Ricart's stepdaughter. Ricart was important in the Yaiza region. Just follow and find out her movements. See what she was up to. She had been seen talking with the journalist. Who else was she talking with?

'*Congratulations on your win last night. I watched the game on the television.*'

O'Grady wasn't trying to lure either Greg or Kenny into some kind of conversation. He was marking time before going back home. Being civil. It was Kenny who finally spoke. Downbeat.

'*You okay?*'

The Irishman nodded, tightlipped. And then, allowing his emotions to get the better of him, teeth bared, leaned over from where all three were currently stood, following the funeral and interment. His voice suddenly became deathly serious.

'But if I ever find out either of you are implicated in what happened to my daughter you will never play again. Do I make myself clear? Have you got that?'

O'Grady let the words sink in as he changed his tone, like some kind of vocal chameleon. His face changed too. A smile emerged for the first time in the day.

He turned to the whole party of just ten, that had ventured from the church to the cemetery and then to the vineyard. He looked around the group, picked up an empty wine glass and tapped it for a ringing sound to command attention. He smiled again as the chatter went quiet. He cleared his throat and began.

'My daughter …'

He looked across to Maria.

'Our daughter … was a wonderful, intelligent, beautiful young woman with the world ahead of her. She had passion, spirit and I am proud to say, some of the Irish about her. She was a cheeky one, of that there is no doubt.'

O'Grady delivered the line in his thick Irish brogue.

'She loved life. And I loved her … as did Maria. That's all I've to say, apart from thank you all for coming.'

And with that he raised his glass.

'To Ciara!'

'He was a good father. He and Ciara were very close.'

Maria had come alongside Greg as O'Grady had left.

'Yurena says you are thinking over whether you can help her …'

This was Maria Cavaleros asking or pointing him in a certain direction.

'We would both be extremely grateful of any help you feel able to give … my sister is the strongest person I know, but I also know her strength is being tested to the limit right now …'

'Matar!'

The word, duly delivered via Snapchat, now saw its purveyor disappear. The recipient had made no verbal reply, just a thumbs-up emoji in response. 'Kill her'.

Gina had parked up. She had left the Seat Ibiza in the harbour car park and was making her way along the footpath that connected the harbour to the bars and restaurants and Santiago's.

It was another fabulous day on the island, sun blazing, a brilliant blue sky and alive with tourists. The rugby league focus of the previous day had dispersed with most Hudderford fans now either making their way to Cesar Manrique Airport, already in the air or back in the north of England, but it was still busy enough in Playa Blanca to make walking along the pathways and promenade a treacherous exercise whether with or without a guitar strapped to your back.

Gina was oblivious of the figure running behind her as she turned the corner from the harbour on to the tightest walkway of the main drag in front of the bars, restaurants and ice cream parlours.

The runner was attired in pink and black running gear, shades and visor. This area was always the most congested and difficult for runners who were seen everywhere along the front at Playa Blanca between the lighthouse to the far west and Papagayos coves on El Rubicon to the eastern tip.

The runner had the advantage over Gina having seen her getting out of her car, having previously received messages as to where Gina was to park. The runner had left their own car and had been limbering up on the other side of the harbour car park when Gina had arrived.

Penny Pickup felt in good nick. She ran six or seven miles nearly every day, clocking up an impressive 120-150 miles per month. And she loved running while she and David were on the island.

She'd nearly reached Gina but typically the numbers in front meant she couldn't simply bob between the foot traffic. It was easier and less stressful to take a short break.

'Hey! Jen!'

Pen had been close enough to attract her attention without shouting. Gina had been intent on getting to the bar, but hearing her 'other' name, she looked up and smiled at her new friend from the previous day.

The runner approaching from behind her swiftly turned and ran back in the direction of the harbour.

'Looking good, Pen.'

'See you this afternoon!'

Pen gave a quick blown kiss towards Gina/Jen as she disappeared back where she had come from, towards the marina, from which Vinny Venus was just emerging on his daily long striding run that always took in at least the lighthouse and back to his apartment around twelve miles.

Vinny would regularly cover that kind of distance without it seeming much effort, as well as putting in the hours at the Estadio.

'Vincent Venus!'

Gina called towards him as he approached. She had instantly recognised the 6ft 4in Eruptor from last night's game, having also just as instantly been attracted to him, both watching him on the field of play and later in the Rooftop Bar. She hadn't made a move on him as she had had enough to deal with at the time, but this time she wasn't going to miss the opportunity.

Normally, Vinny wouldn't have noticed anyone while he was running but he'd also made note of the pretty girl in the red dress at the after-game celebrations. He'd not thought too much more about it since, but had glanced over a couple of times.

The heavy foot traffic meant he'd slowed to almost walking pace.

'How you doing?'

Vinny's standard greeting wherever and with whoever.

Gina was by now at the entrance to the bar where she was due to play again.

'I was at the game last night. You were great.'

She'd decided to make her compliment wholly personal to him. Better first impression. He'd flicked out his bud earphones while he'd stopped.

Vinny had a deep, throaty accent that came from his parents' Caribbean life before swapping it for the UK in the 1960s.

'Thanks. I saw you in the bar, talking with Greg?'

Gina's thought process suddenly moved to wondering whether Vincent was checking out the territory. Whether she was with Greg Duggan. Part of her immediately wanted to play that card, see whether it made any difference. Instead she quickly decided it was best to give Vinny a clear run.

'We were just talking …'

Gina was watching Vinny's eyes. He seemed interested.

'We'd just been introduced …'

She shrugged, as though there was nothing more to tell.

'You did well, spotting me talking with him for such a short time, maybe you'd been watching me?'

Gina cocked her head to one side and smiled. She was playing with him now. It was her style.

Vinny laughed.

'You saying I was kinda stalking you?'

'Yeah … stalker guy!'

She laughed too. This was coming along nicely.

'Hey, you play that thing?'

He'd spotted the guitar case. It wasn't easy to miss, but his eyes really had been dancing on her eyes and smile, rather than taking in anything else.

'Yep. Here.'

She moved her head slightly in the direction of where she was stood.

'Come back later, stalker guy, when you've had your shower. Stinky stalker guys not allowed.'

They both laughed. This had gone well. But then his expression quickly changed.

Vinny raised his chin for Gina to look beyond her.

'D'you know who that is?'

He'd been watching a shifty looking movement of a runner in pink and black from way-off. Kept stopping. Not out of breath. Vinny was curious.

Gina turned and saw the back of the runner, someone she couldn't say she recognised, disappearing quickly from view.

'What the f***!'

Vinny knew instantly from Gina's reaction this wasn't right and set off in pursuit.

He had seen the stalker retreat into premises further along the row of bars and restaurants, but they were all so close together he had no way of calculating which the on-the-run runner could have used. He soon realised his pursuit had been futile and returned to Gina who by now was walking towards him.

'Hey, super try-scorer, stalker chaser guy!'

Gina was making light of what had just happened.

'You didn't catch him then?'

Vinny shook his head.

'Nah … Not even sure the dude was a dude.'

Gina passed it off as of little consequence, but she had been impressed by his spontaneous effort to assist her. She wasn't exactly a damsel in distress, but she liked that he'd immediately thought of protecting her.

The briefest observation Gina had made of the runner caused her to have thoughts on someone she had seen recently.

'Sooooo, Mr Venus …'

She dropped the stalker tag, she didn't want to overuse it.

'How do you fancy dropping by later? I start 1.30.'

'Sounds cool, see you then …'

Vinny had popped his buds back into his ears, his music was back on and he ran off in the direction of the harbour, this time without the same urgency of a few minutes previously and complete with a few side glances and checked whether the real stalker was loitering.

Gina stowed her guitar in the raised corner stage designated for the musicians. The microphone stand and microphone were already in situ with the mixing desk to one side.

She hadn't looked at the time to know whether GPK was late, but Kraft knew – and he was.

'He's on the move. Seems to be heading for the promenade. Want me to stick with him? … yep, will do …'

GPK arrived at the bar around fifteen minutes after he and

Gina had planned. He walked in sporting some of his new apparel.

He was now wearing clothing more suitable to the climate. Hardly height of fashion stuff, but enough to have given his bank balance a whack, as he'd gone for enough changes of outfit to keep him going for a week. He'd taken the rest of the purchases back to the Papagayos Beach Hotel, to the suite now booked.

Greg had made the decision to help Yurena.

He wasn't sure about all of this 'under the radar' nonsense she'd mentioned. He still couldn't get his head around the jabbing of his neck, just so that she could speak with him, especially when she could have easily spoken with him at the funeral for God's sake.

But Greg did understand her frustration, and she was Maria's sister – and Maria was Ciara's mother, and she was owner of the club, and Maria had asked in a kind of undemanding way, and he liked her. In the end, he didn't feel as though he had much choice. Greg Duggan, supersnoop. He shook his head at himself for the thought.

Yurena had been delighted when Greg had told her.

Greg had little idea what he might be able to do, and knew he might be opening up another whole bunch of hostility. What the hell. He'd said yes.

'Is Senor Cuadrado here?'

Greg had gone straight back to the hotel from leaving the funeral. He had then headed straight for Al's. Greg would take this head on, as he did on the rugby league field. No point buggering about. If he was going to do something, just get on with it.

Greg wondered what part Sebastian Dominguez had to play in all of this. Lucia's father. Luis Hidalgo too. If they both loved their children so much what had they been doing the past week?

It was the woman who had warned Greg that Carlos was a dangerous man who was there when Greg arrived.

She was as disparaging about Carlos as she had been previously.

'No lo se, I do not know senor, but I know wherever he is, it will not be something good.'

'What do you mean, Senorita ...?'

Greg had posed his question in such a way that he had hoped the woman would give him her name. She didn't.

'Carlos ... he is a sheet.'

Greg was quick off the mark on this one. He knew the woman meant a different word but looked at her, as though he hadn't understood.

'He works for whoever has this ...'

She made the universal action for having money, the rubbing of thumb with forefinger and middle finger.

'Whoever pays the most. He has no shame.'

'And who is paying him the most at the moment?'

Greg came straight out with it. He wasn't playing some kind of waiting game here. He'd agreed to find out what he could, and he'd gone for the shadiest man on the island first, or the shadiest he'd met so far.

This woman also seemed quite happy to keep her tongue loose.

'Ah, that, senor is something I not know for sure, but he spends more time on that phone than cooking and working this bar?'

'Have you seen him talking with anyone lately? Someone who you think he might be working for?'

She shook her head instantly.

'Carlos keeps his cards, as I believe you say, very close to his chest ... but he was mad, madder than I ever see him this morning when I see him drive off as I coming in today ... I have seen him mad before, but never like this ...'

Kraft. Greg's first thought. Sheet, indeed. GPK had pressed Carlos's button. So much for Greg being under any radar! GPK had drawn attention to himself, but collateral damage would include Greg.

'What do you know about Ciara Cortelli-O'Grady, Luca Hidalgo and Lucia Dominguez?'

Greg felt on borrowed time here already. He could feel that

Carlos was to turn up soon. The woman's face turned from disdain to a smile, reminiscing.

'They were all lovely young people. And they loved the island. Ciara was a party girl, always with a smile on her face and never short of the boys.'

Greg kept his face straight.

'She worked here, but couldn't get on with Carlos, hardly anybody can, he puts on this big me-me-me act all the time.'

'And Luca and Lucia?'

Greg waited. The woman gave a heave of a sigh.

'So sad. About Luca. I hear this morning. And Lucia? Who knows? …

Luca and Lucia were in love. They would often come here. The three of them were friends and were working together … for the island. But they made some people very unhappy.'

'Which people?'

Greg was almost preening himself here, enjoying his new role. He suddenly saw himself as a private investigator.

Maybe that would be a useful career change once he was finished with the game he loved. Probably not, he chastised himself briefly. He focused again.

'Any idea which ones were particularly unhappy?'

Greg had certainly not expected this when he'd turned up. He had been more concerned about how his questioning would go with Carlos, which he had anticipated would end up being confrontational.

'I see people. They come. Some like to come because, well who wouldn't? Some, because It is out of the way … Carlos! …'

She raised her eyes and her hands to the sky.

'… he loves them being here, makes him feel important, but really he is nothing …'

'Except dangerous,' said Greg.

'Dangerous, yes. You be careful senor. And careful how you choose your friends. This island is a wonderful place to live, it is just some of the people who are not so wonderful.'

CHAPTER 40

'Don't you ever answer your phone?'

It was said seductively and playfully as Greg left Al's. He'd felt he'd bled dry any useful information from Adriana Gomez, the lady whose name he had eventually found out before he returned to Playa Blanca.

He smiled. Forget what Kraft had put in his head about her, when he heard Susie's voice he was as relaxed as he could be. He could feel her smile at the other end of the call, but it was without response from him as it was another message he'd just picked up.

'Catch up sometime.'

He sensed a slight disappointment in her voice with the final words. He knew that Susie wouldn't just keep ringing if he never answered. Who would?

'I didn't think you would have come today …'

Ana Cristina Magdalena and Juan Cavaleros were having coffee alongside Ana's pool. Their relationship was business, although several years prior they'd had a brief affair. Juan still carried a torch for her. He looked at her inquisitively.

'… Ciara? The funeral? …'

He held his lips close together, breathed deeply and offered a world-weary shake of his head.

'… you and Maria? More problems? Or same old ones? …'

'Shall we just talk business?'

'For Christ's Sake!'

The exclamation at the other end of the phone conversation was pretty much what Carlos had been anticipating. He knew his future was on the line.

'Get it done!'

There was nothing more said. The caller was gone. Seconds later there was a text. *Just do it!*

'Senor Du-Gan?'

Greg had been quick to answer his phone this time, hoping it would be Susie.

'I know where you will find Lucia Dominguez ... I will send instructions.'

The caller ID had been protected. Hell, news had travelled fast over his involvement in finding Lucia. The only other people that knew he was on the case were Maria and Yurena. The text duly followed.

Greg was now in the car he'd had hired for him. It had been delivered by the time he'd returned to the Papagayos Beach Hotel from having spoken with Adriana Gomez at Al's. Pablo had organised it through Yurena. He was behind the wheel of a top of the range Range Rover Sport. Yurena Aguilar had clearly taken the view that no expense was too great in seeking out her daughter.

Another minute later, another call. Hotline Duggan.

'Senor Duggan.'

Ah, the correct pronunciation of his name from what sounded like an islander.

'I am Det Sgt Alba Marta Arteta ...'

The woman Kraft had mentioned. The copper who had interviewed him last night before the match.

'... I would like to talk with you.'

Greg was more concerned with following the instructions on the text. He had also been hoping to get to Gina's afternoon appearance in the bar. Kraft had sent him a note about it while he'd been at Al's.

'I have a couple of appointments I need to get to. Can we meet tomorrow? Or I could do tonight?'

He hadn't wanted to appear unhelpful.

She went for it. The evening meeting. He'd almost wished he hadn't mentioned that possibility now. Since when was he a guy who had appointments? Like some bloody businessman. He laughed at himself as he drove.

He looked again at the text sent by the mystery caller. Atlanta del Sol was all it read.

Greg had never heard of it, but the caller had also left a Sat Nav reference. It was to the north-west of Playa Blanca beyond the lighthouse.

The final mile and a half had no defined road and was little more than a dirt track. This was the wilder-faced side of Playa Blanca, more exposed to the wind. No beaches, no coves, just the Atlantic Ocean versus small cliffs.

There was no way of getting to Atlanta del Sol, whatever it was, without abandoning the Range Rover and walking what the Sat Nav had given as the destination, around three-quarters of a mile away. The land was too rough. Passing the lighthouse and rounding the corner a hulking great block of concrete came into view looking desolate.

It was only as he approached the derelict building, daubed with all kind of colourful graffiti and looking like some kind of tramp's mausoleum that Greg's antennae went up. Why here?

By then it was far too late.

CHAPTER 41

'... and this next song is for a special person, in a very special team ...'

Gina said it purposely throatily and alluringly, in an almost Marilyn Monroe 'Happy Birthday, Mr President' manner, while looking cheekily over to the table where Vinny Venus was sat with Stu Wainwright, Elton Richards and Jordan Peters.

The other three had come along after Vinny had told Stu about his earlier morning run and what had happened. Stu had then roped in Richards and Peters. They'd all been sleeping off the previous night's celebrations. This was hair of the dog time.

'You're just too good to be true, can't take my eyes off you ...'

Gina sang seductively in Vinny's direction keeping her eyes fixed on him. The trio with him were nudging or nodding him in a laddish, cheeky manner.

There were still one or two Hudderford fans left from the previous day's encounter with a day left of their stay, but otherwise the bar was full of regular tourists on vacation.

'Country Roads' had again proved popular, but it hadn't been sung with quite the gusto of yesterday's crowd.

It had been a much more sedate early afternoon, but Gina had clearly not forgotten to think about the Hudderford supporters even if it was looking like she only had eyes for Vinny.

The Pickups were there again, with friends, so too was GPK who had stuck around after their meeting. Gina had added a couple more recent songs to her set, which went down well with the younger guys from The Eruption, particularly an acoustic version of 'Bridges' by Aussie band Erthlings.

Jordan Peters was particularly taken with it as he proudly announced one of his cousins was in the Sydney-based act. But largely, playing in bars anywhere in the world, Gina had learned pretty quickly that it was the classics that always went down best and she had them all in the palm of her hand with 'American Pie' and 'Son of a Preacher Man'.

'You liked it then?'

Gina had joined Vinny and the boys, after first taking her now customary appreciation from Pen and David 'Pic-Wah' and curtseying comedically towards GPK, as well as receiving several complimentary words from others.

Vinny had loved it.

'Girl, you are amazing!'

The rest of the boys around the table mocked him a little but were all in awe.

'Seriously, great,' said Stu.

'And that one by The Erthlings, wow!' said Jordan.

'How did you even know that?'

As Gina regaled her new fan club with talk of her Australian exploits, one person who had been watching her for some time made a move. It wasn't something that Gina picked up on, just a movement to leave the bar. Phone to the person's ear, there were words, nothing discernible to Gina or GPK.

'… not easy at the moment … she's just finished … talking with everyone … she's not going anywhere … sure, I will …'

Vinny Venus was just what Gina needed. And it wasn't only because he was young, energetic, fit, fun, ripped and attractive, although all of those helped.

Gina counted herself savvy, sassy, intellectually on a par with nearly anyone, fit too, but right now having a partner might come in more than handy. And she fancied him.

This morning. The runner. It had brought home how vulnerable she could be. She wasn't massively afraid, but Gina was a realist, hard-headed like her father. Look after yourself first.

The runner stalker, not much really, but then her chat with GPK. What he'd been through. She now knew that her pursuit of justice for her father's death might be a dangerous pastime.

GPK had put her right earlier, on what he and his team knew – that although George Ramsbottom may have pulled the trigger at what had turned out to be Hopton Town's last game and her father's last breath; the men that had been instrumental in bringing it about had been, they had concluded, but as yet without evidence, Geoffrey Quinigan QC, Julian Jardine and Brent Dugarry. Gina knew nothing of any of them.

Bryan Caill, the owner of Caill's Ales in Hopton, had subsequently sold out to a multi-national and had switched to retirement in The Bahamas. From GPK's team it appeared he had not been involved in the covert operations carried out by Quinigan, Jardine and Dugarry. Hopton Town's ground, owned by his family, had provided the other three with their prize of millions of pounds when they had pocketed it from him due to his increasing debt.

'Can I get you a drink?'

Gina smiled at Vinny's suggestion.

'About time, stalker guy!'

They both laughed. His Eruption teammates looked at each other vaguely, and at Vinny.

'It's alright boys. Just a thing between us, eh Vinny?'

'Jen, we're on our way now,' it was David 'Pic-Wah'.

'We'd just like to thank you again for yesterday afternoon and last night, as well as just now. You've been absolutely brilliant.'

'How's Elena?'

Gina hadn't had the opportunity to ask until now.

'She's completely devastated, David's taking me to her place now.'

Pen had popped up from behind David. Then she noticed who Jen/Gina was with.

'Hey, you're the rugby league player! We saw you on the Canaria TV News this morning. Well done on last night's game.'

She reverted back to Gina. Vinny's teammates were by now doing their version of 'and what about me?'

'I'll tell her you asked about her, Jen, and thank you again, we've had a lovely time listening to you …'

GPK hadn't been idle while Gina had been performing. He'd been texting, emailing, Googling, watching and analyzing social media and getting his house in order for when his team was set to arrive.

His operations would still include a UK-based team – and they'd already been put on alert to track and trace anything relating to Jardine's movements, as soon as his plane had touched down back in England.

In Kraft's experience when you started being threatened or people started lashing out at you that was the time when you knew you were hurting those you were after.

He was watching for everything, taking in every word of memos, notes and reports. One word slightly out of place, one phrase written a certain way and he was on to his people asking why they'd written it that way.

Kraft had clocked the 'other' person who'd been in the bar that had moved.

He knew instinctively that this wasn't someone professional. The same person had tracked him around the shops when he'd been buying his new clothing earlier.

Kraft had gone into two shops and had noted the same person loitering. He'd then purposely gone into two more that he had no need to, in order to track whether that person would be there again. It had been so easy. This was an amateur, but amateurs could be just as dangerous as professionals. They could still kill.

'Did you get it?'

Gina had made her way across to him. He gave the briefest of nods. He'd sent her a text while she was playing. She'd picked it up in between songs. He wanted her to take a photograph of her audience, but if she could take one wide pic and then individual shots around the room, specifically making sure she managed to get this one person the best she could.

Gina had handled it superbly. She'd not taken pictures immediately having read the message. She'd waited a couple of songs and then she'd picked up her phone and nonchalantly rattled off the pics as quickly as she could in a jokey manner, getting everyone to smile.

She'd centred her first shot slightly to the right of Kraft's target and had then added three more as she scanned the room, gradually getting the audience more involved. She'd then swiftly looked at her gallery on the phone to check that the one pic she really needed was okay and had equally swiftly sent it to GPK.

Two minutes later GPK knew exactly who it was. He'd pumped up the photograph on his laptop. If only everything could work out so sweetly. He nodded in reply and answered her without raising his voice.

'Talk later, we're still being watched.'

Gina didn't look. She smiled again, turned and made her way back to Vinny and the boys.

Kraft knew Gina had a plan to stay safe. She was working the Vinny Venus angle, as he called it. He liked that. She was clever. Like her father. He'd met him many times in his position as editor of her father's newspapers.

She'd go back with Vinny, or she'd get to her stepfather's place, still under escort.

That made him consider Ricart. He'd not done much work on him yet. It was time for some preliminaries there at the very least.

He had his own plan. Grahame Pythagoras Kraft was about to use the police angle. He picked up his phone.

'Sergeant.'

It was in his nature to make police officers a little on their guard, put them at their unease if he could. He knew she wouldn't like Sergeant as opposed to Det Sgt.

'I would like to talk with you ... yes, now ... if that's convenient.'

CHAPTER 42

'Que cono crees que estas hacienda?!'

It was fair to say this was not a social call. The person offering the words wasn't noted for going easy in the language department, nor in the physical area either.

'… callate! … eres un idiota! …'

After the vitriol came the instructions. The deliverer was well and truly hacked off with how the aide had been performing or indeed not performing. That much was clear.

'Esta es tu ultima oportunidad.'

Roughly translated, the recipient had been asked what the f*** was going on, to shut up, was an idiot and this was their last chance.

'Si … Si … Entiendo.'

The recipient understood and was duly chastened by all that had been said. There would be no further slip-ups. Lives were at stake, notably the one that was very dear to the person receiving the lecture.

The boys from Eruption had enjoyed their afternoon in the bar listening to Gina and the five of them headed for the beach of Playa Grande, with Gina leaving her guitar at Santiago's where the restaurant/bar owner had now booked her for the next two days. She was bringing in extra people in addition to his regular tourist trade.

'You good?'

Vinny was checking with Gina as they made their way from bar to beach.

'We can do something else?'

It wasn't a loaded question intended to talk Gina straight into his room and all that might progress from there. Vinny wasn't that kind of a guy. He was a gentle young man, although quite different clutching a rugby league football on the field of play.

He was also relatively shy, in the sense that he enjoyed being with girls but hadn't quite realised his own potential as yet. He was good looking, fit in all respects, but also a gentleman. One of his strengths was perception and he detected there was something making Gina uneasy as they left the bar.

She had smiled at him too quickly. There was something, he sensed it.

'Yeah, I'm cool ... yeah ... the beach is calling, Stalker Boy!'

She had decided that her visit to Maria could wait. Vinny would be good for taking her when the time arose.

Kraft watched them go. He was now positioned under the canopy in front of the bar. He'd moved there when he'd seen the other person make their move. In the split second that his eyes moved from Gina and the boys a movement occurred in his peripheral vision.

A split second later he saw it was a runner. The crowds had thinned. The runner could get through quickly. Gina had told GPK about the runner earlier in the day.

Kraft saw something glint. The runner was wearing shades, it could have been the sunlight reflecting or from a ring, but Kraft was on full alert. He couldn't be certain but thought he saw a knife. The runner was moving at a fast pace and getting faster. He or she was a blur of predominantly black running gear heading what would have been directly towards him if he had been a yard or two out of the bar and on the promenade.

Kraft looked quickly again towards Gina and the boys. They were dawdling on the promenade heading towards the next gap in the wall to the beach. The figure was now really going for it, he saw something glint again.

Female, he gathered, now that she was within 15 metres or so from him, but she suddenly slowed, he saw the glint again, put her hand to her wrist and then both hands on her thighs. She'd come to rest nearly slap bang in front of him. She looked up, sweat glistening from her face.

She smiled.

'New PB!'

And with that she started out again, this time at a less

rattling speed. The glint had been from her running watch. Kraft silently cursed the ever-increasing generation of the lycra-clad while at the same time shaking his head and reprimanding himself over perhaps being too dramatic, even though he'd seen everything during his career and fact, he believed, was always stranger than fiction.

In the meantime, three things had occurred.

He no longer saw the person who'd been in the bar, that he'd been monitoring and had their picture; Gina and the boys were now on the beach; and …

'*Senor Kraft, you have something for me?*'

GPK was just coming back down to earth as Det Sgt Alba Marta Arteta arrived with a sidekick she introduced as a detective constable. He wasn't listening to the name.

'*Sergeant, it is really good to see you.*'

Kraft was used to putting on the smile when needed, although he could tell that Arteta wasn't buying it. He cut to the chase.

'*I have some information, but it might be better if we were away from a public place like this?*'

He offered it as a form of suiting his needs.

'*Back at my hotel, perhaps?*'

He had nobody from his team around just yet. There was obviously someone who might or might not have been on his case after his words with Cuadrado and Jardine at last night's game. What better way to keep safe than to receive a police escort back to his hotel.

'*Mi querida … mmm … si …. oh, si … justo aqui … Mmm …*'

Ana Cristina Magdalena may have enjoyed her previous couple of nights with Geoffrey Quinigan QC, but they had merely been an appetizer for today with Juan Cavaleros.

Ana Cristina did not seal deals this way and neither did she take the view this had any bearing on whatever else they had been discussing.

She simply enjoyed Juan for his bedroom expertise. Where Geoffrey was a little kinky or even a lot kinky, Juan was all man.

Where she laughed with, and mainly at, Geoffrey's weird world of sexual gratification without ever reaching the climax she craved, she achieved it time and time again with Juan. Satisfaction guaranteed.

Business was business though, and currently this, initially in the shower and then followed alternately between and then without the sheets, was most certainly not.

Earlier, she and Juan had come to an understanding on many of the items on their individual agendas. They had also discussed the ongoing success of Lanzarote Eruption.

Juan had always respected her business acumen, which she had shown from being in her teens. She was never to be taken in by a man, no matter how well hung or well heeled.

Their occasional 'professional' meetings were generally punctuated by desire. And while neither would say they fully trusted each other, he believed their long-standing relationship was unquestionably based upon a mutual understanding that survival on the island involved pacts and unity. The Cavaleros and Magdalenas had not been noted for this in more recent generations before theirs.

Juan would be there for Ana Cristina if she ever needed him, but the reality had been that she had found herself often having to have been there more times for him over the years.

'Ven dentro de mi, mi querida … si … si … si …'

It was the perfect finale to their meeting.

It was as they showered together afterwards that their talk turned back to the elephant in the room so far as Juan was concerned, so far as he'd always been concerned.

'… so how is El Bastardo?'

Juan continued soaping Ana Cristina's body, enjoying the suppleness of her skin.

Ana Cristina tensed slightly as she stood with her back to Juan, his hands caressing her breasts.

She turned to face him with the shower beating down upon both of them. She laughed. It wasn't an evil laugh.

'Has esperado tanto, mi querida, esa pregunto …'

Roughly translated she had found it humorous that he had waited so long to ask, and wasn't about to bait him with it. She kissed him. The water enveloping them as one, before telling him affectionately,

'*Sigue siendo el mismo bastardo rizado*'.

Then they both laughed. Quinigan was still the same kinky bastard.

Det. Sgt. Arteta did not suffer fools gladly. However, she was more than happy on this occasion to escort GPK to his hotel, since she had already planned to meet up with Duggan later.

She wasn't particularly amused by Kraft's methods, but she mused that he must have been on to something, since their meeting the previous evening, for him to offer whatever he was going to in return for the taxi service. They were now in his suite.

'*Senor Kraft. What is it that you have for me?*'

She believed in being straight to the point. He was of a similar persuasion especially where a life was in danger, and more specifically when it was his own.

'*Sergeant. Since you questioned me my previous accommodation on this island has been ransacked and I am currently being tailed. Would you care to enlighten me over why that may be the case, in the light of me answering all of your questions last night?*'

If GPK had been looking to put the detective on the back foot or under pressure he was going to be sadly mistaken. Alba Marta had seen this kind of approach many times before.

Who the hell did Senor Kraft think the policia were?

There had been an anonymous call made to the island's policia headquarters in Arrecife about a stranger (GPK) who had been acting suspiciously. She'd told him this at the time. He'd been incredulous, as she had found was a common thread with many Britons. For a country allegedly full of stiff upper lips she had seen many drama queens.

'*Senor Kraft. Why don't you just tell me what has happened?*'

Alba Marta was already tiring of him. If he wanted help, why not help her? She remained composed.

'*Do you have any thoughts? You did tell me that you were over here looking into affairs that had taken place back in the UK.'*

GPK wasn't up for giving too much information. She had his back up. He'd felt it the previous night and now.

'As I am sure a man of your experience and your profession will know, if you give me nothing I cannot help you.'

Alba Marta saw Kraft as being disrespectful. Perhaps he was this way with police back in the UK, but she wasn't having it. *'I do not know what your problem is Senor. But whatever it is I will use just one phrase of which you may be familiar. 'Get over yourself' and when you do, I will be ready to help, but until then ...'*

She raised herself up from the chair, smoothed down her black trousers and moved towards the door.

'Det. Sgt. Arteta.'

Kraft recognised he'd overplayed his hand. He quickly reassessed his position. Alba Marta stopped.

'Last night, after our meeting, I had words with two people. What has happened since then are likely to be the repercussions ...'

Arteta moved back towards where she had been sitting, except this time she remained standing, not wanting to give him the impression he was totally back onside with her as yet.

'... the men I gave a hard time were Carlos Cuadrado, who runs Al's and Julian Jardine who is a big noise in rugby league. I can see why both would feel threatened by my actions last night and why they may have both sought to threaten me and scare me off.'

Alba Marta now chose to sit down. She nodded, kept her counsel for a second or two, the index finger of her left hand softly running over her top lip and then bottom lip before coming to rest in the crevice between bottom lip and chin.

'Cuadrado is of interest to us.'

She looked Kraft in the eye. Narrowed her own eyes.

'Why? Why would you be antagonising him?'

'He was the only person I'd had any contact with other than Greg Duggan, since I arrived here when you turned up to interview me last night. Senor Duggan and I had only met for the first time yesterday morning before the game. We went to Al's.'

'Then Caudrado contacted you. It made no sense to me. I saw no

reason for why he would ask you to get involved. Couldn't work it out, still can't. I decided to put some heat on him. I found out more about him through my team back in the UK. I asked him about his passport, implying he was an illegal immigrant. I can see how he might be upset.'

Arteta nodded, raised her eyebrows.

'*... and this Senor Jardine?'*

Kraft proceeded to bring Arteta up to speed with the detail of how he and Greg were involved and how Jardine's presence at last night's game had given him an ideal opportunity.

'*... and Geoffrey Quinigan QC?'*

Kraft had included his name while explaining last year's events. Hearing Quinigan's name now mentioned by Alba Marta was unexpected. He'd mentioned him merely in the telling of the story and hadn't included the QC moniker.

He was warming to the detective sergeant. Initially, he hadn't given out much hope of an 'island copper' on the ball.

'*He is known to us also.'*

'*Why? ... why is Quinigan known to you?'*

Ever since hearing that Quinigan was on the island it had been a source of deliberation for Kraft. Why was he here, particularly now? Kraft wasn't happy with coincidences. They usually turned out not to be.

Alba Marta looked Kraft in the eye.

'*Geoffrey Quinigan,'* she paused, '*... has been known to us for many years. He is regarded as an 'intocable', an untouchable.'*

Kraft raised his eyebrows. He'd already surmised Quinigan was a slippery bastard, but this, untouchable? Surely not?

'*He has friends in high places. And also occupies a high place on the island too. He is a man who makes things happen, for a price ...'*

Alba Marta paused once more.

'*If you have pissed him off, to use one of your wonderful English expressions ...'*

She pursed her lips, raised her own eyebrows and cocked her head. She did not add anything further.

CHAPTER 43

Greg stared down at himself in disbelief.

'*Te ves muy bien, Senor!*'

Under normal circumstances Greg would have been more than happy to receive a compliment about his physique, especially if he'd known exactly what his captor was saying.

'*Me estas excitando. Tu cuerpo es perfecto.*'

Greg looked up. In front of him was a figure clad in black from head to toe. Latex catsuit and full head mask. Latex boots with five-inch stiletto heels. The voice was female. Judging by the way he was tethered, wrists bound together above his head and tether seemingly attached to a metal beam above him, spreader bar attached to each ankle, keeping his legs at least two-foot apart, he appeared to have entered some kind of sexual bondage activity.

The tethering was one thing, his nudity quite another. Greg mused that the body in the latex suit was pretty amazing, even though this was most certainly neither the time, nor the place. Why the hell was he even thinking that way?

Greg's world had turned to darkness as he had approached what appeared to be the Atlanta del Sol. He'd slowed as he'd neared the building, wondering what the hell place this really was. It was most definitely not a hotel. Perhaps it had been. What he knew was that it was a mess, a dilapidated building that was at odds with the rest of Playa Blanca's whitewash walled town buildings and general affluence. It was a mile or so out on a limb, so maybe that was …

And that had been the last his brain had managed for a while as he had blacked out, for how long he didn't know.

The next thing he'd known was his position right now, starkers and bound with what appeared to be some kind of dominatrix in front of him. She appeared to be enjoying his body. What the fuck was going on?

'*Que tu piensas?*'

Greg turned his head to see another figure that appeared from behind him, a hand now lingering on the left cheek of Greg's backside as a metallic red catsuit and full body mask appeared in his vision, this time most definitely male and if Greg had been that way inclined most definitely with a body to match the female in black.

Greg had no words, and certainly none that he could verbalise properly, as he had one item of wear that restrained that department. He was ball-gagged.

There was something oddly familiar about this couple and Greg couldn't put his finger on it. Yes, perverted twats came to mind instantly. But there was something more, something about them.

'*Creo que es un specimen hermoso y lo quiero, eso, creo.*'

The latex duo laughed.

'*Aunque, su pene no es tan grande como esperaba!*'

The male of the pair added now almost in hysterics:

'*Tal vez crecera much mas para satisfacerme.*'

They both moved closer to Greg. The female in black pulling tighter her black gloves before proceeding to run her right hand up from Greg's left calf to his inner thigh. It was becoming harder for him not to respond in his nether regions.

Weirdly, his thoughts turned to some people paying good money for something like this. Fuck sake!

The male in red was now out of his view, but not out of his mind. He placed his hands on Greg's hips and began kissing the nape of Greg's neck.

CHAPTER 44

'Sal de aqui, rapido!'

It was a call, in panic from somewhere in the building. Within seconds Greg was left alone, legs akimbo, bereft of clothing, but in the fortunate position, he thought again about this thought, but fortunate would do, that whatever had caused the Latex Twins to depart had at least preserved some of his dignity. Even if Greg had very little of it presently.

'Jeeessus!'

It was all Kenny could manage as he finally found his star player, having entered every area of the Atlanta del Sol sequentially until he had reached the second storey and his twenty-fifth doorway.

The macabre scene was something Kenny immediately wanted to spare his friend being seen by an on-rushing Det Sgt Alba Marta Arteta and a lumbering Grahame P Kraft. It didn't happen. Within seconds all three were at the doorway. If Greg had wanted to be humiliated, or voyeured, he couldn't have chosen a better way.

'This is known as the Ghost Hotel,'

Alba Marta explained as Greg, now more suitably attired in jeans and white T-shirt, emerged from his bedroom, back in the Papagayos Beach Hotel, into the living area.

'It was the grand idea of an Englishman who was ahead of his time in realising this area of Yaiza had a bright future, but unfortunately he chose the wrong location, the wrong people to deal with and the wrong time.'

Greg couldn't help but feel a slight similarity with that Englishman's plight. Alba Marta continued.

'The Ghost Hotel is the Atlanta del Sol. It is the most remote building in Playa Blanca.'

'And there I was thinking what I'd just had was one hell of an upgrade, particularly in personal services.'

Greg had seen the humour in the position he had been found by the three, especially now that he was back clothed and could see it all in glorious retrospect.

He may well have thought himself not exactly the sharpest tool in the drawer at times but he wasn't as naïve about messages such as 'come to this place or that' for a meet up with someone he didn't know. He had at least learned something from his experiences the previous season with Hopton and

had taken his new role as private investigator seriously.

When he'd received the message sending him towards a location he'd never heard of he'd instantly researched it on his mobile phone. While he had been surprised to see something like 'The Ghost Hotel' given the rest of what he'd seen in Playa Blanca, he'd also had an inkling that he could have been heading towards some kind of trap.

True, he hadn't banked on being jumped when he had, and he hadn't banked on the hessian bag over his head after being fired at by a stun gun.

'*Likely to be a Taser Pulse,*' Arteta had commented.

How could she even know the make and model immediately?

He also certainly hadn't imagined any of the rest of what had happened. Who would?

But what he had done, and it had paid off, was to send a WhatsApp message to both Kenny and Kraft telling them where he was going. He'd hoped they checked their phone more regularly than he had in the past.

Kenny had been first to see it, had set off on his own but had contacted Kraft who had fortunately still been with Arteta. Kenny had arrived at the end of the track before them but had received instructions through Kraft from Arteta, to wait until they arrived. Arteta had alerted officers too.

It had been the siren of the police car approaching that had rid Greg of the Latex Twins.

Kenny had attempted to untether Greg, but the uniformed police had eventually managed it.

'*And what did these people say?*'

Greg wasn't exactly certain what to tell Arteta. She was a copper and while his first instinct should be to tell her everything, his earlier conversation with Yurena weighed heavy on his mind.

'I'd had this message to come here. I'd been asking about someone for a friend and next thing I know I'd received the message saying to meet at Atlanta del Sol because it would lead to learning something more.'

Arteta was not impressed with Greg's reply as it didn't answer her question. She wanted to know what had been said.

For the second time in the day Arteta was about to demonstrate her no nonsense approach.

'Who were you asking about? Lucia Dominguez?'

She saw Greg's instant reaction.

'Then why not simply say Lucia Dominguez. It makes life a lot less complicated.

'Did you know about this?'

Det Sgt Arteta suddenly turned on GPK who had returned with them.

Kraft felt that Arteta was treating them both rather like two mischievous schoolboys. He felt as though he ought to be emptying his pockets for the teacher to show he hadn't anything he shouldn't have. Arteta turned back to Greg. He gave a shrug.

'I thought I recognised them ...'

Greg offered. It was the only concrete piece of news he had over what had happened.

'It was their voices. I'm certain I've heard them before. But I just can't place ...'

'You say you are working on behalf of a friend?'

Arteta wasn't letting go now.

'Who's the friend? Sebastian Dominguez? Elena Dominguez? Yurena Agular? Maria Cavaleros? Stop me when I hit the right name ...'

Arteta had seen Greg's reaction.

'Yurena Aguilar?'

GPK couldn't help himself. He automatically pumped the

woman's name straight into Google. Within seconds he'd completed his first brief check on her, and seconds later he'd informed his team to make a more detailed search.

Arteta was at least happy she'd had a result. She let the Yurena reference ride. Now she went back a step.

'*And your informant?*'

Greg suddenly realised he had informants.

This bit was far easier. Just give the information, get back to playing the sport he loved.

'*The only person I spoke with, from agreeing to help find anything about Lucia, was a woman called Adriana. I'd gone to Al's after the funeral, to speak with Carlos, the restaurant owner. He wasn't there. I spoke with Adriana. She wasn't very complimentary about Carlos. The message came after I'd been with her, but I had no way of checking who had sent it. Came up as private number.*'

'*And that call sent me to The Latex Twins …*'

Greg had given his captors the name when first explaining. Alba Marta had presided over cases previously that had bizarre sides to them and knew it made no difference to the brutality that could be administered. It often made it worse.

'*What did they actually say?*'

She had asked this a few minutes ago, but no matter. Maybe she'd get the answer now.

'*I haven't a clue. It was the most surreal thing. They spoke in Spanish all the time. There were some words … I think they were talking about me … my body … just the way they were talking …and acting … they never talked in English … and yet …*'

'*… and yet?*'

Alba Marta indicated she was keen for him to continue.

'*Like I said, there was something about them … that was familiar …*'

Arteta felt she had exhausted what Greg had to offer. She would follow up the woman at Al's. She was interested in anything that related to Lucia Dominguez and wanted to get to the bottom of what had happened to Luca Hidalgo and Ciara Cortelli-O'Grady.

She also knew how difficult it was getting information from any of the island's big money families. They all had their reasons for keeping things tight. Which begged another question.

'You say you are working on behalf of Senora Aguilar …'

Alba Marta composed herself once again. She knew all the money families on the island. At some stage or other they had all been at least part of some story or other.

'… you are aware of who she is? …'

She paused. Waited. Greg wasn't sure what to say.

'… other than being Lucia Dominguez's mother?' Arteta offered.

'I know she's Maria Cavaleros's sister and that she's concerned about the island losing its World Biosphere status.'

He was matter-of-fact about it. And putting it straight now in his head, what Yurena had told him.

'She wants to find her daughter. That's all I know.'

'So, what really happened?'

Kraft was on to Greg like a shot as soon as he felt the detective sergeant would have left the hallway and on her way out of the hotel.

'You knew their voices. You know their names. They told you more than you've been telling Arteta just now. I know that much.'

Greg said nothing. He stared blankly at Kraft, his lips pursed, folded his arms, breathing calmly. He took a deep breath.

Greg didn't know why he hadn't been immediately forthcoming and had no intention of withholding anything from GPK.

'I'm fairly certain they were Quinigan's kids, well not exactly kids. They must be in some acting school, either that or they just like dressing up, but … and I don't know or understand Spanish … their voices sounded like … like when I heard them last year at Quinigan's place in Scotland.'

CHAPTER 45

Gina had enjoyed her day.

Her second gig at Santiago's had gone well. She'd met a beautiful, gorgeous man in Vincent Venus and she'd spent the remainder of the afternoon on the beach with Vinny and his teammates.

He had walked her back to her car. She'd given him a lift back to his apartment. He'd invited her for a drink at the hotel bar and they were now in his room. Perfect.

But Gina also had no intention of anything further. Call her old-fashioned, she wasn't just going to allow any man a 'home run' on first date, not that this had even been planned as such. She'd had a few like that in the early days and had found it never worked out, not that she was expecting things to go one way or the other just yet.

They talked, had fun, kissed, cuddled, caressed and then he walked her to her car once again.

The front lobby of the Papagayos Beach Hotel was alive with the fresh wave of holidaymakers, all having recently landed at Cesar Manrique. Amongst them were GPK's troops – Ken, James and Jan.

Ken Knott had worked alongside GPK for thirty years. Together they had uncovered corruption in various corridors of power, they had exposed trafficking of minors and bust drugs cartels. Ken was the silent man on the ground, unassuming, an information gatherer, compiling dossiers on movements of targets, what they wore, how they behaved, he was the body language expert and believed you could tell just as much by shape of shoulders, gait of walk and hand placement than words.

James Vickers and Janet Hague made up the trio. James was in his late 20s, good looking with tousled jet-black hair, beard and moustache, a bright young journalist who had started out with Kraft and had moved on to the nationals until he'd decided on a career switch two years ago. He'd left investigative reporting, despite having built up a formidable and impressive CV, for a position on the Solomon Islands in the South Pacific. He'd uncovered the illicit trading in dolphins. Kraft had contacted him specifically as part of this team some months ago on hearing of his desire to be back in the fold.

Janet was the vivacious, attractive girl-next-door whose winning smile and natural good nature masked an uncanny ability to extort information without the target ever realising they'd given it away. She played on the stereotype of the blonde good-time young lady image, which loosened those up who underestimated her. The stories she had broken had earned national and international recognition.

The four spent little time on pleasantries. In no time at all they had turned the three-bedroomed suite next to Kraft's into their new operations hub. Mobile phones and laptops on charge, two printers ordered earlier in the day had been duly delivered. Hire cars had been arranged for all three of the new incumbents.

Inside an hour, after their arrival at the hotel, Ken was on duty outside Ricardo Ricart's villa watching for any movement from Gina. Or Ricart. Everyone on their list was now a surveillance prospect. GPK wanted everything.

The list included Juan and Maria Cavaleros, Carlos Cuadrado, Adriana Gomez, Yurena Aguilar, Gina, Ricart, Greg, Kenny and now Vinny.

Gina's safety was uppermost in Kraft's mind and he was looking for anything that would lead them to Quinigan.

The team was already checking for any of his social media – he didn't have any social media; they'd checked for any mobile phone location – he didn't appear to have a mobile phone number, which was obviously ludicrous. Ken was now working on this through his police contacts in the UK. Someone, somewhere, would have access.

CHAPTER 46

'Hello stranger.'

Greg could not believe his eyes. He'd thought the knock on his door would be Kraft. He'd met the new arrivals an hour earlier and had assumed he may be needed, but this!

She smiled that smile and Greg melted. She'd arrived on the flight that came in after Kraft's triumvirate. She looked fabulous wearing her tight blue jeans and floaty, thin white top and sparkly silver necklace that matched her sparkly eyes.

Their tongues danced on each other as they lost no time going back to what they did best.

'I'd been trying to tell you …'

She was laid naked next to him in bed, their immediate passion having been satisfied, propped up by her elbow with her hand cradling her chin, looking down at him, her eyes sparkling even more. He was smiling back into them.

'… that I was on my way …'

Rugby league in the sun, Susie here. In that moment he wanted nothing more. Forget everything else for now, shut it out.

'… but you never answer your bloody phone!'

She said it playfully as she ran her hands across his matted chest hair. *'I tried so many times to let you know.'*

She softened her voice.

'But I'm here now … for as long as you want …'

Susie sensed something.

'What are you thinking?'

He thought of telling her what Kraft had said, what he'd implied, but no, this was great, what he needed, and he didn't want anything of tonight spoilt. He smiled back into her eyes, shook his head slightly. Took her cheek softly by the hand and as he shook his head even more slightly this time, said simply:

'Nothing. Just that it's great you're here.'

As Susie fell asleep in his arms Greg began trying to work

everything out.

So much was now going on inside his head. Susie was back. That was great. Or was it? It certainly was tonight, but what of tomorrow? What might it mean if Kraft was right? Couldn't be, could he?

He'd also told neither Det Sgt Arteta nor GPK the whole of what had gone on at the Ghost Hotel. Why hadn't he at least done that with Kraft? He had been supportive and wanted the same result. The Latex twins had indeed said far more than he had passed on.

There was only one man, from Greg's experience, who could be behind what had been said.

CHAPTER 47

There were just three days to go before 'El Juego Que Define'. Canaria TV and the island's radio stations had begun billing it in this fashion after they had wallowed in the island's success of the league championship title.

Gina had awoken with Ricardo strutting around as naked as ever with the TV blaring out about the forthcoming game.

Canaria TV had started giving each game a title, adding to the build up. This one was 'The Game That Defines'.

The ticket sales ploy was there for all to see. If the last game had been the most important in the club's short history this was even more vital.

The play-offs and club criteria for reaching Super League had been adapted this season, by the Rugby League Authority.

In recent times these had been complicated to explain but were now a more concise two semi-finals and a final with all of the games shoehorned into the next week.

This made life hectic for players, officials and fans who were looking to book tickets, travel and accommodation with only days to go, but it was great news for Lanzarote tourism as the final had already been planned to be held at Eruption's Estadio regardless of whether Eruption made the final or not.

Rumours within the game had it that Greg's extraordinary feats and meteoric rise in the past fortnight had put him in line for possible selection in the squad for the England team along with Stu Wainwright, not bad at all considering they weren't even playing for a Super League club. But it was only speculation.

Lanzarote Eruption, having finished as league champions, were scheduled to play the fourth-placed team Jaglin Jags, or more accurately Jaglin Jaguars.

The Jags had, it was generally felt, overperformed in finishing as high as they had in the league with a young, enthusiastic team of largely homegrown talent that had come with a rush at the end of the season, denying Leverfield Lynx a place they had held pretty much all season until the last two games. Hudderford Gladiators, having finished runners-up to The Eruption, were at home to Midhaven Mariners in the other tie.

'This will be no walk in the park, Greg.'

Kenny had called him, his mind utterly focused on the task in hand now, whereas Greg, at that particular moment had something else in hand.

He and Susie had awoken to what sometimes happens in a morning. Kenny was oblivious and plundered on.

'Jags have done great. We can't afford any complacency. I'm organising everybody to meet at yours at 11. Do what we did the other day. Run from your place. Run back to yours and lunch there rather than at Al's. Obvious reasons. Then an evening session.'

There was a part of Greg that was certainly ready for action already, but not in the way Kenny had intended.

'Jodidamente te odio!'

Livid did not do justice to the way Maria Cavaleros was feeling as she threw yet another glass in the direction of her husband while hollering words far more than just that she hated him.

She had held back what she had felt over his decision to attend a 'business meeting' on the day of her daughter's funeral.

This morning's news had tipped her over the edge. Worse still, she hadn't even heard it direct from him.

Juan swayed to his left as another missile narrowly passed his ear. Maria wasn't breaking her stride, although she was breaking pretty much everything else in sight.

But she also had an upper hand that Juan would be made acutely aware of later. And it would change everything.

Ana Cristina Magdalena was enjoying her morning run on La Graciosa. She was relieved that she was finally free of her visitors' egos. She may well have known Juan (Cavaleros) and El Bastardo (Quinigan) for years, but love them? Certainly not. She smiled as she ran.

'I will destroy them … all of them.'

Quinigan seethed as Hugo and he shared a coffee.

CHAPTER 48

'Eruption have been sold.'

Ken Knott delivered the news to GPK in his usual mild-manner. Fact over drama. Kraft said nothing immediately, preferring to let the words settle, hear them again in his head.

'Doesn't alter our focus on Quinigan does it? Unless he's the new owner.' Kraft was thinking aloud.

'But why sell now? I was with Juan and Maria Cavaleros when they won the title. Juan was over the moon …

'Maybe that's why. He probably had the deal in the bag on the strength of the result. Cash in while your stock is high. Eruption's price will be right up there just at this moment. From what we know, he and his family have never been precious on holding on to something if the price is right. It's in his DNA. Check out his file. He's done it regularly. He believes everything has its price.'

Kraft gave a brief nod, but he also had a suspicion that every move that happened right now was either triggered by the murders of Ciara and Luca and disappearance of Lucia or some kind of Quinigan effect.

It was time put the heat on Geoffrey Quinigan QC while also asking questions about this sale.

Two hours following Kenny's call to Greg the whole of Lanzarote Eruption's playing squad amassed in the car park of the Papagayos Beach Hotel in readiness for their run to the beach and the Papagayos Coves.

Everyone had made it, even those carrying an injury, not least because all wanted to know what the hell was going on, having picked up the news.

Greg had made sure he was first there even though his bedroom-based activity had not been accomplished satisfactorily for both he and Susie until half an hour ago.

Susie was now all set for her day ahead taking in the rays, soaking up the sun. She looked such a picture, well able to carry off the white bikini with tastefully embroidered gold she was now wearing just as well as girls thirty years her junior. Great legs, fabulous body, very much in trim.

Never, at any time since she had returned had Greg picked up on some kind of suspect mood from Susie, or hesitancy or change of character from what he had known in the time they'd been together. She was the same Susie, he was certain.

He questioned himself over how he could be so definite, but she was there and he was pleased she was back.

'Not a clue.'

Kenny was exasperated about the morning's news when he met with Greg before the others arrived.

'No idea where that leaves us. I've had no words from the Cavaleros. I'd have expected to hear before the media got hold of it, but hey …'

Kenny threw his arms up in the air as he turned away from Greg. He blew, exhaling to calm himself.

'But there might be a good side to this. You never know how these things work themselves out. I've had the same in Oz.'

Kenny saw half a dozen players coming towards them.

'The most important thing for us is to keep focussed on what we do, and that's play with this little bugger on the park …'

He propelled the ball he'd been holding straight into the oncoming Tonito, who caught it in one hand and swooped it out quickly to Baru. The pair were fast becoming as inseparable off the park as they were on it.

Gina had been heading for Maria. They'd WhatsApp'd when Gina had realised she wanted to spend more time with Vinny and they had rearranged their catch-up plans, that Maria had initiated at the game.

Maria Cavaleros's opinion of her husband hadn't been great when he'd disappeared on the day of Ciara's funeral, she hadn't been enamoured by his words at the last game when he'd touted the idea of offloading Eruption, and now she was apoplectic. She was on the warpath. This was not happening.

Whatever Juan had thought he'd done, she was about to

undo. In reality there was also nothing to undo.

'Two Faced Bitch!'

Geoffrey Quinigan's voice was bitter as hell. He spat out the three words. He'd wasted those two days on La Graciosa. Ana Cristina was the bitch she'd always been. He poured himself a scotch. Think.

His day was about to get a whole lot worse.

'For you ...'

Hugo handed him his, Hugo's, mobile. This was not Quinigan's way. He did not answer calls, full-stop, no matter who called. He might initiate them, he might even deign to ring back when he'd heard a message that he felt a reply necessary, but he would never speak to someone calling him direct without first knowing what they wanted and preparing his reply.

Hugo knew this, but Quinigan had already seriously pissed him off by staying longer with Ana Cristina. He knew Quinigan couldn't stop himself, batting for both sides, pleasuring his quirky sexual traits.

Geoffrey would realise why Hugo had passed him the phone, but right now he couldn't care less. Sometimes, he felt, this man needed a dose or two of what he dished out.

Quinigan put Hugo's mobile to his ear. He didn't say a word. The voice at the other end wasted no time. The voice knew that Quinigan would not conform to the norm and give any indication he was there. Standard practice from supercilious twats. The voice had heard Hugo's voice and had heard the transfer of mobile from one hand to another.

'Bad day for you Mr Quinigan. Not what you'd been planning. But at least you're still alive, unlike Jeff Markham and Bob Irvine. You can still walk properly, unlike Tony Estorino. You're still able to have a real life, unlike George Ramsbottom. Want to respond?'

The caller waited a split second.

'I thought not. Not your way. You will shortly be receiving a package. It's not a bomb. Open it.'

The caller hung up.

'Senor Cuadrado?' Carlos spun around from behind the bar

at Al's where he'd been busy getting drinks together for a table.

'*I am Det Sgt Alba Marta Arteta of Canary Islands Policia, this is Det Con Mario Manuel Moreno.*'

Carlos made an easy yet not wholly hospitable gesture, along the lines of asking why she or they were there. He quickly changed his persona with a beaming smile.

'*I'm sorry, can I help you in some way?*'

It was he who had alerted the Department de Policia in Arrecife about a suspicion surrounding GPK. Carlos and the two detectives moved just beyond the restaurant walls, looking out to sea.

'*You have a wonderful place, I loved coming here with my parents years ago when I was a child …*'

Carlos listened, waiting for Arteta to tell him why she was there.

'*… looks like it is still very popular …*'

Carlos knew she was leading on to something, he just didn't know what. He chose to keep his own counsel for the moment. No point jumping into something until he knew which road they were going down. He could pick his answers accordingly.

'*Luca Hidalgo …*'

She was watching his manner now, his body movement, his eyes. Carlos was aware of what she was doing and trying to counter Arteta's discipline with his own. She now kept her counsel, waiting for a reaction.

To make no reply at this point would probably not be his best judgement. Even if Carlos hadn't known the young man, he would have heard his name by now. She waited.

'*Luca, yes … he came here many times …*'

He was careful not to give any other names. He'd been tempted to mention Lucia and that they had a meal at Al's in recent times but had thought better of it.

Arteta looked out towards the sea, lips pursed, wanting more but realising this was the best she was going to get in purely mentioning Luca by name. She switched tack.

'*Luca Hidalgo and Lucia Dominguez were here, at Al's, on the*' day we now know Luca was murdered and Lucia was last seen. When did you last see them?'

It was not an issue Carlos could duck. He had served them drinks. He dealt with the question.

'Around 3.30pm.'

The way he was answering was concise; it was concise to the point of being cagey. Alba Marta Arteta had not thought she had asked anything too pointedly as yet, but she knew Carlos was on edge. She was also aware that he may have many things to hide. This certainly wasn't the first time he'd been questioned by someone from the Policia. And it wouldn't be the last.

Other questions followed, for which he carried on giving answers that added nothing other than confirming everything she had already known about Senor Carlos Cuadrado.

Arteta had taken things gently on this first meeting but as she left, threw in the archetypal detective howitzer just to make sure Carlos was under no illusion that she would be back.

She had turned slightly from him as though leaving.

'Just one last thing Senor. Why did you inform us to question Senor Kraft?'

She looked quizzically at Cuadrado. He had no chance to avoid the eye contact. She saw his brain race, the look that told her he was searching his files for a suitable lie.

'There was something about him, something I did not like. He was with Senor Du-Gan. I like Senor Du-Gan. I did not want to see Senor Du-Gan caught up with someone bad.'

He knew it sounded lame as soon as it left his lips. Arteta let it go.

'Gracias, Senor.'

Arteta said nothing more. Cuadrado watched as she left.

Moreno waited until Arteta was out of sight. He swiftly kicked Carlos hard in the balls, taking out whatever wind might have been in Cuadrado's sails. As Cuadrado doubled over on the floor he squatted down next to him.

'There is something we do not like about you also Senor Cuadrado. Take that as my card. You know where to find us.'

CHAPTER 49

Three days. Kenny knew he had a massive task on his hands.

The Eruption injury list had already been extensive with 8 of the 28-man squad already ruled out of the game including first choice regulars Jordan Peters, Ron Rigson and Victor Borsoni. But now he had also lost Ellard Vellidale, Jose Maria Estapol, Phillipe Longchamps and Elton Richards who had all suffered red cards in the Hudderford Gladiators game.

All four had received an automatic next-game suspension and when their cases came up, due the day following the Jags match, could all find themselves not being available for the final if they reached it.

Kenny was left with just 16 fit men. He'd persuaded himself that Ron Rigson, although injured might be able to play, which gave him just enough for his starting 13 and four on the bench, but the bench would include three debutants of which one was a 17-year-old and two 16-year-olds. Two of them were Lanzarote-born lads and the other a Lanzarote/Spain lad. They were all strapping young forwards.

'*Thank God I called you up and you came over when you did.*'

Kenny had whispered to Greg and Malky in a quiet moment as he had been looking around those who were able to throw a ball around.

'*Somehow or other we've got to get through the next few days with no more injuries and hope these young lads can cope when they come on.*

'*All the senior guys are going to have to be fit enough to give us 70 minutes each. We can't heap that much pressure on young Alliossi, Demorala and Olivera.*'

Kenny and Greg could only nod in agreement of Malky Shannon's assessment.

'*And Ron's really putting his body on the line. You can see he's still not right. He needs wrapping up in cotton wool.*'

Greg was putting veteran Ron's case, as the trio now chatted over lunch at the Papagayos Beach Hotel. Kenny laid it all on the line.

'We've got to be on our game. It doesn't matter what position anyone finished in the league, this is going to be tougher than the epic the other day. Neither us nor Hudderford needed to win that one other than to win the championship. It wasn't life or death, but this one is. Jags will be feeling so good, they've had an easier last few matches than us and they'll know we're not in the best shape due to injuries and suspensions.'

Greg knew his first two games had gone well, but it would all be for nothing if they lost this one.

The players and coaches dispersed with a team call to be at the Estadio for 6.30pm.

'Senor Greg.'

Pablo had intercepted Greg as he'd walked across the hotel lobby after the Eruptors had gone their separate ways.

'I have a message for you. Senora Susie. She says she goes into Playa Blanca. She says she left a message for you on your phone, but that you have left your phone in your room.'

Greg suddenly felt vulnerable. Susie walking along the promenade for nearly a mile shouldn't be a problem, but he couldn't help feeling protective. He hadn't told Susie about what had happened at the Atlanta del Sol yesterday. There had been no sense alarming her, or so he'd thought. But then he hadn't reckoned on her going anywhere other than stopping around the hotel and the pool and bars.

The worst he'd reckoned that could have happened whilst he was away, if she stayed around the hotel, was that she would get chatted up in the bars. She was always so easy with people, prepared to talk with anyone – and her smile, he knew, was always a winning, alluring smile that captivated men no matter what their age, as hers had with him.

This was suddenly very different. He leaped up the stairs back to his suite, tore back into the room, showered, without it almost seemed the water touching him, threw on more appropriate wear and found a note next to his phone.

He needn't have worried at all.

Susie's note had read that GPK had called. They'd introduced themselves to each other and he'd given her a lift into the resort centre where she was going to take in some retail therapy, maybe buy herself something nice to wear for the beach and for later and would meet Greg and GPK at the bar where a girl called Gina was playing from 1.30pm. *'Perhaps you could join us once you've stopped playing with your odd-shaped balls?'* she'd put with a little smiley-faced emoji on his phone.

Greg had other plans before meeting up.

He thought about Kraft using his time with Susie to extricate more information in his quest to link her with last season's events, but at least he knew she hadn't ventured out from the hotel alone. He relaxed.

'I thought you had it all in hand!'

There was exasperation at one end of the conversation.

'Are you saying it is not?'

The voice was trying to stay calm despite panic setting in that things were not going the right way.

'Not at all, my dear chap!'

The other voice was indignant.

'What I'm saying is that we are going to have to make some …'

He hesitated, grasping for the best way of putting the next line.

'… amendments … to our plans in order to facilitate the latest developments …'

Geoffrey Quinigan QC had put on his most conciliatory tone for Julian Jardine, a man he did not rate. He saw him as lacking in backbone. How, he ventured, this man was heading up a sporting empire God only knew!

Having finished up touching base with Jardine, so that the man was aware Quinigan might need some assistance in the form of intervention from his rugby league connections, El Bastardo headed for La Graciosa.

This needed sorting. Ana Cristina could not hang him out to dry like this. And why would she do so?

The other matter was already in hand. Duggan was the key

so far as Quinigan was concerned. It had been his performances in the past two games that had ensured Eruption's success.

He'd already given Duggan a slight tickle, with the events that had unfolded at The Ghost Hotel, enlisting the support of his son and daughter, on this occasion known to Greg as The Latex Twins. It was they who had also 'performed' at the Quinigan country pile in Scotland last year where Greg had been lured.

That was why Greg had remembered their voices when hearing them the previous day, despite their use of Spanish. They'd reported back to their father that they had been successful in luring him to the derelict hotel but had been somewhat limited in their threats given the arrival of the Policia.

'You are to come with us Senor.'

Greg had just finished listening to another message from Kyle, with Diane whispering the words for him to say, prompting him. Greg resisted the temptation to say *'what the fuck?'* even though he had thought it. There was no question, just the directive.

Somehow or other they had entered his suite without the need of his assistance. Their manner was low-key and Greg, determined to act similarly low-key, even though this would set his day back dependent upon the time involved, decided on a brief analysis of the situation that to act like James Bond and disappear through his bedroom window was probably not going to solve anything, and would highly likely result in some kind of injury being two storeys up, nor was the idea of taking on these two men who looked in good bodybuilder shape and somewhere around his age.

Pablo watched on as Greg plus the two left the hotel in a bright red Seat Ateca. Destination unknown. Pablo did not look as though he was surprised at seeing Greg depart.

At least this time Greg had not been injected with some substance, and so far today he hadn't been ball-gagged and spreader-barred. Things were looking up. Civilised abductions here we come!

'I can tell you, Alejandro, and all your viewers that, quite

categorically, Lanzarote Eruption Rugby League Club and El Estadio de Lanzarote is not in the possession of a new owner. All it has is a new minor shareholder.'

Maria Cavaleros had moved quickly that morning following her initial reaction against her husband after hearing the news on Canaria TV. Alejandro Hernandez had responded by turning up on her doorstep just an hour and a half later with Gabriel Garcia. The interview had been set up in their beautiful garden in their house above Playa Flamingo to the western side of Playa Blanca.

'So, Senora Cavaleros, can you tell us exactly what is going on? Lanzarote Eruption has become an island sensation this year, and we all saw the wonderful scenes just two days ago when your team won the league title. Do you want to sell?'

Maria composed herself. She had talked through the plan for the interview with Alejandro, although she was aware he might throw something in to catch her off balance. She beamed at him.

'It was a fantastic night wasn't it. And the end of the game couldn't have been any more exciting with our own rugby league Superman, Senor Du-Gan, as the fans call him, bringing us an amazing victory for Kenny and his boys …'

Maria was determined to be positive, to show those on the island her passion for the club. She took a breath, smiled directly back at Alejandro.

'… but to answer your questions … what is going on and do I want to sell – the answer to the first is I do not know what exactly prompted this morning's story that you broadcast about new owners or a new owner – the second is, no I do not want to sell …'

'But the popular belief is that you and your husband are co-owners of the business that owns the club and El Estadio. If he wants to sell, where does that leave you?'

Maria was ready.

'It is more a question of where it leaves him.' She smiled. *'When he looks back at the contract, as I have once again this morning and have now put into my solicitor's hands, he will see the reality.'*

'And your husband? Can I ask where today's revelation about the club leaves your relationship?'

Once again this had been carefully constructed. Maria wasn't about to play some kind of weeping, wailing wife. Juan was, after all, husband number three, she'd been through marital problems before.

'Who knows? Maybe he will see the error of his ways. And maybe he won't.'

Maria smiled again and Alejandro wrapped up the interview with a piece to camera. He had enjoyed the interview on a couple of levels. It all helped in keeping a story alive and right now anything related to the island's most successful sporting team ever was big news. It was also not without personal sentiment either. He and Maria had become close in recent weeks, as her marriage to Juan had been dissolving. There was potential. Maria was happy he was thinking that way. It helped her case.

The bright red Seat Ateca left Playa Blanca behind as Greg once again found himself back on the road with the hills of Los Ajaches to his right and eventually leaving those in their wake to an incredible landscape featuring volcanoes, the lava landscape they had brought about and thousands of stone semi-circles.

'They are vines.'

One of the two men transporting Greg had seen how he was looking at them inquisitively.

'This is the largest wine growing area in the Canary Islands. The vines are grown this way. It is called enarenado. The way they are grown. You like wine?'

Greg gave a cursory nod. He hadn't expected a tour guide and even though he'd already seen vines at Paddy O'Grady's vineyard yesterday he appreciated the education. This was definitely an upgrade from injections and bizarre outfits.

A couple of miles later they turned into Bodega La Geria, only a couple of miles away from where Ciara had been laid to rest.

Greg had been aware of several bodegas offering wine tasting experiences, but it seemed they weren't bound for one. They drove until a large, sprawling country house came into view where Greg was ushered out of the Ateca.

'Senor Du-Gan, I am Sebastian Dominguez.'

The heavy-set giant of a man with salt and pepper beard and a shock of tousled grey hair held out his hand as a greeting. They shook hands with the grip from both almost akin to an arm wrestle.

'Thank you for coming.'

As though I had much choice, was Greg's first reaction.

'I understand Yurena has asked you to find Lucia.'

Greg was either learning very slowly or was definitely no sleuth, amateur or otherwise. He was leaning very much towards the latter, but there was something, right there, that he felt needed checking. He'd not picked up on Yurena and Sebastian still being on speaking terms, but he guessed desperate times could lead to hostilities being forgotten temporarily when offspring were involved.

'I had the impression you and Yurena …'

'… that we do not talk? It is an easy enough assumption to make given what she will have told you… but still we talk …'

Sebastian Dominguez raised his hands, eyebrows, rolled his eyes and stared directly back into his guest's eyes. Dominguez was calm, hospitable. He was dressed in jeans, linen white shirt, casual-smart. He wasn't at all the horrible man Greg had anticipated.

'Let me get you a drink … have you tried our island wine yet? … we, that is my vineyards, grow vines all along the La Geria region in a way that is unique to our island heritage. We are still using the Malvasia grape, distinctive and full of flavour, although many vineyards along this area are now using a number of other varieties. White or red?'

Greg didn't really want anything. Maybe a beer if that had been on offer, but he was more concerned about keeping his head clear. He accepted a glass of white, not intending to drink it.

'I have seen you play …'

Dominguez signalled for Greg to sit, as he did also, alongside the pool.

'I know little of the game, but I can see you are very good.'

'… But what am I doing getting involved in helping look for your daughter?'

Greg didn't have time for all these pleasantries. Why was he here?

'Your ex-wife asked whether I could help in finding your daughter. Do you have any information that might be useful?'

Christ! He was even sounding like some kind of TV cop show detective. He figured Dominguez must have something to offer, otherwise why bring him out here?

'Wine is my passion Senor Du-Gan, Greg, wine and vineyards. This is what I do. I have very limited purpose in life otherwise. I followed my father and his father before him …'

Greg hoped Dominguez was close to reaching whatever point he was trying to make, because currently this was proving a waste of his time.

'… but I love my daughter and will do all I can to find her … I have been trying …'

'You and Luis Hidalgo, you didn't get on? …'

Greg thought it best to rephrase.

'You were enemies over your daughter and his son being together? You are now married to his ex-wife?'

Sebastian Dominguez took a deep breath. Greg was about to find out how deeply entrenched some of the island's family resentments were held.

Susie was having a great time. She was a real Saturday Girl, a girl who relished getting dressed up for a night on the town back home – make-up, tight jeans or fabulous dress, hair looking fantastic, heels – and she loved being around the city centres with live music in the bars and enjoying either lager or wine, although the wine would go to her head more quickly and so she tended to stick with a San Miguel.

This wasn't a Saturday, she wasn't in some big city, but she looked great sat at a bar overlooking the beach in Playa Blanca. GPK was looking after her, enjoying the company of this beautiful, engaging woman.

They were both now enjoying Gina's third consecutive afternoon at Santiago's.

GPK had been fact gathering, as Greg had suspected he

would. Susie answered all he asked. There was no effort in her answers, as though she was manufacturing them. GPK knew how that was often done.

But was it all a front? And what was her background? His team had been working hard. He couldn't keep asking questions when he was trying to establish a pleasant relationship. He didn't want to make her feel uncomfortable if she wasn't involved elsewhere in what had happened at Hopton, but equally he wouldn't care about that if he felt she was implicated in some way.

'She is what and who she says she is.'

This was Ken Knott's information as he called Kraft.

'I've sent you a text and email.'

The data was there when he looked seconds later. 'L'Oreal divisional manager, north of England, Mrs A. Reuben. Years of service: 22. Age: 55. Marital Status: Married/Estranged. Husband: Mr Ashton Reuben. Children: 3. Grandchildren: 5. All normal stuff.

Next up was James. He and Janet were currently in the wake of Quinigan. James's surveillance on Ricardo Ricart had been abandoned in favour of double-teaming with Janet when she had reported movement at the Hugo Silva residence.

Kraft and his team had earlier ascertained Quinigan's location at his partner Hugo's residence, his perverse habits, his current legal rank as Queen's Counsel, which appeared to be somewhat clouded, his bank records and his mobile phone records for the past two years.

Nobody, other than Hugo, had been a regular. There were contacts with Julian Jardine, but nothing as yet that they could peg as being anything other than brief, sporadic calls to and from a friend. He had clearly also been very careful over texts. There were none, other than the occasional 'darling-laden' messages to Hugo.

'He's heading for Isla Graciosa … and so are we … we're making the ferry crossing now … no, no problem … James and I are playing the happy couple routine, I think he's enjoying it a little too much …'

Janet laughed out loud while James shook his head at her. He was used to her flirty, happy nature. She was great to be around and they'd pulled the happy couple stunt several times previously disarming those they were monitoring.

'Just remember, don't get too close …'

'Oh, I've already told him,'

Janet replied playfully. Of course, Kraft hadn't meant James.

The team in the UK had uncovered Quinigan's long-term acquaintance with Ana Cristina Magdalena and her family's centuries-old ownership of copious land and property on the island. They had also uncovered a black hole in Quinigan's finances. It appeared as though the man they also referred to as El Bastardo was in debt for millions.

'His family estate in Scotland isn't his by right. It is held in a trust. He's asset rich and cash poor. The likelihood is he needs the deals he sets up on top of his existing work as a barrister, which incidentally is reducing every year, just to keep everything afloat.'

Ken reports were always in-depth.

'He has an apartment in London that is valued at £3.5m but even that is involved in some kind of long-term settlement with the previous Mrs Quinigan. And get this, he's also rumoured to be about to lose his QC designation as he's to be disbarred for what they are referring to as misdemeanours.

'It looks as though Lanzarote is more than just a bolt hole and somewhere to satisfy his voracious sexual appetite for all genders whether male, female, bi-sexual or transgender. While he is here, he cannot be disbarred, nor lose his QC, nor be declared bankrupt. He's going nowhere other than here.'

'But didn't he make millions out of the sale of Hopton Town's ground? Surely that is why he was involved?'

Kraft was beginning to see a desperation in Quinigan that he hadn't anticipated, but it also made sense of why he was trying to turn some trick over on the island. He'd been looking for Quinigan's motivation. Now he had it. Running scared, going for the next big bucks.

'If he did then God knows where the money went because there is no record of it in his bank accounts … and we're pretty certain nothing has gone offshore either. It looks like he pocketed nothing from Hopton's demise.'

'*Fuck …*'

GPK put his head to the sky. He'd come away from the bar, excusing himself from Susie, when Ken had called.

'*I know. Much harder for us to show him as being in the frame for what went on. We're still working on it …*'

Vinny wasn't in the bar watching Gina. He and the boys were sleeping off the morning's session, enjoying their siesta, in readiness for the session later.

The Pic-Wahs were absent too. It was a quieter day at Santiago's. Gina wondered whether her residency would be capped at three days because of this, but over the coming two days the Jags' fans and Eruption's own increasing support from the UK would be arriving for El Juego Que Define, which would hopefully swell her attendance once more.

Susie had arrived with GPK at Santiago's just after Gina had started her set. Gina had wondered who the new glamourous blonde was next to Kraft, and why she was there, but had then concentrated in giving the best of herself to everyone.

She didn't see Susie disappear.

CHAPTER 50

Luis Hidalgo was Greg's next port of call. And for once this had been of his own accord. New territory. His first real approach made directly as a supersnoop, or whatever he was.

Getting nowhere fast was where he was at present. He'd not discovered anything that would give a clue as to Lucia's whereabouts and the only time he'd felt as though he'd been on the case had been the contact with the Latex Twins.

He was now beginning to wonder whether it was his questioning skills that were rubbish, or if it was that he was rubbish, full stop.

Having been redeposited back at the Papagayos Beach Hotel on having visited Sebastian Dominguez he'd made straight for Luis, this time in the Range Rover Sport.

He was going to be running late for meeting up with Susie but at least knew she was in safe hands.

'Geoffrey! How good to see you. And so soon after last time. You know, I think those colleagues of yours in London were quite taken with your performance, so much so that I believe they are looking forward to your return ...'

Quinigan couldn't contain his anger even though he was trying to play the disappointment of being an old friend let down unexpectedly.

'Why Ana? Why have you done this – the deal we had? I don't understand ... and now the video ...'

'Video?' Janet mouthed and turned her head with an excited expression to James as they listened in on Ana and Quinigan's conversation from their position about a quarter of a mile from the house under the auspices of being a couple out exploring the island.

The two members of GPK's team had travelled on the ferry with him, but unbeknown to Quinigan who hadn't been able to use the helicopter this time. Janet had managed to land a bug on him as they had disembarked having bumped into him 'somewhat unexpectedly' as she had lost her footing. She had changed her appearance shortly afterwards. She always kept a couple of wigs and shades with her.

Janet mouthed again: *'We need that video.'*

Luis Hidalgo had been the poster boy of Lanzarote athletics in his youth and early twenties. He'd represented the island on the track at 1500 metres and 5000 metres and in the pool at 200 and 400 metres butterfly regularly winning medals at the Canary Islands Games and once memorably reaching an Olympic final in the 5000.

In the autumn of his career he'd won the inaugural Lanzarote Ironman event combining his love of cycling with swimming and running.

Since then he'd carved out a niche as a coach and main protagonist in the island's ever-increasing prowess in producing excellent centres for athletics and sports facilities. He was currently sports director at the famous Club Caleta de Caballe on the island's north-west coast.

The years had been kind to a man who had kept himself in great shape. His gleaming teeth and brilliant smile welcomed Greg as the pair met after Greg had travelled the 25 miles up the coast to meet him. Greg had called earlier to arrange the meeting. Luis's smile dissolved at the mention of his son.

'Mr Duggan, I am a great admirer of your talent. I would certainly never have wished to put myself through the kind of brutality you face in your sport. Personally, I find running is much easier without someone trying to stop you …'

His grin spread right across his face showing an impressive gleaming set of perfectly white teeth.

They were talking from the terracing facing the finishing straight of the bright blue running track. Greg was tempted to give it a try, just one lap maybe.

'But you are not here to talk about athletics, I know …'

Luis took a deep breath. The blond hair he'd had in his youth, that Luca had shared, was now a distinguished white. Luis's shoulders slumped as he mentioned his son by name.

'Luca was a brilliant young man. He had everything to look

forward to …'

This was proving more difficult than he had imagined, to talk about his son knowing he wasn't coming back.

'I loved him so much …'

Luis's voice was breaking, his heart overflowing with emotion.

'I'm sorry … it is all so recent … I am not coping very well … in the background yes, here yes, when I don't have to talk about Luca, but now, like this, it is so …'

Greg could only nod in sympathy. Perhaps this was a fruitless journey. Luis seemed a lovely, caring man, broken by what had happened to his son, as Greg felt he would be too. He remembered when his son Kyle had been in danger last year.

'Yurena Aguilar …'

Greg paused. He wanted to see Luis's initial reaction at the mention of her name.

' … asked me to find out where Lucia might be, if she's still alive …'

He waited for any reaction. *'Would you know anything? I presume you knew about Luca and Lucia?'*

He'd detected hardly a flicker at Yurena's name but was a little taken aback by his reaction to the rest.

'That girl was trouble. Just like her father, but please don't misunderstand, I truly hope she is still alive.

'She and Luca were very much in love. I know they had the island at their heart, the work they were doing on preserving its status as a world biosphere island, but they were making enemies at the same time. I know Sebastian didn't like what they were doing, Juan Cavaleros also. They are fortune hunters.'

Greg felt a bond with Luis Hidalgo. Probably due to sport, but also as a father. He couldn't imagine Luis getting involved in anything away from sport nor having an involvement in disappearances.

And on this visit he was back to enjoying himself. Funny really, for a man of allegedly few words he felt himself taking to this role of asking questions. Perhaps that was it, as he didn't have to be the one who spoke.

He still wasn't sure where any of this would lead, probably nowhere, but he was at least trying his best to piece together information so that he had a chance of helping Yurena. He liked Luis, didn't like Sebastian, didn't really like the smooth operator veneer of Juan. But Luis he felt was genuine. Then again, was that naïve?

'*You know, you should bring your Eruption boys here to train. We have excellent facilities and we are about to expand.*'

Luis had recovered his composure.

'*Athletes come from all over the world. They like it here because they can train in a warm climate, not your English rain.*'

Greg now needed to get back to see Susie, and before Kenny's next session started, but offered up another question.

'*You and Sebastian Dominguez. Friends once?*'

The chiselled 6ft-plus God-like figure didn't miss a beat in replying.

'*We were inseparable as kids. We went everywhere together.*'

Luis looked directly at Greg.

'*During my athletics career too. But then Yurena and Elena came along. We drifted apart.*'

'*Elena left you.*'

It was out of Greg's mouth before he realised. He hadn't meant it to come out quite so quickly. In an instant Luis's demeanour changed. Gone was the gleaming smile. Thunder appeared in his eyes, his jaw set straight and firm.

Greg thought about apologising quickly, but then stopped himself. He wanted to see how this played itself out.

Luis avoided an instant reply. Greg could feel the tension in his silence. Luis, now firm-lipped, appeared to be composing himself from the shock of Greg's statement. Luis sucked in his cheeks, breathed in heavily through his nose, put his right hand across his chin covering his mouth with thumb on one cheek and the other fingers of his hand embracing the other.

This had all been just a matter of seconds but Greg waited for Luis's reaction. Composure back in tow, Luis exhaled softly before replying.

'I loved Elena … I still do … she was the love of my life … is the love of my life … there was never anyone before and there has never been anyone since … we had a beautiful boy, who is now gone … all I have left is this … I hope you find Lucia and that she is safe …'

Luis offered his hand. The two sporting stars of separate generations shook with a firm handshake. Christ, this wasn't getting Greg anywhere quickly and the emotion inside Luis, both for his boy and his ex-wife touched Greg deeply. Maybe he wasn't cut out for this again after all.

'Who the hell owns the club then?'

GPK didn't like things that didn't tie up. The modus operandi of he and his team was to bring the right people to justice for the killings of Jeff Markham and Bob Irvine, but now in the course of doing so they were embroiled in what was happening on this island. He now needed to know what was going on with the ownership of the club, as it could all relate to what they were trying to uncover.

He'd come away from Santiago's and was walking towards the harbour talking with Ken on his mobile.

'It is not at all clear just at the moment. There had been so much press about the Cavaleros owning the club that everyone just assumed they were the owners and that no-one else was involved but Maria Cavaleros's revelation this morning goes against that.

'Juan Cavaleros was clearly under the impression that the ownership of Lanzarote Eruption was wholly down to he and his wife …'

GPK was about to interject.

'… however, that still doesn't make total sense because if they were equal partners he would not have been able to do any deal that meant the club had been sold because, presumably, although we don't know for definite, he would have had to have more than a 50 per cent stake …'

Again, Ken continued before GPK could get a word in edgeways.

'… which means that, from what we've ascertained so far, Ana Cristina Magdalena, reputedly one of the island's wealthiest inhabitants, had bought the club from Juan Cavaleros … and it appears Geoffrey Quinigan QC may be involved in some way as he

and Cavaleros both visited Senorita Magdalena on La Graciosa in the past few days ...'

He paused for breath. Kraft pounced.

'This place gets weirder by the minute. But if Quinigan is on his uppers how the hell is he able to afford to invest?'

'Is he investing? Or is he brokering,' Ken Knott offered.

'Whatever he's doing it's hard to know what it has to do with what we're trying to uncover, Ken. Good work though. Keep digging.'

Greg's quickest route back from Club Caleta to Playa Blanca was through Tinajo and across Parque Nacional de Timanfaya, 'The Land of the Volcanoes', a journey that took in a scene of black lava where not a single tree or shrub interrupts the vista of what is often referred to as a lunar landscape and has just one smooth, straight tarmac road running through it.

The Montanas del Fuego, the Fire Mountains, were the scene of one of the worst catastrophes recorded in the history of the modern world when volcanic eruptions took place on Lanzarote for a six-year period from 1730-1736.

The LZ67 from Mancha Blanca to Yaiza crosses the forbidding malpais, known as the 'badlands'. It is one of the island's fastest roads as there are no intersections for miles.

Greg was enjoying the Range Rover Sport. Its power, comfort and speed. He was enjoying the sunshine, being back out on the open road.

Wow, how different this all was. What a landscape! What a wonderful part of the world! He'd love having Kyle out here – and he'd enjoy some time with Diane again, if that was allowed, if she'd allow it. Surely, she would. If he and Kyle were together he couldn't imagine Diane not being there. And it would be good to be together as a family.

It was also fantastic that Susie was with him too. He was playing great, feeling great, he'd heard the same thing about rumours of an international call-up. He smiled to himself. Just had to get back to Playa Blanca quickly now.

Five seconds later Greg's world went black. As black as the Badlands.

CHAPTER 51

Susie had left Santiago's. She had never intended for this all to go as far as it had, but there was no way back. She'd been the happy-go-lucky girl for much of the past 10 years, long ago having left behind the way of life she had been used to in her 20s through to her 40s when she'd had her children.

She'd never anticipated the feelings she would have for Greg, that would keep drawing her back to him, nor his for her. But this had gone on long enough. This sham. Well, not exactly a sham but something that could never work.

She'd had a fabulous time, hell she'd travelled thousands of miles now to see him twice, but it was time to end it. This wasn't her. It was probably as well that he wasn't here right now, in this moment, when everything had become clear.

'Senora Reuben!'

Susie heard her married name as she was leaving Santiago's. She didn't instantly look around. She walked on.

'Senora! ... Susie!'

She stopped, turned.

Greg had no chance. He had come over a moderate rise on this wonderfully smooth road five minutes after leaving Mancha Blanca with the volcanic Montanas del Fuego in the distance.

That's when he saw it, a cage, no more than 50 maybe 100 metres ahead. The cage was slap bang in front of him. Briefly he saw a flicker of something, human, girl, woman, female, but then nothing.

The screeching of tyres on tarmac were nothing in comparison to what happened next. Avoidance had not been an option as the cage straddled both lanes and whoever or whatever was inside was seemingly alive.

Sunlight was burning down on the tarmac causing glare from the cage, one side of the road was built up into a foot-high ledge as though the road had been hewn into the lava fields, the other side was a harsh rocky outcrop of the black Badlands.

Greg had gone for the option that hadn't been an option. Having hammered steadfastly down on the brake trying to avoid impact with the cage he realised he needed Plan B. With no more than 30 metres to go and briefly seeing the whites of her eyes, wide. Yes, her eyes. Shit, fuck, shit! He turned to swerve off road.

The Range Rover Sport's front wheels avoided the cage by inches, the rear wheels now spinning around to the left and careering ever closer to the cage were corrected by some deft steering wheel action by Greg. The bright shiny gleaming vehicle now mounted the more-than-rough terrain briefly before hitting rock that sent it spiralling in the air, turning over two and then three times on the Badlands before coming to rest on its roof some fifty metres further up the road. No longer bright, shiny nor gleaming. For the next few seconds the only noise was the spinning of the tyres.

CHAPTER 52

'Hola!'

Maria Cavaleros's life was about to turn on the upswing after burying her daughter the previous day and then losing her temper with Juan after hearing the 'fake news' about the sale of Eruption. She had no idea where Juan was right now, nor wished to know.

She had come over to Santiago's after Susie had left and was now about to enjoy a drink or two with Gina, who she had just heard finish her set.

'I decided to come to you,'

Maria announced with a radiance that belied what she had felt earlier in the day.

If Gina had been anticipating some girlie chat from Maria, given the way in which Maria had mentioned her mother when they had met at the game, she was about to be stunned.

Gina sat opposite Maria, a small round table between them. Maria looked Gina straight in the eyes, serious. It seemed to be a day for revelations.

'It was your father I knew, not your mother. You knew this?'

Maria was in no mood for hanging around, there was no affectation over whether this should be a confession or that she should be remorseful in any way, she was here with a purpose.

'I couldn't mention it that way when we first spoke, that's why I chose to say I knew your mother, it sounded more ...'

She searched for the right word.

'Wholesome?'

Gina wasn't annoyed. Her father had been single for a long time. Her parents had been apart many years. Maria splayed her hands, shrugged her shoulders. Lips together.

'If you wish.'

Gina had her father's same forcefulness, his same whirlwind approach to getting jobs done. She'd not stepped into overdrive fully since setting foot on Lanzarote, apart from selling herself to Jason the bar manager at Santiago's.

This was the first fresh news she had found out about her father. She was now eager for more. It was all about to come.

'I first met your father about a year and a half year ago. He had come over for some business awards evening. Corporate event. One of his companies was up for a major prize. They'd flown in a Hollywood movie star to make the presentations.

'Juan and I had been invited but he was busy elsewhere, so I went on my own. No problem there. One thing led to another and …'

Maria flicked the palms of her hands in some kind of abracadabra-style gesture.

'Bedtime!'

Gina's eyes sparkled at the beautiful Maria as he said it. She was enjoying this so far, even if it was about her dad. She'd finally found out something more about him. Not what she'd intended or anticipated, true, and nothing that helped with why she had come, but something nonetheless.

Gina, as well as being playful was also perceptive. She made a swift calculation. Something clicked.

Gina hunched over the table towards Maria conspiratorially.

'You and my father first meet around a year and a half ago. He buys a rugby league club in England at around the same time that you must have been coming up with your rugby league club over here? He's over here just at that time.'

Maria was watching her intently.

'Dad always likes … liked …'

Gina swiftly corrected herself, with no sense of cracking emotionally at the thought.

'… to invest in new things? Then today you mention on TV and radio that Lanzarote Eruption has not been sold, hanging your husband out to dry. And …'

She sat back speculating.

'… and it can't be sold because of something to do with my father? Which is why you wanted to see me.'

Maria finally smiled back at Gina, her biggest smile since Greg had scored the goal that had clinched the championship title.

'You are definitely, as we say 'La Higa de tu Padre', your father's daughter. You catch on quick. We have much to discuss Gina.

'Your father is the major investor in Lanzarote Eruption and the Estadio de Lanzarote. He is the majority shareholder in the business, but not in his own name.'

Maria paused.

'He used yours. He wanted to keep his involvement anonymous. Something about how there may have been problems owning two clubs.

'You are the owner, or at least it is you that owns 90 per cent of the club and the stadium, although your father also managed to use another different name on the records through his solicitors to keep the family name of Irvine out of all the paperwork.'

'Then how the hell does Juan think he has any rights to sell? Surely he knows what he signed up to?'

'Juan is all show. He does not sometimes look at the small print. Juan signed a different contract to the one he thought. When your father set it all up – and your father was an extraordinary man in many ways, he knew his way around, and he also knew what Juan was like. I saw how he worked.'

Gina couldn't help but smile at Maria and shook her head while smiling and raising her eyebrows. Maria smiled back. They held hands across the table. Gina could tell how much affection she'd held for her father. Maria sat back after they'd released their hands of friendship.

'… and so far as Juan was aware he really was a fifty-fifty owner of the club with me. He'd seen something about 50-50 in an earlier draft contract, left me to the paperwork and had assumed that was it. For a man who has been involved in the building of many hotels here on the island he can be very stupid.

'… but if he looks carefully at the contract we have only a 10 per cent share in the club and the stadium … and I don't believe Ana Cristina Magdalena and Geoffrey Quinigan, or El Bastardo, as he is known on the island, would want just that …'

The name brought instant reaction from Gina.

'Woah! Woah! Woah! Lady! Hold your horses!'

Gina toned down instantly.

'*Quinigan? Geoffrey Fucking Quinigan QC?*'

Maria nodded. She could now see Gina's father ever more clearly in his daughter.

'*Well, he and Juan were both at Ana Cristina's estate on La Graciosa in the past few days, separately, from what my sources tell me.*'

Maria raised her eyebrows and cocked her head slightly while she took up her glass.

'*Noooo!?*'

Gina's day had suddenly lit up with new information.

'*She's bedding them? Both of them?*'

Almost instantly Gina realised she was talking about Maria's husband. She winced.

'*Sorry,*' she whispered and winced again.

'*Don't be … and yes, they've been fucking for years. I tried not to think about it.*

'*They've known each other all their lives, I'm sure they don't think anything of it … just sex.*'

She shrugged again, let out a deep breath.

'*But Quinigan? I thought his QC also stood for something else? Isn't he just a slimy perverted fucker?*'

Maria burst into laughter. This was what she needed. The release from what Juan had brought about. She shook her head in dismay.

'*All of those three in one. Fortunately, I have no first-hand experience – unlike Hugo Silva and, I believe, your stepfather …*'

'*Whaat? Whoaaa! Again Lady!*'

Gina's decibel level rose once more. Maria smiled, biting her lip. She was enjoying this but didn't want Gina thinking she was revelling in it, even if she was. She needn't have worried. Gina had seen much of life on the road with her guitar.

Gina looked all around her, but now in more girlie 'let things out of the bag style'. She shook her head, raised her eyes in her head, let them go wide-eyed. Then she leaned over towards Maria and talked about her stepfather.

'*You know he wanders around his villa naked, almost as soon as he walks through the door …*'

She was enjoying this moment of release.

'… all I have in my head of him is his swinging cock and bollocks … he's not badly equipped to be honest, but really … '

'That's Quinigan for you. He loves anything like that. The kinkier the better so far as I've heard. Some like it. Some just play up to him because they want to keep in his favour, both boys AND girls. He gets his share of each … again, from what I've heard.'

Maria became serious once more and Gina sobered up immediately at her next revelation.

'He is not called El Bastardo for nothing. And that is not because of his sexual preference. He is the man who makes things legal, makes people very rich, people who should not be. He finds ways.'

Maria Cavaleros was now well into her stride.

'I imagine he was on Graciosa brokering yet another deal for Ana Cristina. They were at university together in England. That's how he has come to be over here so much for many years, and how he has become the man to go to if islanders want anything legal that is really illegal. He did not earn his reputation as El Bastardo through his sexual prowess.

'Anything to be built on the island, anything not quite the way it should be, and there is much of that kind of thing on here, hotels constructed without fulfilling the necessary criteria, without following the guidelines on size, taking up more of the land than originally planned. All of this is said to go through him.'

The girls were now in serious mode. Gina was in business mode.

'My father was no angel, I'm certain of that, but he would have hated him.'

'Your father DID hate him.'

Another penny dropped for Gina. She smiled at her memories of her father.

'At least I can now make sense of what he meant by some of the texts and cryptic messages he gave on Skype and FaceTime when we talked as I've been travelling the world. Just throwaway things. Now I think about it he was dropping words, maybe clues into our conversations.'

She shook her head as though to bring herself back to today. Gina Irvine, owner of Lanzarote Eruption. Crikey!

CHAPTER 53

Greg's world was revolving, just as the roof of the Range Rover Sport had been for what had seemed an eternity. He was currently upside down, grateful for the seatbelt that had kept him from being thrown about and also for the legendary robustness of the vehicle body. The car may no longer have been in full working order, but Greg swiftly calculated all his limbs seemed to be operating okay.

Next he was being returned to a normal seated position, by virtue of significant power from two exceptionally well-built heavies before being dragged from the vehicle and bound by the wrists and ankles. Greg was powerless.

All energy or adrenaline he may have normally called upon had closed down. He was bundled into a Jaguar F-pace SUV. No expense spared it seemed. That was the last he saw, as he became hooded.

There were no words from his captors this time. No goodwill. What had he got into here? This had to be about Lucia. Was it her in the cage? It had all happened so fast. But the merest glimpse he'd had wasn't that of an early-20s girl, was it?

'*Excelente. Now get him out of the way …*'

The voice now giving the instructions at one end of the line was cautiously euphoric.

'*… where we said … good work … gives me time to decide …*'

He set about laying tables once again at Al's.

Susie hadn't made it back to the hotel, she hadn't even made it beyond the row of bars and restaurants on the seafront where she now sat at another bar with Janet.

Ken's information on Susie had given her a clean bill of health as far as their processed data went, but GPK had still felt there was something more to be had from her. Susie had come across as charming, extremely pleasant company, but it was what she was not saying that had stirred his interest further and when she'd left the bar suddenly he'd sent Janet a message instantly to intercept her.

Janet was positioned a few bars down towards the marina while James was in a restaurant/bar further towards the harbour. They'd been detailed there to watch for anything untoward near Santiago's since returning from La Graciosa and having followed Quinigan back to Hugo Silva's villa.

They had already been full of it having picked up the news of a video of Quinigan, which Ana Cristina had mentioned. Ken was currently detailed on finding a way of accessing any device Ana Cristina may have used and how to get hands on it.

It was Janet who had used Susie's full name. Susie, intrigued and unsure of what to do, had accepted Janet's offer of either a glass of wine, white sangria or lager beer after Janet had explained who she was and that she just wanted to chat if that was okay?

'You and Greg. You've been together a while?'

Janet was trying her level best in keeping things light. She saw Susie's natural hesitation. GPK had also told her that Susie might feel as though this was some Spanish Inquisition, but to keep going, softly.

Susie knew that Greg had either never noticed or chosen not to notice when she had not either answered something directly or hesitated while she made up an answer, but she saw Janet was immediately on the ball.

'You've no need to worry. I'm not about to say anything. I'm just gathering information. This is not about you and Greg.'

The drinks arrived and Susie relaxed again. She clinked glasses with Janet, closed her eyes, laid her head back and enjoyed the sun while she gathered her thoughts.

'Two minutes ago I was leaving,' she spoke inside her head. 'Now look at me.' She breathed out softly and then spoke.

'We were never really together.

We had lots of good times. He's a lovely young man and I know he loved me and still does,' Susie left it like that, but Janet sensed there was more. She didn't know where this was heading.

'*But you didn't? Or you now don't?*'

Susie put down her glass. She put her fingers together in a prayer-like style with her forefingers resting under her nose and thumbs under her chin. She closed her eyes briefly, put her hands back down, then rested her chin on the fingers of her left hand with her left elbow on the table. Her eyes reached to the sky, she couldn't help but smile about him again.

'*I loved him, I still love him, but …*'

Susie smiled again and this time a tear appeared in the corner of her eye.

'*I'm sorry …*' Janet was good at this.

This is why she had been detailed to see what was going on between Greg and Susie. GPK's team hadn't felt there was necessarily anything, but if there was someone who could find out it was Janet.

'*Don't be silly,*' Susie replied.

'*We've had a good time. But it's time to move on …*'

Susie put a smile on once more.

'*Why?*'

Janet was used to coming out with the one question that went straight to the heart.

'*Why now?*'

Sensing that Susie would tire of this quickly she went in for the kill.

'*What's happened Susie?*'

CHAPTER 54

Greg awoke in darkness, not just the darkness from continuing to wear his headgear. The ultra-darkness came from where he was now situated.

There had been no talk en-route to wherever he now was, nothing he could pick up. A little knowledge of Spanish may have helped with the odd word but these two had either been well drilled not to speak or were socially distant.

Greg had been aware of the sound of the sea while his assailants carried his 15-stone body on to a boat, and not a particularly large one at that from what he could gather.

He'd had no idea where they were sailing from or to. He knew Fuerteventura was the next going west along the Canaries.

How the hell had he got into this? 'Greg,' he said to himself. 'What are you doing?' It reminded him of what Susie used to say at one time about their relationship when she'd say, 'What are we doing?'

But now, really, what was he doing? He wasn't some kind of private investigator or private dick. He wondered why they were sometimes called that? Probably summed him up, the last bit anyway.

He wasn't a private investigator, he was a rugby league player finally playing for a good club. 'What are you doing, Greg?' he asked himself again.

'You're the wrong guy, in the wrong place at the wrong time,' he mused. Bruce Willis eat your heart out. This was hardly *Die Hard with a Vengeance*, or whichever *Die Hard* movie that phrase came from.

He wasn't escaping up a small metal service chute or shooting Alan Rickman and his buddies in the Nakatomi building.

His wrists and ankles were still bound. His head was still sheathed in black and it felt as though he were inside somewhere, even though he couldn't see through the fabric. It was fusty, smelled of damp wood and it seemed to Greg more like when he had been inside his father's garden shed when he was a young lad back in Hopton.

'Greg, Greg, Greg. Why do you keep getting into these kinds of situations?' he muttered to himself. Sod you, Bruce Willis! Get out of my head, this wasn't a film.

The knocks, aches and pains of his earlier incident with the Range Rover Sport and the caged girl kicked in. He hadn't been unconscious, but then he thought, 'How would someone know they had been unconscious as being conscious means you're not unconscious?' He'd been okay, fully aware of what had happened throughout, including playing back in his mind the girl in the cage.

He'd had the slightest glimpse. He continually played it over. Why have a girl there in a cage? How would anyone know that he'd be on that road?

He made a lame attempt trying to free his tethers but the combination of their tightness and his body's tiredness brought on sleep.

Wherever he was, whatever was bruised, broken, ached, whoever had arranged this, would all just have to wait.

CHAPTER 55

Susie was back at the Papagayos Beach Hotel. Janet had taken her despite Susie's mild protestations that she would be okay. She was still leaving.

Janet had deposited Susie in the hotel car park, having offered her a lift to the airport. It was GPK's way of making sure they watched her, checked and double-checked. Susie had politely declined Janet's offer, but they would follow regardless.

Ten minutes after Janet had left, Susie rang the number from the card she had left her.

Kenny hadn't initially been unduly concerned about Greg not attending training that evening as his star player had sent a text saying he'd been delayed on an urgent matter and that he'd call in the morning, but there was something about it that rankled with him later on after training had finished.

But then maybe he was imagining a problem that wasn't there. He left it. Didn't pursue it.

Less than one minute after Susie's call there was a knock at her door. GPK was there. He'd returned earlier while Janet and Susie had been talking in the other bar.

He'd been trying to make connections that would give them something concrete on Quinigan and Jardine, hopefully Dugarry too. He was trying to retain his focus rather than get dragged into what also now appeared the island's own problems, although it was proving difficult to keep them apart as Quinigan's name kept appearing in both.

'This is what I found when I got back.'

Susie handed the note that had been slipped under the door to Greg's suite.

It read: 'El no esta muerto. Pero lo estara si sigue hacienda preguntas'.

'I know muerto means dead,' Susie offered.

'It says he's not dead, but he will be if he keeps asking questions?'

GPK purposely accentuated it to see whether there was any reaction from Susie.

'*Come on Mrs Reuben …*'

Kraft was beginning to lose his patience, or at very least that's how he wanted it to come across. There was something about Susie that hadn't sat right with him all day.

'*What is it that you're not telling us?*' He was firm now, no soft soap.

Susie was scared for Greg, but no wallflower when it came to being spoken to like this.

'*I don't know what you're trying to say Mr Kraft, but you're definitely barking up the wrong tree if for whatever reason you think I am involved in that. She pointed at the letter he was holding.*'

Susie steadied herself, biting the inner of her lip slightly.

'*I love him.*'

Those three words bolstered her even further.

'*And I'll tell you this …*'

Before Susie had chance to add anything further GPK slammed her with the words.

'*Then why the hell are you leaving him?*'

'*Because I'm with someone else!*'

It was out before she knew it. She stopped. Calmed herself. Gave in to herself.

'*I have been with someone else for the past six months.*'

She shook her head at herself.

'*But … you know, it's not like it is with Greg … and when he rang me a few weeks ago, told me about here … I don't go back, it's not what I do … but Greg …*'

She shook her head again.

'*Does he know? … about this other guy? …*'

She shook again, this time not a shake of her head at herself, but a definite shake reaffirming her belief that he didn't.

Kraft had finally found what this vivacious woman had been withholding. It made sense at last.

But this note? That was different. He moved on to something now more pertinent.

'*Do you know where Greg went today? Where he was due to be going?*'

'*All I know is that he sent me a couple of text messages telling me he had to see people. Here ...*'

She passed him her phone.

'*Check for yourself.*'

Susie was still clearly offended by the way Kraft had confronted her.

Kraft took the phone. Looked at the messages from Greg, briefly, quickly scanned today's callers.

'*Simon? The new kid on the block?*'

He was taking no prisoners here. He'd seen that name appear. Greg's too, message about seeing some people but no names. That was it. Nothing that helped. Susie had given him another hard look. He passed it back.

'*Are you staying or going?*'

Kraft had received Janet's feedback from her meeting with Susie.

'*How can I go now? Is that what you're saying?*'

Susie and GPK's tones to each other were fast becoming more fractious.

'*I make my own decisions Mr Kraft, for better or for worse ...*'

CHAPTER 56

'Where the chuff? Jeez! Shoulders ache like hell, my wrists, my legs feel glued, my ankles.' Greg drifted off again, but it didn't last. He now ached everywhere. It all gradually came back to him. 'And this bloody hood, so warm. Got to get it off.'

Greg could see the brightness of daytime and feel the heat of the sunshine through the hood. How the chuff could he get it off? All he could hear was the sea, waves, movement, a crashing against rocks.

How long had he been asleep? What day was it? He couldn't have slept a day and a half, so it was the next day.

Cage on the road, the girl, who would do that?

It had to be about looking for Lucia. Was she alive and someone didn't want her found? Why the girl in the cage in the road? He came back to it again. Who was she? Was she Lucia?

Was it Adriana, the woman from Al's. Had her words got her into trouble with Carlos? Was Carlos involved in this? Probably, no definitely. That was his first real tick in a box so far as Greg was concerned. Christ these tethers hurt.

Greg shifted his focus back to freeing himself. He couldn't stand, couldn't see, couldn't move very well with wrists and ankles bound. He ached everywhere from the impact of the car rising up and cartwheeling across the Badlands. He wriggled on the floor, which seemed made of rough dirt, earth and rock. He then tried stretching and found he was able to get some purchase against rock. He then shuffled, using his elbows to get into an upright position on his knees. Better. He could use his hands now to explore.

'First things first,' he told himself. 'Wrists.' Once he had them freed everything else would be easy. The fatigue he'd felt after the car smash, manhandling and subsequent dumping yesterday had gone even if the aches and pains were still very much there.

Sleep had always been drilled into him as fitness's best friend. He speculated how blind people coped day after day and realised just how much more relevant touch, smell and sound became.

He couldn't use his fingers to touch what was binding him because they wouldn't reach, but he could put his wrists to his mouth, albeit with the hood in the way.

'Rope', it was rope that was binding him. He needed to fray it enough so that he could either break it through pulling his wrists apart as it weakened or fray it completely. Probably a long process given its thickness, but right now he had nothing better to do, apart from calling out occasionally, which proved futile as the sound of the sea was too strong. Where the hell was he?

He felt something that was a kind of material, a tarpaulin? He tried to trace each edge to ascertain whether there might be something that could be used to fray the rope bindings.

Stones seemed the only abundant source of anything. After a while of checking out the area around him there proved nothing worthwhile. Try coming out from undercover?

He managed to haul himself up on to his feet.

Who would have known where he was on the road? Luis Hidalgo.

But he could have been followed earlier. Probably was.

The sun was at its height and beating down. Greg's first movement from being under the tarpaulin was a gentle three or four hops and instantly he felt the heat of the day beating down on his head through the hood.

Instant thought. Remember how to get back under cover. Don't go too far. Be able to get back easily. He took another hop and wished he hadn't. Losing any footing he slipped, caught his thigh on a rock as he fell and also his head. Time for blood to flow. He laid in the sun for what seemed an eternity.

'Wrists! Bloody wrists! Sod everything else!' He returned to the task. But hey! This time with renewed vigour. If he'd cut himself, as it had felt he had, because it felt like he was bleeding, then if he could locate the stone or stones or others that had done or were capable of doing the damage, perhaps he might be able to use them. After a few minutes of careful selection, having found several variations of sharp-edged stone he set about trying to free himself.

CHAPTER 57

'It is time we became a little more effective.'

Geoffrey Quinigan QC was holding what was effectively a team briefing at Hugo Silva's villa where the Latex Twins, his son Oliver and daughter Emily, both RADA-trained actors were with him.

Quinigan had come down from his rage of the day previously when he had charged off to Ana Cristina Magdalena as some kind of spoilt child.

Hugo was happier now. It appeared that Ana Cristina was out of the picture at last. He generally watched from afar and hadn't chosen to intercede in any of Geoffrey's actions and involvements on the island previously. Quinigan elaborated.

'Duggan is presently out of the way, and if we're extremely fortunate we may have seen the last of him.'

El Bastardo looked out towards Playa Blanca. He was refreshed from an evening of pure relaxation with Hugo, and back to his scheming, methodical, organisational approach.

'Uppermost now is dealing with these bloody journalists.'

He walked around as he explained.

'They have nothing they can substantiate about last year's events, but they are, I fear, making some progress.'

He walked again. He could see Ollie ready to interject. Quinigan raised his hand to assuage any attempt.

'This is not going to go away. It appears this awful man, Kraft, has a team both here on the island and back in the UK, and he is being bankrolled by the newspaper industry.'

He looked directly at his son.

'Not your wisest move Oliver, eliminating a journalist.'

Quinigan was not damning of his son's impetuous actions, that had seen the shooting of Jeff Markham as he had sat in his car in Hopton Town's car park. He showed Oliver as much by patting him on the shoulder as he passed on his walk and talk.

'*But we are where we are ... and something needs to be done.*'

Ollie had waited his time.

'*... but something not so ... final?*'

He said it with such humour his father couldn't help but smile.

'*Not so final. No.*'

At that moment the button at the gate of Hugo's villa was pressed.

Detective Sergeant Alba Marta Arteta wasn't impressed by anyone. Kraft, Duggan, Cuadrado, none of them had given her everything they knew. She was losing patience.

She knew or at very least sensed Carlos was involved in some way in the murders of Luca Hidalgo and Ciara Cortelli-O'Grady. She also sensed that Lucia Dominguez could be found, whether dead or alive, through him.

This recent news of a takeover of Lanzarote Eruption, involving the Cavaleros and Ana Cristina Magdalena. Was that all part of this? Families on the island. They were a nightmare. She'd visited Yurena Aguilar today and found out precisely nothing.

Yurena, for some reason, would not even confirm what Arteta already knew, that Senor Duggan was trying to find Lucia.

'*Senor Du-Gan, he is missing.*'

Those were the words Arteta heard when she picked up her phone.

CHAPTER 58

'You are our first 'find' in fifteen years of coming here.'

Greg was no longer missing. Try as he might he'd not succeeded in his quest to free his own wrists. Instead he'd used his hands to wrestle free the canopy he'd been under. He'd raised it above his head and had hoped and prayed that someone, somewhere might see movement and come looking. They had.

'You are very lucky. We nearly go to Montana Clara instead. We come for the Canary Gecko and the Egyptian Vulture. This is the only place in the world where you see the Gecko. We look for the lesser spotted Alegranza Gecko and the Chinijo peregrine falcon, but we have no luck yet … fifteen years! But we find you!'

'Leif, this young man does not want to hear about your obsession. Are you more comfortable now? Take your time. We are in no hurry.'

Leif Andersen and his wife Ingrid, Norway's finest rescuers so far as Greg was concerned, had seen his flag waving. They had just come ashore for another day of binoculars amongst the island's flora and fauna.

Greg had been in front of them no more than 100 metres from the island's only beach. A 6ft 2in man with a hood completely enveloping his head waving a large flag-type affair above his head, with his wrists and ankles bound.

Being all set for another day in the wild, knives were a prerequisite on their journeys and the couple made short work of Greg's tethers. While the hood had been breathable it had also been interminably hot and had hampered his progress in trying to break free as he kept having to break off to relax and allow his temperature to return to the norm.

Greg could not believe how thin the roping had been. It was hellish strong, but it had felt much thicker.

'Boat rope is very strong.' Leif had nodded masterfully.

Greg was on Alegranza, known as the Island of Joy, so Leif had said, because someone had felt joy in seeing land. Greg couldn't help but feel he'd be more joyful when he was off it. Right now, he was consuming whatever Leif and Ingrid were passing him from their supplies for the day.

He'd been dumped on an uninhabited island, the second smallest in the Chinijo archipelago, so Leif had informed him in the boat on the way back to Lanzarote.

Alegranza was an island that basically featured a dormant volcano crater, a small sandy beach, thousands of birds and lizards. Human population – zero.

Leif and Ingrid were amazingly generous. Having docked in Orzola they drove to Playa Blanca. They reached Papagayos Beach Hotel. He thanked them profusely and they were gone.

They'd saved his life. Who knew what would have happened to him if nobody had arrived on Alegranza.

It was now the day of the play-off, he knew that much from Leif and Ingrid having put him right on dates and times. Greg had been on Alegranza for two days without food or drink. Leif, who knew about such things, informed Greg that another day or two without water and he would have had little chance of survival.

The couple had found Greg on what was his second morning.

They'd set off early from Orzola, around 6am and had reached Alegranza by 8.30am.

Once they'd unfettered and unhooded him and made sure he was in good health they had climbed back on board what Greg thought an incredibly small sailing vessel for the waters of the Oceano Atlantico. They'd returned to Lanzarote for half past midday and he was back in the hotel for 1.30pm having travelled the full length of the island.

During the course of their journey and having heard the news on the radio, the couple had updated him on the sensation that had been sweeping the world the past two days.

A virus with no cure had started in the Far East. There was worldwide concern and the city of over 1 million where it had begun was quarantined with over 5000 deaths already reported and outbreaks as far as 1000 miles away from its epicentre.

Greg's more immediate concern was his own epicentre.

CHAPTER 59

'*I need another key for my room.*'

Pablo's jaw had hit the floor as Greg had entered the hotel reception.

'*Si, Senor Greg, immediatamente!*'

To say he hadn't been expecting to see Greg was an understatement.

As he passed a new key Greg grabbed his wrist and hauled him up and over the reception desk, headbutting him smack bang on his nose, which splattered various shades of red right across his face.

Greg then hurtled him headlong across the smooth, shiny surface of the reception area like a ten-pin bowling ball where he smashed into a table where ice buckets held bottles of wine and glasses were available for the new arrivals.

He now grabbed the hotel manager by the scruff of his neck and hurled him towards the staircase where his head split open against a metal railing.

Greg hadn't finished yet.

He picked up Pablo and threw him over the railing twenty metres down below. Pools of blood spread on the marbled floor.

Alarms were producing a cacophony of sound as visitors scampered everywhere. Greg made for his suite. He grabbed what he needed and headed for Pablo's car, having taken his keys and phone. He headed straight for Al's. Pablo's phone flashed as he drove.

It took Greg five minutes to reach the car parking area. Another sunny day looking out over the coves of Papagayo and out towards Fuerteventura.

Carlos emerged from behind the bar as Greg entered from the cliff end of the restaurant. Briefly, Greg made a mental note of the canopy. The same material as he'd had been covered with on Alegranza. Carlos needed no words regarding Greg's intent.

He held up his hands, but Greg did not care what he did.

Adriana Gomez appeared just after Carlos. Things were a little different to the last time he'd seen her. In a cage.

He could so very easily have killed her. She was still with him. Working for him. She'd said he was dangerous. How right she had been and how close to her own death.

No words from Greg. Just action.

Carlos was a stocky man. Well-built would be one description, fat another. Greg landed his first debilitating punch square and true right into the man's ample midriff, immediately sending his head down, which enabled Greg to land a haymaker punch to the side of his head that sent Carlos spinning.

Before he could fall Greg grabbed his left arm, which he yanked up behind Carlos's back causing a crunch and popping sound. The man was now in agony, and ball and socket displaced Greg pulled on the arm to bring Carlos out of the bar area.

Adriana had by now retreated, customers had fled. In the far distance Greg could hear the local Policia heading out of Playa Blanca, horns blaring.

Greg dragged Carlos through the restaurant and to the cliff edge looking down on Playa de Papagayo. He twisted the man's now withered arm further. Threw him to the ground. Carlos's shoulders were touching the edge of the cliff. His head over it. Greg bound his ankles with the same rope used on him.

Carlos was desperate.

'Senor! Senor! No! Senor Du-Gan! Por favor!'

Tears rolled down his cheeks. Greg moved him further over the edge.

'Who are you working for you little shit!'

Greg could hear the sirens wailing. The Policia were heading over. Greg edged him further over.

'No lo se! I do not know Senor! I do not know! Someone else … por favor, Senor …'

'El esta mintiendo.'

Adriana. Greg spun round.

'He lies,' she said.

'Tu dices! Tell him!!!'

It wasn't so much the words that had attracted Greg's attention as much as the revolver she was now pointing in Carlos's direction.

'Tu dices, o te matare, and I will kill you! Ahora!'

Carlos held up his hands, as much as he could as they were both now well over the cliff edge. Greg pulled him back a couple of inches. Carlos took a second or two, but finally realised he only had one choice if he wanted to carry on serving sangria and calamari.

Greg, having acquired the information he wanted, released Carlos's ankles from his grasp, leaving them bound, and started towards his car, just as the Policia began arriving in the car park. Greg was ten metres, if that, from Carlos when he heard the gunshot.

He turned instinctively to see Adriana standing over him, revolver in hand, having shot him through the forehead. She followed up by kicking him in the crutch and then pushing him by his bollocks from the cliff.

Greg was back in Pablo's car by the time the Policia had reached the scene.

Being inside the hood for two days had brought clarity to his mind. He'd played everything back, worked it all out.

Susie had teased that Pablo was interested in him. He had been. He'd been monitoring Greg's every movement. Greg had played through every incident since he'd arrived at the hotel. The visit in Pablo's car to Paddy O'Grady. Every time Greg had been around so had Pablo, and on his phone.

Carlos. The woman in the cage had to be Adriana. When he played it all back in his head, he had seen her, clearly, her dark eyes. She had warned him about Carlos and had gone way beyond any safety of her own to tip him off. The two guys who'd taken him from the Range Rover Sport. He'd seen one of them before, serving at Al's.

And now it was time for his next call.

CHAPTER 60

The past two days had seen an influx of Jaglin Jaguars fans. The team had also arrived and was staying at the La Cala, the club's owners having generously splashed the cash.

This match was as exciting for them as it would be for Eruption and being the underdogs they had nothing to lose. Just one match away from another 80 minutes that might take them into Super League for the first time.

Jaglin Jags had been beaten twice in the league by Eruption, who had also dumped them out of the Challenge Cup. All three reversals had been substantial, but in the final weeks of the league season, buoyed by some good results, the management had realised there was a chance of reaching the play-offs and had bolstered the squad with great signings.

Jags' captain and hooker Mick Burke had come in having played for a top Super League outfit. He had been the club's pull in attracting his good friend Mark Lowcock, who had played alongside him.

Clever half-back George Ross had played most of his career in the NRL and had come back to England to help run the family dairy farm with his brothers; and Big Chris Jeffery, a loose forward of now questionable speed but brilliant hands, apparently the same with the ladies.

Big Chris was also a farmer and he had turned around the past two games by harvesting the tries that had pushed the Jags into the play-offs.

Speedy wingers and centres Malcolm Lavery, Charlie Cole, Graham Paddison and Gary Procter were also all on form.

The Jags were at the ground. And now so too was Greg.

'Greg!'

Kenny's exclamation at seeing his buddy and star player approaching him at the ground was fast muted on seeing his face. All he saw was thunder. Kick-off against the Jags was scheduled for 7pm. It was now 2.30pm.

'Where is he?'

Greg was back to limited words. Actions were his true currency.

It was almost as though he'd expected Kenny to know what was going on.

'Cavaleros.'

This had been Carlos Cuadrado's last word to Greg, before he'd been deposited from the cliff by Adriana.

Greg had known Cavaleros was here at the ground, through Pablo's phone. Pablo had been alerting him when Greg had dealt with him in the hotel reception. Greg couldn't work out Cavaleros's message in Spanish, but he'd picked up El Estadio in Juan's response.

'He left about five minutes ago, mate. Like he'd seen a bloody ghost ...'

'You okay, Greg? Where the hell have you been the last two days?'

Pablo's phone exploded back into life. Kenny's also. Both went for their respective phones, like two gunslingers trying to draw first. Pablo's call had been Det Sgt Arteta. Again, Greg couldn't work out the Spanish message.

Kenny's message was in English.

'Cavaleros has just been seen at the marina car park ...'

Janet had been detailed nearby.

James had been monitoring the bugs they had set up around Hugo Silva's villa La Casa Grande de la Flamenco and had picked up talk of the Bella Babe. Ken had done the rest. It was a superyacht. And it had just arrived in the marina.

GPK was presently with Gina at Santiago's. The bar full once again, this time with Jags fans. His team

still didn't have anything tangible with which to nail Quinigan, but the video that James and Janet had heard about when they'd been on La Graciosa, was now in their possession courtesy of some great work by Ken, but it was encrypted. Ken was on the case.

James was on his way to Janet at the marina. She'd sent a

message to the team telling them about Cavaleros having just run and jumped on board Bella Bebe.

Arteta and Moreno weren't far behind. Their Policia colleagues were in the process of rescuing Carlos's body, while also detaining Adriana.

'You know anyone called Pickup?'

Greg's brevity was back. It had been the other name Carlos had given. Carlos was being paid by both Juan Cavaleros and Pickup.

'Owns La Cala, that glitzy hotel next to the stadium. He had a hit song in Spain years ago. English guy, loaded.'

'Has he got a boat?'

'Yep …'

'Its name?'

They were just a minute or so from the marina. Playa Blanca very rarely suffered road blocks. A truck was skewed across the road with vegetables scattered all around and cars parked either side. Greg leapt from the car.

'Bella Bebe!!'

If Greg had hoped finding a boat would be easier because he knew its name, he was to be disappointed.

Kenny saw Janet waving frantically from a pontoon. She pointed at the brilliant-white 72-metre-long, 6-deck superyacht beginning to move away from its berth. Greg ran.

No time for assessing. Bella Bebe was making her way from the marina to open sea. Once she reached it Greg had no chance. Had to get to the yacht before it left the marina harbour. Floating pontoons weren't the easiest to run on, but that's all he had.

Boat traffic was restricted to 5mph at Marina Rubicon, but Bella Bebe appeared to have little concern for such formalities as it charged out heading for Oceano Atlantico. Greg wasn't in the mood for how he might reach it, he just knew he had to. He was also running out of pontoon!

Why the hell was he running for this? What good would it do? Lucia! Had he got this right?

For fuck's sake, he'd been tied up on a bloody desolate island for two days, now he was breaking whatever speed records he held on Strava and Garmin to make it to the boat.

Bella Bebe was fifty metres from open sea. Greg was now running across moored boats and running short of them. Only one option. Dive and swim. He dived. The massive yacht was nearly into open sea. Greg was around ten metres short. Ten metres to make up, for fuck's sake, come on!

Jeez. Stay strong. Stay strong. Stay fucking strong!

Open sea hit with Greg still an agonising two metres short. He could hear the engines start to roar. No chance if he didn't make it in the next few seconds. Dear God, he'd surely not come this far not to get there. These bloody clothes!

One more massive effort. He closed his eyes, speared through the waves that were now starting to come thick and fast as the boat hit open water, and threw out his arm extending his right hand as far as he could reach.

CHAPTER 61

It hadn't been enough. Bella Bebe was now fifteen metres away, now twenty, twenty-five. Fatigue now kicked in. Fuck it. No point carrying on. What a pathetic waste of energy.

'Hey! Get on! …'

Kenny hadn't been idle. He'd 'borrowed' a jet ski from an owner who had just started it up and was currently being dragged out of the harbour by his partner and onlookers.

Bella Bebe was moving further away. Greg grabbed the rope Kenny had thrown.

'I'll get alongside … get on!'

All Greg could do was nod and give a thumbs-up.

Greg held on to Kenny as the pair approached the superyacht, a Sunseeker, built in Poole in the UK, now the world's leading superyacht company.

Kenny had taken the Wavemaster to its maximum speed and they were within metres of Bella Bebe's stern when the jet ski began to cut out. Somehow, from somewhere, he managed to get one flash boost of pace and hit the Bella Bebe with such force that he and Greg were propelled forward, in the air, clear of the jet ski, which was now already ten or twenty metres away and in need of a severe overhaul.

Greg landed unceremoniously on the deck, rolling as he tried to in sport to avoid undue injury. Kenny, less fortunately, had ricocheted off a tubular metal safety rail and was currently hanging on as best he could back in the ocean.

Instinctively, Greg thrust out his hand from the deck and hauled Kenny on board. They had little time for self-congratulation or recovery as a figure loomed at the other side of the doors to the deck.

A gorgeous woman appeared in a white diamond bikini set, that those who know would have recognised as being a 'Hearts of Fire' set modelled by Czech supermodel Karolina Kurkova on the cover of Vogue. Greg and Kenny didn't.

'I really do not know what you two gentlemen think you are trying to achieve, but let me assure you of one thing. You are not welcome.'

She disappeared back through the doors as two deck hands with biceps the size of tree trunks covered in military-style tattoos moved forward towards Greg and Kenny

wielding baseball bats in a fashion that suggested they were used to using them around heads and anatomy rather than playing at Dodger Stadium.

'On one?'

Kenny's words to Greg, who nodded briefly. Kenny shrugged.

'One!'

In a matter of seconds, and with a flurry of arms and legs as they went, the burly duo were no longer on board.

Greg couldn't help but be amazed by the boat. It was a different world. An on-board gym, massive TV screens everywhere, bars, hot tubs, swimming pool, amazing chandeliers – why the hell was he noticing fucking chandeliers? Enough. This was about finding Cavaleros.

They hurried down the corridor of the deck they had arrived on.

'Greg!'

Kenny was slightly ahead of him now. An elevator! It was in use.

'She's taken it. The woman. Has to be her.'

There was a staircase alongside the elevator. They made for the next level and on reaching it saw she was still going up. By the time they had sprinted up another the door was still open and mystery girl had gone, her scent drifting in her wake.

'Down here!'

Greg's first words for a while. They were heading towards the pointy bit of the boat. What was it called? The front bit? What did it matter? Greg's eyes darted around every room they passed. They hadn't encountered anyone else since the two beefy guys.

They were running out of boat and rooms. Still no sign of bikini girl. Through the most amazing bar and sitting room area that Greg had ever seen, sparkling sunshine and blue skies all around. It gave way to the most luxurious, astoundingly beautiful bedroom with probably the largest bed in the world and a breathtaking view of the ocean with windows all around its 180 degrees.

This was the final room.

The doors closed. Automatically. Greg and Kenny looked at each other despairingly. There was no way they were going to let one door faze them.

'On one?'

Greg nodded again back at Kenny. They ploughed into the door with the force of taking out an opposing forward.

What they hadn't reckoned on was that the door would prove just as formidable as some of their opponents on the park. Not the best news for their shoulders.

Kenny pointed at the windows. Greg threw his hands in the air. *'If the door is strong you can bet the windows will be … there!'*

Greg's eyes had been darting around the room, but he hadn't looked up, until now. Ventilation grille. Thank fuck. Now all they needed was to get to it. They tried moving the bed to get to it. No luck. It was held firm.

Greg tried reaching the grille direct from the bed. He was close to reaching but agonisingly just out of reach.

'The table! Hold it firm under me!'

Kenny grabbed up the decadent, marble-topped table that took a great deal of moving, especially for a man still bleeding from his torso from the impact of landing spectacularly and ungainly half on, half off, the boat just minutes ago.

'I don't know where the fuck you think you're going in this tub Cavaleros,' Greg muttered to himself as he managed to lever himself up through the grille, twisting and contorting to squeeze out on to the cabin's roof.

'You're running, why are you running? It has to be because of what you heard from Pablo, and you know about Carlos. That means it has to be because you know about Lucia? What do you know about her?'

Greg was still muttering to himself as he squeezed through and then laid down flat pulling with every sinew, every muscle he had available on Kenny's grip to get him up there too. He made it. Kenny scrambled through.

'You are proving very tiresome gentlemen.'

Diamond bikini woman had recruited two willing deputies, both female, slim and attractive, but carrying armaments, who flanked her now as she held a pistol directly at Greg, who had just jumped over the safety rail on to the main sundeck having negotiated the roof of the cabin below with Kenny following.

'This will not kill you, it will just dazzle you causing temporary …'

Whoever diamond bikini woman was, he wasn't waiting for her trigger finger on the gun.

Unlike the woman herself, the next moment was not going to be pretty.

Greg's head had often been referred to in newspaper reports as having been made of granite. Diamond was about to meet stone in spectacular fashion as Greg launched himself at her chin.

Diamond girl's jaw emitted a thunderous crack. She fell backwards and would have fallen with a slam on the deck floor if one of the two crew behind her hadn't reached out. It was this motion that allowed Greg to take the crew member holding her out too, while Kenny nailed the other. This was no time for chivalry. Greg and Kenny left all three in their wake as they fled for the stairs, making for the bridge.

This had to be the place. There had been hardly anyone on board so far and there had to be someone up here? Cavaleros.

Greg now clutched the dazzle gun he'd impounded from diamond bikini woman.

There were staircases either side of the bridge. Greg and Kenny split. In the far distance behind Bella Bebe, Greg saw a Policia Barco de Agua now speeding towards them.

Going back a year or so ago Greg would have felt no fear right now, but past experience told him to hesitate before reaching the door to the bridge. He was a couple of steps away when he heard another sound, a whirring noise? He looked hesitantly around the corner into the bridge itself.

No Juan Cavaleros. Instead, two women. He'd hoped he would find Lucia Dominguez, but what he'd not expected was …

CHAPTER 62

'Ciara!'

Kenny had appeared at the other side of the bridge. The Aussie stood open-mouthed. He couldn't move. Both he and Greg were momentarily stunned. Ciara. But she was dead, wasn't she? Obviously not.

Greg had little time for this right now. The noise he'd heard was becoming louder.

'Cavaleros?'

Both women nodded, Ciara and this other woman, mid-40s at a guess.

'Just him?'

Another nod.

It was appearing in front of them from the bow of the boat (the pointy bit!) where it had been stored. The whirring Greg had heard had been of the deck opening and the helipad rising 'like something out of bloody Thunderbirds!' Greg uttered not quite under his breath.

Cavaleros had made a dash from the bridge when he'd seen Greg and Kenny escape from the bedroom and inflict damage on diamond girl and her girls. The bridge showed CCTV of every area of the Bella Bebe.

He was now boarding the helicopter already manned by the pilot. Cavaleros turned while still making his way to the 'copter, to see Greg making his way towards him. He was signalling for the pilot to go although he still wasn't quite on board, hoping no doubt to leap on and they would be away.

'For crying out fucking loud, Greg, what next in my crazy life?' Greg again muttered to himself.

He was around 20 metres away when the helicopter lifted off. Cavaleros had leapt to the helicopter's open door and had nearly made it but was not sufficiently in as yet. The pilot, while trying to get the helicopter up safely, dragged him in further.

The 'copter was now around six feet off the Bella Bebe. Cavaleros looked around, back at Greg, a smile developing across his face, as he realised he was on board.

It was Juan Cavaleros's big mistake.

Greg pointed the dazzler and shot infra green at Cavaleros and for good measure at the pilot too. The aftermath was not for the faint of heart. Although temporarily blinded by the dazzler gun the pilot succeeded in lifting the 'copter further. Greg fired more infra-green beams. Somehow this triggered a control failure and then an engine malfunction. The 'copter's momentum meant it continued rising to around 100 metres from Bella Bebe. There was only one way it was to go from there with no engine.

Cavaleros and the pilot leaped from the 'copter before it started its descent. As they plunged so too did the whirring hump of metal and blades.

The forward thrust of the Bella Bebe meant the 'copter wouldn't land in the same place it started. The boat, with a length of 72 metres, would be unlikely to see all of its length through the water in time to enable the whirring metal to land anywhere other than on the boat.

It impacted near to the stern. The wreckage triggered a domino-like explosion heading back up towards the bridge. Greg signalled as frantically as possible to Kenny to get out, but he needn't have worried. Kenny and the two women – Ciara and the other older one were out and rushing towards him as the flames and explosions came their way.

The older woman pointed to where the helicopter had appeared from, in its separate hold. The rest of the boat's glam-kit was there, a multi-millionaire's garage. Greg jumped into the hold, grabbed the lightest floating item he could find, which was still bloody heavy – a dinghy the RNLI would have been proud to have as backup. He held it up while the other three pulled it clear.

With the fires, fireworks, explosions and 185 million pounds' worth of metal set to become the largest and most expensive ship burial ever seen off Lanzarote, Greg, Kenny, Ciara and the other woman threw the dinghy and jumped.

CHAPTER 63

They'd thrown themselves overboard into the open-sea, ocean side of the superyacht and with all of the devastation currently being wrought there was no way any of the now onrushing sea traffic could see them immediately. There was no time for words, but although it seemed much longer they were hauled aboard a rescue boat within minutes.

Kenny, having arrived back ashore with the others, was soon explaining to Det Sgt Arteta why, cataclysmic though this had been, he and Greg had other matters in hand that could not wait, and that they were quite willing to cooperate with the Policia, but after the game.

'How about we catch you later. We've a game to play in under two hours. We're not going anywhere. Come and have a beer and we'll tell you all about what's happened just now. You know where we'll be ... you know how much this game means to the island ...'

Kenny hoped the island pride line would work. He knew he'd made it sound as though they were just running late – which they were – not as though they had just been responsible for the biggest maritime disaster in Lanzarote's history.

Greg had stayed tight-lipped. He let Kenny do the talking. He'd done enough today. Far too much. And yet there was still so much more to do.

Win this game. That's where his brain had now transferred to. He'd found Ciara, okay not his intended target, but it had turned out she was the one to find. The rest would come clear later.

Detective Sergeant Alba Marta Arteta had wanted to question both Greg and Kenny immediately they had landed back at the marina. So many answers were needed, particularly from Senor Duggan. She had never been put in this position before. She made a quick decision. He was playing sport, not running away. She would allow he and Senor Lomax to go. She hoped that she was doing the right thing.

She contented herself with questioning Ciara Cortelli-O'Grady and Penny Pickup right now. She was the other woman. This was all massive. For the island, the club, law and order.

Arteta was also wondering how soon before this was taken up by Policia Nacional in Spain and how soon before she would be taken off the case. This wasn't like anything she'd ever led before.

Social media had gone crazy with mobile phone recordings and cameras from Canaria TV and Cloud TV, in readiness for Eruption's game had filmed and were reporting on 'Desastre Oceanico'.

Holidaymakers and Jags fans had even applauded the fireworks coming from Bella Bebe thinking it was part of Playa Blanca's summer festival that was due to start the next day.

Maria Cavaleros had arranged to spend another afternoon with Gina at Santiago's. They were getting on so well. She'd talked with GPK too.

When the chase had started GPK had joined with Janet and James at the marina. The sea drama had brought Playa Blanca to a standstill. Maria was at the marina too.

Never in her life, had Maria Cavaleros been so overjoyed. She had Ciara back from the dead.

Ciara Cortelli-O'Grady flew into her mother's arms. Maria's phone whistled. A text from Paddy O'Grady, similarly euphoric.

David Pickup walked purposely towards his wife.

'Darling, I thought I'd lost you,'

She could see tears rolling down his cheeks. She held out her hand to affectionately wipe them away. She had been so scared of this moment.'

Maria Cavaleros was ecstatic that her daughter was back. Her smile quite possibly the biggest in the whole of Lanzarote.

'But Senora Cavaleros,' Det Sgt Arteta was keen to reassert some kind of authority and make sense of what had just happened.

'Your husband …?'

'I lost him a long while ago. Whatever has happened has been coming a long while … now, why don't you come to the Estadio and conduct your investigations … that way you will know at least where everyone is … David, Penny? Be my guests … por favor?'

CHAPTER 64

'Jaglin Jags have made a fantastic start to this game Robbie.'

Karen King was teeing up her regular pundit Robbie Robertson after the underdogs had moved into an early six-point lead courtesy of a wondrous passing combination involving veteran centre Gary Procter, one of the very few sportsmen who had ever played as a professional in both rugby league and cricket; centre and ex-Super League player Johnny Ward; second-row and sometime club singer Graham Paddison; industrious team captain Mick Burke who had come up with his own bit of magic with a great reverse pass that had fed Mark 'Lowey' Lowcock who had come on to the ball like an express train and who had basketball-style popped a pass out for speedster and parkrun aficionado Malcolm Lavery to go over in the corner. George Ross had converted from way out on the touchline.

'Yep. We're used to seeing slow starts from The Eruption over the last few weeks, it seems as though they need to go behind in order to wake themselves up. The Jags are the better side right now.'

'That's right Robbie, and with only five of Eruption's regular starting line-up on the park at the moment this will be heaping stress on the likes of ever-so-young 16-year-old islander Francisco Alliossi who has had to come in at hooker to start his first ever game.'

Malky Shannon had made the decision. He hadn't known where the two of them had got to and he'd had to prepare for them not being available. When they'd arrived back at the El Estadio de Lanzarote just 15 minutes before kick-off he'd already given out the team sheet, told the players and was working with what he had. He'd put them both on the bench.

He'd been ecstatic when he'd seen Greg and Kenny arrive, but they had both hardly looked in a fit state and he was adamant that neither were to start the game. He'd reasoned that they would be fitter the longer they had to recover. Neither player could argue with his logic, but going behind, especially in this game, was not something they relished.

'*The Jags are running the ball again here. Oh! That's terrific ball-handling by Jags' loose forward Big Chris Jeffery. He's sold Angel Ramos a real dummy. Oh! And what a step inside. Well, I know he's used to treading carefully around his Whitebred Shorthorn cattle back on his farm in North Yorkshire but that was outrageous.*'

Karen King was in her element relaying interesting facts about players.

'*Fantastic tackle by Fastleigh … but Farmer Chris, that's Big Chris Jeffery, makes an incredible pass before his ball-carrying arm hits the turf and it's captain Mick Burke charging on to the ball with just young Alliossi in front of him … no contest, and he's in! Robbie, Eruption have to get this sorted or their dream will be over before half-time!*'

George Ross had the easiest of kicks in front of the posts. Eruption 0 Jags 12. The Jags' faithful were in full voice. Their fans starting to believe the impossible. It was déjà vu for the Eruption fans.

Stu Wainwright and Aussie loose forward Manny Roberts were rallying Eruption as best they could. Tonito and Popoli Baru, who had both made superb debuts against Hudderford Town in the championship decider, had not yet touched the ball or laid a finger on anyone.

Ron Rigson and Roberto Ortega were injured. Ron before the game had started, Roberto in the first couple of minutes.

'*All over before halftime!? It could be way before then if this carries on. We're only at fifteen minutes,*' Robbie Robertson couldn't help but pin his colours to the mast for Canaria TV.

'*El Juego Que Define. The game that defines the season. Well, at this rate it will be the game that draws a line under it for Eruption … this is brilliant play by the Jags, take nothing away from them.*'

Jags' Big Chris Jeffery relished this kind of game. He'd made the shift from rugby union to rugby league and had played for several clubs that had challenged for higher status.

'*Farmer Chris is laying down the law, Robbie. He's leading this charge.*'

Karen King's comment came as the TV screen for each

viewer at home or in the bars filled with the giant loose forward.

Robbie had been watching even more closely.

'There's something happening down there, Karen. I have no idea what's coming, but they are on it right now.'

Malky Shannon was under the pump, but he'd been under it many times in his career. He knew a twelve-point deficit could easily become eighteen, twenty-four and thirty. He was used to hearing pearls of wisdom from the bench, director's seats and the main stands, but he'd always found it best to go with what he felt, his own reading of the game. He was the same now.

He glanced across at Kenny and Greg. He had to hold them back as long as he could.

Stu Wainwright took the kick-off, launching the ball high into the Playa Blanca sky that was nearing dusk with the floodlights now in operation. The ball disappeared into the lights coming down close to the Jags 20-metre line.

There was only one man of this moment.

Big Chris Jeffery took the ball as the onrushing Eruptors tried to get to him before he could make headway. Angel Ramos and Raul Rodriguez-Perez were no slouches, but Farmers Chris's tail was well and truly up.

FC, as he was also nicknamed, feigned to pass inside, stepped and darted past both Lanzarote-born players. Jeffery, buoyed by how easily he'd managed it once, tried again with Francisco Alliossi and found that the youngster might have been green, but he was up for the game.

'Oh, that's a superb hit!' exclaimed Karen King.

'Welcome to the party, young man,' Robbie Robertson was impressed. *'I don't think Big Chris Jeffery knows which day of the week it is at the moment.'*

'I think you're right Robbie, he certainly put Farmer Chris to sleep there. He didn't even need to count his sheep to get there either.'

The band, that had made its debut at the championship title decider but had been noticeably quiet until now since the kick-off, started up with 'You're just too good to be true ...' The crowd picked up when it reached '... Can't take my eyes off you'.

Another islander was coming good.

One tackle wasn't to change the game, but it had proved a fillip for the Eruption fans.

The band, now increasingly relishing the role they could play, continued with a slightly extended repertoire including a tribal beat in between the memorable pop tunes. The beat inspired the crowd.

Estadio de Lanzarote was coming alive.

Greg's brain was not where it should be. He was watching, ready for when he was needed. But was he ready? His body was a mass of bruises, aches, pains and possibly even an odd small broken bone thrown in somewhere for good measure.

Why the island? Alegranza. Why leave him there? Why the roadblock with the cage with Adriana Gomez? How would they know he'd be there at that time? Pablo. Carlos. They both made sense. But Cavaleros?

What about Luis Hidalgo who he'd just seen? He wouldn't have had the time to organise something would he? No, had to be Carlos. Why would Carlos and Pablo be doing this? Money. Back to Cavaleros.

He'd found Ciara, not Lucia? That was a result, for Ciara. But who had Maria and Paddy buried? Did they know it wasn't Ciara they were burying? Did nobody check? What kind of island was this? Greg's head was spinning.

Susie had gone. Had she? What did that mean? Did that mean anything? Was it involved? Bearing in mind what Kraft had put in his head.

'*And that's a terrific run from Vincent Venus! … Lovely turn of pace from centre Alan Thomas that puts him in the clear, they won't catch him … and Eruption are IN this game at last …*'

'*It all goes back to the tackle made by young Alliossi a few minutes ago, Karen,*' Robbie Robertson was enthused.

'*Sometimes you need that spark to ignite your team and the crowd and it seems to have done the trick. Excellent from Venus. He's becoming more the real deal with every game.*'

Neither Greg nor Kenny leaped out of their seats when

Vinny went over the whitewash for his try. They pumped fists and Kenny smiled his famed gap-toothed grin. Greg was still elsewhere.

Being left on Alegranza, island of fucking joy! Maybe he had never been meant to be found alive. That bloody hood. Two days! He could still feel it around his neck now. That time inside the hood had been like closing his eyes and uncannily, it had made things clear.

'... and that's another fabulous hit from Francisco Alliossi who was actually born right here in Playa Blanca. Robbie, this lad had never heard of rugby league until early this year.'

'You know, Karen, our sport is the best in the world and now, with expansion into areas like here in the Canary Islands, people can see just what a game this is. Big respect to the lad.'

Eruption were holding their own. They hadn't converted Vinny Venus's try and were 4-12 down but the game had changed from a one-sided affair to a war of attrition as both sets of players laid their bodies on the line.

At twenty-five minutes Malky Shannon made his first interchanges. Two more teenagers with no big match experience – another Lanzarote lad, Adrian Demorala and a lad from mainland Spain but who now lived on the island, Carlos Olivera.

In order to keep experience on the park they were interchanged with Angel Ramos and Raul Rodriguez-Perez, which left them with the youngest ever front row trio of Demorala, Alliossi and Olivera.

Malky knew this was ridiculous. The biggest game yet in the club's very short history.

How many clubs succeeded with two 16-year-olds and a 17-year-old spearheading a challenge, against a team that was already in the lead, had players who were poised for their greatest moment and had all the experience in the world? Christ, even Stu Wainwright at 19 and Vincent Venus at 20 now looked like seasoned campaigners for Eruption against these lads he was blooding.

'*Robbie, this game was billed as El Juego Que Define but it could be more like El Cinco Minutos Que Define. I don't mean to be a bit previous here, but this could be sending lambs to the slaughter couldn't it?*'

Robbie Robertson saw the humour and added to it.

'*I think I just saw Farmer Chris licking his lips like some kind of real Jaguar about to enjoy his breakfast.*'

Greg's head was still whirring.

Susie – been, and now gone, for the second time. Ciara – found. He'd been asked to find Lucia – he'd found Ciara instead, what about Lucia? And then Quinigan – not involved in any of this, or was he? If he wasn't where did the Latex Twins fit? Had they been involved in the Lucia thing?

Get back to what he could influence. He leant back, exhaled. Big breaths followed, filling his lungs with air. He made to get up. For God's sake! Everything ached. He stood, moved his head around. Felt like ball-bearings crunching in his neck. Took a few stretches and started warming up.

The Eruption fans responded to what was happening along the touchline. The atmosphere suddenly turned electric.

'*Du-GAN! Du-GAN! Du-GAN!*' rang out all around the stadium that seemed to be close to capacity. The band started up once more with 'You're just too good to be true' and the Lanzarote fans joined at full throttle on the chorus with the 'La-la-la-la, La La la' and substituting 'I love you baby' with 'We love you Du-GAN!'

Gina was watching from the stand, making her official debut as club owner, alongside Maria Cavaleros and Ciara. Paddy O'Grady was there too, making a rare public appearance.

Gina had arranged for the words to the song to appear on Cloud TV's big screen to help the locals with their English. It had been a masterstroke. The buzz that now went all around the ground produced an inspiring tackling spell from the Eruptors on the field. And Greg's strains, pains and tired muscles were re-energised. He was ready. Karen King was loving it.

'*In all my years of commentary I have never heard that kind of reaction merely from a player getting up from the bench!'*

'Absolutely Karen. Definitely the Greg Duggan Factor!' Robbie was similarly entranced.

'But here comes Big Chris Jeffery, charging at the Eruption defence. He's aiming to spoil this party, make no mistake.'

Farmer Chris was in no mood to be overawed and pounded into Manny Roberts but, as he did so, released a deft flick pass out to crafty stand-off John Orange who jinked and made a further five yards before firing out a pass to Mark 'Lowey' Lowcock.

Eruption were covering as quickly as they could, the new boys trying hard to get to the pace of the game.

Captain Mick Burke scooped a ball from a wayward pass, darted between youngsters Demorala and Olivera, and put a little grubber kick through that saw the ball flicking over and over towards the try-line with heavy traffic following in the ball's wake in the form of winger Malcolm Lavery and scrum-half George Ross, but out of nowhere it was Francisco Alliossi once more for Eruption who kicked the ball into touch and out of their despairing hands.

Greg had felt the surge of emotion from the crowd as he had stood. He'd never experienced anything like it. The moment banished other thoughts immediately. He was now itching to get on.

'The atmosphere down here is so intense, Karen,' pitchside reporter Max Sunderland gave his version of what life was like on the benches of both camps.

'Jags' coach and scrum-half legend Billy Smith and Eruption's Malky Shannon. They're both happy with the way their sides have been performing ... Billy says he wants his team to capitalise on their possession ... Malky wants to get his team through to half-time without shipping any more points ...'

'... I cannot remember a single penalty being given in the first half-hour, Robbie ...' Karen King added.

'... that's a tribute to the spirit in which this game is being played, Karen. I can't see us getting through the whole game that way ...

'… *if Jags get the next score, they will be back in the driving seat. If Eruption get it then this place will go mad. But either way neither side scoring next will decide who wins this game just yet.*'

'*Strap yourselves in if you've not done that already folks! This one's got a long way to go!*'

The next minutes was all about Jags' pressure. Jeffery, Lowcock, Paddison and Lavery all went close and Eruption's young boys were holding firm.

Five minutes until half-time. Malky nodded towards both Greg and Kenny.

The pair rose from the bench together. The roar went up from the crowd. The band started up again – and this time with a new tune. Trumpets, drums and steel drums sent the Eruption fans into a summer ecstasy with hips moving and bodies swaying. The words once again came up on the big screen.

'Ole, Ole, Ole, Ole … Feeling Hot, Hot, Hot … Feeling Hot, Hot, Hot …'

'*Well here we go!*'

Karen King's voice now sounded as though she was working on the waltzers in a fairground.

'*Greg Duggan has entered the building – or field in this case – and Kenny Lomax too. Now what can they do?*'

Malky had interchanged the dynamic duo with Ron Rigson and Francisco Alliossi, who received a fantastic reception from the crowd. Billy Smith also interchanged second row forward Richard Clements and winger Mark Webster from his charges, bringing on hard hitting Kendall Jackson and Phillip Holden.

'*Billy Smith is a canny coach, Karen,*' pointed out Robbie Robertson.

'*He's been watching and waiting for when Malky Shannon was going to make these changes and these two guys have been put on with one purpose. They're here to hurt them. This could be explosive.*'

The second Greg's boot had stepped over the whitewash on to the park his whole body had reacted – and not in the best of ways. His legs suddenly felt like lead, his arms weak.

But the crowd! As he loosened up and the crowd had fired up, Greg felt good.

The first penalty of the game had just gone the way of the Jags.

Twenty-five yards out from the posts Jags' scrum-half and kicker George Ross had pinged one straight through the uprights to take his team two points further in the lead at 4-14.

Kenny took no time at all in getting the backs organised.

Greg was setting to kick for the restart. They'd come up with a unique move they hoped would work, but would certainly surprise everyone. Instead of placing the ball on one of its pointed ends and retreating around five or six yards for a run-up, Greg laid the ball flat, kicked it slightly off-centre middle and it span towards the 10-metre line.

The quick play, with the Jags expecting a ball in the air and unready for such a short run-up, let alone short kick-off, had them flat-footed and Vinny Venus had beaten the Jags to it by several metres and had taken it a further ten metres before being tackled by Paddison and Holden.

'Does this man have some kind of new playbook for the game. Greg Duggan comes on to the field and immediately something different happens ... oh, hold on here ... he's on the ball again already ... he's dummied Kendall Jackson and he's in the clear!'

Greg didn't know where this had come from, but he was suddenly transformed. Hurt like hell, yeah, but by God he was going for it.

'He's in acres of space. He's pinned back his ears, he's got Jags' Malcolm Lavery tracking him down and John Orange. He's heading for the corner ... and Greg Duggan has ... has he? Has he scored? ... well, referee John Cloudsdale has gone to the big screen, but he's given the try on the field.'

'This man never ceases to amaze me,' Robbie Robertson added to Karen King's words.

'I don't think there is a more complete player in the championship than Greg Duggan. That try, and it will be awarded, was perfection. Perfect in its unique start and in its execution.'

Vinny Venus had played the ball quickly after being hauled down and Kenny Lomax had immediately appeared at the play-the-ball behind him. He'd played a fast, flat pass out to Alan Thomas who had offloaded one-handed to New Zealand centre Warren Entish who had played the ball back on the inside on seeing Greg hurtling on.

Just how Greg had managed it after the past few days even he didn't know. He'd had three Jags steaming after him and had launched himself into the air as full-back Charlie Cole had appeared from his side attempting to take him out into touch, his right shoulder having spiralled Greg's body towards the whitewash.

The big screen replay showed Greg flying acrobatically, Cole's body mixed with Greg's, with Lavery and Orange also throwing themselves at him. Greg's body had been shifted in the air towards being out of play but critically and crucially the screen showed Greg's right hand telescoping over the top of the mass of limbs and flesh, which now also included the efforts of Procter, and Greg touching the ball down cleanly. TRY! the big screen announced.

The crowd, that had erupted for Eruption a minute ago when it was in real time, then having held its collective breath and having celebrated on seeing the replay, lifted the roof off El Estadio. The band struck up once more with 'Hot Hot Hot'. This was carnival time.

Greg had set up for the conversion attempt way before the pronouncement. He'd known he'd scored. But going over for a try in the corner meant a kick from the most difficult position on the field, wide out to the right and at a tricky angle. They were back within six points now, but if this went over the difference would be just four.

That kind of gap would have been more than Malky Shannon could have hoped for after the opening ten minutes. Greg was composed. He didn't attempt anything other than to hit the ball sweetly. It sailed through. The crowd continued its festivities.

'That sets us up for one heck of a second-half here at El Estadio de Lanzarote. I hope, wherever you are, that you're not of a nervous disposition because this has all the hallmarks of a game that will not go away until the final hooter … but we are not even there yet, we're still in the first half … and with Greg Duggan on the park who knows what will happen.'

Jaglin Jaguars had taken the game to Lanzarote Eruption for the greater part of the first half but knew that pressure without points was never good.

'George Ross has gone the complete opposite route to Greg Duggan's kick-off. He's sent his kick into orbit! It has gone way up into Playa Blanca's night sky. The hang time on this will be one of the longest … and it gives the Jags chance to come up quickly …'

Underneath the ball was arguably the star player of the first half until Greg's arrival, Francisco Alliossi. He'd had to make a swift return as Tonito had picked up a knock.

Alliossi had the fearlessness of youth, his eyes remained fixedly on the ball. He was aware of the approaching stampede. Jeffery, Paddison and the fresh recruits Jackson and Holden were set with one objective.

It was Big Chris Jeffery who wiped him out. Fairly, squarely and sent the young man into the middle of next week. He was spark out. Referee Cloudsdale stopped the clock with one minute 45 seconds left in the half. The crowd was hushed momentarily as the medics came on.

Francisco Alliossi's mum, Liliana, so proud for thirty-eight minutes of the game, was incandescent. She ran on the pitch. Paying no attention to any form of security nor protocol she galloped from her seat in the stand.

Liliana was clearly no slouch, making it across the park to her son before the stretcher bearers had arrived, but on seeing that her boy was already showing signs of recovery and that he was going through the motions of regulatory tests her ire was directed towards Big Chris Jeffery. She slapped him hard in the face and sent her knee into his nether regions. He collapsed to his knees and she threw a right hook, which fortunately didn't land. The Eruption crowd applauded, as well as going into hysterics.

Liliana was shepherded away by the stewards as Francisco made his way somewhat gingerly from the field. Angel Ramos was hastily pushed back into action.

Francisco had collected the ball and hadn't spilled it, in spite of the hit he'd received. There was no penalty. Eruption played the ball from their 20-metre line and there was almost a collective acceptance this would be good enough for the first half.

Stu Wainwright hadn't been noticed for England Lions selection for nothing. He read games and he felt that following the lull there would be those who would have switched off ready for the hooter.

He saw the way the Jags defence had been slow to get back to its mark and had been sluggish coming back to close Eruption down in the first two tackles since Francisco's departure.

The young international hopeful took the ball at dummy-half following a dart from Warren Entish. He waved a hand behind his back just prior which alerted Vinny Venus to come across diagonally from his right side and take a little pass as he ran through on the left.

Vinny ran out wide towards the touchline but had too many bodies around him to make it through. He tried to offload but it proved too dangerous. He went down to the combined tackle of Lavery and Ross forty yards out from the Jags' try line.

One minute of the half was left on the clock. Greg received the ball from Alan Thomas who had been their only player who could stick with Vinny.

Greg had seen the same as Stu. The Jags weren't on their toes. Greg took the ball up five metres, spun as Jackson reached him and made to offload the ball in one of the biggest pass gestures. Jackson thought he had him, so too did Burke, but Greg turned a complete 360 degrees and fled their clutches, freeing his shirt, with a sprint that was not going to get him across the line but was to give the young, fresh, pacy Adrian Demorala a race for the line that wasn't going to be denied.

'What a fantastic way to finish this extraordinary first-half fightback by Eruption. Young 16-year-old Adrian Demorala, playing his first senior game, has gone in for a try that brings the scores level. And, Robbie, it's that man again, Greg Duggan, pulling the strings …'

'You don't need to say the name, Karen, just listen … in these last three Eruption games we have been fortunate to witness the arrival of a player who can turn games on their head …'

In just five minutes Lanzarote Eruption had turned around a deficit to a lead that was to be confirmed with Greg's conversion. 16-14.

Jags Coach Billy Smith had seen it all in his career. He knew his side could play but he also knew their weaknesses. He would tell his lads he was delighted they were still in this game and to go again in the second half as they'd started the first. In Big Chris Jeffery, Mick Burke, Mark Lowcock, George Ross, Graham Paddison and the rest he had players with big hearts who would run all day for the cause.

Eruption's young lads couldn't have been higher than if they'd been on something they shouldn't have been. Demorala had a smile as wide as the ocean between Lanzarote and Fuerteventura, Ramos and Rodriguez-Perez his fellow islanders were ecstatic for the young lad and Alliossi, who still didn't look back to sorts since his hit, managed a fist pump.

As the Eruption players and officials left the field, Greg made his way to the grandstand. He had seen someone earlier.

CHAPTER 65

Greg's movement towards the stand brought about a standing ovation from everyone close by as he approached. Within seconds the rest of the spectators joined in. Greg hadn't been anticipating it but raised his hands above his head applauding them in return. He turned to acknowledge the fans all around who raised up the chant of 'Du-GAN! Du-GAN! Du-GAN' once again.

The band, several of whom had just downed tools for the half-time break, struck up again with 'Ole-Ole-Ole-Ole' and 'Feeling Hot-Hot-Hot'. Greg continued to walk purposefully to the front row of the grandstand where a woman sat with her child who was in a wheelchair. She was wiping his brow. Greg wiped away his own beads of sweat with his arm.

'Mrs Alliossi? Sorry … Senorita Alliossi. Would you like to come and see your boy? Francisco?'

Greg thought maybe Liliana's English was as good as his Spanish, maybe this wasn't going to work, but she smiled.

'He is okay … but if you want to be sure …?'

Greg motioned with his hands and then asked about the boy in the wheelchair.

'Your boy too?'

He rolled his hands around as he tried to get the right words. For God's sake he'd have to learn the language if he was going to stay here. He pointed to her and to her boy.

'Your … chico?' He'd heard chico mentioned along the way for lads.

Liliana smiled.

'Si, Senor, yes … Leonardo …'

Liliana helped Greg as she could see him, his eyes, struggling to ask why.

'Es Paralisis Cerebral …'

'How old?'

Greg asked. He didn't know whether she understood, but she

grasped it as Greg tried to move his hands in some way that denoted growing.

'*Tres.*'

Greg nodded in reply.

'*My son ... my boy ... tres ... Kyle ... come, both of you, see Francisco ...*'

Greg motioned with his hand.

'*Can I ...*'

He put his hand to his chest. '*Can I help?*' He motioned again, this time as though to help Leonardo with his wheelchair.

'*No Senor!*' Liliana explained. '

Leonardo ... is him, he ... drives?'

The trio of Liliana, Leonardo and Greg began making their way in the direction of the dressing room. The crowd responded.

Greg had seen the same look in Liliana's eyes as he'd seen in his wife Diane's last year when she'd lost their unborn child. He just wanted to make sure she knew her son was fine, but he had also inadvertently enhanced his already glowing reputation even further. It had been an emotional moment in the midst of all this other chaos.

By the time Greg had reassured Liliana, by getting Francisco to come out of the dressing room to see her, and then making sure she had someone to take her and Leonardo back to her seat, the half-time interval was nearly over.

Up in the Estadio Rooftop Bar, the ladies that now ran the club, Gina and Maria, were entertaining the Jaglin Jags owner, chairman and officials.

The Jags also had a lady owner Amanda Clarke, a lovely lady with a radiant smile who was getting along famously with them. Amanda had been seen as a breath of fresh air for the game when she had become involved and fervently believed in the expansion of the sport.

Detective Sergeant Alba Marta Arteta and Detective Constable Moreno had been questioning Ciara and, in the light of his daughter's return Paddy O'Grady had also deigned to assist them with their inquiries. Maria had been questioned before the game, with Greg and Kenny to follow later.

Ricardo Ricart and Hugo Silva were present, both seemingly there for nothing more than pressing flesh. Talk was inevitably centring on the day's sea drama.

'And for anyone who has been around this stadium in the past few games you will know that things don't come easy. Lanzarote Eruption have had a tough season in the sun, here in the Canary Islands. And then there's Jaglin Jags, who have been this year's surprise package. Are you ready for part two of El Juego Que Define?'

Karen King was.

'You're both coming off after five minutes, so give me everything, flat out, then get yourselves ready for the last ten,' Malky's calculus hadn't been wrong so far. Greg and Kenny had no complaints as he gave them the news just before the restart.

Malky's plan didn't bring any more points. It was the Jags who had made the better start, as they had in the first half. Winger Malcolm Lavery went close, only to be denied by a great tackle from Popoli Baru; Big Chris Jeffery and Graham Paddison combined to send over Johnny Ward who was adjudged to have been held up over the line, rather than touching down. Greg and Kenny duly scampered off after five minutes as instructed.

The next fifteen minutes saw the game settle into its attritional stage once again. The crowd was quiet after the frenzy at the end of the first half.

With sixty-one of the eighty minutes having passed Shirley Fastleigh took the ball up hard on the halfway line, managed to extend his hand out as he was being tackled and shovelled a pass to Manny Roberts who hammered into Jags' forward, Welshman Richard Clements.

It was a juddering hit with his forearm that referee John Cloudsdale had no other choice but to offer a penalty to the Jags and worse still, a ten-minute sin-binning of Mannion Roberts.

George Ross, one of the league's most reliable goalkickers, had no hesitation in taking the kick fifty-one metres from the sticks. His accuracy was never in question and the length he achieved on his kick showed he still had another ten metres at least in him. The Jags fans, now back all square at 16-16 became more vocal.

Two minutes later and they really did have something to shout about as they hit the lead again with a towering drop-goal from forty yards, again George Ross. Jags fans were not quite up for believing they might win just yet, but their team was giving them hope and the clock was ticking down. Eruption 16 Jags 17.

When a rampant Big Chris Jeffery charged over having made a barnstorming run in which he'd taken no prisoners from twenty-five yards out the island side began to look a spent force. George Ross converted the easy points with a kick bang in front of the posts.

The Jags fans were singing, the loudest they had sung all game. Urging on their heroes. Thirteen minutes left and they were ahead 16-23. Eruption had to score twice. The Jags had no band, but their combined voices were beginning to resonate louder around the ground as Eruption's following looked forlorn.

Malky Shannon looked firmly ahead at the game. His plan had been to put Greg and Kenny on for the final ten minutes. He was tempted to put them on now, but stuck to his plan.

There were another five minutes before they would be back up to their full complement when Manny finished his ten minutes in the bin.

Popoli Baru hadn't really been at the races all game. Eruption were under pressure again. Vinny Venus had scrambled on to a ball two yards from the try line and had been tackled. He played the ball to Warren Entish who had made metres. Alan Thomas and Carlos Olivera had both contributed since. Tackles were running out and Eruption had made little headway. Tonito took the ball from the latest play-the-ball by Olivera and fed Baru.

It was a split-second error. Baru was looking for who he was going to pass to rather than watching the ball and mishandled. Worse still the ball went to ground and quick-thinking George Ross hacked it through towards the Eruption line.

The next few seconds became a mass of bodies, arms and legs once again that referee John Cloudsdale had to decipher, but in the end he opted for going to the big screen, with his on-field decision to award the try.

It was now down to a frame-by-frame playback. The decision took an age.

'*And it's another try for Farmer Chris,*' announced Karen King. '*Popoli Baru is inconsolable. Devastating for Eruption, but a terrific period of the game for the Jags. They've thoroughly deserved this, Robbie. And there's the kick from the impeccable boot of George Ross.*'

From out of nowhere, a lone voice was heard throughout the ground. A female voice. The girl was holding a microphone. She was by the side of the pitch.

'*You're just too good to be true, can't take my eyes off you,*' and then launched into a shout. '*Come on everybody! Get behind us! We need you all right now!*' She sang the lead up to the chorus and the crowd began joining in, when they hit '*I love you baby*' the band was there too.

Malky Shannon put Kenny and Greg back on as Gina Irvine led the crowd. Nine and a half minutes left and Eruption thirteen points adrift at 16-29. Surely this was beyond Greg.

Gina was orchestrating the crowd now.

'*Come on! We're feeling Hot-Hot-Hot ... and on cue the band began with Ole-Ole-Ole-Ole ...*'

Whether or not what Gina was doing would be frowned upon by the rugby league's governing hierarchy, she'd done it. And the crowd was alight. Eruption fans were back in the spirit and having fun, Jags fans were feeling great too. 'Du-Gan, Du-Gan!!' was heard all around the ground as he came on.

Greg's first touch on coming back on was to restart the game. Jags would be wise to his earlier gambit, probably best not doing the same again, but then as he started setting the ball as though to be upright for kicking high he thought, why not?

And without thinking any more, and with no run up he slithered the ball along again for a second time, again spinning, it reached just over the ten-yard line and once again Vinny Venus raced towards it, grasping control before the Jags had reset their minds to what was happening.

This time he picked it up by his fingertips and continued his run, showing great balance as he danced past two and then three Jags defenders. Gary Procter and winger Malcolm Lavery were hurriedly trying to cover.

Lavery launched himself at Venus but Vinny flicked a pass out of the backdoor, the back of his hand, to centre partner Alan Thomas who didn't just go over the line but was able to put the ball down just to one side of the posts.

If the game had felt lost before Gina had taken the crowd in hand and before Greg and Kenny had come back on, then life was very different now.

'*Alan Thomas! Great try by the centre! And what a run by Vincent Venus. These two have been a great partnership all season, but how many players would have thought to use the same trick twice as Greg Duggan has just shown us?*'

Karen King and Robbie Robertson were both shaking their heads.

'*Pure magic! And there's the kick. It's over! And back on to the field comes Mannion Roberts. Wow! This game looked for all the world like it had gone for Eruption, but the girl who sang at the reintroduction of Greg Duggan and Kenny Lomax, the kick-off, the run by Venus, just Wow! Wow!*'

'*Wow indeed! Now, don't go anywhere for the next seven minutes. There are seven points in the game. Eruption need two scores wherever they come from. Jags need to hold firm. Seven minutes for a shot at getting into Super League. If you haven't already made your cuppa, it can wait. If you need to get a beer, get the dog to get it for you.*'

Kick-off for the restart was from Ross. He opted to go deep. The more he could keep Eruption back the better it was for Jags. They'd have to do the yards to get in to position. It would eat up time.

Ross kicked for distance. Tonito took the ball and immediately fed Warren Entish. The New Zealander looked to make ground as the Jags defensive line came up as one. He went to ground fifteen metres out.

Kenny picked up, shimmied to his right then stepped off his left and then his right to send him clear of Paddison and Clements. He weaved his way across the park before straightening up again, dummying stand-off John Orange and scrum-half George Ross to scurry through another opening.

The crowd was going wild. The drums were beating, trumpets blaring. Kenny knew to put his head down and charged on. Thirty metres, twenty, ten to go. He'd not scored a try like this for years.

And he wasn't to now either. With the tryline in sight he felt the clip of a hand against his right heel, which flicked on to his left and he was going down five yards short.

As he was falling he saw an image of red and blue and flicked the ball up in the air. It was Alan Thomas who gathered again and who dived in for the try in the corner.

'Kenny Lomax has just turned back the clock to his Grand Finals days in Australia! That was one amazing, weaving, mesmerising run. And again, finished by master try scorer Alan Thomas. Phew! Now, if Greg Dugan gets this kick over it is down to a one-point ballgame.'

This time it wasn't to be for Greg. They'd needed one more score regardless, but this meant it had to be a try, nothing else would do.

'Three minutes left on the clock, I'm an absolute mess, I don't know what you're like if you're watching at home. Oh, now look what's happening here.'

Malky Shannon had been the ringmaster throughout the game. He brought back Francisco Alliossi. Warm applause added to the fervour around the ground. Carlos Olivera came off to make way.

'Francisco Alliossi, looking as though he was out like a light in the first half, is back and looking fresh. Still strapped in? Here we go!'

The last restart. Three minutes. Three points the difference. George Ross was a wily campaigner and still had tricks in his box.

Ross had his own take on kick-off plays. This time he wanted the ball from it. He wanted it to have an easy hang time and land around twelve to fifteen metres inside Eruption's half for

Big Chris Jeffery to touch it back basketball-style to another of the Jags.

He walked back from setting the ball in position to its underside and set a backspin. Deliberately taking as much time as he could to eat up the clock further, he stepped back six paces and two to the left. He then managed to find reason to tap mud from his boots. He set off, but then mysteriously found another reason to stop and tap again.

'*I've not restarted the clock yet George. In your own time!*' referee John Cloudsdale had seen it all before in his years as a rugby league whistler. He knew how they all tried it on, having been an equally wily player in his day.

Ross smiled, shrugged his shoulders and gave a look that cried out 'can't blame me for trying'. He kicked a beautiful spiralling backspin bomb that Big Chris Jeffery managed to get a hand to and palmed it back for George Ross himself.

'*George Ross has just pulled off one of the most remarkable restart plays, well since the last one by Greg Duggan a few minutes ago! … what a knock back by Jeffery … and Ross is there again … that's not what Eruption needed … and he's feinted left, straightened up and he's gone for goal! … and it's there! It's Eruption 26 Jags 30.*'

Karen King left the next line for Robbie Robertson.

'*It's a fabulous kick and that was perfection from Ross and Jeffery. He's extended the Jags' lead, plus they get the ball back from Eruption's restart.*'

One minute twenty-five seconds to go. Another restart.

Greg had closed his eyes as George Ross's amazing kick had soared through the uprights. For seconds everything in his world stopped. For seconds it was all too much. His limbs suddenly ached again everywhere. Wrists and ankles burnt like hell. Muscles pulled. The lot.

When he opened them he saw Leonardo, who would never have the chance to play, to have these kind of moments, through no fault of his own. He saw Kyle in Leonardo.

There was no way he could pull the same kick-off trick three times in a row. Could he? Nope. He held his right hand up. A sign for where it was going. He kicked it left. High. The chase was on. Whose nerve would break in these final seconds? The kick was received by Charlie Cole. The message had gone out. Don't drop it! Keep the ball alive.

On the fourth tackle kick towards the Eruption line. Three tackles in and down to fifty seconds on the clock, George Ross took the ball from the play-the-ball, not first receiver as had been intended.

Ross played it back to Burke who had Jeffery set to kick. It was going to be tight. He tried to make room to get the ball away. He could go down in the tackle. They would still have one more tackle to go.

Francisco Alliossi hadn't planned on this being a showdown, but it couldn't have worked better. Big Chris Jeffery launched his boot at the ball, Alliossi charged it down. The ball went forward off him. Alliossi ran on to the loose ball that was now thirty metres from the Jags' line, scooped it with one hand and raced over, placing the ball in between the posts. 30-30. Greg's conversion was the last play of the night. 32-30. Eruption erupted!

The celebrations for the championship decider had been muted in comparison to those that came at the hooter in Estadio de Lanzarote for Le Juego Que Define.

CHAPTER 66

'Senor Duggan, perhaps you could give me your account of this afternoon.'

Detective Sergeant Arteta was coming to the end of a tiring day. She had no idea Greg's had spanned the past three days. Greg had showered and changed and had met with Arteta as they had agreed. He was now officially, if he hadn't been previously, totally knackered. He raised his eyebrows, breathed in deeply and started.

'I threw the manager of the hotel, where I am staying, over a balcony because he had put me in the hands of people who were set to kill me. I threw the owner of the restaurant to the ground near the cliff edge because he was involved with people who were set to kill me. I temporarily blinded the previous owner of this rugby league club because he was intent on killing me.'

He stopped. Greg looked directly at Arteta. If she wanted more, she would have to ask. He wasn't being obstructive.

Arteta responded with the same look, straight. They were both quiet. Greg was in no rush. Sleep would have been preferable, but he could do quiet like this.

'Pablo Marizio Gonzalez, the hotel under-manager ...'

Arteta added Pablo's official title for point of reference.

'... has multiple injuries, including possible but as yet not fully diagnosed brain trauma.'

Greg didn't have to try to keep calm. He was almost comatose. Arteta moved on to Greg's next victim.

'Carlos Cuadrado, the restaurateur at Al's or to be exact Chiquitita's Chiringuito, is dead, recovered from the sea and rocks at Playa de la Cera.'

Greg nodded. He knew he was dead.

'I know. I saw Adriana Gomez shoot him and then kick him off the cliff edge.'

Arteta gave a deep breath through tight lips and breathed

out through her nose.

'*Juan Cavaleros is dead, and his helicopter pilot. There are several other people missing from the Bella Bebe ...*'

Alba Marta Arteta was more purposeful here. This had been a gradual walk-up to watching any change in Greg. She was gearing up for her next step, wanted to see how he reacted.

'*... two men managed to save themselves by jumping ship ...*'

Greg remained impassive.

Arteta could feel a certain bristling from Greg. She was ready to drop the bomb. What she felt would give her a reaction. Perhaps then they could start making headway.

'*Are you aware of Bella Bebe's owner Senor Duggan?*'

From what Kenny had mentioned that would have been Pickup, husband of the woman on the boat.

'*Does the name Magdalena mean anything to you?*'

No reaction. Arteta quickly expanded.

'*Ana Cristina Magdalena?*'

Again, Greg looked blank. He was either very good at holding his nerve or he really didn't know. Arteta was now inclined to believe it was the latter. She loosened up.

'*Greg ...*' This was a surprising departure. Arteta coming away from her harder approach and trying to befriend.

'*... were you not aware of Senorita Magdalena, earlier today, having allegedly taken over the ownership of the Lanzarote Eruption club and El Estadio de Lanzarote? ...*'

'*I was a bit tied up at the time.*'

Greg's words were out before he could do anything about it, but was sure she would just see it as him not taking this seriously. If only she knew.

'*Ana Cristina Magdalena was on the superyacht. It was hers. She is, or was, the richest person in Lanzarote. So far as we are aware she was on it during this afternoon's ...*'

Arteta flipped her hands around for the right word. It wouldn't come. Greg wasn't about to help, but he now knew the identity of Diamond Bikini Girl.

CHAPTER 67

News of Ana Cristina's superyacht had reached him. Speculation was that she had been on it at the time and hadn't survived. This presented him with a fantastic opportunity.

He was a great believer that battles were won in a courtroom before legal eagles strutted their stuff. He had work to do. They didn't call him El Bastardo for nothing. Time for his own salvation. Geoffrey Quinigan QC could see light at the end of his tunnel.

Greg wasn't exactly in the mood for a party when he returned from his Arteta experience held in one of the meetings rooms in the El Estadio de Lanzarote, his day having lasted over 72 hours already, but the new Gina Irvine-led party celebrations were much more to his liking.

No speeches, no businessmen sucking up to each other, just lights low, good music and his kind of party spirit, clinking not just glasses but bottles of beer with teammates and others who just wanted to have fun. No pressure on him for words, smiles, inane chatter.

Kraft's team had been working hard too. He put Greg up-to-date on Gina being the new owner of the club; and where David and Penny Pickup fitted into his afternoon of mayhem. He had nothing fresh to impart on Quinigan.

The video was still encrypted. It was proving difficult but Ken Knott had enlisted other help.

Gina – Bob Irvine's daughter as the club's new owner. Greg nodded lightly. He could live with that. Bob Irvine must have been working behind the scenes, sorting a deal in the Canaries for the following season, while also trying to turn around Town's fortunes.

But Bob Irvine had given Hopton Town a belief they could survive. They hadn't, but not for want of him trying and then losing his life. Setting up Eruption in his daughter's name? Fair play. Maybe Gina would be just as positive? Like father, like daughter?

Maria Cavaleros had informed GPK that while the Pickups might be loaded, they weren't that flush to have owned Bella Bebe and neither did they own La Cala. When David Pic-Wah had his hit in Spain with 'Bella Bebe' and a couple of follow-ups that didn't quite dent the Top 20 it had secured he and Pen what had turned out to be a lucrative place on the European festivals circuit to go with their annual royalties. They had met Ana Cristina and become close friends. Ana Cristina had enticed them to Playa Blanca where they had settled over twenty years ago.

David and Penny had been the one couple she had trusted with her boats. She had entered into an arrangement where they managed the crewing and the Bella Bebe would be ready whenever Ana Cristina wanted it. David and Penny could use it whenever they had wished. To those who were unaware of ownerships it added credence for those who believed the Pickups were among the mega-rich. It wasn't an image they attempted to dissuade.

Ciara – Maria explained the story now as she danced with Greg, while continually thanking him and, Greg was now almost certain, coming on to him. There was no doubting she looked fantastic. Ciara was presently wrapped around Kenny on the dancefloor. They were back together and clearly making up for lost time.

Maria was doing a fair impression of wanting to do the same with Greg, she rested her head against his shoulder as they swayed to some sweet ballad. She had enjoyed several glasses of the champagne that had been flowing continuously since the night's victory had been confirmed.

'Thank you again for bringing my daughter back to me,' Maria held him close. Greg couldn't help but enjoy the affections of a woman who was so attractive. But he also needed to know just what was going on. He held her away from him now, to make his point. She hadn't mentioned Lucia.

'But Lucia? Your sister wanted me to find her. Was it Lucia's funeral? Instead of Ciara's?'

Maria looked up into Greg's eyes.

'When Yurena asked you to find Lucia, and when the funeral took place, neither of us had any idea the body we were saying goodbye might be Lucia's. We both thought it was Ciara. Yurena is of course heartbroken. She cannot even grieve the way she should have. It is a bad, bad end to it, to Lucia.'

Greg wasn't unsympathetic, yet it still made no sense. How did she now know for sure it had been Lucia they had buried? And not just anyone?

'Luca, Lucia and Ciara, were passionate in protecting the island's World Biosphere status. Luca and Lucia's law studies helped. Ciara kept them in touch with what was happening while they were at university. They made a good team.'

The music changed to hi-energy party hits that some of the younger players and officials, plus some of the fans, danced to more dramatically, including Vinny and Gina.

Maria led Greg to a corner of the room where she could explain further. They sat on a deep, luxurious sofa. Greg could have gladly closed his eyes and slept.

'Ciara says they uncovered evidence of corruption. Buildings, new hotels mainly, passed for construction, not within the rules of the island's Biosphere status.'

Maria was now talking in earnest. She could see she had Greg's attention but also saw him wincing.

'Do you wish me to carry on? Something is troubling you.'

Greg was sticking with this. Sleep could wait.

He indicated for Maria to keep going. He wanted to hear all of this out before hitting the sack, whenever that was going to be.

'Ciara says they had a list of names. One of them was my husband. Ciara says she tried to talk with him. Another was Ana Cristina Magdalena, who was on the boat. Another was a man called Ricardo Rubio who is Gina's stepfather. The list includes many more ...'

Greg had no idea why Maria had hesitated at this moment. He just thought she'd taken a second to have a drink of her wine. He hadn't realised it had been a dramatic pause.

'… *and an Englishman whose name I am told you* …'

Greg was already there.

'*Geoffrey Quinigan?*' he shook his head immediately. How the fuck did everything in the past year always come back to this fucker!

Maria went on.

'… *they were all young, feeling as though they could move mountains. Luca and Lucia were typical students, full of that innocence where they could see injustice everywhere and wanted to change the world. Ciara was never that innocent. She knew about life – and fortunately still does.*'

Maria told Greg how the three of them had set up their own bank account in the name of Lanzarote World Biosphere Status Action Fund.

'*They took on each of them in turn. Their aim was to hurt them, expose them if they didn't do as they said, and stop them from disregarding planning over future developments.*

'*Lucia lured my husband into bed. I did not know this until now, but the prospect of it having taken place does not surprise me given my husband's tendency towards infidelities. Luca took photographs, recorded their intimacy and they blackmailed him.*

'*Juan, being stupid with women, had told Lucia how El Estadio de Lanzarote had been passed for development through what you English refer to as the 'old boy network', using the legal services of your Senor Quinigan, despite the land having been left barren, for good reason, for decades.*

'*Ricardo Rubio is up for re-election as Mayor of Yaiza. It is his office that every decision on planning in this area goes through. They, Luca and Ciara, trashed one of his priceless Sepago cars. This was before they came up with their new scheme to raise funds, using video and blackmailing their victims.*

'*They found that, as Gina will tell you, he is noted for, as she says, 'swinging his appendages' as she calls them, walking around his home in the nude. They had photos taken of him around his house but Photoshopped him so that they showed him in public places where nudity is not allowed. They sent them to him via WeTransfer and told him they would also appear on Internet websites for gay men. He's not gay, by the way. That's how they blackmailed him too.'*

Greg was seriously flagging, trying to keep up, but he knew this was all starting to make some kind of sense. Young vigilantes. Maria was still going strong.

'Ana Cristina Magdalena had become involved too, with some developments, over the years. She is, or was, the wealthiest woman on the island.

'But when Lucia arranged a meeting with her explaining their actions Ana Cristina was taken with the students, their patriotism and their enthusiasm for their home island. She was also, more importantly perhaps, an islander who had enough money already. She switched, more recently. She joined their operation. This was to be bad news for my husband and Senor Quinigan as deals they had simply disappeared overnight.'

At last! Finally Greg had something more on Quinigan. This might at least make worthwhile this extra, stupid role of private investigator to find Lucia. Maria wasn't finished with talking about her now late husband yet.

'My husband had arranged the development and building of El Estadio de Lanzarote. He was good at this, but never the finances. He always left that to me. It was a huge project and we had only been able to consider it when I met with Bob Irvine last year and we became good friends, close friends, very close ...'

Maria looked Greg closely in the eye, one eyebrow raised just like her daughter, and with a twinkle in her eye. *'Si, senor, that close.*

'We needed a backer. Bob was here on an awards evening. He and I met, we talked, he drove a hard bargain. He liked what we were doing, but said he had to be the biggest shareholder otherwise it was to be no deal.

'He told us of his contacts with the Rugby League Authority, already being the owner of a rugby league club. He was aware of our

island's World Biosphere status and wanted everything the right way. Geoffrey Quinigan was out of the plans and the planning. Bob did not like this man.

'There was nothing wrong with the planning of the Estadio. This was offering something for our own people. It looks even better after tonight's game. But because he already owned a club, Bob, Senor Irvine, put Eruption in the name of his daughter. Gina did not know this because he wanted it to be a birthday surprise for her, sadly we know what happened to Bob.

'My husband was under the impression that he and I were joint owners of the club and the Estadio. He tried to sell the club to Ana Cristina to raise funds to pay his blackmailers, that included Ciara, but he had no club to sell. Gina owns 90 per cent of the club and Estadio. I now own 10 per cent. My husband was embarrassed and very angry when he found out this news earlier today having thought he had sold it to Ana Cristina.'

Come on, give me Quinigan, was all Greg really wanted to hear.

'Senor Quinigan,' she took a breath.

'He first came to the island many years ago and is a master of legal and illegal ways in which construction of anything on the island can get through planning.

'Ciara says there is a video recording, made by Lucia, when she visited Ana Cristina that incriminates Senor Quinigan who was also present at the time, on Ana Cristina's island home on La Graciosa.

'Ana Cristina and Senor Quinigan had been at the same university studying law. That is how he first came to be on the island, I believe. It is the recording of this video and the other blackmails of Senor Quinigan, my husband also, Ricardo Rubio and others that Ciara believes caused Luca and Lucia to be murdered.'

Maria wasn't finished by a long way. Greg's head was swimming.

'Ciara tells me that Lucia & Luca were celebrating their first major success in having had 20m Euros deposited in their new account from their blackmails of Senor Quinigan, my husband and Ricardo Ricart and were looking forward to many more. They had *eaten at Al's. This was their big mistake. Juan had many 'business interests',' she raised both forefingers like quotation marks. 'He had arranged Carlos's illegal immigration and in return Carlos would do anything he asked.*

'Senor Quinigan owns Al's along with several other properties around Playa Blanca. It all goes way back to when the previous owner, Scotsman Alasdair Mackie, mysteriously disappeared. That's where its name Al's comes from. Senor Kraft told me this earlier.

'Senor Quinigan and Juan had people following where Lucia and Luca were heading that day including Pablo and Senor Quinigan's son and daughter. Carlos informed the people he had been instructed to contact that Luca and Lucia had arrived at Al's.

'Lucia and Luca went for a victory swim. It wasn't a lover's thing. They were high on good spirits. They had contacted Ciara to join them ... she was on her way down to the beach, there were only the two of them there ...'

Ciara had appeared with Kenny, as if on cue. They were both taking a break from the dancing, as her mother relayed the last line. She had seen her explaining what she had told her earlier, but she was now ready to tell Greg everything, including why she had visited him the way she had on the night she was subsequently to have died. But she first made sense of Luca and Lucia.

'When I arrived I saw them together. And I wanted to be a part of it. Then I saw their bodies floating in the ocean. It all happened so quickly. I saw their bodies being taken out by the sea. I had made my way down as fast as I could.

'I ran across the beach and into the ocean. I saw blood and much, much more ...'

Finally, the emotion of reliving the scene became too much that her bottom lip trembled and tears came. Kenny held her, but she was determined now to see this through.

'Lucia's face ... it wasn't there ...'

Her tears flowed. Now Maria also hugged her daughter.

'Luca's too, but Lucia must have taken the shot most, if it had been just one bullet. Maybe two. I don't know ... I saw a boat

disappearing in the distance … There was no-one else around … and I couldn't bring them out of the ocean … they drifted …'

The horror of it all was still fresh in her mind and reliving it once again was something Greg imagined she had done every day since.

'Carlos had gone by the time I had climbed back up to Al's. I wanted to let someone know about Luca and Lucia, but I also knew I had to look after myself. They were gone. We had talked about vengeance. That there may be retribution, but we had never thought it would be like this.

'I did not know what to do. I went back to my apartment and changed. I arranged to meet Juan. We had been getting on well, working together at the club and even though we had been blackmailing him it had been done anonymously. He hadn't known I was involved.

'When I told him what I had seen, I could feel something was wrong. I became more worried when he left the bar where we had met to, he said, take an urgent call. Some business call he'd said. I left out of the back of the bar while he went out of the front. I hurried down Avenue de Papagayos as quickly as I could. I went straight to Kenny's apartment and stayed the night. I didn't tell him anything, but he must have known I wasn't myself.'

Kenny knew nothing. He opened out the palms of his hands as though he had nothing to offer. 'I had no idea … I wish I had said something, to help …'

'The next day you arrived.

'Kenny had asked me to pick you up from Cesar Manrique. I took his car, while watching whether I was being followed. I could not see anyone follow me and when you arrived, I took you to El Estadio. When I came back to my apartment everything had disappeared. It was as though I no longer existed.

'I received a text telling me of a safe place. I knew I had to move, but not there. I decided they, whoever they were, would be watching Kenny's apartment, so I decided to go to yours. I did not know what I was doing. It was impulse. Somewhere they might not expect to find me.'

Somewhere under the radar thought Greg. Where had he heard that before?

'I did not want to give you any idea that I was in trouble, so I may have over-compensated for that a little too much ...'

That familiar Ciara and Maria one-eyebrow-raised moment lightened proceedings at this point. Greg felt both of his raise too.

'... and I now know how much I hurt Kenny, but what can I say ... it is history.'

Greg and Kenny looked at each other. They both raised eyebrows at each other. Ciara steeled herself for the next part of her story.

'That evening, while you were asleep, I received another text telling me they knew where I was and again to come to the marina. I knew then that I had to move. I left from the balcony of your apartment.

'This time I went to the marina. When I arrived, someone must have seen me or have been watching nearby because I received another text directing me to Bella Bebe. David and Penny Pickup were on board and welcomed me. They were kind. I was still unsure, but they looked after me.

'They told me I was to stay on the Bella Bebe.

'I still did not know what to do, but I was safe. I was told as long as I did not contact anyone, I would be okay. David and Penny are friends of Ana Cristina Magdalena, who owns ... owned, the Bella Bebe.'

Maria Cavaleros launched herself back in to the tale.

'What Ciara did not know is that Lucia's body had been found washed up ashore in a terrible state. No chance of identification due to the shooting and the ocean's work. But Lucia had been wearing jewellery she had borrowed from Ciara. Before anyone could do anything else and knowing by now that Ciara had also disappeared around the same time, there was an assumption it must be Ciara's. It's all we had to go on. Ciara was dead.'

'I knew nothing of this,' Ciara was nearly back in tears again. 'So far as I was concerned, I was just laying low and being well treated. We went out to sea. We enjoyed wine, good meals. Juan would come on to the boat some days, make sure I was okay. It started feeling natural. I have always enjoyed being at sea. And it was only like a vacation. It felt good not to have to do anything but relax, but I was also not good every time I thought about Lucia and Luca and their faces.

'But today … everything changed … last night we sailed around to La Graciosa. David, Pen, me and the crew.

'Senorita Magdalena does not visit Lanzarote very often and she does not know people like me. David and Pen said they thought it best that she did not know who I was because they had heard of some bad blood between Juan and her.

'They also knew that, by now, to most people, I was dead, even though they knew differently and were helping Juan. They were in a difficult position with the boat being Senorita Magdalena's. So, I became Gabriella Bianco. I quite liked it actually.'

Ciara finally raised a smile. She looked at Kenny who gave a little nod of approval. She kissed him. She came back to her story.

'We sailed back around the island to Playa Blanca and into the Rubicon Marina this afternoon. David had some business to attend to, so he left the boat when we arrived.

'Senorita Magdalena was enjoying the sun, she had just worked out in the gym and had showered. I was with Pen. Juan suddenly appeared out of nowhere and we set off. I did not know why.

'Then you arrived and … well, you know the rest … you found me … gracias Greg! … you brought me back to life!'

CHAPTER 68

'*Buenos dias!*'

Greg heard the words that had been whispered softly but didn't open his eyes. He was in bed. His first time in three days. Sleep had been good, wherever he was.

He kept his eyes closed. This bed was so comfortable, but perhaps any bed would have brought about the same reaction. He'd been that tired. He knew the voice but didn't have the will to acknowledge with either the opening of his eyes or a casual murmur. For now, that would do. He drifted back to sleep.

It could have been hours or just ten minutes before Greg next drifted back into consciousness. He had no idea.

'*Buenos dias, hombre encantador.*'

Greg had no real idea what the last word meant, but the way in which it had been spoken softly and with tenderness told him this woman liked him. He knew now who it was and opened his eyes. How could he not?

Maria Cavaleros. He had found her stunning when he had first seen her while waiting for Kenny to finish up with training when he'd arrived just ten days ago, and he found her even more so now. Her blonde hair and her blue-eyed, beautiful face was his first vision of the day. He couldn't help but return the compliment with a smile of his own.

'*You know, you should smile more, it suits you,*' she offered gently as she perched at the side of the bed wearing a very pretty white MISA Los Angeles Micaela drop shoulder dress.

Not that Greg knew any of that either. He'd just have described it as floaty and pretty. He propped his head up with his hand on his right cheek and elbow on the pillow.

'*You look great,*' his words were softly spoken too. It was a mutual love-in. Greg felt his eyes shutting again. He also felt himself still smiling.

'*Gracias, hombre encantador.*'

There, she'd said it again, that word. He opened his eyes once more, drew a deep breath and asked similarly softly.

'What does that mean? I mean, I know it's nice. I just don't know what it means.'

'It means you are a lovely man, Greg Duggan.'

Maria's tone was sweet rather than seductive. Heartfelt rather than lustful. He looked into her eyes. He felt he could see hurt and pain, but also the joy she now had through Ciara being back. Greg chose not to ask immediately about himself, how he'd woken here. Instead he focused on her.

'Are you okay?'

It was an odd thing to be asking since he'd effectively been responsible for the death of her husband hours earlier. But they had obviously been in love, had feelings for each other, had been a couple.

Maria's smile was still there. She appreciated Greg's concern, nodded and patted the bed.

'Juan.' She closed her eyes now, briefly. She was distressed but not overwrought. She maintained her sweetness of smile. *'Juan and I were good for each other, while it lasted. We put on what you would call a good show together, to others, but ...'*

She took a deep breath now. Gave a simple shrug of her delightful bared shoulders.

'... for a long time we had not been ...'

She shrugged slightly once again.

'I would not have wished him to die ...'

And then swiftly switched their conversation back to a positive tone, smiled at him.

'But I now have my daughter back! ... And that is such an amazing feeling ... And you brought her back to me ... It was what you have done that I will never ever forget.'

Maria's eyes sparkled now.

'That is why you are hombre encantador and ...'

She raised her eyebrows again in flirtatious style but added nothing more. It was cheeky, suggestive and Greg enjoyed the moment.

'Gracias Senorita.' Greg was enjoying being where he was right now, with a beautiful woman and in a comfortable bed. He was contented.

'Your place?' he assumed casually, with a look that asked how he had arrived.

'Last night,' Maria started.

'After I had talked and talked …' she nonchalantly raised her eyes to the top of her head in mild, yet comic exasperation at herself.

'… you fell asleep. None of us – myself, Ciara, Kenny, Gina or Vincent … such a lovely boy, wanted you to sleep back at your hotel. I said that you should come here. Kenny and Vincent carried you. They brought you into this bed, my bed.'

Maria smiled again.

'But I did not take advantage of you, Greg.'

She was enjoying herself. She raised the familiar one eyebrow, then turned serious again.

'Are you feeling any better? We all saw your body last night as we undressed you. Those bruises around your ankles and wrists, the cuts to your legs and arms … they did not come from yesterday?'

Maria was back to tenderness now, her voice more a whisper than truly vocal.

Greg had no wish to inflict any of what he had suffered on to anyone else, unless he had to. He also had no wish to use the 'I was a bit tied up' routine again. He would mend.

'I'm good,' he managed.

'All the better waking up in a beautiful woman's bed. This …'

He motioned in front of him to his battered body with his hands.

'… will all be right in five days' time for the 10 million Euros game.'

'Five? Cinco? No.'

Maria had news for Greg.

'It is now tres. Three days. We received the news by email, text, calls and social media in the early hours of this morning.

'The virus, the epidemic that started a few days ago in the Far

East. There is talk of it becoming a pandemic, there is, so far, no cure. It is all over the news throughout the world.

'There are no cases in Europe or Africa, but there is talk of movement restrictions. There is possibility all sport may have to stop.

'The message we have received is the play-off for next season's place in Super League is to be brought forward. It is the last game of the season and Senor Jardine has said he wants it playing as soon as possible.'

Greg's body ached already at the thought, but he had other issues too. The tameness of the morning had been replaced swiftly by anxiety. He had to make some urgent calls.

'Three days.'

Quinigan accentuated both words with as much fervour as he could.

'Three days to make all of this right,' he spoke sternly, his mouth and jaw set solid to himself as he looked out over Playa Blanca from Hugo's La Casa Grande de la Flamenco.

CHAPTER 69

Cesar Manrique Airport was alive. Jags fans were to make up the next four flights headed for the UK. Holidaymakers were arriving from all parts of Europe and the terminal management was preparing for an increased schedule in the following two days with an influx of Eruption's next opponents' fans for the Super League Showdown.

James and Janet were there to welcome four more to the GPK team since yesterday's sea drama had become front page news around the world.

GPK wanted eyes everywhere, but he also wanted 'that bloody video' unencrypting. Until he'd seen and heard what was said it meant nothing to the case, but it could mean everything.

'Quinigan knows we are getting closer, but he doesn't know how much we know, so he will probably think we are bluffing,' he told his team, now seven plus him.

Det Sgt Arteta had calculated she had one more day in charge with Det Con Moreno in tow before the big hitters from Spain took over.

Greg had no phone. It was either somewhere in the Badlands or in his room at Papagayos Beach Hotel. Either way he didn't have it. He'd always remembered Diane's number, so he rang her and Kyle first. They were good, Diane had heard what had happened and had asked if he was okay.

He'd wanted to call Susie but had never remembered her number. It had been so easy just pressing a button against her name. He had no other person he could contact to find it out. The call would have to wait. He didn't know what to say, even if she had been there.

Maria gave him her sister's number and Kenny's. He spoke with Yurena briefly. There wasn't a lot he could say. Yurena was as distressed as he'd imagined she would be, but thanked him nonetheless. He had at least found her niece alive. Hardly solace for her though, he imagined.

'Perdoneme, Senor Knott?'

Ken was a seasoned, cynical, hard-bitten journalist. He had hardly moved from what had become the team's operations room in their suite at the Papagayos Beach Hotel.

Which Spanish speaking person knew his number? This had been an odd, unsolicited phone call from someone in Ken's speculative journalistic head speaking Spanish but not quite mastering even the opening word. He'd played along. As the woman had continued, he'd become certain. This was a masquerade.

Ken hadn't only been intuitive, he'd also backed up with a recording of the call on his phone. The number she had called on had come up as private, but he had his sources that would locate the number and her location.

'Hola, Senorita, I am Antonio Romero ... I am investigating yesterday's incident?'

Janet Hague was no less intuitive. She had been taking coffee at one of the bars near to the marina, watching for any developments, people moving, boats, anything out of the ordinary.

'May I join you?'

Janet made the slightest of gestures, nonchalant. Her iPad was open, she'd just received the WhatsApp group message, plus for belt and braces a text and email from Ken.

'Who are you working for?'

It was purposefully delivered to cause maximum stress to the man in front of her. To make him think. Would he give anything away by his look? Maybe he didn't understand. She waited.

The young man was sat in front of her now. Antonio Romero was good eye candy. Tall, slim, attractive, well dressed in black trousers and white open-collared shirt. Neat beard, moustache, tousled black hair, designer shades.

'Ah si, El Rubicon Marina. The owners. They are concerned there may be some liability attached.'

'Why me?' Janet enjoyed the direct approach.

Janet bit her lip. She'd seen him coming towards her, he hadn't chatted with anyone else. It didn't make sense. He couldn't have known who she was and where to come, unless he'd already found out through other sources. And if so, which source? Just like Ken, she felt this was the beginnings of a result.

'Midhaven Marauders!? How the hell did they manage that?'

Greg hadn't found out who Eruption would be playing in the play-off final, until now. The morning after the Jags game. He'd assumed, like nearly everyone else except the Marauders, that it would be a return fixture against Hudderford Gladiators.

Kenny had updated Greg.

'No idea, mate. Took us all the way earlier in the season.'

'Yeah …' Greg was ponderous.

Kenny felt the hesitancy in Greg's voice. *'What is it mate?'*

Ken Knott had been an investigative reporter throughout his career and the opportunity to get back in the field, rather than be the stats man, was too powerful to pass up.

He was up for the meeting with this bogus, spurious, pretend-Spanish woman. He wanted to see where this would lead.

Antonio Romero was headstrong. He'd enjoyed talking with Janet. She was bound to check him out. She and her team would be going through files, trying to find anything about him. This had been an exploratory meeting. The next would be the real deal.

'World Biosphere Status.'

Greg was with Kenny at El Estadio.

'That's the thing that links everybody. Luca and Lucia were killed because of their involvement. Ciara was targeted. There's corruption everywhere on the island and Quinigan, he really is El Bastardo.'

'But why bother with Hopton?'

'Probably something that just came up. Remember, it was Caill who was in dire straits. He needed to pay off debts. Quinigan saw another opportunity? He lives off this kind of thing.'

Greg picked up his coffee, but before he drank delivered the news he'd learned earlier from the news on Canaria TV.

'The UNESCO representatives arrive tomorrow from all around the world, and by the time we play the final Lanzarote may have lost its world biosphere status …' Greg looked at Kenny.

'Does it really mean that much?'

CHAPTER 70

Eruption were back in light training in the mid-late afternoon, to be followed by a morning session and full-on training session early evening the next day when there would be just 24 hours before the game that the Canaria TV producers had billed as El Dia Del Juicio Final – Judgment Day!

They were most definitely loving their match titles.

Greg's face was used on screen with Kenny and all of the island-born players, looking stern and with the catchline 'Nosostros Estamos Listos' – We Are Ready.

'This is where we wanted to be boys.'

Kenny and Malky Shannon were alongside each other with the whole squad in front of them on the pitch. Kenny had delivered the opening words.

'But this is not over. We have not won yet,' Malky added. *'Marauders finished third, we've beaten them three times this season, but they turned over Hudderford Gladiators to get here. If we take anything for granted I can guarantee you that we will not be playing in Super League next season. Is that understood?'*

He looked around him.

'Actions speak louder than words gentlemen, let's get to work.'

'Senorita Juniper? Si, I get her for you.'

The call had come direct to Santiago's. One of the bar staff attracted Gina's attention. Gina was taking a break from playing.

Her whole world was to be rocked.

'Are you okay, Jen?'

Santiago's manager saw the instant change in his entertainer. She was trembling. *'Jen?'* She passed out.

It was Gina's first day when none of her new-found friends had been at Santiago's. The Pickups were convalescing after Pen's trauma on board Bella Bebe; Maria Cavaleros was in Arrecife with Ciara; GPK and his team were elsewhere; Vinny was at El Estadio.

'Senor Kraft?'

GPK didn't recognise the caller who had come up as private number. He put the caller on to record. GPK had earlier briefed his now enlarged team with the words that there was nothing as dangerous as a wounded animal and from what he could see that was Quinigan right now.

Surveillance was on Quinigan at Hugo Silva's home. Three of the four new team members were there. Ricardo Rubio's residence was being watched by the other of the four.

Ken and Janet were on standby for any meeting called by Senorita Angelina Diaz, and Senor Antonio Romero.

'*In the next ten minutes you will lose two of your team unless you do as I say …*' The voice waited for some kind of reply. Kraft was thinking. He'd been threatened himself many times. It came with the territory, but this was other people, his people.

'*I'm listening …*' he replied calmly.

'*Stand down your team. Immediately. And then await my instructions.*' The caller hung up.

'*Did you hear?*' Ken, Janet and James were currently all with GPK.

'*He's running scared,*' Ken volunteered.

'*But why?*' Janet followed.

'*We've still nothing seriously on him until this video is decrypted.*'

Kraft was measured, analytical. He brought the thumb and forefinger of his left hand to the bridge of his nose, pulling lightly at the slacker skin. He followed up with rubbing his middle finger and thumb of the same hand across each of his eyebrows, before resting his chin on his left hand with index finger up the left cheekbone and middle finger resting against his upper lip. Contemplation. And then decision.

'*Pull away from your surveillance immediately. Report back to the hotel. Everyone confirm receipt separately and immediately.*'

All responses came back within the minute.

Kraft was composed.

'*We need to be ready. He's done this to give himself breathing space, so that he can move … we need to give him that … for now … and then follow … he's uncomfortable and he's dangerous …*'

Gina had only been out of consciousness for seconds. A couple who had been listening to her earlier had rushed to her aide. Gina had just one thing on her mind as she regained consciousness. Vinny. Her first words: '*Where's my phone?*'

'*Senorita Irvine … Gina …*'

Det Sgt Arteta had arrived with Moreno. '*Are you in trouble?*

'*No, but my boyfriend is …*'

Kraft's phone sprung into life once again, five minutes later.

'*Go home. Today. All of you. Fly tonight. The last flight out of Cesar Manrique is at 21:55, be on it.*'

Kraft was still listening, the caller hung up. He went through the same rigmarole with his right hand as he had with his left.

James asked: '*Was that him? Quinigan? Both times?*'

Kraft shrugged slightly.

'*Could easily have been two different people, neither of them Quinigan. We had surveillance on two properties. That narrows it down to Quinigan, Silva and Rubio.*'

'*Or anyone working with them …?*' Janet added.

'*Why now?*' James entered the thoughts. '*Why start threatening now?*'

'*Because we must be getting closer …*' Ken was feeling positive.

'*If only we knew just how close …*' Kraft was not so positive.

'*But he's making a move, whether it was his voice or not … like James says, why now?*

We know he's been up to all sorts of wrangling on the island, deals, getting properties built where money counted more than the good of the island …'

James took up the rest. '*… and the UNESCO Biosphere Status representatives arrive tomorrow to make a decision on whether the island should have its status removed, which could lose Lanzarote billions of Euros in tourism and potentially hit its tourist trade.*'

It took ten minutes to get to El Estadio. The longest ten minutes of Gina's life. Arteta and Moreno escorted her. Gina and Arteta made calls as Moreno drove. By the time they reached the ground two Policia vehicles were there and the players were being shepherded from the pitch. Vinny was prone, motionless.

CHAPTER 71

Excited Midhaven Marauders fans were landing at Cesar Manrique in the late afternoon, those who had booked flights immediately having learned El Dia Del Juicio Final – Judgment Day! had been brought forward. Odd Shaped Ball Holidays had done a roaring trade selling their two-, three- and four-day packages.

Playa Blanca and the whole of the accommodation in the Yaiza region was booked solid with additional flights now scheduled to arrive in the next two days until just five hours before the match itself.

Midhaven wasn't the most fashionable of cities. It had been one of Europe's thriving fishing ports until the 1980s but in the past forty-plus years its container ship and ferry trade had become its main seafaring business as well as offshore wind farm manufacture and supply.

But Midhaven was also a proud hotbed of rugby league, the only city in the game to support two professional clubs in the north of England. The Marauders had played second fiddle long enough to their local neighbours who went under the simpler name of Midhaven FC. This was the Marauders' moment to rejoin them in Super League after half a dozen seasons in the sport's second tier.

Their heroes were set to arrive the next morning, giving them a day and a half to settle in, take in their surroundings and prepare for what many in the club hadn't in the least anticipated when the season had started.

They had gone back to a team made up of largely local hometown lads with a smattering of Aussie and New Zealand players and had punched way above their weight all season culminating in their play-off semi-final victory against hot favourites Hudderford Gladiators.

Eruption's increasingly excited following, especially after

Greg's three consecutive man-of-the-match appearances, had taken the club's full allocation of 5000 tickets and additional seating and terracing had been arranged at all four corners of the ground to raise the capacity to 8500 with the Marauders' fans selling out their allocation within twenty minutes of going on sale.

Such was the interest in the game all around the island that big screens were to be erected in the main square of the island's capital, Arrecife and in the Rubicon Marina market square in Playa Blanca for those unable to purchase tickets.

El Estadio de Lanzarote was set to rock in just under 48 hours.

Gina's world had already been rocked.

She was now recovering from the shock of first seeing Vinny on the ground as she'd decanted quickly from Moreno's car. The reason for his prone state had been having just completed a sprint training exercise that had developed into a battle between himself, Alan Thomas and Tonito.

Det Sgt Alba Marta Arteta had been on her way to talk with Gina when the new owner of Eruption had received the call at Santiago's.

Gina relayed to Greg, Kenny, Arteta and Moreno what had been said on the phone in Santiago's.

'Your boyfriend. He is next … That's all that was said.'

Gina was far from being a gibbering wreck. She'd recovered having seen Vinny, who was presently on the treatment table in the dressing room receiving a massage.

Greg was all set for starting out after Quinigan. So far as he was concerned there was only one man who was behind all of this. And he would have been on his way but for Arteta's words.

'There is little point …'

It took the wind out of Greg's sails.

'He left La Casa Grande de la Flamenco, Hugo Silva's residence, earlier this afternoon, in a Maserati Levante. We had him followed as far as Arrecife, where he left the car. We lost him in the old part of the city, but we have our officers trying to locate him.'

Arteta could see the frustration in Greg's face.

'It appears there is evidence that will not only disclose his part in last year's events in your country and will also incriminate others who colluded with him, but also show that he has been responsible for much of the illegal building work that now puts the island's world biosphere status in danger of being revoked. We believe he is trying to ensure that whatever this evidence is, it is destroyed.'

Greg would gladly have set off on Quinigan's trail, if he'd known even in the slightest where he might be. But he didn't. He looked forlorn.

Kenny saw Greg's reaction. 'Hey, Greg, we've got this buddy. We'll get him.'

'Yeah,' Gina added, but a little more suspect in her delivery.

'Make sure you do. Vinny's now the one being targeted. I've already lost my dad, I'm sure as hell not going to lose my boyfriend!'

CHAPTER 72

'... *there's something I need to tell you* ...'

Greg had contacted Diane and spoken with Kyle, having been supplied with a new mobile phone by Maria. It was now 7pm, almost exactly 48 hours before El Dia Del Juicio Final – Judgment Day!

This was much needed after what he'd gone through in the past days. His body ached like hell and he could have done without today's training session, however light it had been.

'*I'm pregnant* ...' It was another kick in the stomach that Greg could have done without. In the past few days, when not kicking a ball about on a field or kicking the living shit out of people, he'd been thinking deeply about Diane. He hadn't known quite where to turn, what to do. He'd thought about Kyle so much, particularly during and after the last game when he'd seen Francisco's mum, Liliana, and her other son, Leonardo.

He had been looking forward to talking with Diane. He now slumped on to the bed. So, this was it. If he'd wanted a way back, which he still wasn't one hundred per cent certain he did, this put the tin lid on it. He knew he had no-one to blame but himself, but he wasn't going to feel sorry for himself either.

'*Greg?*' He shut his eyes, took a long breath.

'*Yeah, still here* ...' He didn't smile, but wanted to be good about it. No sense in being stupid.

'*Are you hap ... I mean, when's it due ... how are you feeling?*' He knew he needed to be supportive.

'*Yes* ...' she left a long pause. '*John and I are both really pleased* ...'

She lightened up the mood.

'*Kyle is so looking forward to seeing you. I hope you can get back soon to see us ... There was something here on the news about a millionaire's boat exploding near where you are, worth £137 million*

… did you see it? …'

Better that she didn't know the full story.

'Nah, been too busy playing … you know what it's like out here, it's all sea, sand, sun and what you've been having by the sound of it …'

Greg stopped himself momentarily. He hadn't meant that to sound as though he was pissed off.

'… shit, I don't mean that badly Di, I really don't, I'm really happy for you …'

Diane had a good sense of humour. She'd laughed at Greg's line and the digging he'd then done to try to get himself out of a hole he'd just dug. They finished on good terms, as Greg had hoped. There was no sense in anything else. It was time to move on.

He tried Susie. No reply. Another relationship over.

'Not your most successful evening? Every cloud had its silver lining. This is a phrase I have heard. What do you think, hombre encantador?'

Greg hadn't imagined how quickly his latest down, could very quickly become another almost instantaneous up!

'Maybe Senor Greg is too tired?'

The beautiful woman with a perfect figure stood in front of him wearing nothing but a smile and an upraised single eyebrow, ankle bracelet and jewelled navel, holding two glasses and a bottle of champagne.

Greg's day was brought to a stimulating and satisfying end. Ideal training session for bruising, aches, pains and possible breakages to simply fade away.

CHAPTER 73

'*Julian, dear chap! When you arrive it might be better if we … catch up where I have meetings elsewhere on the island, before you go to your hotel … no … no … nothing at all to worry about … see you later!*'

It was time for Geoffrey Quinigan's planning to start coming together.

Call number two.

'*Do you have everything in place? … good … if anything goes wrong, let me know straight away … I want no loose cannons this time …*'

Call three.

'*Buenos dias mi amigo. Esta toda en orden?*' … *Bueno* … *Y nuestro gran plan?* … *Si* … *nosostros seremos muy ricos …*'

He laughed as his friend responded to the pair of them being very rich, very soon. There were still much that could go wrong in the next 36 hours, but he now felt he had all bases covered.

Julian Jardine was to land at Cesar Manrique on an afternoon flight with his phalanx of fellow Rugby League Authority officials. The game, once billed in the UK as the Million Pound Game, had been upgraded by inflation and was now the 10m Euros Game.

This was an ideal, fitting, although speedily arranged climax to the season for Jardine. His decision, backed by enough of his colleagues who could be bribed or coerced into agreeing to allow Eruption to leapfrog straight into the Championship without ever having played in the lower leagues had been vindicated and it had also been his decision that the Grand Final for the position in Super League should be played at Estadio de Lanzarote.

It gave the sport a sunshine venue for this centrepiece, looked good on screen and on a purely self congratulatory level was a fabulous place for himself, his current partner and to repay those who had supported his motions.

But Jardine was uneasy. Quinigan was 'off his tits' so far as he was concerned; and Jardine was far from the soft operator Quinigan had wrongly assumed, that Jardine had allowed him to think.

Jardine was a man who revelled in power and influence. He squeezed everything he could out of people. When he'd first come together with Quinigan he had seen it as a beautiful arrangement. Quinigan had proved useful. Now he was a liability.

It was near to the end of the previous season that the application from Lanzarote to join the sport had emerged. Unbeknown to Jardine at the time, Quinigan was almost permanently based on the island and pulling various strings over property, land acquisition and buildings. When he'd found out, he'd thought that maybe it wasn't such a bad idea to keep Quinigan involved.

Julian Jardine and his partner loved the island. He had taken full advantage of his position and had booked La Cala as a business expense for the evening prior to the game and the evening of the game and, due to the custom he was bringing to the new hotel in taking at least another twenty rooms or apartments for every visit during the season, he was there as the guest of the hotel management for a further twelve days.

The only problem now was Quinigan. He felt it more in every conversation lately. This wasn't the same man he'd known, even a year ago. The man was losing his touch. Jardine had no time for dead wood.

Jardine was much more than Quinigan had ever anticipated. Behind the scenes he was a manipulative mercenary who would do anything for his own ends. He was neither political activist nor passionate industrialist. He didn't want to take over the world, just line his own pockets and had realised years previously he could do this best by being seen, to those who counted, as inconsequential and impotent.

He also occasionally employed the services of allies who

never appeared on any books and ledgers, and who never submitted an income tax return.

He'd engaged them again, way before Quinigan's call that morning, but having received it he'd felt wholly justified.

'Ohh ... hmm ... mmm ... Si ... huh ...hmmm ... Si ... Si ... Si ...'

The breathing was deep, rhythmic, reaching crescendo.

'Ohh ... ohhh ... ohhhhh ... Siiiii ... Si ... Si!!!'

Maria Cavaleros was not just a beautiful, passionate woman. She was also an amazingly dextrous, supple and energetic lover with a voracious sexual appetite as Greg was now finding.

This had not been at his behest, but he wasn't complaining. Maria's libido was literally on fire and, surprisingly after all Greg had been through recently his body was keeping up, as well as ... well you know the rest!

'You know, I don't think I have ever made love so sweetly in a morning,'

Maria told Greg affectionately. Greg smiled. She was still astride him and only minutes after feeling satisfied, once again felt movement.

'Again? ... Ohh, hombre encantador!!'

They kissed, tongues tantalising each other.

Greg's first night with Maria had been somewhat inactive given what he had gone through previously, but this had been anything but. Following the news from Diane, and Susie's decision to leave again, this had been the perfect antidote. Even if it had all been a whirlwind, like much of the two weeks since he'd first set foot on Lanzarote.

His mobile sparked into life. Having drifted back off to sleep, he now wished he hadn't chosen 'Eye of the Tiger' as his ringtone. Too loud man.

What he was about to hear was to wake him up even more than any Rocky intro!

CHAPTER 74

The meeting of UNESCO officials to determine the island's fate over retaining its World Biosphere Reserve status was to be held over two days, with a decision due to be made by the evening of the second day around the same time as the events at Estadio de Lanzarote. There were those who were looking forward to a double celebration if the island's conservation campaigners and supporters, and Eruption were both successful.

Around 100 representatives were present in the impressive Hotel Volcan in Playa Blanca near the Rubicon Marina, including the Director-General Valentin Pierre Boucher with another 300-400 colleagues present and the world's press.

Yurena Aguilar was the island's spokesperson on behalf of status retention. The island's Cabildo (the government) were all present.

It had been the massive growth in new developments of hotel complexes, with many paying no heed to regulations, that had in part brought about this extraordinary call by UNESCO.

Yurena looked immaculate as she took to the podium to welcome delegates from around the globe. Although still grieving the loss of her daughter she wasn't about to give up on her passion. This was set to be a landmark in the island's history whether good or bad. She intended it would be good.

'Welcome, delegates, to our beautiful, unique island. As our amazing Cesar Manrique once said about life, 'man was not created for this artificiality'.

'Cesar was our inspiration. It is his vision, his artistry, his architecture that brought our relatively small island to international recognition and we still mourn his passing. Of course, our landscape would perhaps never have made quite such a dramatic impact without the volcanic eruptions that occurred from 1730 to 1736.

'We are very proud of our island and its UNESCO world biosphere status and we believe the continued development of the island is due to our success in attracting not just sun-seeking holidaymakers but those who want to know more about our rich heritage and biodiversity.

'I can tell you that we are no different to anywhere else in the world in facing challenges and we are aware of some poor decisions that have been made to meet the demands of tourism, but we are also fiercely loyal to our status and I hope that over the next two days you see that passion and commitment from everyone here. Thank you!'

Midhaven Marauders had arrived at El Estadio having checked in to the Papagayos Beach Hotel. Not for them the extravagance of La Cala. Marauders' local owner, solicitor Glen Hilldue had backed the club to the hilt for the last 15 years and he'd ensured their continuity on the back of prudent investment.

They might not have been the most fashionable club in the rugby league world, but they were a rock-solid community-based outfit and their fans appreciated Hilldue's efforts.

Their focus on local talent had often held them back when there had been a dearth of players of the right ability but this season it had all come together with a mix of senior players and the exuberance of youth as the 'Pride of East Midhaven'.

Greg, Kenny and the rest of the Eruption squad had been under way with their session before the Marauders' arrival. Injuries checked upon, light training and another session planned for around 6pm. After that a final session in the mid-afternoon tomorrow before El Dia Del Juicio Final.

'What is it Greg?'

Kenny now knew Greg probably better than anyone, and he could feel Greg's mumbled semi-reply with its customary, unconvincing non-committal shrug wasn't good news.

'Look. I know you want Quinigan but he's not around. You heard what Det Sgt Arteta said last night. He's disappeared ...'

Greg shook his head.

'The bastard's out there. He's the one who sent that message about Vinny. I need to find him.'

Last night and earlier this morning, with Maria, had succeeded in taking his mind away from everything that had taken place. Now, he was right back on it.

CHAPTER 75

'What have you got on Quinigan?'

Greg's head-to-head with Kenny had straightened his mind. Immediately he'd finished training he'd returned to the Papagayos Beach Hotel and had marched through to Graham Pythagoras Kraft's suite. No pleasantries.

'I want to know everything Mr Kraft. Everything you have.'

GPK steadied himself, leaning back in an office chair from his desk. He motioned for Greg to sit. Greg remained standing.

'We know his son and daughter are playing games with us. Oliver and Emily. They have aliases. It's likely they were your Latex twins. They've been in touch with Janet and Ken, now posing as Spanish-speaking individuals. We are awaiting some kind of meetings.'

GPK steadied himself again.

'Quinigan is in hiding somewhere on the island. We believe that may be in the northern area although he could be on Isla de Graciosa where the late Ana Cristina Magdalena lived. We know he had a relationship with her that went sour.

'We also know that Quinigan was involved, at some stage, with Juan Cavaleros, but that he visited Ana Cristina separately to Cavaleros around the time of the announcement Eruption had been sold. We believe the relationship had also gone sour. We know he has been living with Hugo Silva, with whom we believe he also has a relationship, and from what we can make out that now also appears to be going sour.

'Everyone assumes he is a millionaire through his 'old money' – the estate in Scotland and a London residence – and via his various property dealings, mainly over here in Lanzarote. When he fell upon Hopton's ground being ripe for the picking he couldn't resist a quick kill.

'We can place him in and around everything that went on last year, in some way, but as Geoffrey Quinigan QC would tell us if he was defending his case, it is all circumstantial.

'So far as we can make out, he never made a bean out of the Hopton Town ground sale. And over here? His investments?'

Kraft spread his hands wide.

'*That hotel you were taken to? The Ghost Hotel? His. His mistake. And he's made many.*

'*The 'old money' still exists but, from our sources, it seems the estate in Scotland and the property in London, are not his. It appears his own father – Sir Quentin Quinigan, who passed away last year, also fell out with him.*

'*Quinigan, whichever way you look right now, is a walking disaster.*'

Greg was amazed by the litany of failure.

'*That's what we've got? In reality, nothing that says anything other than he is currently one of the world's biggest losers.*'

Greg shook his head, casting it downwards and closing his eyes as he tried to take it all in. GPK wasn't finished.

'*What we thought we had was a recording that we are told incriminates him absolutely. On this recording he allegedly boasts about what happened in Hopton and other past 'successes' on the island.*

'*The recording we received was encrypted. Unfortunately, we've just found out it is impossible to unencrypt.*

'*Quinigan's son and daughter are arranging meetings with two of my team. We don't know when or why, but it has to be something he is plotting. He wants that recording gone forever, wherever it is, otherwise his career is over.*

'*That's what we have.*'

Kraft moved forward on his chair, hands clasped in front of him. '*Now what about you?*'

'*You know about yesterday? What happened at Santiago's?*'

Kraft's focus had been almost wholly directed at Quinigan, Silva and Rubio and Quinigan's kids. He kicked himself. He'd been at Santiago's most days when Gina was playing, but not yesterday.

Once Greg told him he knew why the star player from Lanzarote Eruption had made a beeline to his suite. Shit. This was getting out of hand.

Greg's phone once again catapulted him into consciousness. It was Det Sgt Alba Marta Arteta.

'*Senor Du-Gan, Greg, we have had a sighting of who we believe to be Senor Quinigan ...*'

CHAPTER 76

Det Sgt Arteta was having a bad day. Her Policia superiors had arrived from Madrid. Moreno was sucking up to them, trying to make a good impression. Good luck to him. They had immediately visited Rubicon Marina and were clearly intending to be all over the boat disaster that they were dubbing 'Asesinato en el Superyate' (Murder on the Superyacht). She was surplus to requirements.

She had been delighted the spotting of Quinigan news had come in. Quinigan wasn't on her superiors' agenda.

The message Gina had received the previous day was separate from the inquiry the big hitters were now running and she relished the opportunity of the Quinigan Chase.

'Where are we going?'

This had not been part of Greg's plan. He'd received Arteta's call having left GPK and his team. Arteta had picked him up from the car park at the front of the Papagayos Beach Hotel.

Greg and Arteta were together now, in her black and white Fiat 124 Spider. Not a standard El Policia issue, her own car. She'd always wanted a sporty number and this had been the best she could afford.

They looked all the world like a couple on holiday, which had been Arteta's plan. She was wearing tight-fitting blue jeans, white strappy top and her hair was tied by a white ribbon making a ponytail. She'd worked on her makeup too and once again Greg was with another very pretty woman. They both wore shades.

'North of the island ...'

Arteta's ponytail was blowing freely as they made good time passing Yaiza and heading through La Geria.

'Our first sighting of him was near Teguise, not Costa Teguise but the town of Teguise, inland. Senor Quinigan is known on the island. People have seen his photograph in newspapers and on Canaria TV. It was one of our, what I believe you call '*neighbourhood watch*' *people, who sent us a WhatsApp.*

'*We followed him. He headed for the mountains of Risco de Las Nieves and is presently in a village called Tabayesco in the valley of Temisa, very picturesque and green. It is where onions, vines, potatoes and fruit trees grow.*'

She laughed as she saw how bored Greg had become with her tourist guide talk.

It hadn't taken them longer than twenty-five minutes to reach Teguise. Greg was focused.

'*Why this village? Taba …?*'

'*… Tabayesco … who knows? …*' Alba Marta Arteta shrugged, while she also smiled in readiness for her next question, unrelated to their search.

'*Maria Cavaleros …?*'

She raised her eyebrows, without looking in Greg's direction. His eyes looked across to hers.

Arteta was laughing now.

'*You are quite the Lothario I understand … mothers and their daughters …*'

She kept her eyes fixed on the road but couldn't resist a smile.

Greg so wanted to say that it wasn't like that but didn't. Instead he looked out of his side of the sports car … and smiled too.

Arteta changed the subject.

'*This is where it can get a bit hairy. We're at Mirador de Haria, and after these hairpins we're on one of the toughest routes of the Lanzarote Ironman. Heard of that?*'

Luis Hidalgo! Yep, that made some sense. Not that Greg was about to impart this to Arteta. But why? Why would it make sense? Just coincidence surely?

'*Do we know exactly where he is? In this village?*'

Jen Juniper was back on duty at Santiago's. The arrival of the Marauders fans had guaranteed a full bar for the afternoon.

'*… and it's great to see some of my lovely friends on the island once again …*'

Jen was soon into her stride and was seriously delighted to see David and Penny Pickup. She had wanted Vinny to be there, this afternoon, so that she could see he was safe, but he

had explained that it was never a good idea if he was in a bar where there might be the opposing team's fans before a match, especially of this significance.

The Kraft camp was in a state of limbo. All of the team had been detailed to various points. GPK was with Janet at Santiago's watching Gina/Jen, but simultaneously checking calls, emails, texts and social media; two of the recent recruits were at the conference, watching for movements from Rubio, who was attending in his position as Mayor of Yaiza. Or rather, he was until now.

'*He's on the move ...*'

The call put Kraft on immediate alert.

'*Sepago Z-102 ... yeah ... we're following ... let you know ...*'

Cesar Manrique Airport was welcoming its latest incumbents. Several flights had touched down within the past half hour, mostly from the UK, carrying ever more Midhaven Marauders supporters. If ever anyone wanted to see how much of an impact the sport was having directly on island tourism this was the moment.

Julian Jardine's phone sprung to life immediately on touching the runway tarmac. He smiled. Everything was under control.

Among those that had arrived half an hour earlier were two quite contrasting characters in both size and shape.

Arteta and Greg were approaching their target.

'*Tabayesco has only two roads ... the village is small as you can see ... our officers tracked him here but with the roads being so quiet they could not drive at too close a distance to see exactly where he went ...*'

She turned her head towards him.

'*But we do have a theory ...*

'*When he first came to Lanzarote, many years ago as a student, Geoffrey Quinigan was a fit young man. His friends were Ana Cristina Magdalena and ...*'

'*Luis Hidalgo.*'

Arteta was surprised by Greg's knowledge, but was more bothered with giving the rest of the story.

'*... yes, the three of them struck up quite a relationship by all* *accounts … quite a relationship …'*

She repeated the final words for greater emphasis. Again, she looked across briefly at Greg. *'… and he fell in love with this village, where Luis was born.'*

'Don't see why he'd come here now. Long time ago.'

It was out of Greg's mouth before he could stop it.

'It's a theory, like I said.' Arteta hadn't snapped at him. She was calm. *'He's running. He's plotting. But he needs somewhere he can be out of the way, out of view. Where would you go?'*

Greg looked blank.

'Somewhere you know? Somewhere familiar? A place where you know better than others? Where your lover may have family who may help? Come on Senor Greg. For an action hero you're pretty dumb.'

'Yeah, but I know what I see …'

Greg pointed towards the far distance, nearer to Tabayesco than they were currently, a car was approaching from the other direction, from the east coast. It made the turning into the village with Greg and Arteta still half a mile distant.

'Mierda!'

Instantly Arteta was not so calm. It wasn't the first time Greg had heard the word for fuck in Spanish, but the first time he'd heard it from her.

They both knew that the speed the car was travelling it had to be someone connected in some way with Quinigan. Arteta took her foot off the pedal.

Greg looked at her. Arteta was rolling the car to a standstill, a perfect view of the village, bathed in the glorious sunshine of another summer's afternoon of 34 degrees.

'What are you doing?'

'What do you think I'm doing? I'm watching. Whoever is in that car, they have arrived before us. We don't know whether they are armed, we have no backup and … they may well be doing just the job you wanted them to do.'

Greg was in no mood for sitting around twiddling his thumbs, or whatever Lanzarote islanders did instead. He opened the door.

'You do what you have to …' He was on the move.

CHAPTER 77

The first day of Lanzarote's UNESCO World Biosphere Reserve status conference was drawing to a conclusion. There was a positive atmosphere around the conference room and the hotel. Yurena Aguilar had been disappointed that Ricardo Rubio had left early, but his Sepago had been tracked since leaving Hotel Volcan.

'We have him. He's parked up. Seems like he's waiting.'

Ann Cummings was reporting to GPK who was still at Santiago's.

Waiting for what or whom? Kraft asked himself. Had to be Quinigan.

'Senorita Hague? Senor Antonio Romero. Are you available this evening?'

Oliver Quinigan spoke with Janet, who had GPK listening in. Oliver could tell someone else was listening but he would have been disappointed if they hadn't.

Their time and meeting place would be decided later on another call.

Senorita Angelina Diaz aka Emily Quinigan contacted Ken Knott at around the same time.

Greg ran.

Christ, he felt he'd run, swum and driven most of this island and its seas by now. He was not in bad shape all things considered, as he neared the village.

Quarter of a mile, maybe less, from the car they'd just seen. Black, Jeep Grand Cherokee.

Two men appeared, both all in black. Conspicuous to the extreme, and they weren't mucking about, to use a good northern expression, in their quest for what was surely Quinigan's whereabouts.

Jeez! Greg saw how his whole world ramp up once again, with fear and danger.

One of the two in black held a gun to a terrified woman's head, her husband instantly changing from resolute and unhelpful to frantic arm movements pointing, thankfully, in the opposite direction to which Greg was approaching.

Greg was 200 yards away, as they turned from having released the woman and saw him directly in their vision as they made for the Jeep. A firearm was raised in Greg's direction, but was withdrawn quickly as the pair stole speedily back into the vehicle.

Greg hadn't been into history repeating itself in taking another bullet and had thrown himself behind an outbuilding as the man had reached for his gun.

The Cherokee sped away up an old dirt track leading to the hills. Greg ran on into the village and to the woman who had been assaulted.

They must have been the only people in Lanzarote who couldn't speak a word of English as Greg tried to get information out of them. Two minutes later Det Sgt Alba Marta Arteta arrived.

'Super hero need any help?'

She shook her head in disdain, explained to the traumatised couple and others that had now congregated, and gave Greg the information they had given her.

'Quinigan came last night. Left about an hour ago when he knew someone was coming. He headed that way.'

She pointed to the Valle de Temisa.

'It leads to hills and then Haria, a bigger village.

'It is four miles on foot to Haria … Get in … unless you're going to run it …'

The thought had crossed Greg's mind. As the thought was also now crossing his mind about Hidalgo. Why hadn't Luis mentioned Quinigan when he had spoken to him?

Luis Hidalgo. Ana Cristina Magdalena. Geoffrey Quinigan. There was a connection.

'Check this out.'

Arteta was now well and truly putting her Fiat Spider

through its paces. She handed him her mobile phone. He clicked on a text that had just pinged through. Told her.

'*Kraft. Wants you to call him.*'

'*Do it! Mierda! Greg, just do it!*'

Arteta was fast losing her patience with Greg.

It wasn't on hands-free, didn't come up loudly enough for Arteta to hear. All Kraft could make out was the sound of wind rushing and the engine of a car.

'*Where are you?*' He hadn't realised it would be Duggan who answered.

'*Somewhere in the north of the island!*'

Kraft was momentarily taken aback.

'*Rubio seems to be heading for a place called Haria. He's in a Sepago …*

We've two of our team following …'

'*Mierda! Mierda!*' was Arteta's response.

She floored the Fiat Spider immediately. They hit over 110mph (180 kmph) on the straightest stretch and were close to Haria within what seemed like seconds.

Arteta made straight for the south of the village. She'd reckoned that if Quinigan had set off an hour earlier, as the villagers in Tabayesco had said, and if he was in anywhere like decent shape, he would be close to the village by now.

She couldn't see Rubio's Pegasos, but she could make out the black Cherokee making slower headway than it would have liked over the hills, still some distance away. The road was a dirt track, and not even that in some places. Tough going for a driver who wasn't used to the terrain.

Geoffrey Quinigan QC had indeed kept himself in good shape and having found that his bolthole in Tabayesco had been discovered had originally laid plans to run to Haria, but had changed his mind and gone for the shorter distance to Arrieta, on the coast. The complete other direction.

He was looking to somehow get hold of the recording that incriminated him. That's where Oliver and Emily came in.

He'd made it to Arrieta in no time at all, wearing running

gear that saw him look like any other regular guy sweating it out on the trails and roads. He'd contacted Rubio to drive straight through Haria and on to the coast.

'*He should have been here by now …*'

Arteta was calmer since they had arrived in Haria.

'*Unless he was never coming … he's a slippery fucker, I reckon he tells people one thing then does the other …*' Greg was right on it.

Arteta went for her phone, issuing instructions to whoever she was talking with rapidly in Lanzarote Spanish.

'*Mierda!!!*'

She shouted again as she finished her call and threw her phone down.

'*We have no backup, every one of our men and women is either at the conference or El Estadio making sure it is safe for tomorrow. We're on our own!*'

'*So, where the fuck is he? And who the hell are they?*'

Greg was watching as the Cherokee lurched forward, and then suddenly disappeared from sight.

CHAPTER 78

The calls had been made. Ken was to meet with Senorita Angelina Diaz at the Lucha Canaria, a Canarian wrestling match taking place on the beach in front of the King's Head bar at 6pm. The kind of place that offered little problem for GPK and the rest of his team. Ken and Emily aka Diaz would be in open view.

Janet's call from Senor Antonio Romero aka Oliver Quinigan had been to invite her to dinner at the Casa Brigida at Puerto Marina Rubicon, also at 6pm.

'A toy boy date for me!' Janet announced.

Kraft and Co could arrange for cover around the marina. What were these two up to?

'Excellent.'

Geoffrey Quinigan was currently catching his breath having run for the past hour and a quarter since leaving Tabayesco.

He was intent on reaching Graciosa, and the rate he was going he might not even need Rubio. The less he had to rely upon anyone, so much the better. He had run way beyond Arrieta. Another three and a half miles and he'd reach Orzola. One quick call.

'Oliver, nothing stupid this time. This is not about smoking guns …'

And Quinigan was on his way again.

Greg and Arteta hadn't stuck around in Haria to find out the plight of the Cherokee and its personnel. They were out of the way.

'What now?'

Greg was at a loss.

Arteta was suddenly driving with a sense of mission once again.

'He's heading for her place. Magdalena's. Has to be. Check the ferry times. She threw him her phone once again …'

'Why?'

Julian Jardine was not a happy man. His 'allies' had caught a flat tyre in their quest.

'Geoffrey, how are you?'

Jardine hadn't intended contacting him directly, but there was a time and a place for everything, and this was it as far as he was concerned.

'I have arrived. You mentioned a meeting?'

Quinigan survived off instinct. Hearing voices, knowing what they were saying carried an ulterior motive.

Why would Jardine want a meeting now and yet seemed reticent previously? What kind of opportunity was Jardine now seeing in meeting him? Fuck! Reality dawned on him. The guys in the Cherokee. Jardine's!

Quinigan was now within a mile and a half of Orzola. He was feeling good, fit and motivated. His adrenaline was pumping. He was now running on the powdery white sands of Las Cocinitas.

Jardine had wanted to know where he was. For the Cherokee boys. Quinigan had set a meeting place.

It had as much likelihood of taking place as he'd had the intention of running to Haria. His next call was to thank Ricardo for his support but to allow him to return to Yaiza.

'He's turning back. Not sure what that means,' was Ann Cummings' report in to GPK.

Kraft tried Det Sgt Alba Marta Arteta. Greg picked up again.

'Rubio's turned around … Ann's still on his tail, but if Det Sgt Arteta wants backup she can turn and follow you …'

Greg relayed. Arteta nodded.

Two ferry companies operate from Orzola to Caleta del Sobo on La Graciosa. Quinigan had timed his run to perfection, but when he was less than 10 metres away it started to move. He gave whatever was left in the tank. The momentum from his sprint and leap took him sprawling on to the deck. One couple applauded.

Greg and Arteta had been a quarter of a mile away. By the

time they'd reached the jetty it was out at sea by at least 100 metres.

'*Graciosa? Why would he want to be back here?*'

Greg was voicing what Arteta was already thinking as they were now aboard the next ferry, making their way across the strait to the island.

'*Looking for something. Maybe that recording, but I don't see the sense, if that is already out there somewhere ...*'

'*But it isn't ...*'

Ann Cummings chipped in. She had joined them in the time it had taken until the next ferry.

'*We had a copy of this alleged recording, but it is encrypted.*'

'*He's aiming to find the original here? Really?*'

Greg was pretty certain, even with his rudimentary knowledge of such things that this was ridiculous.

'*Is he for real?*'

Quinigan had been in no mood to wait for any form of transportation when he arrived in Celeta del Sebo. He'd had twenty-five minutes' rest. He was feeling good. It was back to the road by foot. Run.

He'd be there in less than twenty minutes. He was feeling good about this. In the next hour he could be celebrating, while others would be left clutching at straws and wondering what the hell just happened. Geoffrey Quinigan was back!

CHAPTER 79

'Buena noches querido … has visto un fantasma?'

Shocked didn't do justice to his feelings right now as he was handed a glass of champagne.

He had known the voice instantly.

She had asked whether he had just seen a ghost.

'We jumped,' she said nonchalantly.

'While all of the action was going on, my girls called for help. Ximena is from Playa Blanca and her uncle was close by in his fishing boat. We were lucky. We were all aboard before the Bella Bebe was no more.'

Ana Cristina Magdalena, very much alive but not quite carrying her best look, turned her attention to the pressing matter of her long-term acquaintance's presence.

'So, Geoffrey, why are you here?'

'Ana, darling …' As he began speaking another voice entered the fray. Male. He knew it immediately, but hadn't heard it for years.

'Geoffrey! … Your stats are very impressive today. You really should come to the club, get in some track work. You and I could be a useful part of the veteran 10-mile relay team.'

Quinigan almost felt more out of breath now than when he'd been running earlier.

'Luis …' was all he could offer.

Ana Cristina Magdalena and Luis Hidalgo. He'd known they'd held a thing for each other years ago. Right now he didn't know what to say. Ana was a good degree more clinical, now dropping the forced pleasantries.

'Why are you here?'

Not even so much as Quinigan's name was now mentioned by her. The words were uttered in disdain. She knew. He knew. And he was damned sure Luis also knew.

'The recording. El Gran Error!'

Ana gave a flourish of her arm as she announced it.

'*The Big Mistake! … and you thought, with me out of the way, you would try and find it?*'

Quinigan's phone came to his rescue. This wasn't going according to plan, but everything else appeared to be working from the texts he'd just received. It re-established his confidence somewhat. He looked at Ana and Luis.

'*I admit, I had no idea you were still …*'

He flicked his hand, as though saying the word 'alive' was unnecessary.

'*… but I'm pleased you are, of course … and yes, that blasted recording … as you know, it could finish me …*

'*Is that what you both wanted? … After all these years? … Really? …*'

He was now regaining full flow. They were at least listening.

That's when Geoffrey Quinigan's world stopped revolving.

CHAPTER 80

'*Our young man didn't show,*' Janet reported in to Kraft.

'*I've just had a message to go to the harbour. I'm on my way.*'

GPK had received a similar tale from Ken about Senorita Diaz. Another no-show. Another message about a different meeting place.

'*These kids are enjoying themselves. You might be getting a runaround. Just stay safe. We'll follow.*'

Ann Cummings was next to call in.

'*He's made it to Graciosa, we're here too, heading for Magdalena's place.*'

Kraft repeated his safety message.

El Policia de Lanzarote had just one police officer stationed on Graciosa.

Arteta had phone ahead for him to be ready with wheels.

The sight of the ancient Land Rover Defender, minus windows and roof, leant a new description to air-conditioned.

Island Constable Mateo Bernardino was a young man who knew this small island like the back of his hand. Mateo had arrived just a minute or so before Greg, Arteta and Ann.

'*Everyone on the island is still sad … about Senorita Magdalena,*' he shouted above the noise of the Land Rover's engine and the sand and stone track that led to their destination.

'*Do you know who is in the villa at the moment? Did Senorita Magdalena have people living with her?*'

'*Two female security guards and a caretaker and maintenance man called Miguel.*'

There was little sign of security when they arrived.

Greg couldn't have been more stunned as he, Arteta, Ann and Mateo rounded the corner to the sun terrace, pool and well-tended gardens looking back to Caleta del Sebo.

Quinigan, dead; Magdalena, very much alive; Hidalgo, why was he there?

'*Gracias al cielo que estas aqui,*' thank heaven you are here, were Ana Cristina's first words to Mateo.

'*Detener!*'

Arteta stopped Miguel in his tracks.

'*Esta es una escena del crimen.*'

She wanted to ensure nothing was touched.

'*Moviste el cuerpo?*'

Miguel shook his head.

'*We have not touched him. It was one shot. We had come out here.*'

She put her hands out to indicate the sun terrace. Magdalena was strong-willed, never suffered fools gladly and El Bastardo had fallen into that category many years ago. The shock had been the immediacy. The bullet, his collapse, his life ended.

Quinigan had moved directly in to line, made himself available. Two trained gunmen had been covering relentlessly for a clean shot. It had ripped through his neck. He'd died instantly.

'*He came here looking for a recording … something that would have ended his career … not his life,*' she added despairingly.

'*I have no idea who killed him. It was certainly not my doing. He had many enemies. Here, and it would seem, also back in England.*'

'*When he last came here he had wanted me in on some deal or another. He was desperate. Maybe I was his last hope. We'd been at college together, and we had always enjoyed ourselves in many ways, but he had let me down several times also. He was drunk one evening, had said a few things he would later regret.*'

She shrugged as though there was little else to say. Recognising that she had not, as yet, introduced Luis Hidalgo. She chose her moment now.

'*Luis is here because we run together, we are friends and we are working on something. We have been good friends from school days. Geoffrey ran with us many years ago,*' she now called Quinigan by his first name. It was meant affectionately.

'*Luis and I love our island of Lanzarote and tomorrow we will be making our own representation at the conference. We are hoping that what we are presenting will convince the UNESCO world biosphere officials that our island should retain its status.*'

Magdalena looked directly at Greg.

'I may shock many people by being here, as I shocked you Senor Duggan.'

She smiled at him, raised her hand to her chin.

'I do not blame you for what happened to Bella Bebe. Juan was wrong in so many ways. I had only just found out. When you hit me I was trying to help my friends the Pickups. They had found themselves caught up with Carlos Cuadrado and Juan through no fault of their own.'

Mateo and Arteta had alerted the ferry operators and harbour authorities to search anyone wanting to leave the island, in the vain hope of finding Quinigan's killer.

If this had been as professional a hit as it appeared there would have been backup. Helicopter, small plane, boat. The perpetrators were probably back on Lanzarote already or had made straight for Africa or Europe never to be heard or seen again.

Ann Cummings had informed GPK of developments. Ken Knott and Janet Hague were called off from their respective runarounds.

'You know. There never was any recording, on video, or camera, mobile phone, tablet. He made all that effort, today, for nothing.'

Ana Cristina shook her head.

'We let him believe there was something that would incriminate him. He was having such a bad time that he wasn't thinking straight. He became obsessed. We told him we had sent a copy of the recording to the people who are investigating what happened to your club last year, Senor. We sent something, but it was a corrupted file that was nothing to do with him at all.'

'Do you know what he said? That caused him to be so concerned about the recording,' Arteta was probing.

'All I can tell you is that when he was drunk, he had a loose tongue. How he had made a lot of money out of a sports ground last year, for construction. And how people had been killed.'

Greg felt hollow. He felt cheated that he hadn't had Quinigan before him, explaining what he had done. Was this finally over? Quinigan dead. He hoped so.

CHAPTER 81

El Dia Del Juicio! Judgment Day was upon Lanzarote Eruption when Greg awoke the next morning having returned to his suite in the Papagayos Beach Hotel around 10pm.

'Are you still chasing the bad guys all around the island …?'

Kenny's flippant yet well-meaning introduction to the day, when Greg called him at 10am.

'Or just women again now … Don't suppose there's any chance of seeing you at training? We've only the biggest game of your career coming up.'

Greg considered hitting his red button, not because he couldn't keep up with Kenny's sarcasm, good-natured though it seemed, but because he was totally knackered.

'I'm all yours!'

Greg announced with biggest of yawns, so much so that Kenny couldn't make out the words.

El Dia Del Juicio was just as relevant for what else was about to take place at the world biosphere status conference.

Word had reached all parts through this morning's big news on Canaria TV that Ana Cristina Magdalena was alive and that she intended to speak to the UNESCO delegates.

It was a remarkable united front for the second day of the conference.

David and Penny Pickup performed an opening song they had composed, 'Canta Por Nuestro Futuro (Nuestro Lanzarote)', 'Song For Our Future (Our Lanzarote)'.

Yurena Aguilar once again opened the proceedings, she also welcomed Maria Cavaleros, who spoke about the recent success of Lanzarote Eruption and the evening's massive game; Ciara Cortelli-O'Grady, who gave a sparkling presentation on how young people on the island were Lanzarote's future and how recent 'donations' would ensure the continued education of each generation.

Ana Cristina Magdalena, Luis Hidalgo and Yurena Aguilar stole the show as a trio, laying bare any past family squabbles between three of the island's best-known names and announcing a package of ongoing investment in the arts, culture, sport and above all their commitment to maintain Lanzarote's unique position with UNESCO, backed unequivocally by the island's Cabildo.

Yurena Aguilar addressed the conference and the TV cameras at the end of the two-day event.

'*I am delighted to announce that we have been successful in retaining our status as the only island in the world to continue to be a world biosphere reserve.*' She was as proud as she could ever be. '*I would like to thank Valentin Pierre Boucher and all of the UNESCO delegates and the management and staff here at the fabulous Hotel Volcan. I would also like to dedicate this victory to my daughter Lucia and Luis Hidalgo's son Luca who lost their lives on our island's behalf.*'

From solemn she switched quickly again to patriotic fervour.

'*Wherever you all may be this evening, our best wishes go to the Lanzarote Eruption, our rugby league team with a number of our own island boys playing, in their quest for victory at the wonderful Estadio de Lanzarote.*

'*This is already a marvellous day for our little island. It could be joy unconfined a little later tonight. My personal thanks go to a young man called Greg Duggan who, in his very short time on our island has become much more than just a wonderful player to all of us. We are proud Greg, to call you one of us.*

'*And finally …*'

Yurena Aguilar finished with a reminder of the terms under which the UNESCO delegates had agreed the continuation of the status.

Santiago's was rammed. It wasn't the biggest bar on the promenade but it was fast becoming the most popular. Jen/Gina had a following now, but it was the Midhaven Marauders' fans who were swelling the numbers.

'*All right, all right …*' she engaged with everyone in the bar immediately. *'Now someone told me that you guys know a song called 'I'm a Believer' but with different words.'*

The bar went wild as Gina hit the first lyric and was immediately joined by at least 25 others.

The Midhaven fans kept the verses the same as the original, but when they hit the chorus that would have started 'Then I Saw Her Face, Now I'm a Believer' she left them to it: *WE'RE ALL OVER THE PLACE*, MIDHAVEN MARAUDERS! Not a trace, of doubt in our minds. We're in love, woahhhhh, Midhaven Marauders, MIDHAVEN MARAUDERS ...'

Gina hadn't put a foot wrong all afternoon. She had them in the palm of her hand.

Graham Pythagoras Kraft, while never having had absolute evidence of Quinigan's involvement in Hopton Town's demise the previous season, at least felt his team's mission had somehow brought about his fall from grace.

Quinigan was no longer around. He was happier that was the case, but there was more, he felt this still wasn't over. Nonetheless, he and his team were preparing for a return to England in the morning. Gina had invited him to tonight's big game.

'We shall have every officer available on duty tonight.'

Det Sgt Alba Marta Arteta's pledge was to Gina and Maria Cavaleros when they met for a briefing at 5.30pm.

'Senor Kraft has also offered his team, and some of our special task force who came over from Madrid will be also be here.'

'Do we anticipate trouble?' Maria Cavaleros inquired casually.

'I think we've all had our share of that in the past few days.'

CHAPTER 82

'Good evening and welcome to what they're calling El Dia Del Juicio out here on sunny, hot Lanzarote. The island of lunar landscapes, golden beaches and crystal blue waters. It's only 78 miles off the coast of Africa – and yet it is part of Europe. Everything about Lanzarote is different, enticing and exciting, and no rugby league club in the history of the game has ever been so isolated from the rest yet taken centre stage quite so amazingly as Lanzarote Eruption.'

Joanne Collingwood's introduction to Cloud TV's coverage of 'The 10 Million Euros' game led from the island's natural wonders to a rattle-through of Eruption's best moments with a heart-thumping soundtrack. It was followed by Midhaven Marauders' footage to restore some balance to the programming.

'With me in the studio tonight, before we hand over to your match commentator Karen King and summariser Robbie Robertson, is rugby league legend Ralph McBalingfour ...'

While Ralph ran through the strengths and weaknesses of both teams Greg sat quietly in the dressing room. This had been his only day since arriving on the island where nothing much had gone on in his life.

He had spoken with Diane, went okay. Had a laugh with Kyle on FaceTime. Had still heard nothing from Susie.

Greg had come into the dressing room earlier than the rest. They were all in now. Bits of tape were being used everywhere. Boots being tied.

This was a much-changed side from the starting line-up that had begun the season and even since Greg had arrived.

Malky Shannon took the lead.

'This is just a game of rugby league. Forget it being anything else. You will win this, we will win this if we leave the emotion to the fans and play properly. Go and do your jobs.'

'And here they come,' Karen King announced to the Cloud TV and Canaria TV viewers.

'Eruption have just one change to their starting line-up from the Jags game four days ago. Jose Maria Estapol returns at right wing for veteran centre Ron Rigson; and on the bench Elton Richards adds experience, with 17-year-old Carlos Olivera dropping out through no fault of his own.

'Our referee tonight is Paul Caden.'

Greg was starting from the bench again, as he had been now in all four games.

Karen King was laying down markers for the way the game may go, based on recent form.

'Eruption have been slow to hit their straps and consequently have found themselves behind early on, whereas the Marauders are known for their swift, aggressive start to games.'

'That could well be what's happening here,' Robbie Robertson analysed.

'Scrum half and stand-off duo Mick Taylor and Mike Peachey have linked up beautifully there and they've sent full back Gav Floater right through the middle. It's a great tackle by Tonito that finally stops him, but not before they've made thirty metres.'

The Marauders ran hard and strong. Ian Rose, Pete Lamping and Duggie Smelt all going close. The first 15 minutes were a hard hitting, smash fest of testing each other out until a play broke down. Jez Ellis, Marauders' prop, had run hard over the halfway line and was spinning in the tackle to release one-handed when the ball inexplicably slipped from his grasp.

'… and Popoli Baru, who only made his first start less than two weeks ago, has kicked it on … it's gone into acres of space behind the Marauders' defence as they were all coming up in a line … Baru is 25 metres out … he's kicked it on … centre Martin Champs is covering … wing Neil Gower is on the charge … it's bounced kindly … Baru launches himself at the ball, oh and Gower too, and Champs … well, for me that's a try … referee Paul Caden might want the fourth official to take a look … yes, he's ruled a try on the field, but …'

The big screen came to life. Mr Caden had wanted to see whether Baru had downward pressure on the ball or whether a Marauders hand had beaten him to it. The slow-mo replays were played backwards and forwards.

'Baru is in no doubt, but when do we ever see a player who isn't …' Robbie Robertson added.

'It's a fabulous run and he showed great control.'

'YESSSSSSS!' The crowd collectively emphasised TRY shown on the big screen.

Estapol, another of the Lanzarote-born players kicked the conversion. Eruption 6 Marauders 0.

Marauders' Mike Peachey tried a cheeky kick-off, but Stu Wainwright was on it like a flash. Warren Entish, who had been getting better with every game, was in support and his centre partner Alan Thomas took it on the kind of burst that only one other man on the field could live with, Vincent Venus.

'And just listen to this …'

The band was already playing 'Hot Hot Hot' before Vinny touched the ball down under the posts.

'This is sensational rugby league from Eruption. They could be out of sight by half-time at this rate, Karen.'

The conversion, bang in front of the posts, was a formality. Eruption 12 Marauders 0.

Marauders' coach Peter Gatens made a triple substitution, bringing on Big Barry Twedell, terrier-like centre Jon Bramley and Man Mountain Adrian Worsfold.

The game settled into the arm wrestle it had become during the first 15 minutes and as the clock ticked to 20 minutes Greg was ready to play his part. He and Elton Richards came on for Tonito and Popoli Baru.

'Du-GAN! Du-GAN! Du-GAN!' rang out. It was as though a tremor was going through the terraces, an expectation. Everyone had heard Yurena Aguilar's words, that Canaria TV had replayed on the big screen before the game.

'I cannot properly convey the warmth being felt here for a rugby league player who many had never heard of until four games ago.'

Karen King could feel her eyes glistening over.

'… and referee Paul Caden has stopped the clock! This is so touching … and the young boy that Duggan went over to in the crowd *at half-time in the Jags game is by the touchline with his mum. They're both cheering him on and applauding as though their lives depended on it …'*

Karen King was close to tears. '*Robbie?*'

Words failed the 17-stone ex-forward.

'*Amazing,*' he eventually managed.

'*I've seen some things in my time young man,*' Referee Caden told Greg.

'*Usually for my colleagues in the army through Help for Heroes, whatever you're doing, keep doing it …*'

The game restarted. Marauders had the ball just inside their own half. At 12-0 down and only half way through the first half they weren't out of it, but they knew two more scores for Eruption with nothing on the board themselves would be a massive task.

'*Duggie Smelt, he's a wily campaigner,*' Karen King was trying to ensure that the Greg Duggan Effect was not bringing a biased commentary.

'*He's offloaded to Big Barry Twedell. He's turned in the tackle, down now though. Peachey takes it up. They're ten metres from the Eruption line. He plays the ball to Taylor who throws a long pass out to Floater. Five metres away, camped in Eruption territory. Bramley's on the charge. This could be a try. Ohh, but Kenny Lomax has ripped it from his grasp one-on-one. He's now galloping for all he is worth.*

'*Tremendous break. Eruption have their tails up. Richards is in at acting half, he's darted away, offloads to Ortega at pace. He's tackled by Lamping.*

'*… but that's an amazing stretch of his arm, keeping it off the ground, flicking it up for Duggan … we didn't need to tell you that …*'

The crowd had reacted immediately, '*Du-GAN! Du-GAN!*'

Greg's first touch of the game. He'd had to bend to collect but pivoted on his right and cut inside, through a hole.

'*Duggan has been on the field less than a minute. He's over the halfway line and 15 metres into Marauders territory, but here's traffic – Floater, Champs and Gower.*'

Greg handed off Champs, his knee went into Gower's groin and his left shoulder into Floater's chest as he was coming down.

Carnage.

'*Now that's a* collision.'

This was tough going for Greg. His body felt every knock, blow, tackle.

'*It's Entish. One of the unsung heroes. He finds Rodriguez-Perez, who runs the ball. Takes the tackle. Wainwright now shapes to pass right, switches the play and it's Roberts who loses his footing. He's swamped.*

'*Last play in this set. Twenty-five metres out. Roberts to Lomax to Fastleigh to Ramos. Quick hands but little ground made. Ramos is smothered by Peachey and Rose, offloads to Wainwright, who shimmies to his right, creating space and threads the ball through with a grubber kick that is heading for the try line! Wainwright follows his kick, with Entish and Thomas … the ball has hit the padding at the base of the left-hand goalpost … Duggan has come from nowhere! And it looks like he may have got it! … this one's going to the screen, Robbie.*'

Greg couldn't be sure he'd scored. Bodies had flailed everywhere at the base of the post. Referee Mr Caden went to the big screen, as Karen King had surmised. He signalled no-try on the field.

The crowd drew breath. Slow-mo replays from at least four cameras. Greg had picked up the ball cleanly, one-handed. Had he been stopped just before the line, gone over and then been held up? Two cameras were close to being definitive only to be obscured from the final act of whether the ball had touched the whitewash or Floater had managed to save the try.

'*Three scores down if this is given and the conversion will be another gimme. I don't think Marauders have come back from that kind of deficit and still won the game all season … I think it's going to be given,*' Karen King was on the edge of her seat.

'Here we go …'

The screen had changed to 'decision pending' complete with the five second timer counting down and the obligatory beat to heighten the tension. Everyone waited. But neither TRY nor NO TRY came up.

Instead of graphics, a Facebook 'Live' video appeared of a woman. Blonde, attractive but dishevelled, bound, as Greg had been. The crowd fell silent, hushed.

'*Susie …*' Greg couldn't believe what he was seeing.

'*Hi Sweetheart …*' She was trying to hold it all together, eyes darting to one side and also nodding nervously at the person holding the recording device.

'*… I'm okay …*' She so clearly wasn't.

'*… they say you have to come …*'

Another voice, male, out of shot.

'*You have 15 minutes.*'

The screen went black. It had lasted less than 10 seconds. Back in the mobile studio at Estadio de Lanzarote there was already an investigation under way into what the hell had just happened.

The decision pending flashed on the screen. TRY!!

The crowd, that had been variably either shocked, stunned or had taken the short video as some kind of weird advertisement were in uproar! The Midhaven Marauders fans could not believe it had been given. The Eruption fans were ecstatic.

Greg was already leaving the field. Malky Shannon put on Francisco Alliossi. Greg headed straight for the exit.

He was on his way.

Det Sgt Alba Marta Arteta was at her car with Det Con Moreno as Greg appeared.

'*Get in.*' They both knew exactly where they were headed. There had been no mistaking the building.

'*We'll be there in five minutes … rapidez!*'

Arteta was armed. Moreno too.

'*Si. Ahora. Todos.*'

While Moreno drove along the largely deserted streets of Playa Blanca, Arteta was issuing instructions for everyone to follow.

'*We're on our way,*' the next call had come from GPK.

Moreno had picked up speed on the main street of Avenue Faro de Pechiguera but had lost a little on the dirt track, which led to the Ghost Hotel.

Greg could feel time slipping away. Susie. For God's sake, he thought she'd left the bloody island. Left him. They were over.

He knew that, but this! This needed sorting. He'd only heard the male voice for a second, nothing more, but he'd known it instantly. Bastard.

'Greg. *We do not know what this person has planned ... be careful ...*'

When their eyes met there was an understanding. Greg realised for the first time, in that one look, just how beautiful Arteta was. They had come through so much together in the past few days. He smiled, gave a little nod and as

Moreno stopped the car was out like a flash, just as Alba Marta had thought. They had stopped the car around 300 metres short of The Ghost Hotel.

Greg was one man, one goal, yeah one vision. Where had he heard that line before? Fuck, concentrate. Another 100 metres. He was now looking directly at this hulking horrible haunting edifice.

'Susieeeeee!'

Greg let out a wail like a banshee into the early evening as he was within 50 metres.

'Susieeeeee!'

As Greg made it to within 20 metres of Atlanta del Sol there was a gigantic click and lighting all around the base of the building lit up The Ghost Hotel. Seconds later an amplified voice, the same voice Greg had heard earlier.

'Hello Duggan, or should I say, Hola! ... *you don't have much time ... this place was meant to be my father's greatest work, the grandest hotel complex on Lanzarote, but in the end it cost him everything! Tonight, it will do the same for you ...*'

Areta and Moreno were close to Greg, there was a wailing of El Policia approaching and GPK and his loyal band of Ken Knott, Janet Hague and James Vickers had just fled their car.

'*This hotel cost my father his life. Tonight it disappears and as you were the man responsible for him no longer being alive, you can feel the pain before you die. This whole hotel is rigged with explosives. Your girlfriend is here. You can walk away. Leave her to die. Or you can try to save her. You have 5 minutes before this hotel, your girlfriend and you are no longer.*'

There was no sinister laugh. The voice was clearly hurting and wanting to hurt Greg as a form of retribution.

'*Susieeeeee!*'

Greg ran the length of the hotel. He'd been bound and held on the second storey. He went there next, clambering up where there had once been a staircase. There couldn't be more than three and a half minutes left now.

Instinctively Greg decided on making for the third storey. Oliver Quinigan would have made this as difficult as possible.

His boots from the game hadn't been a problem along the rough track but suddenly left a great deal to be desired. By the time he'd made it to what had been designated the hotel's top floor Greg reckoned he had about a minute to a minute and a half left. If this was to be it then fuck it, he would at least have done the right thing.

When Greg reached the third level he stopped, hadn't wanted to, had no idea what time was left, whether he'd calculated correctly or not. Hoped he'd counted too quickly rather than slowly.

Greg heard something, like a scratching noise. He couldn't be sure, but it was all he had. Shit. Which way? He felt it as front, left. Went that way. All or nothing. Must have been in the final minute now. Fuck, this was worse than the last minute in a game. Far worse. He ran. There must have been 30 rooms either side all the way along.

'*Greg!!*'

His name echoed around the building.

'*Greg!! … We have him, Oliver! …*'

It was Arteta's voice. Quinigan's son. Then he saw her.

Her face spelt it out as boldly as it could have been. Frightened, afraid, petrified.

Oliver Quinigan had used the spreader bar once again. Susie was wearing what appeared as though she may have been wearing for a few days. How long had she been like this? Forget that, get her out and get out fast!

Susie's wrists were in similar leather bracelets in which he'd been held previously, the bar between her ankles similarly bound by leather. He had nothing with him to free her. He kissed her briefly after removing her ball-gag, another of Oliver's trademarks. Susie couldn't say a word. Shocked beyond anything. Her eyes said fear!

'*Up here!!!*'

Greg appeared at what would have been a window but was merely a space. Within seconds a team of El Policia officers appeared carrying equipment that released her from her bindings.

Susie collapsed as she was released into the arms of the police officers who sped her away. Greg followed. The rescue party was just fifteen metres away from the Ghost Hotel when the first explosion ripped through the building and started its instant demolition with concrete breeze flying in all directions, landing within inches of Greg. The second explosion came when everyone had made it to fifty metres clear. They still needed more ground. A third explosion followed.

Greg was on the floor, some 100 metres from the now close to rubble Ghost Hotel. Gathering his breath. Susie had been transferred to an awaiting ambulance and was heading for hospital General de Lanzarote in Arrecife.

'*Thank you, Greg,*' was all she had said. Nothing more.

'*You okay?*' was the most he could manage. She had been leaving him, or had she? No, she had been leaving him. Did he feel the same about her as he had when she hadn't been leaving? None of that mattered at present.

'*I'll come and see you,*' she smiled a weary, weak smile in return.

Greg watched as the ambulance departed. Arteta was by his side. GPK close by too.

CHAPTER 83

'… and Kenny Lomax is in trouble here, my goodness, things just keep getting worse for Eruption … and he's off, 10 minutes in the bin …'

'This game is sliding away from Eruption, Karen. Ever since they took that 18-0 lead in the first half it has been downhill all the way …'

Cloud TV and Canaria TV producers and directors had given a strong directive that no reference should be made over the errant video that had been shown at the ground. Fortunately broadcast delay of around seven seconds had meant the video had not been shown into homes and bars.

'… but at the same time it has been an amazing display by the Marauders, Robbie, who did not let those early scores deflate them …'

Eruption had gone in 18-6 up at half time, seven minutes after Greg had fled the ground. Marauders' scrum half Mick Taylor had combined superbly with stand-off Mike Peachey once again with Gav Floater kicking the conversion.

Not long after the restart Elton Richards had been given a straight red card for violent conduct over a tackle on Pete Lamping. The twelve-man Eruption had held firm for the first 10 minutes of the half, but then the floodgates had opened with tries from Twedell, Peachey and Taylor. Floater had been successful with all conversion attempts. Peachey had popped over a drop-goal with 15 minutes to go. Kenny had flattened him off the ball which had brought about the yellow card. It was now Eruption 18 Marauders 25.

'… but there's big news coming from the Eruption bench, let's go down to our pitchside reporter Max Sunderland.'

'That's right Karen. Greg Duggan is back, from wherever he has been in this second half. Malky Shannon is reorganising for one final push for 11-man Eruption. This isn't over.'

There had been a growing murmur around the ground as the information was passed on and fans had started noticing Greg's presence back in the Estadio.

Greg's head was a complete shed. He'd just saved Susie. But they were over. Diane was pregnant. They were over too, but he still felt for both. He wanted so much to see his son Kyle. What about Maria? All these thoughts were about to disappear for the next 12 minutes.

Greg had pulled on a fresh kit after being escorted to the ground by Det Sgt Alba Marta Arteta.

Malky Shannon also had Francisco Alliossi readied to reappear.

'*Last throw of the dice, Robbie,*' Karen King was excited once again.

'*Can Greg Duggan turn this game? He's done it every time so far, but nobody can just keep doing it can they?*'

Robbie whistled through his teeth, gave a long audible exhalation. '*One thing's for certain, Karen, there's going to be no let-up from either side in these last minutes.*'

'*That's right. Hold on to everything wherever you are. This is all set to be a bumpy ride – but what a prize!*'

Estadio de Lanzarote, which had gone from ecstasy in the first half to near despair around the hour mark, was now a cauldron of noise.

'*We're feeling Hot, Hot, Hot!*' rang out from the crowd, to the band's increasing volume.

Greg's first touch was to charge on to the ball from a pass by Manny Roberts. He broke through tackles from McIntosh and Raper, and was hauled down by Rose. The roar that accompanied his run was deafening, but it was soon quelled when Eruption lost the ball two tackles later.

Marauders then continually stretched the 11-man Eruption defence for the next five minutes, pounding their line. Finally a flailing arm thrown out in desperation by Angel Ramos caught Ellis high. No card was shown but Referee Caden put the incident on report and awarded a penalty. Gav Floater converted. Eruption 18 Marauders 27. Five minutes left.

Greg took control.

'*There's something brewing here,*' said Robbie Robertson.

'*Those two points could be crucial, but Greg Duggan looks ready to pull a few strings as he now needs to. Unless Eruption score inside the next two minutes this game is over.*'

Eruption were to kick the ball back to the Marauders. In their last training session he'd tried something with Jose Maria Estapol and Stu Wainwright. It was time to give it a go.

Greg placed the ball on the centre line. He had retreated, ready to kick flanked by Estapol and Wainwright. The other eight players were all set to the right flank ready to charge for the ball. Nobody was left at the back. If this all went tits up it was game over.

Greg, Jose and Stu moved in unison toward the ball. Greg ran from the right as though to kick the ball left, made to kick the ball but didn't. Half a second later Stu did the same from the left, as though to kick high towards the right, but also didn't. A split second later, co-ordinated like a Red Arrows fly past, Jose tapped the ball towards the 10-metre line and continued running. The other eight players, knowing exactly what was happening, ran diagonally from right to left towards the ball.

Karen King shook her head in disbelief.

'*... and Jose Maria Estapol has regained possession from his own kick! ... the Marauders were, like the rest of us, mesmerised ... they cannot in a million years have anticipated something like that ...*'

The crowd was on its feet. Greg was at acting half as Jose was tackled. Greg signalled behind his back for Francisco. The 16-year-old was fresh, all energy and with a great brain. Greg had had another move up his sleeve.

'*Oh, this is like watching a magician. Greg Duggan has just shown a slight of hand that has somehow seen the ball come out of the back of his hand, around his back and young Alliossi has charged around him, now he's straightening up ... ohh, that's electrifying pace from the youngster ... he's in the clear ... he's going all the way ... amazing ... and what a tremendous finish we have here ... 16-year-old Francisco Alliossi, product of Lanzarote, excellent ...*'

The try had been scored out wide, the conversion was tricky and Jose Maria missed. Eruption 22 Marauders 27.

'*You're just too good to be true, Francisco we love you!*' rang out from the crowd to the band's lead. A new star was born.

Kenny Lomax returned to the field. Eruption now had 12 men. Three minutes left. Six points would win it. Any Marauders score would pretty much seal it for them too.

Two minutes 45 seconds. Marauders hammered the ball high into the night sky. Tonito was underneath it, just five metres from his own line. He found Entish who spun away.

Three more tackles followed as Eruption made their way into the Marauders' half. Less than two minutes on the clock. Stu Wainwright shovelled a pass to Alan Thomas who fended off two Marauders and was 25 metres from the line with just the fullback to beat. Vinny Venus was just a metre or so behind, ready for the pass. It never came. Thomas sold Floater an outrageous dummy and scored near the sticks. The crowd went wild! 'Hot! Hot! Hot!' reverberated around the ground once again. This was it. Eruption 26 Marauders 27. The kick was a formality.

'… *and inexplicably Jose Maria Estapol has missed it! … He's inconsolable … what a poor lad …*'

The crowd, that had been in festive full swing, was hushed.

'*Referee Caden has stopped the clock,*' said Robbie Robertson. '*He saw the Marauders slowing everything down for the restart … it shouldn't alter much.*'

The Big Screen clock showed the time as 79 minutes 48 seconds. Only 12 seconds left in the game. Greg's heart was pounding so hard. He'd come to the island less than two weeks ago, for what should have been a relaxing time!

Marauders had done it. Seconds left. Their supporters were baying for the final hooter. Mike Peachey booted the ball as high as he could to take up at least another precious second.

It came down with Raul Rodriguez-Perez underneath it, but with an over-eager Duggie Smelt charging in and dumping him to the ground. Referee Caden was about to blow for a penalty but as Raul fell, he one-handed a pass out to Greg who flat-footed Jez Ellis and found himself in the clear! Greg had made it just short of the halfway line when the hooter sounded.

There was a collective groan from those in the ground, who felt it was all over, but Greg continued his run. He sidestepped Lamping and Gower before fending off the attention of Champs. The crowd roared him on. It was Jon Bramley, covering, who grimly held on to his shirt and Greg offloaded to Vinny who made a mazy run crossfield before he too was nearly stopped.

Vinny shrugged off the attentions of centre McIntosh, stepped back and 20 metres out from the Marauders touchline – and with Marauders expecting a drop-goal attempt to bring the scores all square – he created the space to send a spiralling kick as high as he could manage. It was all or nothing.

Greg reappeared, eyes fixed on the ball. He had this play for the match and Super League.

The ball was high. He was in full flow. Legs pumping. The ball was still going up, it would only take a second for it to come down. He had to collect it, he just had to. As it began its descent Greg flew in the air, just catch the bloody thing!

The crowd gasped as one, home spectators and opposition fans alike. Greg had gone airborne with around three metres to reach the line, collect the ball and touch down.

Greg's eyes never flinched from the ball. Greg twisted in the air to maintain eye contact. He'd gone too early! He was descending before the ball, but at around two feet off the ground the ball was in his grasp.

Underneath him was Gav Floater, laying his body on the line too. Greg landed with a jarring crack but with presence of mind to place the ball to his right side. It was the last movement he would feel.

Pandemonium took over at the Estadio. Referee Caden signalled a try. The big screen lit up with 'Eruption 30 Marauders 27 – We are in Super League' before playing back the try.

The band played 'You're just too good to be true, can't take my eyes off you' and gradually the euphoria changed to concern.

Greg hadn't moved.

Enjoyed Tough Season in the Sun?

Read on for an exclusive extract
from the third Greg Duggan crime thriller
by Chris Berry

TOUGH WORLD

CHAPTER 1

The Dressing Room
He was nervous. He'd taken ages to get ready. It was the excitement. His debut. He'd never played in a match like this. Couldn't even lace up his boots, his hands were shaking. Everyone else seemed much more confident around him. He wanted to do well, make a good impression. So many had turned out to see him.

The Dressing Down
'Beyond belief!'
Greg's best mate had been used to being contrastingly astounded by his on-field brilliance and his regular off-field dramas. He'd stood proudly alongside him through all of the highs and had been confounded by the mess in which Greg constantly found himself. This was another calamity alongside a recent catalogue of moments that seemed to have picked up momentum.
'You're your own worst enemy, mate. But this …?'
He threw his hands up in despair, as he'd done many times in the past.
'Just what possessed you?'

The Dressing Down (Part Two)
'Vamos! Y no vuelvas!'
She had rasped out the words when she had found out. 'Go and don't come back' had been the translation. He'd had no defence. It had been another chapter drawing to its close for a while. He knew only too well he'd not been very clever, but his world had not been right for months. He'd not been thinking straight. Too much going on inside his head and sometimes, as ever, elsewhere in his anatomy.

'*Estas despedido!*'

It was more than all over. She'd sacked him too. As he always seemed to, he'd gone from hero to zero.

Dressed to kill

'*I don't bloody well care! Just get off your fat arse and do something about it!*'

Her heels clacked as she made her way purposefully and stridently from the building. This was fast becoming a living nightmare rather than the grand celebration she had planned and overseen throughout. Touching buttons, she moved straight to the next call. Similar vitriol. She was on the warpath. Woman in a man's world, she was taking no prisoners. She wanted action.

'*It's me. Just what the hell do you think you're doing?*'

She stopped while she listened.

'*Listen to me. Hold your nerve. We are only days away … okay? … right, gotta go.*'

One second later, incoming call. Personality change. Switch off hard, badass powerful. Switch on tender, sweet, romantic, seductive.

'*Hiiii! … I'm on my way … you had better be ready for me, because the day I've had I'm so ready for you … now that would be telling …*'

She smiled. As she turned off her phone, watched her screen go black. Then her world took a similar turn.

Balance redressed

When the charred remains of a body were found on the island of Efate in the south Pacific archipelago nation of Vanuatu there were initially no questions asked by the local authorities. It was simply another body, another day, another unexplained death. That was until investigations began into the disappearance of the partner of the Rugby League International Authority just days prior to the start of the Rugby League World Cup to be held in Australia.

Dressed to thrill

'Don't say a word,' she whispered, wearing a smile that meant everything to him and an electric blue off the shoulder dress that hid nothing from sight, showing off her stunning legs and cleavage. *'We have all night to talk, but so much time to make up.'*

Debutant

When blond-haired, 6-year-old Kyle Duggan appeared from the dressing room with the rest of his team and their opponents there were cheers from all of the parents. The red and white Hopton Under 7s were about to play their first game of the season against Ludding Vale and Greg was back to watch his son. His world might have been falling apart, but this was the one bright spot right now as he stood on the touchline alongside Diane.

Never before had Greg been so proud. Never before had he realised how important this all was. Thirty minutes later he was also extremely angry. But also even more proud if that could have been possible, as Kyle showed his dad that he'd learned a thing or two.

Debutant (Part Two)

Greg's world was rocked just minutes later. Samuel Duggan was in the emergency ward in Byron Central Hospital. Judy, his mum had called.

'Greg, I think he's going to die. How soon can you get here?'